MW00943190

# BROTHERS IN BLOOD
# AN UN-CIVIL WAR

Copyright © 2019

Robert Daniel Mumford

All Rights Reserved

ISBN: 9781076645760

# Acknowledgements and Credits

A great many people made this book possible. First, my wife and better half, Becky, who encouraged me to keep going, edited the first rough drafts and provided much needed input.

I owe many thanks to Josh Langston, author and teacher who convinced me that I might be able to write and showed me how to go about it. My critique group headed by author and teacher June Converse, helped keep me on the straight and narrow. My Beta readers, Katie Huffine, Becky Mumford, Christy Woodard, Barry Pencek and Bob Williamson deserve a big thank you for reading and critiquing the whole book. I know the investment in time it took. Thanks for doing that for me. I hope I can return the favor soon.

Cover designed and created by Josh Langston.

Contact Josh at:
druidjosh@gmail.com

# Disclaimer

This book is a work of fiction. It is loosely based on actual historical events in the State of Missouri during the Civil War, but the main characters and the 15th Missouri Cavalry MSM are products of the author's imagination.

Confederate irregulars, guerillas and bushwhackers did, in fact, roam the state almost at will, and caused great harm. Some of the Unionist Missouri Militia units were every bit as bad. Bloody Bill Anderson, William Quantrill, Sterling Price, Jo Shelby and Todd Young were actual historical figures, and are mentioned only in passing. Confederate General Sterling Price's first and second invasions were very real events and caused great stress and hardship to Missourians of the time. These historical events and personages are the backdrop and not the subject of this novel.

## Please follow my blog or contact me at:

## robertdanielmumford.com

*General Order Number 2*
*St. Louis, Mo., March 13, 1862*

*...Major General Sterling Price has issued commissions or licenses to certain bandits in this State authorizing them to raise "Guerrilla forces," for the purpose of plunder and marauding. Gen. Price ought to know that such a course is contrary to the rules of civilized warfare, and that every man that enlists in such an organization forfeits his life, and becomes an outlaw. All persons are hereby warned that, if they join any guerrilla band, they will not, if captured, be treated as ordinary prisoners of war, but will be hung as robbers and murderers. Their lives shall atone for the barbarity of their General...*

*By Command of Major General Henry W. Halleck* [1]

# Part 1

## Lincoln County, Missouri

## August 1864

HEADQUARTERS TRANS-MISSISSIPPI DEPARTMENT
                    Shreveport, La., August 4, 1864.
Maj. Gen S. Price,
            Commanding District of Arkansas:
 General: You will make immediate arrangements for a
movement into Missouri, with the entire cavalry force of your
district .... You will scrupulously avoid all wanton acts of
destruction and devastation, restrain your men, and impress
upon them that their aim should be to secure success in a just
and holy cause and not to gratify personal feeling and revenge.
Rally the loyal men of Missouri, and remember that our great
want is men, and that your object should be .... to bring as large
an accession as possible to our force.
        By command of General E. Kirby Smith: [2]

# Chapter 1

Will Tanner felt the pounding of horse's hooves on the hard-packed dirt road long before he could hear them. The tremors pulsed through his worn-out brogans into his legs and up into his gut. *That's a whole lot of horses,* he thought. *And they're movin' awful fast.* Were they Yankee Cavalry? Or were they Rebels? The rumble of their hooves reached him—like distant thunder, faint but growing. They were headed his way.

He jumped off the road into the trees and crouched behind a massive old oak just in time to watch the horsemen gallop by. Eight of them galloped by before the dust they raised obscured the rest. Will sneezed into his sleeve as the cloud enveloped him, but not before he caught the musky scent of sweaty horses, the stink of unwashed bodies, and the acrid smell of burnt gunpowder.

Some of the riders wore blue coats, others wore gray. Some had no uniform and wore civilian clothes. Polished metal flashed in the bright sun—pistols and knives mounted on their saddles. Blue and gray coats mixed with civilian clothes—and all the guns—meant these men were Rebel irregulars or guerillas. Or worse, bushwhackers! An ice-cold hand squeezed his heart.

Could these men really be bushwhackers? *No, no, no!* He shook his head in disbelief; his mind rejecting the thought. Bushwhackers, heartless, merciless men like Bloody Bill Anderson and William Quantrill, did their burning and raping and killing way out west, near the Kansas border. They'd never come this far east, would they? Will knew, though, that whoever these men were, they were dangerous, and his family was in peril.

Obscured by their own dust, the riders raced down the road toward his farm. The thunder of their hooves echoed from the hills long after they were out of sight.

Will thought frantically. If those riders were aiming for his farm, they were already there. Ma and his baby brother, Nate, were alone at the house, and it was already too late to warn them. Knowing Ma would have to face those men alone terrified him, but he convinced himself she could handle them—she had to. She was smart, and a tough old bird, as she often described herself. Even so, he prayed the men would just ride on by and leave them be.

His younger brothers Jake, Ike and Seth, were fishing and swimming down at the river below their house. Will hoped that Jake—younger than Will by two years—was alert and watching for trouble. He worried, though. Things had been quiet for so long now. Had they both become careless?

His brothers had been told to hide at the first hint of trouble. If Jake spotted the horsemen, and they didn't turn down the river trail, or search the woods too closely, his brothers should be ok. There were good places to hide all up and down the riverbank and in the tangled woods and canebrakes.

Still, Will worried about them. They might both have been careless, but Jake was reckless, hotheaded and rash. Quick-tempered and quick to act, he often plunged in headlong before thinking about the consequences. He had an old shotgun with him—useless against all those men, all those guns. Will hoped Jake wouldn't even think about using it. He hoped he would stick to the plan Ma had made them agree to. *Don't play the fool this time, Jake! Hide! And take Ike and Seth with you!*

If he couldn't warn Ma, at least he could warn Jake and Ike and Seth. Will turned away from the road and scrambled down the hill toward the river, dodging trees and thick underbrush, shifting the heavy old Kentucky rifle between his hands. Briars tore at his shirt and scratched his arms. He ignored the pain.

As he ran, Will's heart fell. He knew what those men were here for. They were here for him and Jake.

More than two years ago, on a cold and dreary late winter day in the spring of 1862, another band of riders—Confederate Missouri State Guard—had surrounded their home. When the Rebels left that day, Will and Jake marched off with them—at bayonet point. Like thousands of other young Missouri boys, they had been conscripted, marched south and forced to fight for the Confederacy.

The raw, untrained and ill-equipped Rebel army they joined was badly beaten and routed at a place they called Elkhorn Tavern. In the panicked retreat afterward, most of the newly conscripted boys—Will and Jake among them—melted away like snow in the hot sun. They just quietly slipped away and went home.

It had taken Will and Jake three weeks to make their way back home; walking only at night, hiding and sleeping during the day, eating when they could. They'd been laying low ever since, hiding from Yankees and Rebels alike. Wary of strangers, friends and neighbors. Always looking over their shoulders for trouble.

The cold hand in his chest squeezed harder and his blood seemed to freeze in his veins. Will feared what the riders might do this time, if they caught him or Jake. Confederate soldiers would proclaim them to be deserters from the Rebel Army and drag them off to go fight again. These men were not soldiers, though. They were bushwhackers; bloodthirsty, savage, heartless killers. Will had heard the stories. He knew if bushwhackers caught them, they would do worse than make them fight. Much worse.

Charley Porter pulled the reins back hard and the black gelding he rode skidded to a halt in the dirt road, bucking and bobbing its head in complaint. The horse looked sideways at him and neighed. Charley ignored it.

The other riders halted and spread out to both sides. Dust enveloped them all. Charley covered his nose and breathed through his sleeve until the dust drifted off with the breeze. He dusted off his coat and hat and rubbed the grit from his eyes.

Before them sat an old farmhouse surrounded by cornfields on three sides. An unpainted, two-story barn stood further down the road. Missing shingles on its roof made it look snaggle-toothed. The usual assortment of outbuildings—pigsty, smokehouse, corncrib and outhouse completed the farmstead. Tools lay scattered here and there, and animal skins were stretched for drying on the open barn door.

"Porter!" said Henry Perkins, the leader. "That the place up ahead?" He sneezed and wiped his nose on his coat sleeve. "Goddam dust!"

Charley spat dirt from his mouth and glared at Henry. He hated taking orders from that old gray-bearded fool. Henry was too soft and sentimental, in Charley's estimation. He didn't have the stomach for killin' Yankees. Yet, Bill Anderson had put him in charge, so Charley had to take his orders. For now.

Charley broke off his stare and looked over the farmstead. The only movement was the thin wisp of smoke rising from a stovepipe and drifting toward them in the breeze. Charley smelled ham frying; his stomach rumbled and his mouth watered. They'd been riding hard all week in enemy territory, and he couldn't remember his last hot meal. He aimed to have one soon, though.

Henry looked his way again. "That the house or ain't it, Porter?"

Charley ignored his hunger pains and took his bearings. The dusty road continued east to cross a wooden bridge, about a quarter mile away. He figured it must cross over the Cuivre, but from here he couldn't see the river itself. "It's the last farm before we cross the river, so, yeah, that's it," he said.

"Well, all right then," Henry said. "Boys, check your pistols and let's go pay 'em a visit."

Charley smiled, ignoring the order. His guns were always ready.

The silence gave way to the snick of pistols being drawn from leather and the metallic clicking of cylinders spinning. The horses clopped slowly forward.


Will reached the edge of the bluff looking down on the river and saw his brothers Ike and Seth below as they splashed around in their favorite swimming hole. A tiny creek entered the river here, and a sandbar had formed which made a perfect place to swim. The boys were naked, and when they dived underneath the water, their white bottoms glowed as their heads dipped under and their legs flipped up into the air. He didn't see Jake anywhere.

Before he stepped out of the woods, Will scanned the bluff and the riverbanks, looking for any sign of the riders. None were in sight and his panic eased a little. Scooting on his legs, he made his way down the loose scree to the swimming hole.

He didn't want to alarm his brothers, so he took a deep breath and released it slowly before he spoke. "Where's Jake?"

"He heard somethin' and went up to check it out," Ike said, looking up to the brush line above the river. "He's up there."

Will nodded. "Good. We got company. It's likely nothin' to worry about but get dressed anyhow. Put your shoes on, too."

Ike waded ashore and used his shirt to dry himself before putting on his pants. "Who do you think they are?"

"I don't know just yet. You 'member where to hide out and where to go if it gets dark?"

Ike's eyes widened, and his shoulders tensed. "Who are they, Will? Are they bushwhackers?" Ike, too had heard the gruesome stories about Bloody Bill Anderson and William Quantrill's raiders.

"Don't worry," Will said. He gestured with the rifle up to the brush line. "We'll be watchin' from right up there. An' I got this." He shifted the old gun to his shoulder and patted it. It wouldn't be much good against eight mounted men with revolvers, but it reassured Ike.

"Out of the water, Seth," Will said. Seth had ignored him the first time and looked to be ignoring him the second time.

Ike threw on his shirt and brogans. "Come on, Seth, we gotta get dressed."

"Aww," Seth whined. "I wanna swim some more. It ain't even suppertime yet." Sulking and dragging his feet, he sloshed ashore.

Will ignored the whining and scanned the bluff once more before kneeling and handing Seth his pants. He pondered for a moment what he was going to say to him; Seth was only five and easily scared.

"That's right, it ain't suppertime yet," Will said. "We're gonna play hide an' seek. Me an' Jake, against you an' Ike. Ike knows a real good place to hide. Why, I bet me an' Jake won't never find you, no matter how long it takes! You wanna play, don't you?"

"Sure!" Seth was excited now.

"All right, put your clothes on. Shoes too. Go with Ike an' do what he tells you to do, ok?"

"Ok." Seth threw on his pants and shirt, grabbed his hand-me-down shoes and threw them on over his mud-caked feet. "Come on, Ike! Let's hide!"

As the pair ran off, Will jumped the creek and scrambled up to the brush line. He heard a low whistle just before he reached the top, and he crouched down and crawled up to Jake, who lay on his stomach, well-hidden by the low scrub. Will knew the spot well, It was on the crest of a long gentle rise, and had a clear view of the farm spread out below. "

Jake peered down at the house, fingering the old single barrel shotgun that lay next to him. "Riders, down at the house," he whispered. "I cain't tell who they are."

"Yeah, I saw 'em," Will replied. "They came by me on the road. I think there's eight or nine of 'em. I saw blue coats, but some of 'em had gray coats."

Jake bristled. "I can see they ain't Yankees. You reckon State Guard or guerrillas?"

"I ain't sure," Will lied.

"Which means you think it's bad."

"Maybe." Will studied his brother. Could he trust him to keep his cool? If he went off half-cocked today, things might get bad, real quick.

Down below, the riders spread out in front of the house. Will counted them again—his first count was wrong, there weren't eight riders. There were eleven. Eleven heavily armed bushwhackers. The cold fist of fear squeezed his heart again.

Charley eased his horse to the right of the group and pushed back his coat, the quicker to pull out his pistol. He wore a Colt Navy revolver in a holster on his right hip. He laid his hand on it and thumbed it absently. Another Colt was tucked into his belt on his left side, the handle facing forward. Two more revolvers were secured in holsters mounted to his saddle, one on each side.

The gang stopped just outside shotgun range, and the men spread out sideways facing the house. A dog barked at them from under the porch. No other sounds broke the quiet.

"Hallo the house! Hallo the house!" yelled Henry.

Charley saw a curtain move in the open window, and a moment later, a tall, gray-haired woman came out of the open door and stood on the porch. She wore a blue apron with flour dust all over it and a white smear marked her forehead. On one hip she carried a toddler, who tried to squirm out of her grasp. She hoisted the brat higher up on her hip.

As Charley observed her, he realized she wasn't as old as he'd first thought. Hard life on a Missouri dirt farm had aged her before her time. Not too many years ago, she'd have made a pretty woman, all cleaned up. Still, her steady manner showed that life hadn't yet beaten her down and used her up. Her clear eyes scanned each of them without flinching until she locked them on Henry. In her free hand, the woman held a rolling pin. Charley smiled at that. *She's got gumption, that's sure. But what use is a stick of wood against pistols?*

"Who are you and what do you want?" she said.

Henry swept off his filthy hat. "I'm sorry to bother you Ma'am. Where are your men-folk?" He scratched at something on his neck.

"When I know who you are and what is your business here, then I might tell you," she retorted.

Henry's face turned red underneath the dirt, and a few of the men sniggered, amused by the woman's sass.

Charley laughed at Henry's discomfort. *This might get interestin', watching an old woman outfox Henry.*

Henry replaced his hat and leaned forward in his saddle. "Well now, Missus Higgins. Our names are not important. We're from the Missouri State Guard—he pronounced it 'Missoura'—and we're out here looking for runaway slaves an' deserters an' such." He scratched his neck again.

More sniggering. Charley laughed out loud and shook his head in mirth. Henry had just let slip they knew who she was and were looking for her boys.

Henry's face turned a deeper red. "And I'm the one that'll be askin' the questions, here," he said, in a sharper tone. "So, I will ask you again, where are your men-folk?"

The Higgins woman scowled at Henry for a long moment, her eyes never leaving his, until finally she sighed and looked away. "My husban' went to town to fetch some things at the general store. He'll be back d'rectly," she said.

Charley knew she lied. He knew she'd been a widower for years now.

"Where yore boys at?" asked Emmit Hayes, staring right at her. He pulled his coat back, exposing his two pistols and a huge Bowie knife and spat tobacco juice to the ground.

*Now we're gettin' down to it,* thought Charley.

The woman tried to hide her fear, but her eyes widened, and she took a faltering step backward.

Emmit was a huge man with a barrel chest and a bulging belly. With his thick, hairy arms, full black beard and wild black hair to match, he looked like a bear and acted like one too. He had unnerved many an otherwise brave man just by brandishing his big Bowie knife and glowering at them. He was unpredictable and violent—qualities Charley admired in a man.

Henry attempted to regain control, glaring at Emmit. "I'll do the talkin' here."

Charley sniggered again; he couldn't help himself.

Henry glared at him before turning back to the woman. "Missus Higgins, where are your boys? As you can see, we're gettin' a mite impatient here."

The Higgins woman sagged like the wind had been let out of her sails and she looked down at her feet. "My oldest two boys are off ridin' with Jo Shelby an' his cavalry," she said, pronouncing it 'calvary.' She looked up at Emmit then quickly switched her gaze back to Henry. "My next two are not old enough to fight. And this one on my hip cain't hold a gun yet. Now, he is a biter, though."

Some of the men sniggered at her joke. Charley wondered at the woman's nerve. He knew she was trying to defuse the tension. It was liable to backfire on her. She might get by with poking fun at Henry, but Emmit was a different story.

"Now, Missus Higgins," said Henry, "We know that ain't the truth. Things will go a whole lot easier if you'll just tell us where your boys are."

She looked down again, a sure tell. "I just told you."

Henry sighed and shook his head. "All right, Missus Higgins, we'll do this the hard way." Turning to the gang, he ordered, "Search the place."

All but a few of the men dispersed, some to the outbuildings, some to the fields. The dog barked frantically now. Leather creaked as Emmit dismounted and strode to the porch. Charley remained seated and watched Emitt and the woman. This was liable to get interesting.

The Higgins woman backed away, eyes wide with fear. "I done told you all, my boys ain't here!"

Henry motioned to Emmit. "Go on, search the house. You know what to look for."

"Whiskey!" said Emmit.

Henry ignored Emmit. "Porter," he said. "You go with him. You too, Harris."

Charley smiled and dismounted, handing his reins to Henry. Behind him, Charley's friend, Darnell Harris, did the same and they both strode up to the porch.

"No! You ain't comin' in here!" yelled the Higgins woman, brandishing the roller.

From his vantage point up on the bluff, Will could see the whole farmstead spread out below him. A red checkered apron flapped gently with the breeze from the back door of the house — Ma's danger signal. He could hear their old beagle Chigger barking from up way up here. He hoped the toothless old dog would just stay under the house.

The leader doffed his hat and motioned with it, talking to someone on the front porch. He couldn't see who from this angle, but it had to be Ma.

Jake sat up. "I cain't tell what's happenin'!"

Will pushed him back down. "Stay down. They'll see us." He felt Jake's glare but ignored it.

Down in front of the house, a big man with a thick black beard, brushed back his coat, exposing the bright flash of sun on the polished steel of a big knife.

Some of the riders scattered and searched the outbuildings. Three dismounted, walked toward the porch and disappeared from view. One rode his horse to the barn.

"Dammit," said Will, shaking his head and looking at his brother. Jake's eyes went wide, and Will felt his muscles tense up. They had been sleeping in the barn loft since spring and their blankets and spare clothes were hanging up there in plain sight of anybody who cared to look. That was a mistake, and now they'd pay for it.

When the horseman ducked out the back door, still mounted, Will was able to breathe again. The rider hadn't been in there long enough to check the loft. The man rode back to the leader. The others straggled back one or two at a time, except the three who'd gone into the house.

The leader talked and gestured and barked an order, and the men all dismounted and tied their horses to the fence rail. All but one trickled to the porch and disappeared. Will shuddered. Ma was now alone inside with ten dangerous marauders.

Jake snorted in disgust. "Dammit, Will, we got to do somethin'!" He pushed up again.

Will lay a hand on his shoulder. "No. You know what Ma told

us. We stay right here an' watch. We protect Ike and Seth. We run an' hide if we have to. You know this is what she wants us to do."

Jake sagged back down and cursed, his jaw grinding in frustration.

"Take a good look down there," Will said. "Those men are bushwhackers. Hardened killers."

Jake cursed again and looked away.

"There's only the two of us," Will continued. "There's eleven of them, and they got six shot revolvers, an' they got three or four apiece. We cain't take 'em, Jake. We got to wait 'em out. Ma's smart, an' tough. She'll be all right."

"But what if….?" asked Jake.

Will couldn't answer him. He didn't want to even think about it. What if something bad was happening down there? They might be forced to act. He knew if they tried to take those men in a gunfight, he and Jake would be killed. One Kentucky rifle and a shotgun would not be any use against eleven men armed with six-shooters.

Jake cursed under his breath and shook his head in disgust. "Dammit! Dammit! Dammit!"

Will turned his eyes back down to the house and shrugged off his brother's frustration. His mind churned, searching for a way out of this. Try as he might, he found no answer that didn't end in him and Jake getting caught. Or killed.


Charley stepped up on the porch right behind Emmit.

"I already told you, there ain't nobody here," yelled the Higgins woman. "Ain't no need for you to come in my house!" The dog, alarmed by the woman's angry voice, barked frantically.

"Shut that damn dog up, or I will," said Emmit.

"Chigger! Quiet!" yelled the woman, and the barking subsided into a low growl.

Emmit stepped up to the door, his hand on his pistol.

The woman blocked his way. "You ain't got no right to go in my house!" she yelled. She set her brat down behind her, who started crying. She raised the rolling pin like she might use it on Emmit.

Emmit pulled out his knife and turned it in the air so the woman could see it flash.

"Put that away, Emmit," said Henry. Emmit cursed but lowered the knife.

"Now Missus Higgins," Henry continued, "General Sterling Price of the Confederate State of Missouri has given us orders to round up deserters and bring 'em back. Your two boys is deserters. If it were up to me, I'd just as soon hang 'em."

The woman paled and took another step back.

"But, it ain't up to me." He shrugged. "So I am gonna ask you once again to step aside. We will have a look inside your house." He pointed to the door. "Go on in there, boys."

Emmit sneered at her and took a step forward. The woman stood her ground, but he grabbed her rolling pin and yanked it from her grasp.

Off balance, she stumbled back and fell through the door frame into the house. "Well come on then, damn you," she said. "Ain't nobody here, you'll see that quick enough." She rose and stepped aside, muttering as she did.

Darnell stepped ahead of Charley and doffed his hat, his head hung down as if ashamed of something. Darnell was an odd boy, touched in the head — slow, as some would say — and he didn't have any family or friends. Charley had taken him under his wing a few years back and looked out for him. In return Darnell performed whatever task Charley asked of him without complaint. He was the nearest thing to a friend Charley had.

*Darnell might be ashamed,* Charley thought, *but I ain't, 'specially by no damned Yankee woman.* He stomped into the cabin. Emmit was already rifling through the pantry, looking for drink. Darnell went into the kitchen and rummaged through the pantry.

Charley went to the rope-frame bed near the fireplace, stripped the quilts from it, and poked the bedtick with his hunting knife. He found nothing there, but he sliced open the bed-tick anyway, just for the hell of it. Grinning, He yanked open the door to the back bedroom, his gun half drawn. Inside was nothing but another bed and a few boys clothes hanging on pegs. The bed received the same treatment from his knife, but there was nothing hidden there either. He ripped the clothes from the pegs and threw them on the floor, and returned to the main room empty-handed. Eying the unlit fireplace, he felt around up inside the chimney. His hand found something soft on the ledge inside. He grinned at the woman when his sooty hand came back gripping a small leather purse.

"Looky here, Darnell!" he said, smiling. His joy was short-lived when he counted out only a few dollar's worth of coins. "Damn it! You got more money here somewhere. I know it! Where is it?" He glared at the woman.

"No! That's all we got, an' you cain't take that!"

He smiled. "We call this the Yankee tax, an' we're the tax collectors."

The woman was furious. She glared at him with daggers for eyes, then looked away and said no more.

"Where's the god-damned whiskey?" Emmit roared.

"Charley, they got some biscuits makins and some ham," yelled Darnell from the opened pantry. "You got any coffee?" he asked the woman.

She answered him with only a stare. Darnell shrugged and turned back to his search. When he opened the cook stove and peered inside, the heat made him flinch and he slammed it shut. From the cupboard, he withdrew two cloth bags and grinned. "Coffee! an' sugar," he said.

Charley grinned again. The woman could fix them some good eats. "Boys," he yelled to the men outside. "Come on in and get some breakfast!"

The woman started to say something, then bit her lip. Her head fell, and she looked away.

"I know what you're thinkin'," Charley said.

Her eye-daggers aimed his way again.

"You're were hopin'," Charley continued, "that we'd just take the food an' money and ride on out. Ain't that it?"

Finally, she nodded.

Charley smiled. "Not likely," he said.

*****

18

# Chapter 2

Joline Higgins looked up from her skillet at the marauders who'd invaded her home. Some of the men wore blue sack-coats, and some of those had bullet holes and bloodstains on them. Others were wearing civilian garb, and a few wore gray. All were in need of a meal, clean clothes and a bath.

She recognized none of them, though the yellow-haired man called Porter—just a boy, really—looked somewhat familiar. But she couldn't place him, and she had more important things on her mind.

They were a scruffy gang and stank of body odor, horse sweat, and rotting blood. Their cloying reek mixed with tobacco smoke from their pipes and the greasy smell of frying ham and bitter coffee. In the small house, the stench overwhelmed her, and she almost gagged on it.

She moved to the back door and opened it. She saw her red apron still hanging there, her sign to warn the boys to stay away from the house.

The older man called Henry looked up and shook his head.

"I just need some fresh air," she said.

"You can stand by the front door, leave that one shut."

She knew she had to be careful, these were cruel men—murderers and thieves for sure, probably worse. She shut the door and moved to the window. Henry watched her closely.

And they knew her name! They must know Will and Jake were nearby, too. She hoped they did not know that Will and Jake were Tanners, from her first marriage. It often caused confusion, her last name being Higgins now. *That might stand in my favor though. Might be I can use it. I have got to protect my boys!*

Henry wiped the grease and crumbs from his gray beard with a sleeve, and asked, "Where's your other two boys? The ones that ain't already in the army?"

"They're down at the river," she replied. "Fishin' and trappin'." Joline hoped the boys would remember not to come home while the red apron was out. She relaxed a little, Will was not one to be easily surprised, and he'd see to the younger ones. She forced herself to smile. "They got some muskrat traps out, they're hopin' to get some more skins to trade over in town. An' maybe catch some fish for supper." She paused. "They'll be down there 'till suppertime."

Henry scratched his neck and pinched something he'd found there. He flicked it onto the stove, where it sizzled and popped. He looked directly at her. "Now, Missus Higgins, we know who you are, and we know you're a widower, so you done lied to us once. Don't do it again."

Joline's heart skipped a beat and she looked down at her feet.

"You say your eldest are ridin' with Jo Shelby? What's their names?"

"William... Uh, Will and Jake are my two oldest, they're the ones off with Shelby. Last I heard, they were down in Texas." she lied again.

"Watt, you know Shelby's outfit," said Henry. "You know of any Higgins in that outfit?

Joline thought she might have fooled them, until the Porter boy smiled at her.

"Will and Jake Tanner," he said. "Not Higgins."

Joline turned white. She glared at Porter. Where did she know him from? He must be from around here somewhere, he knew too much.

Porter just smiled back at her.

"Well, Watt, you know any Tanners in Shelby's outfit?" asked Henry.

"Nope, can't recall any. Now I don't know everybody...."

The big man, the one called Emmit, got up from the log bench. "Well ain't that just dandy, Henry. She lies to you like that an' you just sit there and take it. We need to get on with it. If you ain't got the backbone for it, I do."

20

Joline feared this man most of all. He was a big, big man, and there was malice in his pure black eyes. And in that knife he like to flash.

Henry rose and walked to the stove and poured more coffee into his tin cup. He gave Emmit a wide berth.

Emmit stomped over, carrying his own cup and loomed over her. "Where's your whiskey?" He asked. "You got some stashed somewhere, I know it."

Joline saw Henry stiffen but he did nothing, only sipped his coffee. The other men sitting at the table perked up at the mention of whiskey. The Porter boy smiled again, like he was looking forward to something.

Joline shook her head "No, we ain't got no whiskey. We frown on such in this house, we don't hold with it, so we don't...."

Before she could finish, Emmit threw his cup, coffee and all, at the cupboard. Joline flinched but remained calm. Tin plates crashed to the floor, and the cup rolled out. Joline noticed a new dent in it. She moved to pick it up, which also got her away from this angry mountain of a man. She wiped the cup and put it away, out of habit, and moved toward Nate, who had begun to cry again.

"I don't see no bible layin' 'round here, so you ain't no goody-goody. Everybody's got whiskey." Emmit took a step forward, leaned over her and bellowed, "Where's yore God-damned whiskey?"

Joline flinched at the man's rage. Trying to mollify him, she said, "Sir, we ain't got none, take a look for yourself...." She stepped back and moved away from him, trying to find a safer place. Emmit chased her around the table and cornered her at the bed where Nate lay bawling now, frightened by the noise and angry voices.

Henry sighed and shook his head but made no effort to intervene. The other men egged Emmit on. "Get 'er, Emmit!" one said. They laughed at her plight.

Joline wanted nothing more than to run away, but there was Nate to think about, and now the men were between her and either door.

"I've had enough o' this," Emmit yelled. "Let's get to the business at hand." He hitched up his pants, took a step forward and back-handed her.

She yelled and fell backward onto the bed. Stunned, she lay there for a moment, eyes watering, until the sting faded. Nate crawled over to her, wailing now. Holding her face where Emmit had struck her, she tried to shush him. "It's all right, Nate, it's all right. Shhhhh."

The other men hooted and watched to see what Emmit would do next.

"I don't know what you men want," Joline sniffed. "My boys are already fightin' on your side, and we ain't got no more money. An' we ain't got no whiskey. Why don't you-all just ride on out of here? Take the food, take it all if you want, please, just leave us be." She fought back her tears.

Emmit walked over, pulled her up by her hair, and struck her again, this time with his palm. The slap knocked her back across the bed. This time she rolled off the far side and pulled Nate to her.

Henry threw down the rag he'd been wiping his hands with and stood up straight. "They ain't got nothing more we need, Emmit. Leave her be. We got bigger fish to fry."

The big man glared at him instead. "Naw, Henry, she's a liar, you know that. She lied about her husban' and them boys. She's lyin' about the whiskey. I know they got some. Everybody's got whiskey or some corn-liquor. Even them that say otherwise. She'll tell me where it is, or else...." He pulled his knife from his belt and waved it at Joline. "Where's that whiskey?" he demanded. He whacked the bed frame with the knife, like a hatchet, knocking out a chunk of wood.

"I... I told you, we ain't got none!" she stammered, her heart racing. She crawled backward, into the corner away from Emmit, pulling Nate with her. She made herself as small as she could.

Emmit chopped furiously at the bedpost. Chunks of wood flew to the floor. He stopped chopping and moved around the bed toward Joline. Her heart nearly stopped.

"Emmit," Henry said. "Let's go. They ain't got no whiskey, or money, an' we got business elsewhere. Let's go."

The men's hooting died down to silence. The big man continued to stare at Joline for a moment, then his eyes turned to glare at Henry whose hand now rested on his pistol..

Henry's eyes remained steady, watching Emmit.

Emmit cursed and stabbed his knife into the bedpost, where it stood straight out. You'd shoot me, Henry?" He pushed back his coat, exposing his own gun.

"I will. If you make me." Henry said, in a calm voice. His hand was steady on the gun, his eyes unwavering.

Joline thought for sure Henry would shoot the big man or be shot by him. The men stared at each other for what seemed like forever, Emmit's eyes full of spite, Henry's steady as a rock. Emmit's hand shook ever so slightly, otherwise nobody moved.

After an eternity, Emmit's hand moved away from his gun. "All right, Henry, lets ride," he said, leaning forward on the table. "You're the boss. For now. They'll be whiskey elsewhere anyhow." He turned and stalked to the door, grabbed his hat from a peg, and went outside.

The men muttered, some in relief, some in disappointment. Joline heard only her own heart pounding in her chest.

Henry kept his hand on his gun for a minute, then he relaxed, too. "Boys, take all the food you can carry."

The Porter boy rose, cursing. He stared at Henry a moment, shook his head, and stalked outside. Another boy, the slow one, grabbed the remaining biscuits, ham and coffee beans, threw it all into a flour sack and made his way out the door, looking sadly at Joline as he left. The other men grabbed what they could find and filed out, cursing and muttering.

*Henry has robbed them of a show,* thought Joline.

Henry turned to Joline, and his features softened just a little bit. "My apologies, Missus, for my friend Emmit's behavior."

Joline could only stare at the man. She touched her cheek below here eye. It was already swelling.

Henry continued, "He weren't a bad man before the Yankees strung up his brother. He's still a bit raw on that account, as you're likely to understand. Still, it's best that he didn't find any liquor. He can be a mean one when he's had a pull or two." He pulled the knife from the bedpost, threw on his own coat and hat and followed the men out the door.

Joline rose from the floor and tried to comfort Nate who was still wailing. Her cheek stung and throbbed, and her eye was swollen nearly shut. She carried Nate to the window, pulled back the curtain and watched the men with her good eye as they filled their saddlebags with the hams, bacon, corn, molasses, and tobacco they'd stolen from her family.

Henry flipped the knife in his hand and gave it to Emmit, handle first. "We got everything we can carry?"

When the men assented, he mounted his horse. "Price needs men. There's two here somewhere, probably watchin'. Let's see if we can flush 'em out." He looked directly at Joline. His eyes, now emotionless, locked steady on hers for a moment before he turned to the Porter boy, "Burn it. House and barn. Burn it all," he said.

Porter's scowl turned into a grin and he headed back to the house.

"No!" Joline screamed.


Will was getting really worried now. It had been the longest hour he had ever spent, waiting on the men down there to leave. Nothing happened, except that a man came out and relieved the guard, and some of the men had visited the outhouse.

Then something changed. The men came out of the house carrying sacks stuffed with... *What? Food?* It had to be food, they didn't have anything else worth taking. Others raided the smokehouse and the corncrib, and came away with their sacks filled. One man grabbed a chicken, wrung its neck, and hung it on his saddle. Another raided the hen house and came away with a basket of eggs and two more chickens.

"Dammit Will, you see what they're doin', they're takin' our food."

"I know, I see it.

Jake cocked his shotgun. "We just gonna let 'em?"

"Yeah, we are. If they'll just leave us alone it will be worth it."

"You know they won't."

"I don't know that, Jake, I'm hopin'," Will snapped. "For the last time, think about what will happen if we go down there. We'll be killed, for sure."

Jake uncocked his shotgun. "Dammit!"

Will agreed. "Yeah, dammit!"

Jake shook his head. "I don't understand you, Will Tanner. Not one bit."

"I know that, too," said Will.

*This is more like it,* Charley thought. He strode back up onto the porch where he met the Higgins woman, her rolling pin in her hand. She swung it at his head, but he ducked the blow. She did knock his hat off, which enraged him. He wrenched the pin from her grasp, and she fell to her knees.

"I'll teach you, you old shrew!" He raised the wooden roller like a club.

"No, Porter" yelled Henry. "Just burn the house."

"Dammit Henry, she hit me. I got to teach her she cain't do that." He raised the pin again. The boom of a pistol shot stopped him in midswing. Charley looked back. Henry was now holding his pistol aimed straight at his face. Smoke still trickled from the barrel and the bore looked as big as a barn door. Time seemed to stop, and the hair stood up on Charley's neck. Everything was still and quiet, even the dog had stopped yapping.

"Porter, I said no. You will not do that, not while I am here," said Henry.

Charley dropped the roller, and it bounced off the porch with a clatter, and rolled under the house. The other riders were watching intently, but none made a move to defend him. He thought long and hard about his next move. Henry had the drop on him—there was no next move. Better to be shamed and live another day. *Someday I will kill you for this, Henry Perkins.*

"All right Henry, goddammit, you win," Charley said. "This time." The men behind Henry guffawed and Charley's face burned with anger. He snatched his hat up from the porch and put it on, smashing it down on his head.

He turned and kicked the Higgins woman back into the house. She rose to her feet and backed away, her eyes looking around wildly. Charley figured she was lookin' for a knife. Or a hidden pistol.

She either thought better of it or there was no weapon. She backed further away and put herself between him and her brat. "Please don't do this, there ain't no cause for it," she said. Tears filled her eyes.

"You been harborin' Yankee scum. That's cause enough. Besides, I got orders." Charley laughed—he'd do this without orders if it came to it.

He saw the cookstove, still full of hot embers, and smiled. *That will do,* he thought. He gave it a hard kick, and it fell sideways but didn't quite fall over — the stovepipe held it up. Charley knocked it off with a stick of kindling and kicked the stove again. This time it fell on its side, the door flew open and hot coals spilled out onto the wooden floor. Flames sprouted up immediately.

The Higgins woman jumped backward, grabbed her brat and ran out the back door.

Charley spotted something on the floor that wasn't there a few minutes ago. A leather bag had fallen from the bottom of the stove. He picked it up. It was hot to the touch and it jingled with coin. *That lyin' bitch! It was hid under the damn stove!* The flames were growing larger and Charley grew nervous. He ran out the back door himself, bag in hand. As he walked by the woman, he grinned and shook the bag. "Lookee what I found!"

If her eyes could have killed, Charley would be dead. Her glare bored right through him. But it had no effect on him, and he danced around her, jingling the bag of coins in her face. "More Yankee tax," he said.

Tucking the bag into his pants, he strutted to the barn where he found a coal-oil lamp and a box of matches. He smashed the lamp against the wall of the feed stall next to the hay. The coal-oil soaked deep into it while he struck a match. When he threw it into the hay-pile, flames leapt up and licked the side of the stall. He watched the fire until the wood caught. Only then did he turn away, satisfied there'd be no saving the barn now. The mule smelled smoke and kicked at the stall door. It brayed and panic filled its eyes.

*Too bad for you, old mule,* he thought. Turning away, he left the barn.

Back outside, he saw there was no saving the house now, it was already too far gone. Yellow flames licked from the open door, and thick, black smoke rose high into the sky, contrasting against the white clouds in the blue sky.

The woman threw a bucket of water into the fire through the back door, doing little good. She returned to the well for another bucket but dropped it when flames erupted from the open windows. Her brat sat by the well and howled for his mama. She reached to pick him up, but when the mule screamed again, she instead ran to the barn and emerged leading the mule.

"You'd burn the mule to death?" she shouted at him. "You're a damned cruel man. No, you're a damned cruel little boy!" She spat the words out at him.

"A boy? I'll show you how much you know." He pulled his pistol and shot the mule in the chest. It brayed, took a step and collapsed to the ground, its legs flailing about. He shot the mule again, and then a third time, until it lay still. He looked straight at the woman before holstering his gun. "Don't think I won't kill your boys just like that mule. I've killed men before and I'll do it again."

The woman sagged to the ground next to her brat. She keened and wailed loudly for a long minute. Then she seemed to stiffen her resolve and clenched her jaw. She picked herself up, sat the crying brat on her hip and walked straight up to Charley. She looked him right in the eye and didn't flinch. He could feel her hatred for him like it was a hot poker aimed for his face. It only served to stiffen his resolve and he returned her stare with a smirk of his own. She never looked away and in the end, it was his smile that faded and his eyes that looked away.

"You'll pay for this, Charley Porter," she said. "Someday soon, you'll get what's comin' to you for this. I know who you are and what you are. You'll pay."

Taken aback, Charley backed away from her cold fury.


Up on the ridge, hope flooded Will's body and removed some of the weight from his shoulders. The riders had left the house and mounted up. It looked like they were gonna ride on out. There was some conversation, a yellow-haired man dismounted, walked back to the porch and disappeared. Will started when smoke puffed up into the air and a second later the sound of a pistol shot reached his ears. Beside him, Jake jumped. Will at first thought the worst until he spotted the gun smoke moving straight up into the air. Was that a warning shot? Or a signal for us to come out? Both?

A minute later, Ma ran out of the back door with Nate in her arms. She set him down by the well and lowered the bucket. The yellow-haired man exited from the back door, walked by her and headed to the barn.

Will's hopes for a peaceful end to the encounter died when smoke boiled out of the house's open back door. *No, no! They're burning the house!*

Beside him, Jake gasped and cursed.

Ma drew a bucket of water from the well, ran to the back door and threw it inside. Behind her, the man went in the barn and after a few seconds, came back out. Wisps of smoke escaped through the gaps in the boards of the barn walls.

"Will!" Yelled Jake.

"I know, Jake! I see it!"

"Goddammit, Will! They're burnin' it! Goddammit!" Jake's voice rose, and he struggled to rise from the ground. Will grabbed a fistful of sleeve and held him down.

Jake's eyes bored into Will's with a look of pure rage. "Dammit, Will! We gotta do somethin'!"

Will's eyes moved to the rifle he held, and he stared at it, his shaking hands gripping it so tight that his knuckles had turned white. *We cain't do anything*, he thought, *they'll kill us both.*

Tears formed in Will's eyes and he wiped them on his sleeve. "Jake!" he said, still holding his brother's arm. "Jake, listen! We cain't go down there! It's what they want! Don't you see 'em down there, waitin' for us?" His voice cracked as he choked up.

Down below, flames burst from the windows of the house and black smoke billowed high into the sky. The house was already too far gone to save. Atop the barn, flames now licked up through holes where some shingles had been ripped away by a spring storm.

By now, Jake had turned purple with rage. Again, he tried to get up and again, Will held him down.

"Damn you, Will, we have got to go down there and help them!"

"No," Will croaked, wiping more tears on his sleeve. "No. Listen to me. I want to go down there and shoot those men as much as you do but we cain't do it. We might get one or two, then we'll be killed. We don't want Ma to see that. An' we cain't save the house now. It's too late already."

Jake cursed under his breath. He stopped struggling and lowered his face into his arms. "Dammit, Will. We shoulda' gone down there when I told you the first time."

Will had no answer to Jake's accusation, so all he did was shake his head. He kept a firm grip on his brother. *Why cain't he see it would just get somebody killed? And not just us?*

Will clenched and unclenched his fists, and tears streaked down his cheeks as smoke and flames poured from the house. Flames were leaping from the barn now, too. The smoke from both fires, black and thick, rose high in the blue sky and mingled into one column.

Through his tears, Will watched Ma run to the house, throw another useless bucket of water at it, then return to the well and drop the bucket. He watched her rescue Missy from the burning barn and watched smoke puff again and heard three distant booms as the yellow-haired man shot the mule.

They both cursed. Will had to hold Jake back yet again. Why did they shoot our mule, he wondered? For what possible reason? Will couldn't understand the cruelty. To shoot the mule like that made no sense. It was an act of pure meanness.

They had owned Missy for as long as he remembered—she was part of the family, and to see her killed like this brought sobs to his throat. *How're we gonna plant next spring?*

Chigger, their old beagle, waddled out from under the house and turned to bark at the fire. If they shot Chigger it would be the last thing he could stand.

By that time, the men had ridden around back. There was some discussion, some gestures were made, and the yellow-haired man put away his gun.

Beside him, Jake trembled with rage. "God-damn them sonsabitches!" he sobbed. He cursed them over and over and ripped off his hat and slammed it to the ground.

Will didn't know how much longer he could hold Jake back, and he didn't know how much more he could take himself.

He too, wanted to go down there and kill those men, though he'd never killed a man, and he never thought he'd want to. He wanted to beat them to a pulp, to shoot holes in them, to cut them up with his knife—to watch them bleed and suffer and plead for their lives. He wanted them to be sorry they'd ever come here.

It wasn't in his power to do it and trying to would only get him and Jake killed. Where would Ma and his other brothers be, then? At the complete mercy of those merciless men.

Flames shot up from the windows of the house and smoke billowed. Now, the wind shifted, and the crackle and roar of the fires reached all the way to where they lay hidden atop the bluff. Down by the well, Ma sank to her knees, sat there and put her head in her hands. She was crying, and Will couldn't go to her, couldn't help her. It broke his heart to watch, and tears rolled down his own cheeks, but he clenched his jaw and set his mind to bear it. They had to bear it. He had to bear it. For Ma's sake.

The Higgins woman's words had given Charley a chill, but he shook it off. He felt her hateful eyes boring into him just the same.

Henry, Emmit, Darnell and a few of the men rode around to see what the shooting was about. Darnell dismounted and knelt by the mule's body. He put a hand on it and turned to look at Charley, a puzzled look on his face.

"What the hell, Porter?" asked Henry.

"Just an old broken-down old mule. Nothin' to get excited about," Charley replied.

Henry shook his head. "Porter, that mule might've come in right handy in Price's supply train. Or else they might've et it. You ever think before you go poppin' off your guns?"

Charley snorted. "That old mule wouldn't have made it five miles before it died."

An old dog crawled out from under the burning house and barked at the fire. Charley considered shooting it to spite Henry and the damn Higgins woman. He looked at Henry. "Can that there dog carry anything for Ole Goddam Price?"

"Don't shoot that dog," said Darnell.

Charley looked over at his only friend. Darnell had a soft spot for animals in general and for dogs in particular, and he was plainly upset by the dead mule. Charley felt the need to placate him, so he holstered his pistol. "All right, Darnell, I won't shoot the damn dog. It's just another mouth for them damn Yankees to feed, anyhow."

Darnell crouched and whistled the dog over to him. It waddled over and licked him in the face, his whole rump wagging as if Darnell was its long-lost master.

Charley could only shake his head in bewilderment.

The horses were getting nervous from the flames and smoke and the smell of the mule's blood. They pranced and sidestepped restlessly. Darnell stopped petting the dog long enough to soothe and calm them all. "Whoa now, easy, easy," he said. Soon they settled down again, and the dog wandered off into the cornfield.

Charley felt the need to reload, so he walked around the house to his own mount. The others followed him, walking their horses slowly.

"Well, I reckon them boys ain't gonna show," said Emmit.

"Let's give it another minute," said Henry.

As Charley was reaching into a saddlebag for powder and balls, a mule brayed from the road behind him. When he turned and looked, a wagon and a team of mules pulled up, followed by the inevitable dust cloud. In the driver's box sat an old man and a girl, both wearing yellow straw hats. In the back stood three negroes, buckets held tightly in their hands.

He forgot the powder and swapped pistols with one of his spares. He mounted up and faced the wagon as it came to a creaking stop. The negroes jumped out, buckets in hand, and made for the well.

The girl caught his eye right away. Dark, auburn hair fell from under her hat and made a pretty contrast with her lightly tanned face. She wore a red gingham skirt, stained a reddish-brown on the bottom from dragging in the dirt. A dark blue shirtwaist, gathered in by her apron strings, did little to hide the fullness of her figure. Rolled-up sleeves, stained the same dirty color as her skirt and apron, revealed well-tanned arms and hands. Her worn-out brogans were caked with dried mud of the same color. She was no spoiled child, this girl, she'd spent long hours working outside in the fields and gardens.

Despite all that, she was the prettiest girl he'd ever seen, and he could not take his eyes off her.

*****

# Chapter 3

Lucy Carter had never been so terrified. Smoke filled the sky, flames reached high into the air, crackling and popping, and a gang of vile men milled about on their horses, pointing guns at everyone. A dead mule lay on its side near the well, its blood soaking into the raw dirt.

Joline Higgins knelt nearby, cradling her crying youngster, Nate. When she spied Lucy, she ran over and handed up the toddler. Lucy took him without hesitation and set him in her lap. Nate shivered and shook as he cried, and Lucy tried to soothe him.

Papa alighted from the wagon and approached a gray-bearded man on horseback. The man pulled his pistol and pointed it at the negroes. "Hold it right there!" he yelled. "First one of you darkies to draw water gets a bullet!" The negroes dropped their buckets and backed away, hands up in the air. He turned his gun on Papa, who stopped in his tracks.

"What is the meaning of this outrage?" asked Papa.

"Who are you to be askin'?" asked the man.

"Benjamin Carter. I own the farm right over there, next door. I saw the smoke and we came to put this fire out."

"Well now," said the man. The pistol pointed downward. "These your slaves, Mr. Carter?"

"Yes, those are my negroes."

"You are not a Lincoln man, then. I'd rather not harm you or your property. You all should just get back in your wagon and ride on home and put this behind you. This ain't your affair."

Papa insisted. "Who are you men?"

"Mister Carter," he sighed. "We are the Missouri State Guard. That's all you need to know."

Papa looked them over good. "I doubt that," he said.

"Never you mind, then, who we are," said the man.

"Why are you burning these poor folks out? They ain't harmed no-one," said Papa. "I've known them for nigh on thirty years, and they're good folk."

"That may be," said the man. "But they got two boys that deserted an' General Price needs men. We're here to round 'em up." Henry motioned with the pistol. "Now you go on back to your wagon."

The negroes did as they were told, but Papa stood his ground.

"I mean what I say," the man said. "I will shoot you if I have to. That house will burn."

Lucy's blood turned cold. That man had threatened to shoot Papa. Maybe they should just go home, like the man said. But that would leave poor Joline all alone to deal with these ruffians.

All eyes turned as two young boys ran up from the cornfield. Lucy recognized them as two more of Joline's five boys. *Is that Ike and Seth? They have grown a foot since the last time I saw them!* A skinny boy with yellow hair pointed his pistol at them but lowered it when he saw they were un-armed.

"Ma!" yelled Ike. The boys ran to Joline and she sank to her knees and hugged them to her. Time seemed to stand still as flames shot through the roof of the house and smoke billowed high into the air. The fires snapped and popped, and Joline sobbed.

The roof of the house collapsed inward with a crash of noise and sparks. In the wagon, Lucy felt a blast of heat and she covered Nate with her arms and turned her head until it died away. Sparks flew high into the sky.

Papa looked at the burning buildings, removed his hat, wiped the sweat from his head on his sleeve and replaced the hat. The fire crackled and hissed. Turning back to the gray-bearded man, he said, "I don't know who you are, but you, sir, are an evil man. And evil only begets more evil, and violence only begets more violence."

The yellow-haired boy laughed out loud. "Henry, let me put a hole in this bible-spoutin' old fool. Shut him up for good."

"No, Porter, I'll handle this." The man named Henry turned back to Papa. "It may be harsh, Sir, but these are harsh times. I do what is necessary for Southern independence. You bein' a slave-holder, you ought to understand that. Now go on back to your wagon." Henry raised his pistol again and motioned with it for Papa to move.

Papa raised his hands. "I ain't armed." he said. He backed away toward the wagon and stood with the negroes. He glanced into the wagon box.

"An' don't even think about usin' that scattergun you got layin' there," said Henry.

"You won't harm my daughter, will you?" Papa asked.

"We don't molest women nor children. We ain't animals."

Papa backed away from the wagon box.

The boy called Porter looked at something off in the distance. He raised his gun and fired a shot off into the air — Lucy jumped at the sharp crack even though she'd seen it coming.

Then he aimed his pistol right at Ike Higgins and Lucy nearly stopped breathing.

"Will Tanner!" he yelled loudly in the direction of the bluff. "Come out now! Or else I start shootin'!"


Will spotted the two small figures crossing the cornfield, heading right for the conflagration — and the marauders. Panic struck him like a hammer blow and the blood drained from his face. Ike and Seth were heading straight into the terrible danger down below. *How did they get by me an' Jake?*

Jake gasped and pointed. "No!"

Things were getting out of hand fast, and Will was sure someone was going to get hurt. His whole family was now in mortal danger. He racked his brain for way out of this mess. Nothing came to him.

More movement below grabbed his attention; a mule-drawn wagon had pulled up and stopped. It was their neighbor Ben Carter and some of his hands. They'd seen the smoke and come to help.

And now, a man was holding a gun on Ben Carter. And who was that woman with him?

There were too many riders down there, too many guns pointing in too many directions. Someone was bound to start shooting any time now. His mind raced and his hearted pounded until he thought it would burst.

The man who shot the mule drew his gun again and fired a shot into the air. Then he pointed it directly at Ike. Will heard him shouting something but he couldn't make it out. No matter, he knew what it was. A warning. The second one. A warning for us to come out. There might not be another.

That was the breaking point, the last straw. He had to do something. Now!

"Will!" said Jake.

"I know, Jake, I know!"

There was only one thing left for them to do.

Jake had long ago come to the same conclusion. "We gotta go down there," he said through his tears. He stood up and cocked the old shotgun. "Don't try and stop me this time."

"Yeah, Jake. We gotta go down there," replied Will. "If we leave the guns here, go down and surrender, maybe they'll just take us and leave Ma and the boys alone." He paused and pondered a moment. "On second thought. I'll go down by myself. I'll tell 'em you are off some other place workin' as a hired hand. Maybe that will satisfy 'em and they won't look for you. Ma will need you to help out now."

"No Sir," said Jake. "You ain't takin' this on yourself. We go down there together. Besides, they won't be satisfied 'til they catch us both. You know it. It won't work anyhow."

Will cursed again, there wasn't time to argue, and Jake might be right anyway. "Ok, we both go." Now that he had decided, some of the tension left and the helpless feeling eased. He wiped his eyes on his sleeves and took a deep breath. He looked at Jake, who had gone white. "You ready?"

Jake nodded. They slid the guns into the brush, out of sight, and stepped forward with their hands up. Will yelled, "We're comin' out! Don't shoot!" He hoped the riders below could hear them over the noise of the flames.

"No sudden moves, Jake," he said to his brother.

Jake nodded again.

They walked down the rise and into the cornfield, yelling out their surrender every few steps. The waist-high stalks swished as they walked through them, almost drowning out the noise from the fire.

Soon they were close enough that one of the riders noticed, and several pistols moved to cover them. He stopped. Now was the riskiest time. Would they simply shoot them and be done with it? Will shuddered, his hands shook, his knees wobbled, and his throat tightened. "We ain't armed!" he yelled. It sounded more like a croak.

Will looked at Jake, who looked as scared as he felt. "Well, Jake," he said, "this might be the end of us."

Jake's eyes went wide as the reality of what could happen set in.

*Better us than Ma and the boys,* Will thought.


Charley looked at the girl again. Fascinated, he eased over to get a closer look, keeping his gun pointed at the oldest Higgins boy.

He noticed the slight reddish tint in her hair. He saw her big brown eyes, that were for the moment locked onto the drawn guns. She trembled ever so slightly, not from fear, but from anger, he figured. Her scowling eyes met his own, and she didn't look away.

She held her stare and her lips compressed into a scowl and she ground her teeth, her anger and disgust plain to see in her eyes.

*She's no shrinking violet, this one,* Charley thought. He doffed his hat to her, in defiance, no longer caring what she might think, and rode back to face the Higgins family.

"Any sign of them deserters?" Henry yelled.

"Yeah, Henry. They're comin'," said Emmit, laughing. He pointed to the field behind the house with his pistol.

Charley looked. Sure enough, two young men were walking through the waist-high corn, un-armed, hands high in the air. He hadn't seen them in two years, but he recognized them right away — Will and Jake Tanner.

He forgot the girl as he grinned and rode out to meet them, his pistol now aimed their way.


Right away, Will noticed the scraggly yellow hair and the thin features of the man who trotted his horse over, his pistol aimed their way. But it was the wild cackle of laughter from his lips that gave him away. He knew him! It was the Porter boy! The last Will had seen of him was at the battle at Elkhorn Tavern when he'd seen Yankee soldiers marching him off as a prisoner or war. What the hell was he doing here?

Porter was thinner than before, if that was possible, and his eyes were sunk back into his head, leaving only dark shadows where his eyes should be. He looked thin and sickly, like he hadn't eaten in a long while.

He looked dangerous too. He was no longer a scared teenage boy. There was a swagger and a cockiness about him that was not there before. He looked like a rattlesnake. Coiled up and ready to strike.

Will eyed the bullet holes in the blue coat Porter wore and realized that he'd likely taken it off a dead Yankee. Did he kill the man himself?

As if in answer, Porter rode around behind them and Will heard the click of a pistol being cocked. Will's knees gave way and he kneeled in the dirt. *This is the end. I'm gonna die right here in front of Ma. Well, ain't nothin' more to be done about it.* An odd sense of calmness overcame him, and he closed his eyes and waited.

"Porter!" yelled the leader of the gang. "Alive, I said! We need 'em alive!"

"All right, Henry, I won't shoot 'em," said Porter. "Not yet, anyhow."

Will had never heard sweeter words. He opened his eyes and stumbled to his feet. They might live a while longer.

Porter rode up in front of them, his pistol still cocked. "You boys are lucky Henry's in charge," he said. "I'd shoot you now, if I had my way, you damned Yankee scum."

Jake stared at Porter as if he had two heads. "Once a liar, always a lair, right Porter? We ain't no Yankees and you know it."

"Just keep quiet," said Will. "Don't provoke 'im."

Porter's eyes flashed. "Oh, I'm provoked, all right. An' you boys are gonna pay for what you done. You owe me an' I'm here to collect."

Will racked his brain, trying to understand what it was they'd done to Porter to deserve this anger, this ferocity. Then he recalled the fist fight Jake and Porter had just before the battle. He'd never bothered to ask what that was all about, but surely that couldn't be it, could it?

Will's thoughts were cut short when a big man with a huge dirty beard threw him a rope. "You," he said, pointing to Will. "Bind that 'uns wrists in front. An' it better be tight when I check."

"Sorry," said Will as he tied Jake's wrists together. Jake winced as he tightened the knot. Their eyes met and Will caught a glimpse of something in his brother's eyes just before he turned away. Guilt? Remorse? He put the thought aside for now.

The big man dismounted and bound Will's wrists in the same manner. He checked Jake's ropes, looked at Will and grunted. Porter sat on his horse nearby, still holding his pistol.

"You got two minutes to say your goodbyes," said Henry.

They walked over to Ma and the boys who had gathered around Carter's wagon. When Will saw the bruises on Ma's face, his heart fell. "What did they do to you, Ma?"

Jake bristled with anger. "I'll kill 'em for this, Ma, I swear it," he growled.

"Hush up, Jake," said Ma, looking nervously to see if any bushwhackers had heard him. None had. "It ain't nothin' that won't heal. Don't you worry about me none." She started crying again. "Why did you come down here? Why didn't you stay hid up there?" she asked through her tears.

Will hung his head in shame. "We had to. When they pointed that gun at Ike, we couldn't just sit up there and watch." Will choked up. "We had to do somethin'...." He couldn't say any more.

Ma shook her head. "They wouldn't have hurt us no more now that the Carter's come to help. I wish you'd just stayed up there. Now you'll be drug off to God knows where an' I might not ever see you again." She hugged him.

"It'll be all right Ma," Will whispered into her ear. "We got away once, remember, an' we can do it again. I ain't dyin' for no Rebels if I can help it. Jake neither."

Ma nodded into his shoulder. "You do that, Will Tanner. Wait for a good chance, an' be careful. An' watch out for your brother."

She hugged Jake and said something to him. Two men grabbed the ropes and yanked them roughly away from their mother.

"Ike," yelled Will. "Watch out for Ma and your brothers." As he was being led past the wagon, he said, "Thank you, Mr. Ben, for coming to help."

Then he noticed the woman in the wagon and stopped in his tracks. It was Lucy, all right. He'd not seen her in two years and…she'd changed—grown up. She was beautiful. The rope yanked him roughly forward.

"Don't dawdle," warned Henry. "We ain't got time for laggin' behind. Keep up or get shot."

Will couldn't keep from looking back at Lucy as he was being dragged away. He could swear she was looking right back into his eyes. She was the prettiest thing he'd ever seen. And she had smiled at him.

*****

# Chapter 4

All Joline could do was cry. It had all come to naught; the house and barn burned to the ground, their mule killed, and worse, the boys captured and hauled off like pigs to market.

"My boys! My boys!" she sobbed. "Why didn't they stay hid out like I told 'em!"

Lucy came over and held her hands, trying to console her. "I know, Miss Joline, I know," she said, kneeling and hugging her. "They'll be all right. I'm sure of it. But right now, we got to take care of your other boys. They're right here, safe and sound."

Through her tears, Joline watched her youngest son play in in the dirt nearby. Oblivious to his crying mother, Nate herded a june-bug around with a stick, until the beetle had enough and opened its wings and buzzed off. He started to cry again. Lucy picked him up and helped him find another one.

*Lucy's right,* thought Joline. She had to be strong for her boys, and she made up her mind to get control of her emotions. She looked up at the sky, where black smoke still twirled in the breeze, took a deep breath, and released it slowly. Her boys had come through the ordeal unscathed, and that was something to be thankful for. Her sobs gave way to sniffling, and she wiped her eyes on her apron.

Joline looked at Ike and Seth who clustered around her. Ike tried his best to look confident and fearless; he'd fetched Ben's shotgun from the wagon and stood guard over them all. She could tell he was still shaken by what he'd seen today—his eyes stared off, unfocused, into the distance, and a stony frown was etched on his face.

"Ma, where are we gonna sleep tonight?" asked Seth. He clung to her skirts and picked at some mud that was stuck there. She didn't have

40

an answer for him.

Ike looked down at his feet. "I'm sorry, Ma," he said. "Will, he told us to stay hid, but when I heard the shootin' an' saw the smoke I didn't know what to do."

"You were supposed to stay hid, Ike, you an' Seth," she said. "Till dark. Then you were supposed to go to the Carter house."

"I know, Ma. I'm sorry."

Joline watched him shuffle his feet in the dirt. She figured he'd suffered enough for one day and she couldn't bring herself to chastise him further. The bushwhackers — for that's what they were, she was sure of it — were far more violent and unpredictable than anyone could have expected. It was no wonder their plans fell apart.

She sighed. "It's all right, none of this was your fault," she said. She struggled to get the words out, but Ike needed to hear it. "An' nobody got hurt. We can always build another house. It's gonna be all right."

"You got hurt, though," said Ike. He looked up to meet her eyes.

"It looks worse than it feels. It'll heal up right quick. Don't you fret none about that." Joline saw the angry look that crossed his face, just before he looked away. *When Ike sets his jaw like that,* she thought, *he looks like Frank.*

Joline sighed. She missed Frank Higgins, her second husband and father to her three youngest boys. He'd been a good man and a good father, even to Will and Jake, and she'd loved him dearly. Things might have been different today if he were here. But he wasn't, the flu had taken him a few months before Nate was born.

There was already too much sadness in this world. Then along came this damned war, and the sadness doubled. Far too many young men went off to fight and precious few came home. The ones that did were the wounded, the maimed, the armless, legless and worse. Some, like Ben Carter's second boy, Patrick, simply vanished — gone missing in some far-off place named New Hope Church. *Of all the places in the world,* she thought, *why fight a battle at a church?*

Thinking of Will and Jake facing those same dangers made her shudder. She'd tried hard not to let her boys get caught up in this mess. But the war had found them, sure as the world. It had come knocking on their door and Will and Jake had answered and they'd suffered for it. Twice now. They'd been lucky the first time, would their luck hold? She had to shake off this melancholy! Nothing good would come of such dark thoughts.

Maybe Will was right, after all, to come down and surrender like he did. Would those men have really killed Ike if he hadn't? She couldn't know now, for sure. They might've, she decided.

And that yellow-haired boy who pointed the gun at him. What kind of a boy threatens another child? And that huge black-bearded ruffian that beat her. She shuddered again. It was best not to think about what might've happened.

Suddenly, Ben appeared in front of her and said something, but she wasn't listening. She'd been staring into the flames, lost in her world of what-ifs. She focused her eyes on Ben and rose to her feet; her knees were weak and wobbly and almost failed her.

Ben gripped her hands and steadied her. "I sent my man Tom to town to fetch the sheriff," he said. "The authorities need to know that there's bushwhackers about. Maybe the militia or the army will be called out to look for them and your boys."

Joline nodded through her tears. Ben continued talking, and she heard him say something about bushwhackers being bad out west, near Kansas, but they'd not been this far east in a long time. Everybody heard about what was going on out west. But there had been little of that here since they dragged Will and Jake off the first time.

Ben and his negroes had been pouring water on the house since the riders rode out of sight. There wasn't much else they could do. The flames had worked their business and the house was gone.

She thought about her mother's old cupboard, by now, a part of the ashes. It made it all the way out here from Kentucky in an old wagon, through storms and across flooded rivers, under dripping wagon tarps only to get burned up in a fire like so much kindling. She sighed, resigned to its loss. It was gone, forever, nothing to be done about it.

She took some solace from knowing everything else could be replaced. She wiped her eyes on her apron again. *Time to quit cryin' and start doin'.*

When the slaves returned to the well for more water, she walked over and said, "Thank you for helping, but it's no use. It's too far gone. Rest yourselves."

They looked at Ben, waiting for his instructions. He nodded, and they began putting the buckets back in the wagon.

Ben cupped his hands and took a drink from the last bucket they had drawn. He poured some on his head to rinse off the sweat and soot. "You'll stay with us until we can get you rebuilt," he said. "And we will help you rebuild."

She shook her head. "You're a kind man, Ben Carter. We cain't impose on you like that. With the war an' all, it's too hard on everybody these days."

"No, no, no," he replied. "We have the room, plenty of food and spare clothes. and you are welcome to it. Martha will make you welcome." He lowered his voice. "Fact is, she'd tan my hide if I did otherwise." He laughed. "You can stay in the carriage house as long as it takes to get you fixed up."

Taken aback by the kind offer, Joline was at a loss for words. She knew Ben had another son, James, off fighting, right now, for the South. Yet here he was, offering to help, even though Will and Jake had been avoiding conscription for a long time now. He must know it too, it was an open secret in the community. She felt somehow ashamed.

As if he'd read her mind, he said, "I don't hold with what those men done. That man was wrong. I ain't no Lincoln man, sure enough, but I didn't vote for no secession neither. In my eyes, those men ain't nothin' more than murderers and thieves. They ought to be hung for what they did, and I aim to see it done if I can." He spat on the ground.

Once again, Joline was speechless. But she finally found her voice. "Thank you. I don't really know what to say. We'll only stay as long as it takes to get a roof over our heads." If Will and Jake could escape those men, things might still work out all right.

Ben waved away her thanks with a flick of his hand. "It's settled then."

Joline found her spirits rising from Ben's kindness. *There is still goodness in the world, after all,* she thought.

Ben took another drink of water from the pail and slung the excess water from the dipper. He waved his arms around at their farm. "Your crops look good; the corn will make well, the tobacco will do, and you got some pigs and chickens left. You'll be able to start again."

"Yes," she said. "We can start over." She made herself smile, just a little. She put an arm around Ike's waist and the other across Seth's shoulders and hugged them both.

"Now," said Ben. "Let's see what we can salvage from these ruins. Rhett! Tom! Check the smokehouse and see if those damned thieves left anything."

Joline looked back at the remains of her home. The chimney looked more like a tombstone than part of a house. It stood there looking lonely and sad against the clear blue sky. *It is a gravestone,* she thought, *a gravestone for a burned-up house.* That made her sadder than ever. She was suddenly very worried about Will and Jake.


While Nate napped in the wagon, Lucy poked around in the smoking ashes of the house with sticks, looking for any metal items they could find. Lucy's mind was not on her work. She couldn't stop thinking about Will.

He was no longer the clumsy, gangly boy that she remembered. She couldn't say exactly why, but she thought he'd somehow grown up, turned into a man. It wasn't just that he'd filled out, his shoulders broadened and his features more defined, it was more the way he acted.

He might have been trembling with fear, but he faced those savage men for the sake of his family. It was an act of bravery. Some would have run away — many had, she knew. Will didn't run. He faced his fear and did the right thing in spite of it.

She recalled the surprised look on his face when he saw her. His steely blue eyes had locked onto her own and held her mesmerized. She couldn't look away even as he stumbled off with those men.

She sighed and forced her mind back to the task at hand.

There wasn't much to be found. The iron cookstove would be salvageable but the thin metal flue had burned through and was useless. An iron kettle and a frying pan also survived the heat. There were tin cups and plates, warped and scorched, but fixable — they could be straightened and scoured.

Her mind wandered off again, all of its own. Right back to Will Tanner.

She'd last seen Will and his brother Jake at a barn dance — it must have been at least three years ago. She sighed, remembering how there used to be barn dances and shucking bees and other things all the time. The war had put an end to that. Again, she pushed images of Will out of her mind.

She found a few fork tines and knife blades that had their

handles burned off. Papa's man Tom was good at carving and would fix them, too. Over by the fireplace, the iron pothooks had also survived. She found nothing else.

She moved her efforts to the barn, where Papa and the negroes were wrestling the iron plow from the ashes. It had survived unscathed except for some scorch marks. There were a few smaller pieces of iron, an ax-head, a few hoe-heads, a shovel, and some iron rings from harnesses and such. Everything else was gone. Hay, oats, blankets, buckets, leather, ropes—all gone. There was nothing more to do here.

Two of Papa's negroes were hitching their mules to the Higgins' dead one, dragging her off to be buried. Missy, she thought they called her. Poor old Missy. Lucy shook her head in disbelief. Those men had no call to shoot the mule.

That man—that Porter boy—was pure evil. And rude. He'd sauntered over and just stared at her like she was a sack of potatoes. He frightened her; his eyes looked like hollow pits. They looked like there was nobody in there, like there was no soul in there. He frightened her even more than those other men, and they were frightening enough. She shivered despite the heat of the day. She put him from her thoughts.

She looked back at the remains of the house. The fireplace and chimney had withstood the heat, they still stood straight and tall. Someone who took pride in his work had built them thick and strong. She knew they'd be able to re-use them. They might be scarred and soot-stained but they were still solid, and the new house would be built right around them.

Her mind again wandered back to Will. Lucy saw his face in her mind, just as if he were still there. Saw his neatly trimmed hair, thick and dark, and saw the two days-worth of stubble on his face that somehow made him look handsome. She felt herself blushing.

She saw again his blue eyes—like his mother's, she now realized. Today they were rimmed in red like he'd been crying. She supposed he had been—who wouldn't, watching your home go up in flames and your kinfolk threatened like that?

She shuddered again, remembering those dangerous men and those guns, pointing at everyone, ready to shoot! *It's over,* she thought, *why do I keep thinking about it?*

Will had defended his family, the best way he knew, at the risk of his own life. To come down and face those men like that took courage. He'd make a good husband and father, someday. She felt herself blush

45

yet again. Such thoughts! Where did they come from?

Confused by her own feelings, she forced herself to think about other things. Her mind moved to Will's brother, Jake. He had changed too, at least physically. Unless he'd changed a lot, he would still be full of himself, always eager for a fight. He'd often fought with other boys over some silly provocation or other. Some of that was just being a boy, she knew, but Jake got into more fights than most.

She recalled the fight Jake had gotten into at the barn dance, the last time they'd all been together. Jake had argued with someone, she couldn't remember who, and it had led to blows. The other boy's friends had jumped in, and Will stepped in to help Jake. She didn't recall who 'won' that fight or even if anyone did, and she didn't care. She wasn't impressed by fighting—so childish and so unnecessary. Other girls her own age might be impressed by such things, but she wasn't one of them.

Will brought a peaceful end to it, and as far as she knew, the boys remained friends afterward. Just like he'd put a stop to the violence today.

Porter's evil, leering face jumped into her mind. She shivered once more, then resolved to forget about him, certain she'd never see him again.

It was getting dark by the time they had loaded up the wagon with the smaller items they'd saved. The wagon creaked and popped as they moved up the rutted road and turned right on the lane to their farm. No-one talked, the day's events had drained all their energy.

Then she had a horrible thought. *Will I ever see Will Tanner again?*

*****

# Chapter 5

"Slow down up there!" yelled Will.

The rider ahead ignored him. The rope jerked him forward and he stumbled, almost losing his footing again. He knew if he fell, the bushwhackers would drag him over the rocks until he got back up. And laugh about it.

Beside him, Jake struggled to keep up. Will glanced at his brother and saw the sweat dripping from his hair. He wondered why he was hatless, then he remembered. Jake's hat was still up on the bluff where he'd tossed it away in a fit of anger. Luckily for Jake, the thick canopy of trees provided shade from the August sun.

Will stumbled again and moved his gaze back to the path ahead.

"Keep up or get run over!" shouted someone, from behind.

The rope bit deep into his wrists and soon his hands were numb. He wriggled them trying to get blood to his fingers, but it didn't work, and he soon gave up. The slow-walking horses were still faster than Will could walk, and he had to trot just to keep slack in the rope. Already, he was tiring and out of breath. If he or Jake slowed the column too much, these men would shoot them — or hang them from the nearest tree.

Porter dropped back to ride next to Will. "You remember me, now, dontcha? You an' Jake and me, we fought together at Elkhorn Tavern. I know you recall that?"

Will ignored him.

"Yeah," he continued. "You two cowards run off and left me behind to get captured." He smirked. "You two deserted. That's why you're down there draggin' along an' I'm up here ridin', free as a bird."

47

"Yeah, Porter, I remember," said Will. "I remember you froze up, scared solid. I told you to come with us!"

"I was wounded," said Porter. "An' you and your damn brother left me there to end up in that prison camp. We was supposed to be brothers, Tanner! And you left me!"

Beside him, Jake stumbled, and an elbow jabbed into Will's ribs. When he looked at his brother, Jake shook his head and mouthed the word "No."

Will couldn't let Porter's lie go by. His rage built and his voice rose. He knew he was baiting the man, but he couldn't stop himself. "Porter, you're lyin'!" he yelled, loud enough for the other riders to hear him. "You wasn't wounded—the only blood on you was from other men!" He took a deep breath. "You pissed your pants and froze up like a damn jackrabbit when I told you to run. You could've come with us, but you were too damn scared. It's your own damn fault you got captured."

A nearby rider guffawed at Porter. "Jackrabbit Charley! We done got a new name for ye, Jackrabbit!"

Porter turned red and his eyes narrowed to slits. He turned to the rider. "You best shut your mouth! You don't know nothin' about it." He pulled his pistol out and aimed it at Will's face.

"I spent six months in a Yankee prison camp, starvin' an' freezin'. An' worse, all on account of you, Tanner! You and your goddamned brother. I hate you for it. An' I hate every damn sumbitch who wears a blue coat an' them as helps 'em. I've killed me a right smart of 'em. Today, I'm gonna kill you two."

The other riders went silent.

Will thought he might have pushed Porter too far. *Is he gonna shoot me, now?*

"Well, look at you, Porter" Jake said, "You're wearin' a blue coat yourself! Gonna shoot yourself, Porter?" The riders nearby guffawed again.

"You're no soldier," continued Jake. "Just a yellow-belly coward. An' now you're a bushwhackin', murderin' thief to boot. If you were a real soldier you wouldn't be wearin' that blue coat. Did you kill that man yourself, Charley Porter? Or somebody else do it for you?"

Porter had a crazed look in his eyes. He moved his gun to aim at Jake and cocked it.

The laughter ceased and the column came to a stop.

Charley came close to shooting Jake; his finger twitched on the trigger, and he almost pulled it. *All I gotta do, is just tighten my finger a little more and the gun will buck and it'll be done. Then I'll shoot Will too, an' be done with the both of 'em.*

And then what? He didn't know what Henry would do about it. Would he do anything? *No, Henry won't have the guts, not after it's done. Oh, he'll report me to the Colonel, and he'll raise hell with me, on account of ole General goddamn Price. Then I'll leave this so-called State Guard and go back and ride with Anderson. I never signed no papers, no how.*

Bloody Bill Anderson wasn't one to quibble about killin' Yankees. He hated them even more than Charley did. He hated Unionist civilians just as much and had killed many of them, too.

Henry appeared from nowhere just as Charley's finger was tightening on the trigger. Henry was yelling at him, pistol drawn and pointed his way. Beside him sat Emmit with his own pistol out. It was only then he noticed the column had stopped.

It was two against one. He couldn't count on the others; they would just watch. Once again, the odds were against him and he reconsidered his options.

Will's pulse pounded in his temples and he felt his face drain. *Jake's pushed him over the edge. Porter will shoot him now, sure as the world!*

"Porter! Alive! I need 'em alive! Put your damned gun away," shouted the leader, the man Porter had called Henry.

More laughter came from the gang. "Charley," said one. "They're baitin' you. You ain't the smartest dog in the pack, are ye?" More laughter followed.

"Quiet!" ordered Henry. "Keep it down. We ain't in real friendly country here."

Pointing the gun back at Will, Porter lowered his voice. "You keep your damn mouth shut, Will Tanner, or I'll shut it for you." He uncocked and holstered the pistol, but he continued to glare at the brothers. "This ain't over yet."

"Heard that once before," said Jake.

Porter glared at them both, his jaws clenching and grinding, his eyes flashing with anger.

Will nudged Jake in the ribs and shook his head. "Don't provoke him no more. Leave it be."

"Got 'im off your back, though, didn't I?"

Will nodded. "I reckon so." He had goaded Porter too, and it could have got them both shot. *We gotta be smarter than this*, he thought, *there ain't nothin' gained by arguing with Porter, not while we're tied up like this.*

Cursing, Porter spurred his horse to the front of the little column, which then moved forward again.

Will returned his own gaze to the ground so he wouldn't trip, and his eyes briefly focused on an odd hoofprint in the soft dirt, but his mind was already moving on to more important issues. They might be safe enough while Henry was around, but he knew Porter would kill them if he got a chance. They needed to get away from him.

He knew this country well; they were still within a few miles of the farm. He racked his brain for places where they might be able to slip away, and he knew some. While their ropes were tied to bushwhacker saddles, there was no chance to break away and run. Their only hope was to catch the riders off guard.

There was no more talking for a long while, just the sound of horse's hooves clomping on the hard dirt road. They walked about two miles, by Will's reckoning, then veered off on a faint trail that led south through the brush.

Will knew this trail. He'd hunted it often. The forest here went on for miles, and the trees were so big they shaded out the undergrowth. If they ran here, there was no place they could hide. They needed a better spot.

The track narrowed and filled with tree roots and rocks. The horses had to go single file, and the pace slowed. The brothers were now separated, Jake's rope was handed to a rider behind Will, and he could no longer see him. Will was able to catch his breath, but he stumbled some on the rough path.

They came to a curve and Will twisted his body to look back at Jake. He saw the man holding Jake's rope, and behind him was one last rider. The rider saw him looking and he smiled and shook his head in a silent warning.

Will turned his gaze frontward just in time to get slapped by a low hanging tree limb that whipped back at him. It stung his face, and he felt blood trickling down his cheek He wiped it as best he could on his sleeve. The rider in front of him turned back and laughed at him.

*He did that on purpose,* Will thought. *That sonofabitch!*

After another two miles, they came to a small stream that crossed the trail at right angles. The line halted while there was a discussion at the front. Half the riders, including Porter, crossed the stream and moved on down the trail.

The remaining half, with Will and Jake in tow, turned into the creek and walked downstream. The water was only ankle-deep, but it was cool and felt good on his sore feet—for a few minutes. His waterlogged shoes soon got heavy and his legs ached from lifting them. After a while, it was pure torture.

He stumbled on a rock he didn't see and fell face forward, the rope twisting him sideways and over onto his back. He sought to push himself back up, but it was useless on the slippery rocks, and he was dragged for a long time. His hat came off and he glimpsed it being crushed by a horse's hoof.

After a few guffaws, his captor stopped long enough for Will to get back on his feet. He spurred his horse and they moved forward again.

Will's clothes now dripped with water and weighed a ton. He was tired, hungry, cold and miserable, and his back was bruised and scraped raw. And now he had lost his hat.

He stumbled onward. There was no other choice.


Charley knew why he'd been assigned to Emmit's bunch. Henry wanted to get him away from the Tanner boys. Henry was right to do it, but it still infuriated him. "Where we goin'?" he asked.

"Don't you worry 'bout that none, Porter, just ride," said Emmit.

"Why the hell is everybody on my back?"

"Cause yore so easy to ride?" said someone, from behind him. The men guffawed.

"God-damn all of you," said Charley. "You can all go to hell."

"Probably will," said another man. The men laughed again.

"That's enough," said Emmit. "We're in Yankee country. I reckon we need to be quiet."

A few men snickered but the laughter soon died away to be replaced by only the muffled thumping of hooves in the dirt.

The tall canopy and open forest floor gave way to smaller trees and thick under-brush. The trail narrowed, and the trees arched overhead, blocking out the sunlight. It was like being in a tunnel. Charley felt boxed in. Trapped. He much preferred the wide-open prairie to this dark, spooky woods that made his nerves jangle. He wished they'd break out of it. He wished they were already back at camp, with some hot food.

There might be hell to pay when they got there, though. Their mission had been a failure; they'd not been able to recruit any men for General Price. Henry hadn't been stealthy enough, and word had gotten around. Almost every time they came to a place, the men had already run away and hid. And the towns were full of Yankee troops, they didn't dare go into any of them to recruit.

Porter figured nobody wanted to fight for General Price. Not in these parts anyhow.

It had been Charley's idea to detour by the Tanner place. He knew about where the farm was, and he figured the Tanner boys would be there, hiding out somewhere nearby. That old fool Henry had latched right onto it, as dangerous as it was, to have something to show The Colonel. It had been a huge effort for only two men. They'd have done better to just keep raiding supply trains and such. But it had suited Charley's purposes well. He had the Tanners right where he wanted them.

Charley's daydreams of revenge were interrupted when the trail crossed a badly rutted wagon track. Emmit led the men west onto it and they spread out to fill the much wider space. Charley felt better out in the open, even though it made them more visible to anybody that might happen by.

After another mile, they saw an old barn up ahead. Half-hidden behind it was an even older house. There was no smoke coming from its chimney, but they could hear the ringing noise of a hammer striking metal. The riders halted.


Will's brogans felt like bricks on his feet, his socks had bunched up and blisters had formed on his feet. The riders splashed on, and he forced himself to keep up.

After another half mile the column climbed the streambank and stopped in a small clearing. His captor dropped his rope and Will collapsed to the ground.

Jake plopped down beside him. "My legs feel like they're made of lead."

Will just nodded, saving his energy. He heard the riders talking about a road that lay ahead.

Henry rode back to where Will and Jake sat. "Watt! Scout that road to the west, make sure it's clear." Watt trotted his horse forward and the others dismounted.

"Take a drink, boys. Might be your last chance for a while," said Henry. "Fill your canteens too." He nodded to the brothers. "Let 'em drink," he said. "Watch 'em close."

Will and Jake crawled to the water, cupped their hands and drank. The water was cold and sweet and helped a little with their hunger. They splashed some on their heads to help them cool off.

The bushwhackers filled their canteens nearby. Will looked at the nearest one and said, "I gotta piss. I'm gonna walk just over there."

The man nodded his assent, hand on his gun. "Don't try nothin'."

Jake went with him. They turned their backs on the riders and clumsily undid the buttons on their pants. It wasn't easy with their hands tied. Will's fingers were so numb they felt like they were made of wood.

While they were relieving themselves, Jake inclined his head at the thick underbrush, and looked at Will, silently asking if they should make a break for it.

Will took a good look around, then back at their guard, who was carefully watching them. He gave Jake a slight shake of his head. "No, not yet," he whispered. "I know this country. I've hunted this creek before." A plan began to form in his mind.

Jake rolled his eyes and inclined his head again.

Will shook his head again. "No. There's a better place up ahead," he whispered. That seemed to placate Jake for the moment. When they were done, they walked back and sat on a tree root.

Henry walked over, stretching his legs. Will didn't want to make eye contact with him and avoided his gaze.

That didn't matter to Henry. "You know your mistake?" he asked. "See, I knowed you was around somewhere. Your fields was too clean, wasn't near enough weeds growin' in 'em. I seen me a lot of farms lately, most of 'em ain't kept up like yours, 'cause the men are off fightin' for one side or the other. A couple of little boys like your brothers won't keep them rows clean like yours was. That's how I knew you two was there. An' I figured you was watchin', too.

*He likes to brag,* thought Will.

Henry pulled out a pipe and tamped in some tobacco from a pouch. He lit it with a match from his shirt pocket. Will smelled sulfur, and the sweet aroma of tobacco smoke. Henry puffed a bit on the pipe to get it going. He looked right at Will. "You were right to come in like you did. Ida' let Charley kill one of your brothers if you hadn't. I don't like killin' young'uns, but these are hard times, and sometimes I gotta do hard things."

Will just stared at him, stunned. Would he really have shot Ike or let Porter do it? Had they killed boys like Ike before? How many farms had they burned? How many women molested? How many men forced to go to war for the South?

"You sonofabitch," Jake said.

There. Jake had said it for him.

Henry laughed, blowing smoke from his nose. "You're right. An' damned to hell, too, I reckon. I got nothin' left to lose. You'd best not forget it."

Before Jake could say any more, Watt returned from his scout. "Looks clear to me, but there's some fresh tracks headin' west on the road. I cain't tell how many horses. Several."

"Let's ride," said Henry. "I think we will keep to the creek a while yet. We'll meet up with the others at the camp."

Will and Jake were hauled up and herded back to the line of horses. His rope was looped loosely around the horn of Watt's saddle. Jake was hitched to the horse behind. The riders mounted up.

"No talkin'," said Henry, still puffing the pipe. He entered the stream and headed down it. The others followed, single file, their horse's hooves splashing in the water.

Soon they halted again. Will saw another road up ahead through a gap in the brush. He heard conversation from the front but he couldn't make out the words.

Henry eased his horse forward, took a long look in both directions, trotted his horse across the road, and stopped just inside the trees on the other side. He looked around, and after a moment motioned to the next rider who urged his horse forward.

The rider was in the middle of the road and the next was just stepping out, when there was the deep boom of a rifle. The first rider slumped in his saddle and his horse jumped forward into the trees where his body fell off. The second rider tried to back his horse into the cover of the creek-bed but was blocked by Watt's horse.

Boom went another rifle shot. Then another. Watt dropped the rope so he could pull his pistol. Reins in one hand and pistol in the other, he returned fire. His pistol made a sharp popping noise and smoke puffed out with each shot.

The bushwhackers were firing now in all directions, and the attackers, whoever they were, were shooting back. Blue smoke filled the air and the deep booms of rifles mixed in with the sharper popping of pistols. Bullets were zipping all around. A second man fell from his horse.

A bullet grazed Watt's horse's rump. It jumped and Will was jerked forward into Watt's leg. The rope came loose from the pommel, and Will bounced off into the heavy brush and fell on his back. He figured now might be a good time to run. He looked at Jake who was also loose from his rider's horse. "Now!" he yelled, to be heard above the din.

Jake dived over Will's head and they both crawled deeper into the brush. They found a dense growth of cane and backed into it. Amidst the booms, pops, and zipping bullets, they heard a thump and someone screamed. There was a splash as something heavy fell into the water. The shooting slowed, then stopped.

"You men in the creek!" yelled a new voice. "You are surrounded. Give up now or we will kill you all!"

Will heard galloping hooves splashing back upstream. There was a series of booming rifle shots, but the horse continued running.

The voice returned. "We have killed two of you for sure. We will kill all of you unless you surrender. Throw down your guns and come out to the road with your hands up. Do it now!"

"Who are you?" yelled Henry.

"15th Missouri Militia!" came the answer. "Give up or be shot to pieces."

"I ain't givin' up to no militia! You'll hang me anyway!"

"Have it your way, then!"

Boom, came a rifle shot, followed by more pops from Henry's revolvers. A horse crashed through the brush, and hooves pounded the roadbed as a rider galloped away.

"Shoot that man!" yelled a voice. Several rifles boomed. The pounding hooves slowed to a walk and then stopped.

"I got that son of a bitch!" yelled a second voice.

"No, that was my shot!" yelled a third.

"Make that three of you that we have killed!" the first voice yelled. "Throw down your guns and walk out on the road, hands up."

"All right, I am comin' out!" Will recognized this one as Watt, the man who had held the rope tied to his hands. Will heard more splashing as Watt walked downstream to the road, hands upraised.

"Any more of you sumbitches givin' up?"

"They all been shot! Or run off! I'm the only one left!" yelled Watt.

Jake looked at Will. "Let's go," he said.

"Hold on." He placed his still-tied hands on Jake's shoulder and held him there. "Stay down." Then he yelled, "Hello the Fifteenth Militia! We're prisoners and bound up with ropes! We want to come out now. I think the bushwhackers ran off."

Before they could move, three rifle muzzles appeared, aimed right at their heads. "Hold still right there, boys," said a soldier with three stripes on his blue coat. "Don't even twitch."

*****

# Chapter 6

Charley pulled out his pistols and spun the cylinders, making sure there was a cap on each nipple, and each was ready to fire. They were. The gang rode on toward the house.

He scanned the farmstead. On the left was a rail-fenced pasture holding three swaybacked horses and a thin, worn-out mule. The pigsty held one huge sow, cooling herself in the muck.

The house looked abandoned and was in dire need of repair. Its roof sagged in the middle and the chimney needed chinking. The porch was missing planks and the door was wide open. No smoke rose from the chimney. No smell of cooking food filled the air, no wash hung from the clothesline. There was nothing to show anyone lived here.

To the right sat an old barn that leaned to one side like a drunken man about to fall over. Whole planks were missing from its sides and the roof needed shingles. An old wagon sat in front of it, the front axle propped up on a stump, one front wheel missing.

The clang of hammer on iron rang out from the barn. Someone was working in there. The riders stopped in front of it and spread out sideways.

"Hallo the barn! Hallo! Anybody home?" yelled Emmit.

The clanging stopped. An old man wearing a leather apron walked out of the barn, holding a hammer in one hand and a shotgun in the other.

He looked as run-down as the house. A scraggly gray beard covered his face and his hair poked out in bunches from beneath his old straw hat, which was coming apart. His worn-out clothes were filthy and shot through with holes.

Some of the men drew their guns. Charley didn't move, he wasn't worried about one old broken-down dirt farmer.

Surrounded by armed men on horseback, the man's eyes widened, and he moved to the wagon and stood behind it. "Who are you?" he shouted. "Whadda ya want?"

"Are you a Lincoln man?" asked Emmit.

The man studied them a moment before he answered. "Hell no," he said. "My sentiments are Southern."

Charley figured he'd seen the blue coats and the bullet holes. "He's lyin', Emmit."

Emmit ignored Charley. "You got any negroes?" he asked.

The man shrugged. "I had me one," he said. "Harry run off in sixty-three an' I ain't seed him since. You know, after that damn-fool Lincoln done his damn-fool proclamation."

"Well, that's too bad. If I see a negro named Harry, I'll shoot him for you," said Emmit. The men sniggered.

The man's eyes narrowed, but he smiled and nodded.

"Anybody else here?" The men spread out a little more. Emmit looked at the house, then back to the man. "Don't lie, I'll know if you do."

"No. My wife died last year. She's buried under that tree out yonder in the pasture. My son's went to California in forty-nine. I run this place by myself. Well, since Harry run off, anyhow."

"Got any food? An' these horses need hay and corn," said Emmit. "An' you ain't told me yore name yet, mister...."

"Johnson. Jack Johnson. I ain't got much but I reckon I can share it."

Some of the men dismounted and tied up to the fence.

Emmit smiled. "Johnson, you got any whiskey?"

Normally, Charley didn't care if Emmit got drunk. But now, he felt uneasy for some reason. He looked over his shoulder back the way they'd come and saw nothing. Still, he felt they should take what they needed and just ride on. "Emmit, we need to be movin'."

"Scared, are ye Charley?" Emmit laughed and sneered at him. "Go round up them horses."

His face red, Charley turned his horse and rode over to the fence where he dismounted and tied his horse to a post.

Behind him, Johnson was protesting. "You cain't take my horses, I'll starve if you do that."

"Surely a Southern man like yourself wants to help the fight, right Johnson?" said Emmit.

Charley tuned out the rest of the conversation. He looked over the horses in the pasture. They were old, underfed, and their ribs were showing. *They aint no use to anyone,* he thought, *might as well shoot 'em now.*

The mule was in worse shape—it limped along on a sore leg. It looked sideways at him as he jumped the fence, then walked over and sniffed at him. Charley ignored it. Behind the horses, he saw three wooden grave-markers under a large poplar tree. He couldn't read them from here, so he ducked through the fence and walked out into the field. The mule brayed at him. "Shutup, old mule," he said.

Charley couldn't read but he knew his numbers. He stooped over and read out the years carved on the crude wooden markers. 1824 - 1863 was carved into one. Another one had 1851 - 1861 and the last one had 1862 - 1863 cut into it. Two pups and a wife. The graves reminded him of his mother, dead since before the war. His sadness turned into anger all over when he recalled how she'd died—murdered by some cheap rake in a hotel room. Charley often fantasized about what he'd do to the man if he ever found him. But now was not the time to dwell on it. He turned and walked away.

Four halter ropes hung from the fence and he gathered them up, but he looked again at the mule and put one back. The mule would be too slow. *Hell, these sorry-ass horses will be too slow,* he thought. He roped them anyway, led them to the fence, kicked out the rails and tied them next to his own horse. He didn't bother to replace the rails. Let the damn mule wander—it would be better off anyhow.

Yells and hoots erupted from the house where most of the men had gone. He could hear Emmit yelling about something. An uneasy feeling settled in Charley's stomach.

One man had stayed outside as a picket and was watching the road. He nodded toward the house when Charley neared and spat tobacco juice on the ground. "Emmit's getting' tight."

"Yeah," Charley said. "An' we'll be stuck here a while. We need to be movin' on."

The picket nodded and spat again. "Yep." He moved his gaze back to the road. "I think I'll stay out here and keep me a lookout. Too many horse tracks in the road. Makes me nervous."

Charley was on edge too but said nothing. He strode to the house and onto the porch and looked inside. The interior was dark, so he waited for his eyes to adjust. After a short time, he could see the men sitting around a greasy old table, passing around a jug. The Johnson man stood near the stove, pacing back and forth.

As Charley watched, Emmit took two swigs when the jug came his way. He was well on his way to being falling-down, mean, and stupid drunk, which was his usual habit.

"More whiskey, god-dammit!" Emmit yelled.

Johnson cringed. "I only got the one jug."

Emmit pulled his knife out. "You sonafabitch," he said. "You are a liar. You dirt-farmers always hide yore money and yore whiskey."


Will raised his still tied hands slowly. The bores of the rifles aimed at his head looked to him like cannon. Beside him, Jake did the same. The guns lowered some when the ropes binding their wrists became visible to the soldiers.

"No quick moves, now boys," said a man in a dark, sweat-stained slouch hat and a worn frock coat with three faded yellow stripes sewn loosely on the sleeves.

Another man appeared in the circle of soldiers. This man wore a fancy black hat with yellow crossed swords embroidered on the front and a long dark blue coat with yellow piping on the sleeves and yellow bars on the shoulders. A gleaming sword hung from his belt. *An officer,* Will thought.

The officer smiled with a kindly look. "Stand down, Sergeant. These boys look harmless enough."

"Yes, Sir," said the sergeant. "We was about to untie 'em." He motioned to the other soldiers and they lowered their rifles. "It's all right boys, you can stand up. You're with friends now."

The waterlogged rope had swollen tight around Will's wrists. When a soldier tried to loosen the knot, the pain in his wrists flared and he let out a yelp.

Beside him, Jake cursed. "Damn that hurts!"

"Sorry," said the man fumbling with Jake's rope. "Have to cut 'em off."

Another man pulled out his knife and sawed the ropes off Will's wrists. Throbbing needles of pain shot down into his hands as the blood returned to them. He rubbed them together and flexed his fingers.

"Now, who are you boys?" asked the officer.

Will hesitated. He wasn't sure how much he wanted to tell this man.

Getting no answer, the officer continued, "All right, I will go first. I am Captain Phillip Stevens, Fifteenth Missouri State Militia Cavalry." He waited for Will to say something. "That was an introduction, son. It's customary for you now to tell me your name."

The words 'Fifteenth Missouri State Militia Cavalry' meant nothing to Will. But the Yankees had set them free, so he answered.

"I am William—Will—Tanner, from Millwood in Lincoln County, an' this is my brother Jake. We was taken prisoner at our farm this morning. These men, bushwhackers I reckon, burned us out and took us prisoner. They were takin' us south to make us fight for the Rebels. We sure are glad to see you!" It was more than he meant to say but the words had just spilled out.

Stevens offered his hand, and Will shook it. After hesitating, Jake followed suit.

"You boys were lucky. We were out on patrol and just happened to be in the area. A scout heard you splashing down the creek there and we set up an ambush. We got our trap set up just in time to bag you."

"Well, I don't feel so dang lucky, bein' burnt out, hogtied an' dragged over half the state an' all," said Jake.

Will elbowed him. "Shut up, Jake. Let me do the talkin'." He felt Jake's glare bore right through him.

"Well...." Stevens frowned and cleared his throat. Then he broke into a smile. Nodding to the bodies, he said, "Well, it was bad luck for them."

Will smiled back. "Yes, Sir."

Stevens continued, "We've heard rumors that Price and his army are moving up from Arkansas. Guerrilla activity has picked up all over the state. These men are a long way from where they usually operate, though." He removed his hat and ran his fingers through his hair. "Still, this confirms the rumors we've been hearing." He replaced the hat, tugged it down on his head and beckoned them with a hand. "Come with me."

They followed Stevens to where a body lay in the road. A blue-coated soldier bent over it, searching his pockets.

There was no doubt Henry was dead. He lay face-up in the road, his head twisted at a strange angle and his vacant eyes focused on nothing. Blood formed a large circle where it soaked into the dirt around him. Will had to look away.

"Broke his dang neck when he fell off'n his horse, Captain," said the soldier.

"No matter," said Stevens. "What knocked him from his saddle was a bullet." Turning to Will, he asked, "Do you know this man?"

"I don't know him, but he was in charge. They called him Henry," Will said, forcing himself to look.

Jake walked over and kicked Henry's body, hard. "Sumbitches beat up my Ma."

Stevens looked at Jake, a puzzled expression on his face. But he didn't protest.

Will just shook his head at his brother's antics.

The soldier pulled out a folded, blood-stained paper from Henry's coat pocket. "Sir, I found this," he said, handing it to Stevens.

Stevens gingerly unfolded the letter and read from it silently, his lips moving from time to time. He frowned. "This is an order from 'General'—he spat the word out—Sterling Price to one 'Captain' Henry Perkins. Hah!" He frowned and shook his head. "The Rebels are promoting bushwhackers to officers now? Damn them! They should all hang, just for that."

"Ahem," he continued. "This so-called 'Captain' was ordered to recruit soldiers and round up deserters and runaways for the so-called 'Confederate State of Missouri' and meet up with Price in Jefferson City. I guess that's you two boys. You were the only two prisoners?"

Will shrugged. "Yes, sir. We didn't see nobody else."

The Lieutenant rubbed his jaw for a minute. "The Colonel needs to see this right away," he said before calling for a dispatch rider. In a moment, the courier galloped off with the letter.

Stevens took a long look at Will and Jake; a stern look on his face. "You boys are deserters from the Rebel army?" he asked.

Will looked at Jake, and with a slight shake of his head warned him to keep silent. Will looked down at the ground and pondered the situation. *How much can I trust this man? If I tell him the truth, are we headed to a Yankee prison?*

He looked at the rope marks on his wrists and thought for a moment. No Yankees had ever hog-tied him, burned down his farm, beat up his Ma, threatened his brothers, or forced him to fight. Only the Rebels had done that—twice, now. *So, which side do I trust?*

Will raised his eyes and studied Stevens, who stood patiently waiting for an answer. From what he'd seen so far, Captain Stevens was stern but fair. His men followed his orders without questioning or griping and they seemed to respect and trust him. In turn, Stevens treated his men with respect.

Unlike the quarreling and back-biting he'd seen among the bushwhacker gang. There was a tension there; an unspoken undercurrent of resentment and violence that was absent amongst these Union soldiers.

Will looked around him, there must be fifty or more men here. If these men trusted Stevens, why shouldn't he?

His mind made up now, Will began to tell his story. Once he started, the words seemed to flow like water from a pump. "It's a long story, Lieutenant. We was conscripted against our will two years ago this past spring and forced into a Reb infantry outfit down at Elkhorn Tavern. We was put under Colonel Jo Shelby. After the fight, we got separated from the outfit, so we left and came home. We been layin' low ever since."

He took a deep breath, looked at the ground again, then back up into Steven's eyes and continued. "Sir, we never wanted to fight for the Rebs. We was forced into it. They marched us off with rifles aimed at our backs."

Form the corner of his eye, he saw Jake nod his agreement.

Stevens studied them both for a moment, his eyes moving from one to the other. Finally, his eyes locked onto Will's. "This is what I will do," he said. "I will take you to see the Colonel and he can decide what to do with you two. If he stays true to form, he'll let you go home—if you're willing to take the Oath of Loyalty. That's something for you to think about on the way."

"Yes, Sir. Thank you, Sir," said Will.

"Do you know these other scoundrels?"

"The one you took prisoner, they called him Watt. He's the one who had my rope. I never heard the other's names. You know 'em, Jake?"

"Nope," said Jake. "I was at the tail end and I didn't hear too much."

"Sergeant!" yelled Stevens. "Make sure we search all the dead men, make note of anything that might identify them, then assign a burial party. Share out their pistols if anybody wants them."


Charley saw Johnson's eyes widen as he backed away from Emmit's knife. The knife glimmered in the dim light as Emmit turned it this way and that. Johnson re-considered his answer — wisely, thought Charley — and sighed, his head hung down in resignation.

"All right. Wait here and I'll go fetch it," he said. The man walked around the table, giving Emmit a wide berth, and went out the door.

"Follow 'im, Porter." Emmit turned back to his drinking. "And pass that damn whiskey!" He grabbed the jug, tilted it up to his mouth and took a long drink. He grimaced before holding the jug out. "Have a…. have a drink, Charley."

Disgusted, Charley said, "Well which one you want me to do, drink or follow Johnson?"

"Oh," said Emmit. "Alrigh', follow the damned man then." Emmit's glazed eyes wandered away. "Make sure he don't do nothin' s… stupid.

Charley turned and followed Johnson out the door. The man strode to the pigsty, climbed over the rail fence, and slapped the sow on the backside to move her out of the way. The pig ambled off to the side and plopped down into the mud with a grunt. The rich, half-sweet stench of pig shit assaulted Charley's nose, and he stayed outside the sty to keep his boots clean.

Johnson slogged through the muck, moved one end of the pig-trough over a few feet and brushed away a few inches of damp dirt. He pulled back an oiled cloth covering a shallow hole and reached down into the hole. When he straightened back up, his expression had changed to one of surprise and he pointed to something behind Charley. "What the hell's that?" he asked.

Charley turned to look behind him. A pistol cracked and he felt the wind and heard the buzz of a bullet that whizzed by his ear. He ducked down and turned back to Johnson, who now held a rusty old pistol in one hand, its barrel still smoking. "You lyin' Yankee sonofabitch!" Charley pulled out his own pistol just as he heard Johnson's pistol click. *Misfired! You're a dead man now!*

Charley's Colt did not misfire, but his aim was off. His shot hit the man in the upper thigh and he fell sideways into the muck. Charley's second shot blew a chunk of wood from a fence post in front of Johnson.

Johnson jumped up and limped to the far side of the pigsty and crashed through the fence, knocking off the rails and falling again. He stumbled to his feet and limped out into the cornfield. The panicked sow squealed and grunted and ran out of the gap toward Charley.

Charley sidestepped the frantic pig, and followed Johnson into the cornfield, his senses heightened now, his heart pumping. This was a game he'd played before and he loved it. *Oh the chase is on now! Run rabbit, run!* He stalked him through the corn, a smile plastered on his face. "You like to shot my damn ear off!" he yelled, laughing. "You'll regret that, in just a minute or two!" Footsteps thumped behind him. Charley half turned and yelled back to the men, "He's mine! Nobody else better shoot him!"

The footsteps stopped. He heard someone say, "Keep back boys, that's Charley's man."

Charley stalked Johnson, who had fallen again after only a few more yards.

Johnson stood up straight and faced Charley, grimacing with pain and putting his weight on his good leg. "Well, I reckon you'll kill me now, sure as rain. I'll tell you the truth, an' you can be damned for it. I ain't no secesh, I am a Lincoln man through and through." He raised the old pistol again and pulled the trigger, but again there was only a metallic click from his gun.

Charley smiled and held his fire.

Johnson looked at his gun, confused and disgusted, then threw it at Charley.

Charley easily ducked it. He walked toward the man, who

trembled but held his ground. "You're pretty cool for an old farmer. You been shot at before?"

The man' shoulders fell, but his eyes remained steady on Charley's. "I was in the Mexican war, under General Winfield Scott," he said. "I fought with him all the way from Vera Cruz to Mexico City." He smiled. "An' I fought alongside your own General Bobby Lee." His eyes turned skyward. "It sure was hot down there, but I had me some good times." He looked back at Charley. "Bury me by my wife, would you?"

"Sorry, old man. Ain't got no time for diggin' no hole."

Charley pulled the trigger and his pistol jerked. This time his aim was better; the ball hit the man in the center of his chest. His eyes went slack even before he collapsed backward in the dirt. His feet twitched twice then went still. "It's gonna be even hotter than Mexico City down where you're goin', I expect," Charley said. He stuck his pistol back in his belt and turned away.

Several men had come out to watch the excitement. "Had a gun hid, did he?" asked the picket.

"Yeah. An' his powder got wet. I reckon he left it under the dirt too long."

"Or maybe the pig pissed on it," said someone. The men guffawed. Most turned back to the house. Emmit had not even come out.

Charley made a mental note. He had three shots left in this gun.

The picket had returned to his post and was watching the road toward the east. Suddenly he yelled, "Riders! Comin' fast!"

Charley ran to the road and looked, sure enough, there were horses, coming fast, lots of horses. Above them flew a guidon that flashed red and white and blue. *Dammit! Yankee Cavalry! Where the hell did they come from?* Their hooves rumbled like thunder on the hard-packed road.

"Emmit!" he yelled. "We gotta go now! We got Yankees!" He didn't wait for a response—he ran to his horse, untied it and mounted up.

The picket and another man had already spun their horses and were galloping down the road away from the Yankees. Charley followed them, but then he thought of a better plan. *Let the Yankees chase them and forget about me!*

He jerked his horse right into the cornfield and raced across the rough furrows. The cornstalks ripped at his legs as he headed for the tree line off in the distance. The deep furrows between the rows threatened to trip his horse, and it stumbled once and almost fell.

He risked a glance back over his shoulder and saw that Emmit had fallen trying to mount his horse. The Union troopers were concentrating on the small group still near the fence and ignoring Charley, so he stopped and wheeled his horse about to watch the gunfight.

Emmit was trying to mount up when smoke puffed again from the Union carbines, the booms reaching Charley a split second later. The horse reared up and jumped sideways and Emmit was knocked to the ground once more.

More puffs of smoke belched from the Yankee's guns followed by more booms, and another man fell from his horse. The horses had had enough of gunfire and ran off. There was only a lone bushwhacker left standing—he let go with his pistols, but there was no effect. The sounds of shouting and screaming and horse's hooves mixed in with the gunshots.

As Charley watched, Emmit rolled over and rose to his knees. Two pistols appeared, one in each of his hands, and he fired at the Yankees. A trooper leveled his carbine and fired—the smoke and boom almost as one now—and Emmit fell backward into the dirt. He pushed himself back up on one elbow, raised a pistol and fired again. Once again, there was no effect on the Union troopers.

The Yankees were within pistol range of the fence now, and they reigned up and milled about. Most were reloading, but an officer— Charley saw the yellow bars on his shoulders—leveled his pistol at Emmit and popped off a round. Emmit fell back into the dirt again, and this time he didn't move. The officer fired another shot into his still form.

The remaining bushwhacker now had his hands in the air. Blue coated soldiers surrounded the man and he was lost to Charley's view.

A trooper pointed at the cornfield where Charley sat atop his horse. Another boom rang out, and a bullet ripped through the corn stalks nearby. Charley had seen more than enough, so he wheeled about and raced for the tree line. More carbine shots boomed behind him, but none came near him that he could tell. When he neared the trees, he risked another glance backward, and saw that the troopers were not chasing him. He wondered why but didn't dwell on it too long. Instead, he guided his horse into the trees and put them between him and the Yankees.

He didn't stop until the sun was low and the shadows were long.

*****

# Chapter 7

Will jammed his shovel into the hard clay yet again and threw a bit of dirt to the side of the grave he'd been digging. The pounding of hooves on the road announced a rider, and he stopped his work, wiping sweat from his brow with his sleeve. When he saw the rider was a blue-clad Federal trooper, he edged closer and leaned on the shovel.

The rider jerked to a stop, dismounted and saluted Captain Stevens. "Sir!" he said. "A message from Campbell. He found some bushwhackers at a farm up the road. Sir, he plans to attack and requests you come up and reinforce him." He held out a paper in one hand.

"You mean 'Lieutenant' Campbell, don't you, Private?" asked Stevens.

"Sir?" said the private, looking confused.

"Never mind, Private. Let's see the message." He opened the paper and read to himself. He looked up with a smile and turning to Burnes, he said. "Never mind the burial, Sergeant, leave them where they lay. Tie that prisoner to his horse, get the men mounted."

"Yes, Sir!" The sergeant yelled out, "You heard the man, mount up!" In seconds, the shovels had been packed away and the troopers mounted and ready to ride.

Stevens turned to the Tanners. "Can you boys ride? We need to assist Lieutenant Campbell."

Will hesitated.

"Yes Sir," answered Jake.

"Good," said Stevens. "Sergeant Burnes here will find horses for you."

"Yes, Sir," said Sergeant Burnes, walking away.

Will gave Jake his evil-eye. He could have hit him. They didn't own a horse and Will did not consider himself a good rider. What was Jake doing? Why so quick with his answer?

What little riding they'd done before was on their mule Missy, bareback, and at a slow walk to town or to the grist mill. Will had ridden a horse a few times with his friend James Carter, but it had been many years. These men intended to ride hard and fast. Will wasn't sure he could keep up.

It was already too late to say no; Burnes was bringing two of the dead bushwhacker's horses over to them. He shrugged. There was no help for it now. Besides, he didn't relish walking any more today. He stuck his left foot into the stirrup, stepped up and swung his right leg over the saddle and plopped down. His right foot found the other stirrup and he settled back in the saddle. At least he had remembered how to mount up.

The sergeant handed him the reins and the horse began to sidle rightward.

"Hold him right there, use the reins!"

Will pulled too hard on the reins and the horse bucked in protest.

Burnes grabbed the halter and steadied the horse. "Well, just hold on and keep up," he said. "We can't wait on you."

Will felt his face reddening.

Jake made it look easy. He stepped up into the stirrup and swung his right leg over gracefully and grabbed the reins and turned the horse to face the right way. Will wondered where he had learned how to ride a horse like that.

The troopers took off at a trot, which soon led to a gallop. Will bounced around in the saddle until he remembered how to use the stirrups. After a while he got into a kind of rhythm with his horse and it got easier. The best part, though, was that the moving air cooled his hatless head.

Riding beside him, Jake looked more at ease in the saddle than Will felt. Again, he wondered when Jake had found time to learn to ride. He shrugged it off as unimportant.

Still, they fell behind the more experienced troopers, and Sergeant Burnes dropped back to ride with them. After a half-hour that seemed like forever, they caught up with the rest of the company at an old run-down farmhouse.

Will pulled too hard on the reins and the horse stopped too quickly and bucked sideways. He had to grab the pommel to keep from being thrown. When the horse felt the reins go slack, it walked over to some grass, bent its head to the ground and cropped some grass.

Burnes laughed and shook his head. "Well, at least you didn't fall off." He grabbed the reins and led the horse over to the group.

Will felt his face redden, and he felt Jake's eyes on him. "When did you learn how to ride like that?"

Jake just shrugged.

Then Will saw the bodies. His eyes first locked on the dead horses, then he saw the human arms and legs splayed out amongst them.

Another officer rode up. "Captain!" he yelled. "We got two of 'em! Three o' the bastards got away, though."

"And your men?"

"No casualties, Sir. A scratch here and there. They did kill the old farmer, though." He pointed to a body lying behind a pigsty.

Stevens sighed and rubbed his chin. "Only the old man?"

"That's all we found. It looks like he lived alone, there's no sign of anybody else."

"Well, good work, Lieutenant." He waved Will and Jake over. "Know any of these men?"

Will dismounted before walking over. His legs felt rubbery. "That big one there, they called him Emmit. The others...." Will shook his head. "No, Sir."

"The same bunch?"

"Yes, Sir."

Loud whoops of laughter reached them from the pigsty, where several soldiers were milling about. Stevens and Campbell wheeled their horses around and rode over. Will followed out of curiosity.

Some soldiers were dragging things from a hole in the ground. A jug of something was already being passed around. There was an old hunting knife, wrapped in a greased cloth, and a small bag of coins, that clinked when a trooper shook it. It appeared to be heavy.

"Sergeant, confiscate that jug!" yelled Stevens.

Burnes did as ordered, replacing the wooden stopper. He gave it to Lieutenant Campbell, who removed the stopper and smelled the contents. "Whew, stout stuff, that."

"I'll take that, private," said Stevens, pointing to the bag of coins. The soldier handed it up, Stevens opened it, and his eyes widened. "Must be two hundred dollars in here. I wonder why they didn't take it?"

"I think we came upon 'em before they cu'd find it," said Campbell. "Matter of fact, Captain, we heard shots and that's what alerted us. I looked w' me spyglass, and I saw only a handful o' men. I knew we c'ud take 'em so we charged up. There was more of 'em in the house, includin' that fat one who lies yonder. We killed him and one o' the others. Two of 'em hightailed it down the road that way, he pointed west. "Another other one lit out across the field t'ward that tree line there." He pointed north. "I didn't chase 'em, cause o' what happened to the Third Militia last week."

Stevens nodded. "You were right to be cautious, Lieutenant. Have you searched these men?"

"Aye, we did. Naught to be found."

"Captain Stevens, Sir," said Will. "I don't see the one called Charley Porter among the dead ones. He must have been one of 'em who got away. I don't know who the other ones were. We know Charley from Jo Shelby's outfit. He was with us at Elkhorn Tavern."

Stevens took out a pencil and made a note in a little book.

"These bastards were at our place back in Millwood this mornin'," said Jake. "They beat up our Ma, an' burned our house an' barn. Killed old Missy, our mule. They threatened to shoot my other brothers and some other folk that came to help. Them dead ones over there, and them back at the creek, they got better'n what they deserve."

"I am sorry for your troubles, son," said Stevens. "Like you, I'd rather see them hang myself. Don't you worry, we'll write it up in our report and we'll do all we can to catch the others. Maybe by the time we get back to camp, you'll remember more."

Jake walked over to Emmit's body and kicked it.

"I believe he's a mite annoyed," said Sergeant Burnes.

Will nodded. Jake was always annoyed at something. Or somebody.

Some soldiers wrapped the farmer in a blanket and buried him in the small graveyard under the big tree in the pasture. Will and Jake pitched in with the digging.

Lieutenant Campbell gave a brief prayer in his strange accent. One soldier knew the old farmer, so he carved his name—Jack Johnson—and the date on a sharpened board and pounded it into the dirt at the head of the grave.

After some grumbling and much cursing, the soldiers drug the dead outlaws across the road and buried them in shallow graves. It took three of them to drag Emmit over. There were no markers made and nobody said any prayers for them. Will figured wild animals would soon dig them up, but the soldiers didn't seem to care. He wasn't sure if he did either.

After the burying was done, Captain Stevens ordered the whole command back to the first skirmish site where they buried Henry and the other dead men in the same hasty manner.

The bushwhacker's horses were gathered up and roped together. A wounded mare had to be taken out to the field and shot. Will knew it was coming but he still flinched when the shot was made.

A trooper brought over a big knife and turned it this way and that, admiring the shine. "You want this 'un? I already got one. Doan' need another 'un."

"No. Thanks anyhow." Will didn't want any reminders of their ordeal. He just wanted to get back home.

The man looked at Jake. "How 'bout you, you want this 'un? It's a big ole Bowie—Arkansas Toothpick, they call 'em."

"Sure, I'll take it," said Jake. "Thanks," He tested the blade with his thumb and grinned at Will, before sticking it in his belt.

Will shook his head. "That knife will get you in trouble."

"Why do you always do that?" asked Jake.

"What?"

Jake's eyes flashed. "Everything I do, no matter what, you gotta have your say about it." He turned and stalked off, leaving Will openmouthed and without an answer.

Stunned by the sudden reversal of his fortune, Charley pondered what to do next. For the first time in years, he was alone and on his own. He had no friends to watch his back — not even Darnell — and he was deep in Yankee territory. And those damn Yankees were likely on his trail.

He shivered as he realized the sun had disappeared and night was fast approaching. In his panic, he hadn't kept track of his direction. The trees here were thick and mossy, and water squished from the ground. He couldn't tell east from west; what faint light there was didn't seem to come from any one direction. There was no trail to follow, and the thick canopy of leaves overhead made it impossible to see moon or stars.

The wind picked up, leaves rattled, and somewhere a limb crashed to the ground. Panicked, he spun his horse around, pistol drawn, looking for the source of the noise.

*Is that the Yankees? No! Calm down, Charley, it's just the damn wind!*

Forcing himself to think, he picked a direction he thought might be west and rode that way, dodging the low-hanging limbs. The light got dimmer and he dismounted and walked his horse, picking his way through the brush. He stopped when it was too dark to see, tied off the horse and sat back against a fallen tree. The dark woods closed in around him.

He couldn't make a fire, the Yankees might see it or smell the smoke. So, he sat in the utter blackness and trembled despite the blanket he wrapped around himself. The darkness around him magnified every small sound. A twig snapped nearby, and his heart leapt into his throat. Somewhere off in the distance an owl hooted.

His eyes strained to see in the gloom, and soon every dark shadow became menacing and hostile. Every tree might hide a blue-coated soldier ready to shoot him, or a bear or panther with claws extended, ready to rip his throat out. He panicked again and pulled out his gun. The heavy, cold steel in his hand was reassuring, and calmed him somewhat.

It was so quiet he could hear his own heartbeat; it was getting louder and louder. Soon, he realized what he heard was not his heart, but the muted thump of a horse walking in the soft forest dirt.

Charley cocked his gun with shaking hands. He cringed; to him, the metallic click sounded like thunder in the silence. *That was a mistake!*

*Now they'll know I'm here, for sure.* The sound of the approaching horse grew near and a shadow darker than the surrounding gloom materialized in front of him. He raised his pistol and tightened his trigger finger.

Will ignored his brother's angry glare. Jake would go for days sometimes in one of his moods. Will learned long ago to just let him be.

The troopers mounted up again and headed west on the narrow road. Captain Stevens sent scouts ahead and off to the left and right, and two trailed behind to guard that direction. He stopped at every crossroad and every farmhouse or barn and sent troopers to check them out.

Sergeant Burnes explained to the brothers why the Captain was being so careful. Last week, Bloody Bill Anderson had lured a company of the Thirty-Ninth Mounted Infantry into an ambush. The Thirty-Ninth fought on foot with single shot Springfield rifle-muskets, while Anderson's men were on horseback and armed with six-shot pistols, several each. Once the bushwhackers got in close, the infantry had no chance against such firepower. Anderson had massacred the whole company, including the wounded and those who tried to surrender. Then he mutilated the bodies.

Will watched for his brother's reaction to the tale, but he only saw him shake his head and frown. It didn't seem to cross his mind that Will had been right, back at the farm, that the two of them couldn't have taken on eleven mounted bushwhackers with an old Kentucky rifle and a shotgun. But Jake was already annoyed and now wasn't the time to start that fight.

The Captain's precautions slowed them down and it got dark long before they were near any town. The troopers made camp for the night near the farmhouse of a known Union man.

Stevens and Campbell were invited inside to have supper with the farmer. As he headed to his meal, Stevens called out, "Sergeant! See that these boys get fed and have a bedroll."

"Sir!" replied Burnes. "This way boys, I'll introduce you to hardtack, salt beef, and camp coffee!" He took them to a campfire where several men sat around, making their supper.

Will smelled coffee and meat frying and his stomach growled. He knew what salt beef was but had never heard of hardtack. He and Jake found a space on a log and had a seat. They were each handed a square cracker that was hard as a rock.

Some of the men snickered and nudged each other when Jake tapped his on the log. "I think you could drive a nail with this thing," he said. More laughter followed.

Will tried to bite off a corner, but only managed a few crumbs.

Burnes laughed. "Careful, now, that thing will break your teeth." Handing him a tin plate and knife, he said, "Soak it in some of this meat grease, or maybe your coffee, and it'll soften up some." He poured coffee into tin mugs and handed one each to the brothers.

Jake had bitten off a small corner of a cracker and he crunched on it a while. The noise carried clear across the fire. Will decided he'd settle for just some meat and coffee. The beef was tough and stringy but at least you could chew it, sort of, if you worked at it a while. The coffee was strong and bitter. A soldier dumped a handful of sugar in it, which helped. He already felt better.

While he ate, Will listened to the soldiers talk. The soldiers seemed to know their business. They had abundant confidence in their abilities to fight the Rebels. They joshed and ribbed each other and showed off their captured pistols, bragging about the feats they would do with them.

Will learned that this was Company G of the Fifteenth Cavalry. There were about eighty troopers altogether in the company, including officers. Of that number, only about sixty-five men were present for duty. Burnes said there were eight other companies in the regiment.

Altogether, there were over eight-hundred men in the whole regiment. And it wasn't even up to full-strength; they were still recruiting men. Will was impressed. Eight hundred men was a lot more men than Jo Shelby had with him at Elkhorn Tavern.

And, unlike Shelby's ragged and shoeless troops, these men had real uniforms. They all wore sky blue wool pants, short coats made of dark blue wool, and knee-high black leather boots. Their hats, though, were not all the same. Some wore what they called 'bummers,' short-brimmed wool caps with a flat top that leaned forward. But most of them wore floppy round hats like Will's had been. 'Slouch hats,' they called them. Will thought they'd keep the sun and rain off better than the bummer caps.

Will heard some soldiers grumbling about 'picket duty' and he asked what that meant. Burnes explained that pickets — guards or sentries — would be on watch all night. Pairs of men would stand guard all night in several places around the camp. Every few hours, the pickets would be relieved by other so that no-one lost a whole night's sleep. With so many soldiers in the company, Will felt the danger of an attack was small, but it comforted him to know that men were on guard all night.

Jake perked up when the talk turned to guns. The troopers were equipped with model 1859 Sharp's carbines, a short breechloading, fifty-two caliber rifle. It used pre-made silk cartridges, inserted from the breech, and it shot something called a Minie-ball. Burnes passed a cartridge to the brothers and they were intrigued by the conical shape and the heft of the bullet. It was much bigger and heavier than the thirty-two caliber round ball used in their old Kentucky rifle.

"One of these can tear an arm off," Burnes said. "It shatters bone into little pieces. That's why so many legs and arms are gettin' cut off."

Will believed him. It was a wicked looking bullet.

Other soldiers bragged that a trooper good with a Sharp's could fire six shots a minute from the ground. It was a boast that impressed Will. Their old muzzle-loading Kentucky rifle took a whole minute just to load — then you had to prime it before you could shoot. The troopers conceded that it was much harder while riding, though. Will couldn't imagine even trying to load his old rifle while riding a horse.

As the campfire died down so did the talk. Sergeant Burnes produced tobacco and a pipe from his coat pocket and lit it from a burning stick. He stared at it a moment and said, "You boys were lucky indeed today. You know, we didn't know anybody was around until we smelled tobacco burnin'."

Will cocked his head. "Smelled tobacco?"

"Yep," said Burnes. "We smelled good Virginny tobacco. This tobacco." He showed Will a pouch. "I took it off'n that dead one, back yonder. He don't need it no more." He puffed a moment. "You cain't get good tobacco like that here in Missouri. When we smelled it, we knew there was a Johnnie around somewhere. Then we heard horses in the creek, so we set up our ambuscade, and shore enough, boom! There you was."

Will recalled Henry lighting his pipe. "You mean that if Henry hadn't lit up his pipe…."

"Yep," said Burnes. "We might not have know'd you was there. The whole thing might've come out different." He puffed again.

Will smelled the pipe smoke from across the fire and shook his head in disbelief.

Burnes continued, "Sometimes, win or lose, fight or not fight, live or die, comes down to a small thing like that."

Will's mind replayed the events of the day. It came down to tobacco smoke, of all things! Will wondered what small thing had caused Charley Porter to lead a vicious gang of bushwhackers to his doorstep. What tiny thing had led to his farm being burned to a pile of ashes. He became morose and tuned out Jake's questions about rifles and horses and such.

After a time, his thoughts turned to home, and he wondered how Ma and the boys were doing, where they were sleeping tonight. He recalled how Lucy Davis had smiled at him as he was being dragged off

Will felt his ears burn as he thought about Lucy, about her seeing him like that. *I was tied up like a dern trussed-up hog ready for slaughter!* He was glad she couldn't see him now. He felt filthy. His clothes were torn and bloody, his back scraped raw, his shoes were wet and smelled like manure. He was dirty, hatless and bedraggled. He fell into feeling sorry for himself.

But he and Jake had survived the day, and that was what mattered.

Burnes left and returned with two wool blankets. "Sorry boys, best we got for tonight."

Jake took off his shoes and set them by the fire. He wrapped up in a blanket, laid down nearby and was almost immediately snoring. *How the hell does he do that?* thought Will.

Will made a trip to the nearest tree and relieved himself. He returned to the dying fire, set his damp shoes on a nearby log to dry, and found some soft grass to lie in. With experienced soldiers all around him and armed sentries on guard, he felt as safe as he could be. He wondered what tomorrow would bring, then, exhausted, he was fast asleep.

"That you Charley?"

Relief washed over Charley like a cool blanket, and he found he could breathe again. Darnell! It was Darnell!

He lowered his pistol and un-cocked it. "Yep, it's me. Damn am I glad to see you! I came near to shootin' you just now, you prob'bly ought to yell out before comin' in on a man like that. How the hell did you find me?"

"I dunno. I came across your tracks a while back and been followin' you ever since."

"Where's Henry and the men?"

"Dead, Charley. They got shot."

"Shit! What happened?"

Darnell related the story of the ambush at the creek in his halting, stuttering way. Charley had to ask questions just to keep Darnell talking.

"Who was it that ambushed them?"

"They was Yankees."

Charley became annoyed. Sometimes it was hard to get anything useful out of Darnell. "I know that. Did they say what outfit they was?"

"Uh, yeah. Fiftieth somethin'"

"Fifteenth? Fifteenth Cavalry?"

"Yeah that was it. Fifteenth Cavalry. They was Yankees," said Darnell, repeating himself.

When Charley had gotten all he could from Darnell, he told his own similar tale of woe and death, adding a few embellishments. In the story he told Darnell, Charley fought off the Yankees for as long as he could, trying to save his comrades. In his tale, Charley was a hero.

In his usual manner, Darnell only grunted, which irritated Charley. What else could you expect from a half-wit like Darnell? "Fetch me some of that jerky you got," Charley said sharply. "An' some water."

Darnell rose and retrieved the beef from his saddlebag and untied his canteen. He handed half the meat and the water to Charley. They were quiet for a while, then, chewing on the tough dried meat.

Darnell broke the silence, asking, "What do we do now, Charley?"

"First thing is," said Charley, "We get some sleep. We cain't go nowhere till dawn anyhow. Then we ride west an' find Anderson."

"Ok."

Charley took a swig from the canteen and stood up to relieve himself against a tree. "One of us needs to be awake all night," he said. "You get first watch. You stay awake and I'll sleep a while, then I'll relieve you."

"Ok."

"Well, all right then," said Charley.

Darnell simply grunted.

Charley made himself as comfortable as he could on the cold, damp, leafy ground, wrapped up in his blanket. He had no intention of relieving Darnell and he slept all night, only waking when the birds began to sing, greeting the morning sun.

Darnell was still wide-eyed and awake.

\*\*\*\*\*

# Chapter 8

It was only mid-morning, but the sun was getting high, and Jake felt its rays boring through his hair and burning his scalp. Sweat ran down his face; he wiped it from his eyes and flicked it away.

As they rode west, the dense canopy that shaded the road yesterday gave way to gently rolling hills covered mostly with knee-high grass. Clumps of shorter trees dotted the hillsides and lined the creek-beds, but the road they traveled was in full sun.

Sergeant Burnes looked at Jake's and Will's hatless heads, then up at the sky. "You need a hat," he said. "Both of you." He yelled to a nearby soldier, "Hey, you, Simmons! Find these men a couple of hats."

"We ain't got no dang hats, Sergeant," replied Simmons.

Burnes looked over at the prisoners. Both wore dark blue slouch hats.

"Well then," he said, pointing. "Take theirs."

Simmons rode over and ripped the hats off the two prisoners. One cursed him bitterly for doing so, but Watt just hung his head.

Simmons rode over to Jake and tried to hand him a hat.

Jake stiffened in the saddle "No, I ain't wearin' no damn bushwhacker's hat." His anger began to rise.

"Jake, don't be stupid, put the hat on," said Will. "It's August for Pete's sake. Your brains are gonna boil."

He ground his teeth a moment before responding. "It's your words make my brains boil. I ain't wearin' that man's damn hat. And don't you be callin' me stupid. I ain't stupid."

"It's all right, he won't be needin' it much longer, anyhow," said Simmons. "It's a Union Cavalry hat. Likely he took if off'n a dead trooper." He handed Jake the hat and threw the other to Will before trotting back to his place in the column.

Before Jake realized it, the hat was in his hands. He inspected it —

there was no blood on it, no bullet holes, and it was in good shape. It looked almost new, and only had a small band of sweat stain around the brim. It was much better than his old, worn-out straw hat.

"Wear the dang hat, Jake," Will repeated, tugging on Watt's hat.

"Shut up, Will!"

"Fine." Will shrugged and rode away.

Jake knew Will was right, being out in the summer sun without a hat wasn't smart. But a bushwhacker's hat? A dead man's hat? It just didn't feel right.

Burnes was looking at him with an amused expression on his face. "You'd be honorin' the dead trooper if you'd wear his hat," he said.

Jake stared at the hat for a moment. Did a bushwhacker taking it from a dead trooper make it bushwhacker's hat? He decided no; it was a Union Trooper's hat after all, no matter who wore it last. When he put it on, it fit him well, and he felt cooler right away. The hat felt good, like it belonged up there on his head, and his mood improved.

He liked being around these blue-coated soldiers. They sure used a lot of cuss-words, but that didn't bother him at all. The cussing made them seem more honest than most folks back home, who wouldn't cuss in public, but would swear up and down like a sailor out of hearing of the women and children.

These boys had a sense of humor, too, unlike his brother Will, who was always so damn serious and so damn bossy.

They had horses, too. Good horses, provided free of charge by the United States government. And those guns — those brand-new carbines — were sure something to see. Jake wondered what it might be like to shoot one of them.

Thinking of guns turned his mind back to Ma and what had been done to her, and how he wanted to avenge her. Jake recalled their house and barn in flames, Missy the mule laying there dead, the way Porter had aimed his pistol at Ike, and he became infuriated all over again. He wanted nothing more than to see Porter and all those men dead.

Some of them were already dead and beyond his revenge. They were lying back there in shallow graves. Jaked hoped coyotes dug them up and scattered their bones. He hoped the the ones who had gotten away were caught soon. Or killed.

These troopers — these Yankees — were doing something about raiders and marauders and bushwhackers — chasing them down and killing them, two or three at a time. He'd seen the proof of that with his own eyes. Not like his brother, who just wanted to sit back and watch and hope the war would just go away. He gave Will a glare, but it was wasted as he was looking the other way.

The column moved on and everyone grew quiet in the mid-day heat. Jake had lots of time to daydream about shooting bushwhackers.

Will had almost nodded off in his saddle when a chorus of cheers and yelling erupted from the men around him. He soon saw what the commotion was about.

They crested the top of a long slope and spread out below them was a sea of white tents. Amongst them, blue-uniformed men milled about like ants. Here and there, buildings and houses poked up above the tents, and smoke drifted up from stove-pipes and tinted the air a light blue. A huge Union flag flapped loosely in the breeze from a tall pole near the middle.

Sergeant Burnes saw him staring at it. "Thirty-five stars," he said. "They added one for West Virginny last year."

Will was confused. "West Virginny?" He didn't know anything about any of the states except for Missouri and Arkansas, and California, where the gold was.

"Yep. West Virginny split off from the Confederates and Ole Abe made 'em a new state." Burnes searched through his pockets for something. Not finding it, he reached behind him for his saddle bag. "Where's my dad-gum pipe?"

"Where are we?" asked Jake.

Burnes now had his pipe in hand and was filling it with tobacco. "Camp Fremont, home of the Fifteenth Cavalry. The town is Mexico, Missouri," he said. "County seat of Audrain County."

Will studied the town below. Steeples rose from a couple of churches near the center, and another rose from a large, two-story brick building set just behind the flag-pole. A group of large tents with several smaller flags stood just outside its doors on the lawn.

Burnes must have noticed Will staring at it. "That's the courthouse," he said. He lit his pipe and the sweet aroma of Virginia tobacco filled the air.

The courthouse was the biggest building Will had ever seen, and its white brick gleamed in the harsh sunlight. It dwarfed the Lincoln County courthouse, in Troy. The lawn surrounding it was filled by white tents. Hundreds of smaller tents were laid out on a grid in a large pasture across the dirt street. Smaller flags and guidons flapped here and there. Men in blue coats were sitting, walking, currying horses, drilling, moving about, doing whatever soldiers do.

The scene reminded Will of their talk last night about the small things. Here was a big thing, this camp with its hundreds, maybe thousands of Yankee soldiers. Amazed, he realized that this camp was just one of many scattered across the state. How could the Rebels win a war against so many bluecoats?

The smell of manure and woodsmoke filled the air, but there were other smells too. He smelled coffee, fresh-baked bread and bacon being fried. There was the cottony smell of canvas baking in the hot sun. He got a whiff of the latrines, then it was gone with the breeze. Off somewhere in the distance, rifles boomed in sequence; Boom, Boom, Boom.... Will searched for the source.

Burnes grinned. "Just shootin' practice, boys. The Johnnies ain't gonna attack us here."

Will believed him. The Rebels would have to be insane to attack this place.

The column halted and the troopers dismounted. "We'll take these horses now, boys," said Burnes. "Keep the hats, though."

When they had dismounted, the horses were led away and Burnes led the brothers to a large tent, near the front entrance of the courthouse. A smaller Union flag hung from the main tent-pole, snapping and fluttered in the wind. The flaps of the tent hung loosely in the sweltering heat.

"Wait here," said Burnes.

Logs had been placed in a circle around the remains of a still-smoldering campfire. The wispy tendrils of smoke smelled of ash and something else that had been burned — coffee? Will took a seat and stretched out his legs.

Jake paced back and forth nervously in front of the fire-pit. "What are we gonna tell 'em, Will? If they find out we shot at the Yankees, they'll make us prisoners and send us off to prison."

"They won't do that," said Will. "They got papers you can sign now, an oath or somethin' to swear to, and then we can go home. Besides, we was drug off against our will, and we came home soon as we could. That has got to count for somethin'." Will paused. "I figure the truth is the best thing. Let me do the talkin'."

Jake made a sour face. "I hope you know what you're doin'." He took a seat and pulled up a stem of grass and began chewing on it. He soon stood up and paced back and forth again. "What's takin' 'em so long?"

Will ignored him.

Finally, Sergeant Burnes came back out. "It'll be a few minutes," he said. "Colonel's finishin' up a letter." He tamped ashes from his pipe, refilled and lit it, and took a seat on a log across from Will.

While Burnes smoked, Will studied him. Burnes was short, stocky, and well-muscled. His reddish hair was graying slightly just above his ears and his short beard was mostly gray, tempered with a little red. A long, faint scar crossed his left cheek and disappeared into his beard. He wore the same uniform as most of the troopers; sky-blue wool pants and black leather boots that came halfway up to his knees. His short coat, however, had three yellow stripes and a yellow diamond sewn on his sleeve just above the elbow.

Will was curious about the scar but didn't want to pry.

That didn't stop Jake. "Sergeant Burnes, how'd you get that scar?"

Will kicked him lightly on the leg. "Don't be nosy, Jake."

"No, it's all right, I reckon," said the sergeant. "I got that scar from a Minie-ball at a little hill called Kennesaw Mountain, down in Georgia. It grazed my cheek, that's all. I was lucky." He puffed on the pipe.

"I've heard of New Hope Church, but not Kennesaw Mountain," said Jake. "I know somebody who fought there, on the Rebel side."

Burnes nodded. "Was there, too. Them Rebels down there, now, they know how to fight. There weren't none of this guerilla bushwhackin', shootin' and runnin' away crap, like we got up here. Them boys stood up toe-to-toe and held their line 'til we flanked 'em and they had to leave. Ole Billy Sherman usually flanked 'em that way instead of hittin' 'em head on. He saved many a boy's lives thattaway, and we all was grateful for it."

He paused for another puff. "But at Kennesaw, he got tired of flankin' 'em. The Rebs was dug in good at the top of that hill, and Billy Sherman ordered us to march straight into 'em."

Burnes looked at the ground, silent for a moment. "Many a good boy lost his life that day. An' we didn't take that hill."

Will didn't know what to say to that, so he kept quiet. An uneasy silence held for a moment. Even Jake was silent.

Burnes puffed again and blew the smoke up into the air. "Next day, we flanked 'em again and they pulled out for Atlanta. I reckon generals is just like us, sometimes they're smart and sometimes they ain't."

He took another draw from the pipe. "Then my enlistment was up, an' I came home to Missouri. And somehow I got hoodooed into signin' up with Captain Stevens and this gang of misfits. I ain't none too smart either. Don't that beat all?"

Burnes grew silent and for a long time there was no talking and the only sound was of him sucking on the pipe. Will was lost in images of battles far away and a sadness came on him. Their friend, Ben Carter's youngest son Patrick had gone missing down at New Hope Church. He wondered if anyone would ever find out what happened to him.

The tent flap flipped opened, and another officer said, "You can come in now, Sergeant."

"Well, come on boys lets go meet the Colonel."

Will entered the tent, and his eyes were immediately drawn to a tall, clean shaven man standing behind a small table. His wavy hair was silver and contrasted with his deeply tanned and slightly wrinkled face. He had on a dark blue waistcoat and dark pants with a yellow stripe down the leg. His hat, hanging on a nail driven into a tent pole, had even more yellow piping sewn to it than Captain Stevens'. Other than the hat and some bright brass buttons on his coat, his uniform was unadorned. He stepped around the table and shook hands with him and Jake.

"I'm Colonel Nelson Owens, and this is my adjutant, Lieutenant Don Morrison. And you've already met Captain Stevens. He's told me all about your little adventure."

Will hadn't seen the two officers standing at the side of the tent. Stevens nodded. Morrison stepped forward and shook hands with the brothers.

"Let's get right to business, I have lots of work to do today," said Owens. You boys were rescued from some of Bill Anderson's men, correct?" He didn't wait for an answer. "And you were taken from your home in Millwood, Lincoln County. And these same men burned your farmstead? Was anyone hurt?"

Before Will could answer, Jake said, "Yes sir. Ma was roughed up and got some bruises on her face."

Will interrupted before Jake could go off on a tirade. "But that's all I reckon," he said. "We was lucky. They threatened my younger brothers and some folks that came to help put the fire out."

"And these men claimed to be under orders from Sterling Price? Rounding up deserters?"

"Yessir."

"Well, some of those men have been dealt with," said Owens. "And I'm sure we'll soon catch up to the others. That brings me to you two men." He motioned to Morrison, who took a seat at the table, opened a ledger book, dipped a quill in an inkpot, and began writing something in it.

"Let's start with your full names." He looked at Will. "You first."

"William Edgar Tanner. I go by 'Will."

"Jake Tanner. Jacob Tanner," his brother blurted.

"One at a time now, boys," said Owens. He looked at Morrison, who nodded. Nodding at Will, he asked, "And how old are you?"

"I'm twenty-one, now, and Jake is nineteen."

"And you two were conscripted in sixty-two by the Confederate Army?"

"Well, I guess so, sir," said Will. "That's what they said, anyhow. They came to the farm and took us south and made us fight. We didn't want to go, they made us."

Morrison continued to scratch in his ledger book.

"Do you recall who it was that took you?"

"No, Sir. We wound up with Jo Shelby's outfit."

"Now this part is important, boys, so think hard about your answer. Did the men who took you in sixty-two point their guns at you or otherwise threaten you?"

Will was not likely to ever forget that day. The soldiers carried muskets with huge bayonets like swords mounted on them. And, yes, they had been pointed their way. "Yeah. Yes sir, that is. They had bayonets on their guns an' they did point them at us."

"Yes, sir, they did," agreed Jake.

"And you say you were in the fight at Elkhorn Tavern? We call it Pea Ridge, but never mind that. Did you shoot at anyone?"

Before Jake could say anything to the contrary, Will looked right into the Colonels eyes and said, "No Sir. We were ordered to load and shoot, but I aimed my gun way high so as not to shoot nobody. I told Jake to do the same."

Jake nodded. "Yes, sir. That's what we did, fired high or wide. We didn't want to be shootin' at nobody."

Owens rubbed his jaw for a moment, then sighed. "Well, speaking strictly from the law, you boys have 'borne arms' against the Union. Therefore, in the eyes of the law, you are Rebels. But there is a way we can fix this. Are you willing to take the loyalty oath?"

Will looked at Jake, who nodded. Will said, "Yes Sir, we can take the oath."

"Good. After that you can go home, if that is what you want."

Owens nodded at Morrison, who opened another ledger. He began scribbling in it. He nodded back at Owens.

"Ok, boys, repeat after me: 'I, Will and Jake Tanner,' he whispered. 'Of Lincoln County, of the state of Missouri, do solemnly swear in the presence of God Almighty, that I will henceforth support, protect, and defend the Constitution of the United States....'"

He paused before finishing the pledge. The boys repeated his words, then Owens added "....so help me God."

There were a lot of big words in there that Will wasn't sure he understood, but again, he looked at Jake, and nodded. Jake nodded in return. They said, "So help me God," almost in unison.

"Can you sign your names?" asked Morrison.

Will shook his head no.

"Well, then come make your mark, and we will witness it, and that will do."

Will took the quill handed to him and made an X on the paper where Morrison pointed to. Jake did the same. Morrison then signed his name and Owens did the same.

"Now, you boys have sworn not to take up arms against the Union again, and that's all well and good. I'd like you to think about something else. I need men that will fight against these bushwhacking sons of.... These scoundrels. I think you two are good men who want to protect your homes and families against them. I want you to think about joining up with the Fifteenth."

Will was surprised at Owens's offer. He hadn't even thought about joining up, he just wanted to go home and be left alone to tend his farm.

"Sir," he said. "I figure the best way to protect our family is to go home and tend to our business. We don't want to get involved in the war, on either side."

Jake had a funny smile on his face. Will ignored him.

"Think about what might have happened at your farm yesterday," said Owens. "There was how many of them? Eleven? Is that right?"

"Yes, Sir," said Will.

"Eleven of them, then, and two of you, and if things had gone bad, you'd be dead and buried today, and probably some of your family with you." Owens stood up and walked to the front of his desk and leaned back on it. "Many farmers, just like you, have been killed. Their families killed. Bushwhackers like those men have been running amok all over the state, burning, murdering, raping. They need to be stopped. Caught and hung, if I have my way. The only way to do that is to chase them down, one band at a time and fight them. We need men like you to ride with us, to catch these men and to hang them, if necessary. We need men like you to help us restore peace in Missouri. Think about it, boys, that's all I ask."

Jake looked funnier still, like he was about to say something stupid. Will shook his head again and Jake looked down.

"And another thing," Owens continued. "You will get paid to do it. Thirteen dollars a month." He glanced at Morrison. "Isn't there a bounty on?" he asked.

"Yes, Sir. There's a federal bounty of three hundred dollars to sign up for the duration." Morrison paused. "The duration can't be much longer than a year or two, now that Sherman is at Atlanta's gates."

Will didn't know what a bounty was and was too embarrassed to ask.

Jake looked up. "What's a bounty?"

"The Federal government and the State of Missouri will pay you three-hundred dollars to sign up," said Morrison. "That's in addition to your normal pay of thirteen dollars per month. Plus, you'll have a uniform, a horse, a Sharp's carbine for a weapon, and we'll train you how to use it. And, of course, we'll feed you. Best of all, you can help us catch these damn bushwhackers or run them out of the state."

Jake looked at Will, his eyes wide. Will shook his head again. Jake frowned and looked away.

Owens added, "Just think about it. Go home if you want for a day or two. If you decide to join up, come back here and see me or Captain Stevens."

Three hundred dollars? Will had never seen that much money — had never known anyone that had that much money. What about the farm, who'd do the work? And what would Ma say? Will decided it wasn't possible. What he said was, "We will think on it, Sir. We need to go home and see about Ma and the farm, first."

Owens immediately lost interest in them and waved them way. "Very well, dismissed.... You can go."

They left the tent, followed by Sergeant Burnes. "If you boys do come back, come see me," he said. "I want you in my company. I'll make good troopers of you."

Will and Jake shook hands with Burnes. He led them to a half-loaded wagon being driven by two negroes. Both had carbines stashed alongside them in the driver box.

"Toby here will give you a ride as far as he can, then you'll be on your own," said Burnes. "Remember what I said."

Will simply nodded and the brothers piled into the back of the wagon and nestled in amongst some half-empty bags.

Jake huffed. "Three hunnert dollars! Damn, Will, that's a lot of money."

"Yeah, but who'd be there to protect Ma and the boys?"

"Jesus, Will! It's a dang fortune!"

"Drop it Jake, we ain't joinin'. You know what Ma'd say."

Jake cursed again, laid down and put his hat over his eyes. The wagon jerked forward, and they were bounced hard by the badly rutted road.

Even Will was impressed. Three hundred dollars! Hard cash money! He was about to lay his own head back and think about what three hundred dollars would buy when he saw something from the corner of his eye. A group of Yankee soldiers were marching in formation toward a big oak tree. Sunlight flashed off bayonets mounted to the rifles they carried.

Two men in civilian clothes were being prodded along in the middle of the soldiers. He recognized them as Watt and the other bushwhacker, whose hats they now wore. The prisoners had their hands tied behind them. Watt appeared to be praying, or crying, Will couldn't tell which.

Will nudged Jake, who sat up and looked where he had nodded.

"It's them two bushwhackers," said Will.

"What are they.... oh hell!" said Jake.

Will knew what was about to happen to them. There was a rope, tied into a noose, draped over a big limb of the oak tree. The other end of the rope was tied to the saddle of a horse that another soldier held. He and Jake watched as the noose was placed around Watt's neck, followed by a black hood.

They were almost around a curve when he saw the horse jerk forward and Watt was lifted into the air, his legs clawing, searching, reaching for the ground. Then mercifully, Will lost sight of his swinging body.

Jake's mouth hung open. "They mean business, don't they?"

"Yeah, Jake. They mean business."

Will swallowed hard. He looked at the hat he held in his hands. Watt's hat. He looked at it for a long time.

*****

# Chapter 9

Will was still worn-out from his ordeal. The late summer afternoon was hot and stifling, and with his weariness, it made him sluggish and drowsy. He laid back on the sacks in the back of the wagon and covered his eyes, but sleep wouldn't come. Each time he closed his eyes, he saw the hanging all over again in his mind. He saw the way Watt's legs kicked out and his toes searched, desperate to find purchase and support himself. The scene played over and over in his mind as if it was carved there in stone. He thought about how awful it must be to die that way.

He gave up trying to sleep, sat up and turned forward to face the teamsters. The negro driver was short, stocky and well-muscled, and his skin was the blackest Will had ever seen. Like his companion, he wore civilian clothes, but his hat was the same style and color that the cavalry troopers wore.

"So, you're Toby?" Will asked.

"Uh-huh," came the reply.

"Where you headed to?"

Toby didn't answer, he just flicked the reins and clicked to his mules. His gaze was fixed on the road ahead, and he never turned to make eye contact. It was clear to Will that Toby didn't want to talk. This was no real surprise; the only negroes he knew were slaves, and they seldom talked.

Jake, as usual, had not noticed or maybe he didn't care. "What's in these here sacks?" he asked.

"Now that might be none yo bizness," replied Toby, turning around to stare at them both. His eyes were like two bottomless black pits, and he stared directly at each of them in turn. Now Will was surprised; he had never known a negro to be so bold as to speak and stare like that. After a time, Toby turned back to his driving.

Jake started to speak again — Will elbowed him and shook his head. Jake being Jake, he ignored the admonition. "I'm just makin' small talk, that's all."

Will shrugged. Let him make a dang fool of himself.

The other negro turned around and smiled. "Doan mine Toby, he sulky today." He paused, then laughed. "He din' get to poke his gal las' night like he wonted to." This man was taller and thinner than Toby, and his color was lighter. His unruly hair poked out from under his worn and dirty slouch hat. His wide smile was genuine and friendly, in contrast to Toby's scowl.

Toby glared at Bo. "You need to mind yo mouth. Ain't nobody's bizness."

"My name Bo," said the other man, ignoring Toby. He stuck a hand back to Jake.

Jake took it and shook for a second. "I ain't never shook the hand of a colored man before."

"It doan rub off." said Bo, smiling back at Jake.

Jake looked down at his hands. When he looked up his ears were red.

"That's okay. Gits 'em every time," said Bo, laughing.

Will rolled his eyes. *Well, that didn't take long.* He shook hands with Bo, then extended a hand to Toby, which the man ignored. Will broke the awkward silence by introducing himself. "I'm Will Tanner, and this one here who ain't got no manners is my brother Jake."

Jake gave Will the evil eye. "Shut up, Will."

Bo guffawed. "Yeah you two be brothers, all right," he said, when he recovered.

Toby shook his head. "You ain't goan laugh when them bushwhackers come a callin', now is you?"

Bo's smile faded. "I reckon not."

"Then mine yo job and be lookin' all round," said Toby.

Bo leaned forward and picked up his carbine, cracked open the breech, peered into it, and snapped it shut again. He made a show of scanning all around for trouble, one hand shading his eyes. "That better Toby?"

Toby spat over the side of the wagon. "One these days, goan be real trouble, an' you goan git me and you both killed. Mark my words on it."

Bo smiled again. "Everybody die sometime, I reckon." He turned back to Jake and Will. "We carryin' some dispatch and some mail over to Army headquarters in St Louie. Might be some money in there. Might be somebody around who think some money in there, somebody that wont that money. We got to be careful. That why Toby all cranky today." He turned to Toby and glared at him. "That doan mean we got to be unfriendly."

Toby glared at Bo. "Hush yo mouth. We doan know who these boys be, they might be bushwhackers themselfs and goan knock us in the head, take this money fo the Johnny Rebs."

"I reckon they ain't no such thing," said Bo. "Colonel Owens, he'd a hung 'em if'n they was." Bo looked back to Jake and Will, looking into each boy's eyes for a second. "Jes like he hung dem las' ones you saw. He doan waste no time with go-rillers. He hang 'em pretty quick."

Turning frontward, he continued, "'Sides, I heard these boys was captured by bushwhackers. If they was captured by bushwhackers, then they ain't no bushwhackers. These boys be all right."

"An' if you wrong?" asked Toby.

"Don't fret none, we ain't bushwhackers," said Will. "They burned us out yesterday and hauled us off to fight. But we ain't fightin'. We just gave our loyalty oath."

"See?" said Bo, "I tole you. I ain't wrong."

"Doan mean nuthin'," said Toby.

"You in the Cavalry?" asked Will, trying to change the subject.

"Nope," said Bo. "They doan 'llow coloreds in the Fifteenth. We hired out to 'em, though. We teamsters. This here is our mules and our wagon."

"We ain't good 'nuff to ride with 'em," spat Toby. "We good 'nuff to follow behind 'em an' get shot at when there's a fight."

Bo asked, "Still better than hoein' cotton and shuckin' corn, ain't it?"

Toby spat again. "You the one who know that. I ain't never been no field hand."

"Yep, I do know that for a fact." said Bo, nodding exaggeratedly. "I do know that," he repeated.

Toby said, "It may be jes a little bit better — if we doan get killed."

Bo grinned. "That right, if'n we doan get killed."

"Well, I hope you don't get killed," Will said. "Not today, anyhow. If you get killed today, we get killed too."

Bo laughed at Will's little joke. Toby ignored it. Jake just stared at Will with a perplexed look on his face.

The banter dispelled some of the gloom Will felt. But after another long lull in the conversation, his mind returned to the hanging, and his smile turned downward into a frown.

Bo was watching him, and his eyes narrowed. "Now, you take them last 'uns that was hanged back there," he said. "They deserve it. I heard Cap Stevens talking 'bout it. That one man, he was a mighty bad 'un. He raped a woman over to Fayette. A white woman. Other stuff too, bad stuff. An' the other one too, he killed a farmer over to Carthage. They got what they deserve to get. Don't be frettin' none over they sorry souls. They down in hell right now, all burnin' up, an' rightly so."

Will sighed. "Maybe they did deserve it, then." He forced his thoughts away from the hanging and his mind wandered back to home, and Lucy. He hoped everything there was all right and that he'd soon see her again.

The wagon creaked on in silence. Will daydreamed of Lucy a while, and again found himself nodding off in the heat, so he lay back in the sacks.

After what seemed to be only a few seconds, he woke with a start when Toby yelled "Whoa now! Whoa now!" to the mules and the wagon clanged to a stop.

"Lordy Jesus!" said Bo.

Alarmed, Will sat up and spun around. Up ahead sat two men atop their horses, blocking the road. Toby and Bo pointed their rifles.

Charley Porter halted his horse when he saw the wagon coming up the road. Darnell pulled up beside him and they watched it come to a halt well out of pistol range. Two rifles came up and pointed in their direction. The driver's faces were dark blurs under their hats. Negroes. As he observed the wagon, two more heads popped up from the back of the wagon. In the shimmering heat, all he could make of them were their dark hats.

Charley was tempted to attack. He figured they were only teamsters, carrying mail or some other goods between towns. If they had mail, there might be money in some of it. Bill Anderson would be impressed if Charley rode into camp with captured Yankee mail — Anderson would read Yankee mail just for the fun of it. If there wasn't mail, well there might be other things worth stealing.

The teamsters had rifles against his and Darnell's pistols. Pistols could shoot six bullets without reloading, and they had several apiece. The rifles had better range and accuracy — if the men in the wagon were good shots, he and Darnell would be killed or wounded long before they could get within range. *Or just as bad,* he thought, *the horses might get shot.*

The more Charley studied the wagon, the less he liked his odds. If there was anything of value in it, there ought to be cavalry with it, and there weren't any. And he was still skittish from yesterday's fight where most of his companions were killed or captured, and that figured into his calculations. Besides, he liked to have more men on his side when he fought. He felt alone and exposed out here with only Darnell at his side.

He decided. "Come on Darnell, let's ride," he said. "They ain't got nuthin' we need bad enough to get shot over." They turned their horses and cantered north across an open field toward the woods in the distance. Charley's shoulders tensed as he half-expected to be shot at any second, but the men in the wagon held their fire.

Charley relaxed only when they reached the tree-line. Slowing their horses, he and Darnell entered the woods and continued north until they reached a small creek that flowed westward. Spooked now, Charley decided to ride downstream in the shallow water to hide their tracks. After a few miles, they left the stream on some rocky ground and turned north again, staying off the roads whenever they could.

The few farmers they came across all carried guns or had them leaning nearby. Word of Anderson's raid must've gotten around, Charley thought, and the farmers were ready for trouble. After the debacle at Johnson's farm, Charley's confidence had taken a blow, and, besides, they had food enough for now. There was no need for a confrontation, and they gave them a wide berth.

It had been a relief when Darnell had found him last night, and the panicky feeling had eased off. Yet something about Darnell puzzled Charley — he wasn't sure of him in a hard fight. He tried to remember if he'd ever seen him shoot anybody, armed or not. He'd seen Darnell shoot his guns when fighting armed soldiers, but he'd never seen him actually hit anyone.

In the killing at Centralia, Darnell had just sat there, eyes averted, and he had not even drawn his pistols. Charley had participated with gusto, so it amazed him that Darnell had not. He found that odd. Didn't Darnell hate the Yankees too?

After a while he decided that no, Darnell had never killed anyone. Charley resolved to fix that deficiency the next chance they got. He had to be sure Darnell would cover his back in a tight spot.

After a few more miles, the afternoon heat began to make Charley lethargic. He removed his hat and wiped the sweat from his brow with a sleeve. "Let's hole up somewhere for a while. There's too many people around anyhow."

Darnell simply nodded.

They found a copse of stunted oaks next to a small creek where the horses could get some water and a little grass. They hobbled the horses and lay back in the grass and slept for a while. Charley woke once, his hearth thumping in panic, when a coon-hound bayed off in the distance. He listened for a minute, and the dog soon quieted. *Just an old hound treein' a squirrel,* he thought. He dismissed it and was soon sleeping again.

Jake knew right away who one of the riders was. Even from so far away, he could make out Charley Porter's long yellow hair and the black horse that he rode. He wasn't sure about the other man, but it didn't matter. He only was able to breathe again when the pair moved off toward the woods.

"Doan know who that was. They don't wonna to talk to us, look like," said Toby.

Bo blew out a relieved breath. "Dat a good thing. They look like hard cases."

Jake agreed. He leaned over to Will and whispered, "You make 'em out?"

"Yeah, Charley Porter, for sure," said Will. "And that other one too, I don't know his name, but he was at the farm."

"Shit!" said Jake. He looked down, slowly shook his head and cursed under his breath. He'd hoped they'd seen the last of Porter, but he'd been right there in front of them, in plain view.

Will gave him a funny look. "What?"

"Nothin'," he said. "I was hopin' Porter'd be long gone and we'd never see him again. But yeah, that was him. That yellow hair's a dead giveaway."

Bo looked back at the two. "You know 'em?"

Will nodded. "I think they were two of the bushwhackers that burnt us out two days ago. Not sure though. Best to keep a good eye on 'em."

Four sets of eyes watched as the two horsemen disappeared into the woods. The bushwhackers never looked back over their shoulders and never drew their pistols. Toby and Bo both un-cocked their rifles.

Bo looked back and asked, "You boys know how to shoot one of these?" He pulled a Colt revolver from his belt and held it up.

Jake opened his mouth to answer and, as usual, Will butted in. "No, we ain't never shot one of those."

Annoyed, Jake quickly said, "I can shoot it. One of the troopers showed me how."

Jake felt Will's eyes staring at him. "Why'd you say that?" asked Will. "You ain't never shot one!"

"I didn't say I shot one," he hissed back. "I said I could shoot it. A trooper showed me how it worked. That's more than you know about it, ain't it?"

Will's mouth fell open, but thankfully, no more words came out of it. Jake was tired of bein' belittled by his big brother.

Bo offered the pistol to Will, who declined with a shake of his head. He handed it to Jake, who took it.

"It already loaded," Bo said. "You got six shots. We worry 'bout reloadin' later, if need be."

"Careful where you point that thing. Don't shoot yourself. Or me," said Will.

"Well that's a tempting thought," said Jake, only half joking.

Shaking off his annoyance at Will, he studied the six-shooter, and though it was a little rusty, the heft of it felt good in his hand. He pulled the hammer back to full cock to get the feel of it, then let it back down slowly, just like the trooper had showed him.

Bo now had a grave look on his face. He scanned the trees where Porter had disappeared, before he turned back to Jake. "You watch out behind us. They might circle back on us. Toby, give Will yo rifle."

"What? No," said Toby. "That cost me two month's wages, I ain't...."

"He ain't gonna steal it, he just goan borrow it. 'Sides, you cain't shoot it while you drivin'."

Toby cursed under his breath, and reluctantly held the rifle up for Will to grab.

"I'll be careful with it," said Will.

Toby cursed again, clicked his tongue and slapped the reins. The wagon lurched forward.

"You got one shot," said Bo. "All you gotta do is pull back the hammer and let fly."

Toby slapped the reins and clicked his tongue and the wagon lurched forward. There was no more small talk.

Jake had some now time to think about things. He looked sideways at his brother and avoided eye contact. Which was just as well, because Will was doing the same thing.

He'd let Will get him riled up, yet again, over a small thing. He knew Will was right, he'd never shot a pistol before, and it'd be pure luck if he hit anything when he did. Will was usually right about these things, but did he have to be so damn bossy about it? Why the hell did he always do that? Why was he always on his back, riding him, telling him what to do and what not to do? Will acted like Jake was still a little kid.

But Jake soon realized it was really Charley Porter who had gotten his goat. He'd been rattled by his sudden re-appearance two days ago. He'd tried hard to forget Porter and the lies he'd told him back at Elkhorn Tavern, more than two years ago now. He'd kept that secret for so long now he'd almost forgotten it, but it was still there, deep inside his head, and Porter had brought it back to the surface. Now, it was like a heavy stone in his belly, gnawing away at his gut.

Jake knew he ought to tell Will, especially now that Porter had re-appeared, but he couldn't bring himself to do it. He didn't even want to think about it, much less tell his brother. Telling him would be like admitting the words were true, and he could never admit that.

He'd hoped Porter would just disappear and he wouldn't have to deal with it. But Porter was still out there, and that meant trouble.

He stole a furtive glance at his brother, who had turned away from him to scan the horizon. When Will turned back, he scowled and he looked away again. No, now was not the time to tell Will. Not while he was so annoyed.

As Jake pondered these things, the torpid afternoon wore on, and the miles rolled away behind him. No more riders appeared. Here and there Jake saw farmers out working in the fields. A few waved at the wagon, but most just glared at them with suspicious looks. All carried guns or had them stacked within reach. He could almost feel their eyes on them as they rolled by.

After a long while, the sun lowered and the heat eased off. Toby turned the wagon off the road onto a well-used track that led to a wooded creek. Bo turned around and said, "We'll camp here 'neath them trees."

After a few hundred yards, Jake spotted the stone fire-ring and the wagon creaked to a stop. He and Will unharnessed and hobbled the mules. They spoke to each other as little as possible. Jake could feel the tension between him and Will, like a wall of some sort. It saddened him, and he didn't know what to do about it.

While Toby gathered wood, Bo started a fire and cooked a meal of fried corn bread, salt beef and coffee he produced from one of the sacks. They ate in silence. Everyone was too hungry and heat-sapped to chat. Afterward, Toby produced a jug from under the wagon seat. He took a long swig and offered it to Will, who declined and passed it to Bo.

Bo took a swig and offered it to Jake.

"No, Jake. You know what Ma would say," said Will.

Jake felt his anger rise again. He had to take a drink now, just to show Will he wasn't the boss. He took the jug from Bo.

"You drink rotgut befo'?" asked Bo, grinning.

"Naw. How bad can it be?"

"Jake…," said Will.

Jake cut him off. "Shut up, Will. Mind your own dang business."

He took the jug, wiped the mouth and took a big gulp. Immediately, his throat was on fire and he gagged, snorting whiskey out his nose. Fumes shot up into his nose and down into his lungs, burning and choking him even more. Gasping for air, he handed the jug back and bent over and coughed up the burning liquid. "Jeez!" He croaked.

Bo guffawed and slapped his legs. "Good stuff, aint it," he said. He offered the jug again. "Hair of the dog dat bit you?"

Jake didn't know what the words meant but he knew he didn't want any more of that wretched stuff. After a while the burning eased, and he could breathe again without coughing. He didn't dare look at Will who he knew was giving him one of his smug looks.

Toby just watched with a scowl on his face. "Waste of good whiskey," he muttered.

The night grew silent except for Jake's occasional wheeze, the crackle of the fire and the chirping of crickets. Soon, Toby stood up, grabbed a blanket, wrapped himself in it and lay down. "Bo, you got first watch."

"We'll take our turn too," said Will.

Jake hadn't even thought about it, but after a second, he agreed.

Toby pondered for a minute. "Ok, Jake, you get the first two hours," he said. "Then Will can take two hours, then wake up Bo. I get the last watch."

Bo handed him the pistol again. Jake stuck it in his belt, found a tree and sat with his back to it, facing the road. His wheezing eased off and he gazed up into the sky. By now, the evening star had set, and the Milky Way was a bright smear across the moonless sky. The stars were brighter tonight than he'd ever seen them, except maybe in winter. He watched them twinkle until he got drowsy. He made himself stand up and walk around to stay awake. When he estimated two hours had gone by, he woke up Will, and took his place in the bed of the wagon. He was asleep in seconds.

A buzzing fly lit on Charley Porter's nose and woke him from his nap. He swatted at it, cursing, then remembered where he was. It was time to ride again. The sun had gotten low and it had cooled down. He nudged Darnell. "Time to go," he said.

Darnell grunted, wiped his face and rubbed his eyes. "Ok." He stood and brushed the grass from his shirt.

They retrieved the horses and tightened the cinches. Charley's stomach growled. He retrieved some ham and biscuits from a saddle bag and tossed some to Darnell.

"Eat quick," said Charley. "We got to ride."

The biscuits were hard; cool water from the creek helped to wash them down. The salty ham was good, and his hunger eased off, but it made him thirsty again. They drank their fill, topped off their canteens and mounted up.

The biscuits and ham they stolen from the Tanner's farm reminded Charley of how much he hated Will and Jake Tanner.

He didn't hate them because they had deserted from the Rebel Army, he could care less about state's rights, secession or slavery. Charley was not a deserter himself, but only because he'd been captured. He, too, had run away from the fight back at Pea Ridge. It wasn't his fault, he had decided, his whole company had been nearly wiped out by cannon fire. He recalled the moment when he had looked around and there was only a handful of men left standing to face a whole Yankee regiment. *And those damn cannons still a-firin' at me!*

He shuddered at the memory of the man standing next to him, the sickening thud of the cannonball that caught him square in the chest and tore him in two. There was more blood than he'd ever seen, and some of it had splashed onto his own face. The smell was awful. He never knew that the insides of a man would smell so bad. It was more than he could take. Something snapped inside his mind that day. He had dropped his rifle and run away.

He wasn't the only one, many a Rebel soldier had run away from that fight, and when he jumped behind that log, there were others already there. There was that damned sergeant who tried to get him to go back into the fight. Some of the boys, ashamed of themselves, got back up and paid a heavy price in blood for it.

A Yankee shell fragment took off the top of the sergeant's head, ending his exhortations, his arguments and his shaming. The man fell back into Charley's lap, his body quivering and eyes fluttering until after an eternity, he finally lay still, blood everywhere, and his eyes rolled backward and stared up at him.

Charley shivered remembering that awful sight. He couldn't remember the sergeant's name, but he couldn't forget his eyes — surprised, puzzled, pleading and accusing. As if Charley himself had sent that piece of iron careening over the field and into his head. As if it should have been Charley that got killed instead of him. As if Charley could have done something about any of it.

He hated to admit it, but Tanner had been right about one thing. He did freeze up that day. He couldn't move — his legs just wouldn't work. The worst part was that his bladder had let go, and them damned Tanners were right there and saw it. Saw his shame. He felt their smirking eyes on him even now. But that wasn't why he hated them, either.

They'd left him there! Just up and left him to get captured and drug off by them damn Yankee sumbitches. He'd pleaded with Will to help him get up. All he needed was a hand, but Will wouldn't help him. Instead, he and his damned brother slunk off like the cowards they were and left him there alone. Left him there so they could run home and hide behind their momma's skirts. Left him there to face those Yankee bastards all by himself. Left him there to be drug off to that damn prison camp where he almost starved and died.

He shuddered again. The Yankees treated them, not like soldiers, not like men. More like animals in a cage, to be laughed at, tormented, beaten, abused. In a Yankee prison camp, there were things worse than dying. Dying was the way out, living was the hell.

He shuddered again and buried those memories deep in his mind and covered them over with hate, like a dog buries a bone, to be dug up when needed. Like when Yankees needed killing.

He hated them for that, but even that wasn't all of it.

*I trusted Jake! I told him the truth. An' all I got for it was a beatin', from him and his damned brother.*

Charley's memories angered him, and his anger distracted him. It had gotten darker as they rode, and he hadn't even noticed it. He heard horses and when he looked up through the gloom, they were surrounded by armed men. The clicking of pistols being cocked brought him up short.

"Hold right there or git shot!" someone shouted.

Charley's hand moved toward his own gun as he considered his options. A whole slew of cocked pistols pointed straight at him, each one glowing faintly in the dim starlight. He knew he couldn't win if it came to gunplay.

A voice yelled, "Don't do that, if you want to live!"

He breathed a sigh of relief as he recognized the voice. "That you Bose?" he asked. "It's Charley Porter and Darnell Harris. Damn, you like to scared the bejeezus outta me!"

"You deserved every bit of it, bein' out in the open and against the sky like that," said Bose. "Hell, you tryin' to get killed?"

A retort came into Charley's mind, but he quickly thought better of it. Bose Lewis was well known for his quick temper. Metallic clicks sounded in the dark as pistols were un-cocked and put away.

"Anybody else with you?" asked Bose.

"No, just us two."

"Where's Henry an' the rest?"

"Henry's dead, killed by goddam Yankees. Darnell saw it. Emmit's dead too, I saw him git killed. Some of the others too. Me an' Darnell is all that's left. That I know of, anyway. Some might've run off."

"Well, damn!"

The men surrounding Charley grumbled and cursed from the darkness. Someone said, "Dammit! Bastard Emmit owed me money." The man's poor fortune amused the others and they laughed and guffawed.

"Good luck collectin' it!" snickered another. The men laughed harder.

"Quiet!" yelled Bose, and the men went silent. He turned back to Charley and said, "Well, if anybody else made it, they'll find us. Let's go. You can fill me in while we ride."

Bose turned his horse westward, and Charley fell in beside him. He told Bose about Henry splitting up the company and the fight at Johnson's farm. He left out the part where he ran off and hid in the woods. "There must a been a hunnerd of 'em," he lied. "I killed a few, but there weren't nothin' else I could do for the boys, an' I barely out-run 'em as it was."

"What about Henry, what happened to him?" asked Bose.

"Darnell told me they got jumped crossin' the road and they shot Henry off'n his horse, and a few others too. Darnell ain't sure which ones were killed or what."

"That right, Harris? Henry dead?" asked Bose.

"Yeah," replied Darnell.

"You see what happened to anyone else?"

"Nope."

"Why not?"

Darnell hesitated. "The Yankees was shootin' at me."

"How many Yankees?"

"A bunch."

"Dammit, Harris, don't you know more'n that?" asked Bose.

"Nope."

"You're about useless as tits on boar hog, you know that Harris?" Bose spat over his horse's withers.

Charley defended his partner. "Bose, now you know he's daft. Ain't no need to...."

Bose cut him off, "Shut up, Porter. Wasn't talkin' to you."

Charley leaned back in his saddle, perplexed by Bose's attitude. He didn't want to get on the man's bad side, so he shut his mouth. For a while, there was only the sound of horse's hooves thumping in the soft dirt or clopping on a rocky surface.

After a while, the silence got to Charley and he risked another question. "Where we goin', Bose?"

Bose did not answer and neither did anyone else. Charley felt something was wrong. Bose was down at the mouth and more touchy than usual. The men seemed to know it and were edgy and tense. Charley could feel the tension in the air, and he figured he'd be better off to keep quiet.

After another long silence, Bose answered Charley's question. "We're supposed to meet with Anderson at Rocheport. It's gonna be a long ride." Silence again. "After that, who knows?"

Only then did Charley notice there were no new recruits or conscripts with Bose's party, and his curiosity got the better of his caution. "You pick up any new men?"

"Nope," said Bose. "Most everybody was already in the brush
105

when we rode up. Word got around, I guess. We only caught one man, an' he tried to run off, so he got shot."

"Well, shit." Charley leaned back in his saddle, and it creaked with his movement. The raids had been a total disaster. "Whose damn fool idea was this anyhow?" he asked, not expecting an answer.

"General Sterling Goddamn Price," said Bose. "And Bill Anderson for goin' along with it." He spat again and spurred his horse ahead and away from Charley.

Charley was taken aback by Bose's remarks. It was the first time he'd ever known him to find fault with Anderson. Few men would ever criticize Bloody Bill Anderson, even behind his back. Those that did quickly found greener pastures or were buried under them.

Another rider pulled up beside him. "It's a sore spot," he whispered. "It was a cousin o' his what got shot. Best leave 'im be."

"Damn!" Charley's eyes widened. "Damn!" That would explain Bose's surliness.

"Yeah, it'll be hard goin' home again after that," said the rider. The man pulled out a rope of tobacco and cut off a chaw.

Charley's eyes narrowed. "Well, the cousin was a damn Yankee, anyhow," he said.

"Ain't that simple," said the rider, spitting over his horse's mane.

"Why ain't it that simple?"

"Bose is the one what shot 'im."

"Oh," said Charley. He didn't know what to say to that. He thought at first, that it might be a hard thing to live with. On further reflection, he came back to the fact that Bose's cousin was a Yankee and so he deserved what he got. "Still," he said to the rider. "The man was a damn Yankee."

The rider just grunted, spat again, and moved away, leaving Charley alone with his thoughts. He rode in silence the rest of the night, and his mind soon wandered from Bose's problems back to his own. With a gang of well-armed men around him now, his spirits rose, and his courage returned, his loneliness and apprehension forgotten. He rode all night thinking about what he'd do to Will and Jake Tanner if he ever got the chance.

Late the next morning, the gang rode into Rocheport. When he saw Anderson's camp, Charley felt like he was home, for the first time in a long while.

*****

# Chapter 10

Will sat up from his bedroll, heart pounding, confused about where he was. He'd been dreaming of Watt as he swung from the hanging tree. In the dream, Watt tried to tell Will about something, but he was being strangled by the rope and his words were garbled. He tried over and over to make himself understood — it seemed to be important, and he grew ever more agitated with Will.

Skittish and tense from the strange dream, Will's heart thumped again when something moved in the shadows. He felt sheepish when he saw it was just Toby, out there on watch, and he took a deep breath and calmed himself. *It was only a dream!*

Will was wide awake now, and a lightening eastern sky hinted of dawn. There was no use trying to go back to sleep. He flung off the blanket, stood up and padded over in his sock feet to a nearby tree and relieved himself. The crickets and katydids went silent as he neared them. Through the trees he saw a thin sliver of waning moon low in the crystal-clear sky. The day would be another sunny, hot and still August day.

Toby moved again, and Will tiptoed over to and squatted down beside him. Toby turned his head slightly, looked away and said nothing. The whiskey jug lay beside him. Will wondered if he'd been drinking all night.

Keeping his voice low, Will asked, "Want me to take over? I cain't sleep anyhow."

"Naw. It'll be daylight here shortly. No need."

"Mind if I sit here, anyway?"

Toby shrugged in response.

Toby's indifference was puzzling to Will. Toby didn't want to talk to him; that much was plain to see. Will didn't understand it; he hadn't done anything to him that he knew of. "It's ok, I can go back to bed, I reckon." He turned to walk away.

"Naw, it's all right." said Toby. "You sit if'n you wont. Jes don't 'spect no conversation."

Will sat on the ground and said nothing. Somewhere nearby a whip-or-will sang his eerie call, and way off in the distance a pack of coyotes yipped.

"Coyotes got 'em a rabbit cornered, I reckon," Toby said, starting the conversation he said he wouldn't start.

"Sounds like it."

"Sorry 'bout yo farm bein' all burnt up an' all."

"Yeah. Thanks." Maybe Toby wasn't as irritable as he seemed at first. Will took a chance. "Where you from?"

Toby turned to look at him. "What you need to know that fer?"

"Just askin'. You don't have to tell me."

"I know I don't have to tell you, if'n I don't wont to." Toby's voice rose a little.

Will didn't know what to say now. Once again, he was confused by Toby's up and down moodiness. He felt like he should leave but he was too embarrassed to get up. So, he sat a while, quietly enjoying the night sounds. He'd always enjoyed the night; he wasn't afraid of it like some folks were. Nothing bad had ever happened to him out in the dark, not yet anyway. After a minute, the crickets started their chirping again. Will knew that while the crickets chirped, nobody was out there trying to sneak up on them. It was when they got quiet that you needed to worry.

"Arkansas. Jonesboro, Arkansas," Toby said.

Will had almost forgotten he'd asked. "You got family back there?"

"You ask that question from every black fella you see? Cause if you do, you doan know much, do you?"

Will felt his face flush. It was true he didn't know much about black folks. The only negroes he personally knew were Ben Carter's slaves, and he'd never talked to them. And they'd never offered to talk to him, they barely looked at him when they did speak. Toby's resentfulness was not something he'd experienced before.

"You're right," Will said. "I don't know any negroes except for my neighbor's slaves and I ain't never talked to them. I didn't mean to offend." Will moved to get up and go back to bed.

Toby sighed and spoke again. "It ain't you I'm mad at," he said. "Not you yourself, anyhow. I jes got my mind on other stuff. Ain't nothin' to do with you." He sighed again and took a swig from the jug. "I don't even know who my daddy was. An' I barely remember my Momma, cause Massa need money an' he sold me off when I was a child. Took me nigh on twenty year to buy myself from my new Massa. Thank the good Lawd he 'llowed it."

"Sold you? When you were a kid?" Will asked, not sure he'd heard right.

"Yeah. I don't even know how old I was." said Toby.

Will was taken aback. He'd never thought much about slavery; it was just something that was. Everybody knew it was part of what the war was about, but it didn't have anything to do with him. His family didn't own slaves; the thought of owning slaves had never occurred to them, never even been discussed. That was for rich folks. He'd never wondered what life might be like from a slave's point of view, never wondered about their feelings, their pain, their suffering.

"I do got family back in Arkansas," Toby continued. "Got a wife and a young-un I ain't seed since the war started. They's still slaves. Abe Lincoln done freed 'em, but ain't no Yankee Army down there, so they's still slaves."

Will was stunned. He'd never heard a story like his before.

"I had to leave 'em," said Toby. "I didn't wont to, but them damn slavers start roundin' up freedmen like me and puttin' chains on us an' sellin' us again. It was plain as the hair on my haid if I didn't run away they's gonna get me next and sell me off. I might never see my family again if'n I didn't run off." He paused for another sip. "I ain't seed 'em in three years. Someday soon, I goan go back and get 'em. Gonna buy 'em or steal 'em away and we gonna go somewhere we can jes be let alone." Toby's voice had grown hoarse and his eyes glinted in the soft moonlight.

Will sighed. He felt sorry for him, but he was sure Toby wouldn't want his pity. He didn't know what to say, so he said nothing for a while.

Toby corked the jug. "Getting' to be daylight," he said, chuckling. "Here I done went an' said no conversation, and then I just spit out words like I bit a worm in a apple."

Will found enough courage to ask, "How you gonna get your wife and kid back?"

"I been savin' my money an' gonna buy 'em. I know a white man might can buy 'em and den sell 'em to me. Or maybe I have to sneak 'em away. It might be I have to wait till the war over." He paused again. "It cain't last too much longer," he said. "An' I believe the South gonna lose, too. Then black folks be free an' I'll go find 'em."

"I never knew, Toby. We never owned no slaves."

"I know that. Most white folks, they doan wonna know, either. They just turn they heads and say it's just the way it is. So, I guess I am mad at white folk in general. A little bit, anyhow."

They were both silent a while. Toby had given Will a lot to think about.

"California," said Toby.

"California?" asked Will.

Toby smiled. "Yeah. That's where I'm takin' my family once I git 'em."

"Oh yeah, where the gold is."

Toby shook his head. "Don't care nothin' for gold. They can keep all that. Gonna find me a little town where people don't care 'bout my skin and set myself up in a little freight haulin'. Feed my chile and raise up some more."

"Sounds like you got it all figured out," said Will.

"Yep, I do," said Toby. "I jes get a little down sometime, get a little sad. I ain't seed 'em in three years. Doan even know for sure if they's still livin'." He looked at the glowing sky. "But the sun come up each day, an' I be one day closer to seein' 'em."

"I hope you do just that, Toby," said Will. "I surely do. An' I'm sorry for your troubles." *His troubles make mine seem like small things.*

They sat in silence for a while. Will was lost in his thoughts, trying to understand the war and what it was really about. Why did people have to be so damn mean to one another? He hadn't figured out any kind of answer when he noticed the birds were singing and the sky had lightened to a cool blue.

"Well, I reckon we lived another day, then," said Toby.

"Yeah, we did."

"I make a mean cup of coffee. If you'll stoke us up a fire, I got some bacon too, an' we'll have us a little breakfast." Without another word, Toby walked off into the woods.

Will stood up and stretched the stiffness from his bones. The night air had been warm and humid, and he knew the day would be a hot one.

"Time to get started," he said to no-one. Soon, he had a good fire going and he kicked Jake awake. He let Bo sleep until Toby woke him.

Toby was right, the coffee was good, and the bacon was delicious.


Three hours after they left the camp, Jake found himself nodding off in the heat. He tried anything he could think of to stave off the torpor; he shifted the rifle from hand to hand, crossed his legs the other way, shifted his butt to one side. Nothing worked for long.

He jumped off the wagon, hoping the walk would help. He soon found himself falling behind, and he had to run to catch up. It was too hot to be walking, much less running, so he climbed back in, rocking the wagon bed. Will raised his hat, gave him the evil eye, then covered his face again.

"Bo, you got any water?" Jake asked.

Bo threw a canteen back to him. Jake uncorked it, took a long drink, and splashed some in his face. He poured some into his hat before putting the cork in.

He was handing it back when Will intercepted it. "Hold on, gimme a swig."

"Yeah you prob'bly need it, too," said Bo.

Jake put his wet hat back on. The air moving through the wet felt cooled his head.

Will performed the same routine, splashing his face, wetting down his hat, taking a long drink. He passed the canteen back to Bo, before covering his face with the hat once more.

Jake's little run had helped to get his blood moving. He managed to stay awake until, after another hour or so, they came to a crossroads.

Toby stopped the wagon. "This be as close as we get to Millwood. Be about—hmmm—about ten mile or so. You boys gonna have to hoof it from here."

Bo handed Jake the canteen again. "Here, take some mo, you goan need it."

He took a good long drink and passed it to Will who eyed it for a second, looked at the sky, took a long drink and passed it back to Bo.

Jake jumped out on Bo's side. "I reckon you want this back?" He handed over the rifle.

Bo looked down at Jake. "Good luck to you boys. If I was you, I'd jump in the brush mighty quick if you hear riders a comin'."

"Good idea," replied Jake, as he stuck out his hand.

"It doan rub off," Bo said, shaking his hand and grinning.

Jake laughed but didn't look at his hands this time.

Bo chuckled. "You learnin'."

Jake extended his hand to Toby, but again, the driver ignored it. Instead, he flipped the reins and said, "Giddyap, mule!"

Jake had to jump back to avoid getting run over, and the wagon lurched forward, leaving a small cloud of dust behind. He wondered if Toby had done that on purpose, or as Bo said, he was just cranky.

"Ten miles…." Will sighed loudly. "We better get started, gonna be a long walk." He walked up the road, leaving Jake there.

Jake looked up at the mid-afternoon sun and started walking. His footsteps were muffled by the inch-thick layer of dust, and little clouds of it kicked up with each footfall. *Will's right, it's gonna be along walk. A long, hot walk.* He was already thirsty again. And hungry.


Will thought about food and water—or the lack of it—for the hundredth time since they left the wagon. *It's my own dang fault. I know better, and I didn't ask for any. I bet they'd have given us some if we'd asked. Lord-a-mercy, it's hot!* He looked up at the sun, high in the sky, and wondered how far they'd come and how much farther they had to go.

Jake trudged along behind him. "Ain't there a creek west of this

113

road?" he asked.

"Yeah but it's pretty small," said Will. "Might be dried up this time of year. We'll see right soon. It crosses the road up ahead. See that tree-line?"

As Will had expected, the little creek was dried up and dusty where it crossed the road. Upstream, near a thicket, the creek-bed looked damp. Will figured they might be able to dig and get a little water there, so they walked up the creek and found a shady spot. Jake plopped down in the soft grass.

Will dug a hole in the creek-bed with a stick. A little water started to seep into it as he watched. "Gonna be a while," he said. He sat down beside Jake and removed his hat.

"How much further, you think?" asked Jake.

Will ran his hand through his hair and wiped his forehead with a sleeve before he answered. "Not sure," he said. "I ain't been this way in a long time." He looked at the angle of the shadows. "I'd say we been walkin' an hour and a half. So, I think maybe we're almost halfway home. About five, six more miles."

Jake pointed. "Look, apples!"

Will looked up and sure enough there was an old apple tree in the thicket. Small green apples hung from it here and there. "They look green to me," he said.

Jake jumped up, picked one and took a small bite. He immediately spat it out. "Whoa, that's one dang sour apple."

"What'd you expect," Will said. "It's August. They don't get ripe till October."

"Well, I had to try!" he laughed and threw the apple at Will.

Will blocked it with one hand, "Yeah, I reckon you did. You always gotta try, no matter what."

"What the hell's that supposed to mean?" Jake asked, his smile disappearing.

"It means you never listen," said Will. "I could tell you that a snake's gonna bite you, and you'd still poke your finger at it. You always gotta learn things the hard way. It's in your blood."

Jake sulked for a minute. "How would you know if it's in my blood? You never knew Pa. You was only, what? four, when he left? So, tell me Will, how would you know if it's in my blood?"

"I just know what Ma says, and she knew him pretty well, I reckon."

Jake looked down at the ground. "It makes me mad, when people say I'm like my Pa. I ain't like Pa, I just ain't. I won't never run out on my family like he did."


Will stiffened. *Is that why he's so mad all the time, so easy to rile up? Is he mad at Pa for goin' off and gettin' himself killed like he did?* He knew where this conversation was going and where it would likely end — in a fight they didn't need right now, so he tried to ease the situation. "That ain't what Ma means when she says that. She just means that you get riled up too easy and jump the gun when you need to slow down and think a little before you go rushin' in. That's all."

Jake bristled. "Maybe you need to rush in a little faster sometimes."

Jake's words stung — there was some truth in them. Will decided not to reply and looked away.

Jake seemed to soften. "I didn't mean that like it sounded. I know you're always gettin' me out of scrapes I shouldn't have got into. An' I appreciate that an' all." Now Jake looked away. "But I ain't Pa. And you ain't neither."

Will didn't have an answer for that. *Is that the way he sees me? That I'm trying to be Pa? I'm just tryin' to take care of everybody like Ma says and keep the farm goin'.*

Will was silent for a few minutes, thinking about what Jake had said. Wasn't he only doing what the man of the house was supposed to do? Take care of everybody else? *Somebody's gotta do it; Pa ain't here, and I'm the oldest, so it's on my shoulders, ain't it? Or is Jake right, an' I'm trying to be a father to everybody?*

When the silence grew too long and got uncomfortable, Will said, "Maybe you're right, Jake. I am the oldest and that's what I'm supposed to do, take care of you all and keep the farm goin'. Maybe I am too hard on you sometimes, but I got to try an' keep you out of trouble, at least 'til you're all growed up."

Jake jumped to his feet and glared down at Will, his fists tightening. "Why'd you have to say somethin' like that fer," he said. "I am all growed up, damn you."

Will realized he'd made things worse; Jake was now ready for blows. He raised his hands in surrender and smiled. "Cool your heels, Jake," he said. "I didn't mean to rile you. Besides, it's too dern hot to fight."

Jake sat back down, still glaring at Will.

They were silent for a time, and Will had time to think. He wondered why he and Jake clashed all the time. Maybe Jake was right, maybe he was too hard on him sometimes. On the other hand, his brother didn't always show good judgment. Maybe they were both wrong and both right at the same time. Maybe the truth was somewhere in between.

"Ok, Jake," he said. "I didn't mean that like it sounded. You are growed up. I reckon it just snuck up on me. You're a good man, an' I'm glad you're my brother."

Jake relaxed. "You mean that?"

"Yeah, I do." As Will said it, he realized it was true. For all his faults, Jake was a good man; kind, loyal, hard-working, protective of his family—traits a good man ought to have. Jake had a good heart and would give you the shirt right off his back if you asked. He could do worse for a brother. "Yeah, Jake, I do mean it," he repeated.

Jake laughed. "Well, all right then."

Will laughed too and picked up the apple. "Well, I'm holding out for some real grub," he said. He tossed the apple back at his brother, who dodged it, grinning.

"Whoooee, some of Ma's fried chicken sure would be good right now," said Jake.

"I'd settle for some beans and a biscuit. Hell, I'd eat that hardtack them soldiers had," said Will.

Jake shrugged. "Well, there ain't no fried chicken here. Let's go, it's only five more miles." He put his hat back on and shoved it down hard.

Will sighed and rose from the ground. When he checked the hole he'd dug in the creek-bed, there was only enough silty water for a sip each. When Jake had taken a sip and spit most of it out, Will decided he could hold out for clean water. In five more miles, they'd be home, with all the cool, fresh well-water they could drink.

After checking the road was clear in both directions, they left the creek-bed and set out again.

"Five miles," said Jake, starting off.

*Five long, hot miles,* thought Will.

\*\*\*\*\*

# Chapter 11

Joline Higgins swung the ax and it bit deep into the log. Ben Carter's negro, Tom, waited for her to lift the ax, then turned the log slightly with an iron cant-hook. On her next swing, a large chunk of wood flew from the cut. "Time for some water," she said, wiping her face with her apron.

She leaned the ax against the log and made her way to the well where she took a dipper from a bucket and drank it. She washed her hands and splashed her face with a second dipperful. Tom took a drink from his own bucket, removed his worn-out straw hat and poured some on his head.

"Ike!" she yelled. "Come get a drink."

Ike dropped his hand-ax, picked up the old flintlock and trod over to the bucket. The rifle had never left his side since he'd retrieved it from the river bluff. Seth followed him from where he'd been trimming branches with a hatchet. They both took long drinks from the same dipper.

Chigger huffed, raised himself up from his dusty bed, shook a cloud of dust from his fur and waddled after them. He looked expectantly at the water and wagged his tail. Ike poured some into his hand and let the dog drink.

Joline marveled at how Ike had grown; he was almost as tall as Jake. And she was proud of the way he'd taken on Will's duties around the farm. He took it seriously and she was thankful for it. With the help Ben provided, they would have a roof over their heads before winter set in.

Using her bonnet as a fan, she created a little breeze to cool herself. The four of them stood for a moment in the shade provided by the roof of the well. Once again, she was reminded of how kind the

Carters were to them. It would not be possible to build a cabin without Tom's help.

"Ma, where do you reckon Will and Jake are now?" Ike asked.

She shook her head. "I don't know. I wish I did."

"I heard Ben sayin' that the Rebels is a comin'. He says they're tryin' to take Missouri back for Jeff Davis. You think they'll come here?"

Joline didn't know how to answer. She was worried about it herself, but she didn't want Ike and Seth to worry. So, she settled on a version of the truth. "I don't think they'll come here. Right now, they're fightin' over at Pilot Knob but that's a long way south of here. There's a lot of Yankees fightin' 'em and I think they'll get beat a long time before they get here."

"You think Will and Jake are there fightin'?"

"I don't know," she replied. "I hope not. Only thing I know for sure is that if they can, Will and Jake will come back to us."

"Missus Joline," said Tom. "Look yonder." He pointed to a large cloud of dust over the main road toward town.

Joline's gut tightened. "Everybody, into the corn field, now!"

Tom grabbed the axes and disappeared into the corn.

Seth ran to Joline and she grabbed his hand and quickly followed Tom. Ike picked up his gun and stood behind the well, as if he was going to make a stand.

"No! Ike! In the corn!" she yelled.

"I ain't gonna let 'em burn us out again!" he said. His jaw was set firmly, and his eyes had narrowed into slits in the bright sunlight.

Joline beckoned him with her hand. "They ain't nothin' left to burn! Get over here, now, Ike!"

Ike stood there another moment, a puzzled look on his face. Then he lowered the gun and ran over to the corn.

Joline sent the boys off with Tom deeper into the field while she watched the road through the stalks.

By now she could hear the distant clopping of hooves. A moment later, she heard the pounding of those same hooves on the wooden trestle that crossed the river. A large group of riders dressed in civilian clothes filed past the house. Many were only boys, and few had guns.

Those that did carried old rusty muskets or shotguns.

Even though they were walking their horses and mules, the dust they kicked up wafted high into the sky. A dust devil crossed the road and a funnel of dust twirled high into the sky. Most of the riders held on to their hats, but one lost his in the gust. The hat twirled high into the sky before it plopped down near the well.

The rider led his horse over to retrieve it. Joline could see he was no more than a teenager, younger even than Seth. She wondered what his mother thought about him being off with this bunch, obviously bound for the war. The boy dismounted, retrieved his hat and shoved it back on his head. He spied the newly cut logs and peered out into the cornfield.

*He knows*, Joline thought, holding her breath. Finally, with a shrug, the boy's eyes moved back to his horse and he mounted up and rode on.

She counted riders until she got to a hundred, then she gave up—there seemed to be no end to the column. She wasn't sure who these men were, but she was glad they weren't interested in her farm. Nobody even stopped to drink from the buckets that were sitting out in plain view.

The column began to thin out, and the last stragglers followed their fellows westward on the road. After waiting a few minutes to make sure there were no more riders, she yelled for Tom and the boys to come back. She could hear them rustling the cornstalks as they did. Still, she hung back just within the corn.

Ben Carter rattled up in his wagon and stopped in the yard. Lucy rode next to him, Nate asleep on her lap. Joline stepped out from the corn.

Ben saw her and grunted as he climbed down. "Everything ok here? I saw the riders pass by."

Joline nodded. "We're fine, they never even looked at us."

"Rebel recruits, I expect," said Ben. "Goin' to join up with Price. I heard Caleb Dorsey had rounded up several hundred."

Joline shrugged. "I stopped countin' at one hundred. They was a lot more."

Ben pulled out his pipe and gestured with it. "Well, it was smart move hidin' in the corn. I hear tell they been robbin' folks of horses and clothes and guns and such."

"We ain't got anything left to steal, so maybe it was a blessin' they came by today."

Ben eyed the two foundation logs they been working on. "Makin' progress, I see. That 'un looks good and flat." He knocked the ashes from his pipe on a log.

"I want to thank you again for your help, Ben. We couldn't...."

"You've thanked me plenty," Ben interrupted. "I just wish there was more I could do." He put some fresh tobacco in the pipe and struck a match.

Joline knew she might not want to know but she had to ask. "Ben, have you heard any word on my boys?" Ike edged closer and cocked an ear.

Ben puffed on the pipe to start it. "No, Missus Joline, I have not. I'm sure the Sheriff passed the word on to the Yankees, an' I'm sure they'll keep an eye out for 'em." He paused for a puff. "They don't generally tell anybody what they're up to. An' right now, they are more worried about General Price an' where he's headin'. They're gatherin' up all the men they can find right now just to fight him off." He waved the pipe at the road. "That's why them Rebel recruits can just ride down that main road there and not have a care in the world. Ain't no Yankees nearby."

Joline, looked down. Tears formed and she wiped them away. *I will not cry today. I don't have the time for it.*

"I am sorry for that," Ben continued. "This damn war, it just ain't fair a'tall."

She nodded, ashamed of feeling sorry for herself. "Here I go feelin' sorry for myself when I know what you're goin' through yourself. I want you to know how sorry I am about Patrick."

Ben held up a hand. "No, don't you worry about that none. We ain't givin' up on him just yet. He might..." Ben looked away quickly and swallowed hard. He shook his head before he said, "He might be in some prison camp or hospital somewhere. I'm sure of it. He'll show up yet."

Joline doubted that was true; he had gone missing three months ago, and there was still no word. But she would not hurt Ben by saying it.

Despite his words, Ben looked upset. "Well, let's get to it, these logs won't hew themselves." He puffed his pipe and strode off.

121

Joline took another drink, wiped her face, replaced her bonnet and picked up her ax.

Lucy looked up to see two stick figures walking through the pasture across the road, their images shimmering in the late-afternoon heat. In the glare, she couldn't make out who they were. She picked up Nate, who'd been making mud pies at her feet, and shaded her eyes.

Only when one of them removed his hat and waved it in the air did she recognize Will Tanner's dark hair, slim build and rolling gait. And there beside him trudged Jake, a bit shorter and with lighter hair.

Her heart leapt and she couldn't hold back her smile. How could this be? Not more than three days before, she'd watched in horror as he and his brother were trussed up and drug off by those awful men. She'd thought she might never see them—him—again. She squinted, trying to force the image into focus. "Miss Joline! Papa!" she yelled. "They're back!"

Papa said, "Who's back?"

"Will! And Jake!"

"Well, I'll be danged," said Papa, standing upright from where he'd been shaving a log.

Miss Joline dropped her ax and ran down the lane to greet them, little puffs of dust marking her path. "Jake! Will!" she yelled as she ran. She hugged them each in turn. "Lordy, I feared the worst! How did you get away?"

Lucy followed right behind her, Nate balanced on her hip. Ike and Seth ran up from where they had been chopping firewood.

"Ma, we're hot and tired and thirsty," said Will. "Can we get a drink first? Then we'll tell you all about it." He looked directly at Lucy with his sky-blue eyes and smiled.

The day suddenly felt much hotter than it already was. Nate squirmed and when Lucy set him down, she noticed to her horror that her white bodice was stained brown from his muddy hands.

Will didn't seem to notice the dirt. He smiled at her with that lopsided grin of his and wiped his sweaty face on his sleeve. He hugged her, and she felt the heat from his body radiate through her clothes. She felt her face burning but she couldn't stop smiling.

"William Tanner," Miss Joline said, "Where's your manners?

You're filthy from travel and you've no call to be gettin' familiar with Lucy." Her tone was serious, but she smiled. "Let's get you some water, and we'll hear your story out."

As they walked toward the well, Miss Joline hooked arms with her two oldest boys. Fresh buckets of cool well water were drawn up, and Will and Jake took dippers-full and drank them down. They poured some on their heads and shook the excess out.

"Never thought well water could taste so damn good," said Jake.

"Jake! Mind your mouth," said Miss Joline. She stared at him, mouth agape. But she shook her head and then smiled.

Jake blushed. "Sorry, Ma."

Will rolled his eyes. "We got rescued by some Union Cavalry," he said. "It was just dumb luck that they happened by."

"Those men, the bushwhackers," asked Papa. "Are they captured or kilt?"

"Most of 'em got killed," said Will. "The leader, the one called Henry, he's dead. An' that big un, that looked like a bear, he's dead too. Two of 'em got captured. Some got away, though."

Lucy thought the dead men had gotten what they deserved. She had only a moment's shame that she felt that way about the dead.

Will started to add something, but he looked at Ike and Seth and closed his mouth.

"What about that Porter boy?" asked Miss Joline.

"He got away. He wasn't among the dead, anyhow." Will paused for another drink.

Jake took over the story, relating how they had to go to the Union Camp and how they had to take an oath before they could come home.

"What oath?" asked Miss Joline. "You boys didn't join up, did you?"

"No, nothin' like that," said Jake. "We just swore that we'd never fight against the Union Army. We don't want to fight against 'em anyhow, so...." He shrugged.

"Good," said Miss Joline. "I don't want you fightin' on either side."

Jake frowned and looked away.

*Jake wants to fight,* Lucy thought. *He's got that same look my brothers had before they joined up and went off.*

Will asked, "Did a big bunch of horses come this way? We saw some tracks."

"Yep," said Papa. "Rebel recruits, we think. Did you see 'em?"

"No. We saw the tracks where they turned off the road. It spooked us, though, and we took to the woods and cut across pastures an' such. Stayed off the road."

Papa nodded. "Yep, it's best to be careful right now. Any riders you see now are apt to be recruits, irregulars or worse. The Yankees are concentratin' down south to deal with Price."

An uncomfortable silence held for a moment. It was clear to Lucy that Will and Jake weren't telling everything they knew.

Papa lit his pipe and chewed on the stem. "Missus Joline," he said. "These two need clean clothes and a bath. We can take them to our place and take care of that. Might be some of James's or Patrick's old clothes that will fit them."

Joline nodded. "An' then they'll need feedin'."

"Reminds me," said Lucy. "If you got an old hen that's quit layin'. Mama said she'd fry it up for supper tonight."

"Fried Chicken! I love fried chicken!" said Seth, his eyes lighting up.

Miss Joline spotted a chicken and snatched it up by the head and wrung its neck in one fluid motion. She caught another and did the same. "Here's two for the fry pan. Might as well eat 'em before the foxes do," she said, flinging the still flopping birds into the wagon.

Will looked over the new cabin. The new walls were three logs high. "I'm impressed," he said. "We'll have a roof on it in no time."

Papa nodded. "Yep, I reckon we got a respectable day's work done here. We can start again tomorrow."

They threw the tools into the wagon and Papa climbed up into the driver's seat. Lucy sat next to him, Nate once again in her lap.

Miss Joline sat next to her and began to pluck the chickens. She looked up with shining eyes. "My boys are back, Lucy! My boys are home!"

"Yes, they are," replied Lucy, smiling. It was all she could do to get her mind off one of them.

Tom jumped into the back and sat against the seat back. Will and Jake jumped on the tailgate and dangled their legs from it.

Ike and Seth walked behind the wagon, Ike balancing his rifle on his shoulder. He marched along like he was trying to be a soldier. The Tanner's old beagle waddled along behind him.

Will turned sideways and glanced at Tom and said something Lucy couldn't hear over the creaking wagon and the clopping hooves. But she heard Tom's reply.

"I just do what Massa Ben say I do." Tom then pulled his hat over his eyes and was silent.

Will's eyes met Lucy's again and he smiled. She looked forward so he wouldn't see her blush. Papa noticed and gave her a wink, and she blushed even more.

It was a short ride home. Papa stopped the wagon at the carriage house and the men hopped from the back. Miss Joline took her chickens to the main house to help with supper. Ike and Seth took Nate inside to finish his nap.

"The tubs on the back porch," Lucy said. "Already set up. Tom can heat up some water. You boys go on, I'll bring clean clothes and towels."

When she came back, towels and clean clothes in hand, Tom had a fire blazing under the big iron kettle. The extra heat on an already hot day made him sweat as he poured buckets of water from it into the tub.

"I'm goin' first," Jake said, as he began stripping off his clothes and throwing them aside.

*Well*, thought Lucy, *Jake's not shy.*

Will didn't appear to hear Jake. He just stood there, looking at Lucy. "Oh," she said. "I guess I ought to turn my back or something." But she didn't. "I've got brothers, you know, and I've seen everything. So, don't be shy about it. Get those dirty clothes off and I'll see they're cleaned."

Will blushed, shrugged and laid aside his hat and unbuttoned his collar. When he pulled the shirt over his head, he winced with pain.

Lucy at first only noticed his tightly muscled chest and arms and his farmer's tan. Then she saw the angry red scrapes and purple bruises on his chest and back. They contrasted starkly with the white skin that never got any sun. She saw the rope burns on his wrists that had been hidden by his shirt sleeves. It made her angry to see how he'd been treated. "Those ruffians," she asked, "what did they do to you?"

"Not what you think. I fell and they drug me over some rocks," he said. "It'll heal."

"I'm sorry, I shouldn't be staring," said Lucy, turning her back to him.

"I thought you had brothers," teased Will.

"Yes, and none as bashful as you. Now quit foolin' around and throw me your clothes." She heard the sound of clothes rustling, and a pile of them plopped down at her feet.

"I could just go on down to the river. Jake got the clean water, anyhow," Will said.

"That water'd be cold!"

"Might feel good on a hot day like this one."

Lucy risked a quick glance behind her. Will stood there with only a towel wrapped around his waist, his arms crossed, waiting for Jake to finish. She tried not to stare at him, and she averted her eyes when he looked her way. For his part, Will would take a shy glance at her, and if their eyes met, he'd smile, then blush and look away.

Lucy wished he wasn't so shy. He didn't need to be, he was quite handsome with his blue eyes, wavy hair and friendly smile. Several days' worth of stubble only enhanced his strong jawline.

She liked the way he smiled most of all. He smiled with his eyes as well as his lips, and she knew it was genuine. He held back nothing when he smiled.

They both stood there in bashful silence while Jake bathed.

When Jake announced he was done, Tom brought in another bucket of warm water and poured it over his head to rinse out the soap. Jake shook his head like a wet dog. "No peekin'," he said, as Tom handed him a towel and he stood up and stepped out.

Lucy averted her eyes and quickly turned back around, picking up the pile of clothing as she did. With a parting smile at Will, she headed to the main house.

In the kitchen, Mama was cutting up a chicken while Miss Joline poured boiling water on the one she'd plucked.

"Here's the boys' dirty clothes, Miss Joline," said Lucy. "I gave them some clean ones. We can wash tomorrow, if you want. I'll put them in a basket."

Miss Joline smiled. "Thank you, Lucy."

"Will's got some bad scrapes. He's banged up pretty good too," Lucy said. She hadn't meant to scare her, but Miss Joline looked up from her work and a furrow crossed her brow. Lucy quickly added, "Nothing too bad. Nothing's broken, anyhow."

"I need to go see for myself," Miss Joline said.

"Wait," said Lucy. "We got some salve you can put on him. Mama, is Chloe upstairs?"

"You'll have to fetch it yourself, Lucy. Chloe's out back in the garden," replied Mama.

Lucy bounded up the stairs and was soon back with the salve. She handed it to Miss Joline, who ran out the door with it.

Lucy plucked some pinfeathers while she waited.

Miss Joline was gone only a few minutes. She handed Lucy the salve jar.

"Why don't you hold onto it a while," said Lucy, handing it back. "you might need it again."

"Thank you. Lucy." Joline pocketed the jar and sighed. "It could a been worse. I reckon we were lucky, no ribs is broken, though he'll be sore a few days."

"Yes, it could be much worse," said Mama. She stopped her work and sighed. "I need the outhouse." She wiped her hands on her apron and went out the back door.

Lucy knew Mama was upset about Patrick, and her own happiness at seeing Will was tinged by sadness. She missed her brother, too, and wished she could do something about it. The only thing they could do was wait for word. It was hard on Mama, and sometimes the least little thing would send her into tears.

Joline looked upset too. She knew why Mama left.

"I'm sorry, Lucy. I know it don't seem right, some folks havin' the good luck while others have the bad."

"Mama will be all right," said Lucy. "It's just the not knowing that's hard on her at times. Besides, I hardly think havin' your home burnt and your sons taken away is good luck. It's all bad luck."

Joline stopped her work and said, "I hope this damned war ends soon an' puts a stop to all this misery. What's it all for, anyway? I don't understand why men got to fight each other like they do. What good is it, in the end?"

Lucy didn't have an answer. She didn't think anyone did. Well, maybe the Almighty did, but she wasn't even sure of that.

The kitchen filled with silence. Mama came back in and picked up the knife and resumed cutting the chicken.

Chloe came in with a big bowl of green beans from the garden, and Lucy helped her string them. The work helped make the sadness recede, and soon it was all she could do to keep her mind off Will and help with supper.

*****

# Chapter 12

Will was famished and the sight of so much food made his stomach growl. The table was covered with fried chicken, biscuits with butter and molasses, fresh green beans and squash from the garden.

Ben said the blessing, and everybody dug in. They were all hungry and there wasn't much talk.

Will ate every crumb on his plate and licked his fingers, then washed it down with some cool buttermilk. He took another biscuit and slathered butter and molasses on it, and soon, it too was gone.

Jake practically inhaled a chicken leg, then chewed the gristle off the bone while he reached for another piece. Will had to chuckle; Jake might drag his feet when there was work to be done but he never wasted time with a meal.

When everybody had their fill, the women rose to clear the table. Ben motioned for Will and Jake to follow him to the front porch. The sun had set and the air had cooled. They each took a chair and took in the cool breeze.

Ben tipped his chair back to lean against the wall. "I got Tom watching the road in case anybody comes," he said.

Will nodded. It hadn't occurred to him to post a lookout. By now it should have. He kicked himself mentally. *I got to be smarter from now on than I've ever been.*

"Now tell me the whole story," Ben said, lighting his pipe. "Includin' the parts you didn't want the women-folk to hear."

Will told Ben everything, except the part about the Yankees inviting them to join up. He worried that might upset him. Ben had always been a good friend and neighbor, but his sons had gone Confederate. It somehow didn't feel right to accept Ben's hospitality and then talk about joining the Union Cavalry. Will had no intention of joining anyway.

When Will finished his story, Ben puffed a minute. "I ain't one to meddle, but if you boys were to ask me, I'd tell you that there's several Rebel recruiters working Pike and Lincoln Counties. You need to keep one ear to the ground. Them we saw today was easy to spot. Others of 'em work in small gangs an' might sneak up on you."

"Thanks, Ben. We'll do that."

Seth and Ike came out, followed by Ma, carrying Nate.

"Time to go home," said Ma. "Supper was good, Ben. Thank you, and good night."

Lucy walked out on the porch, drying her hands on her apron. Will saw her eyes seeking his own before they looked away. *It's a good thing its dark,* he thought. *Or else everybody'd see my ears turnin' red.*

There was an awkward silence for a moment until Ma tugged on his arm. "You need some rest after your ordeal."

Will knew she really wanted to talk and there'd be no rest anytime soon. He was tired, and re-telling the story wasn't what he wanted to do right now, but Ma deserved to know. Tipping his hat to Ben, he tore his eyes from Lucy and walked off with Ma.

In the carriage house, they gathered around an old table that Ben had sent over, and Ma poured mugs of cool buttermilk for everybody.

For the second time, Will told the story of their escape from the bushwhackers.

Ike and Seth listened intently. Their eyes widened when Will talked about Henry and Emmit being killed. Will glanced at Nate, who was off in a corner, oblivious to the conversation, playing with a corn-shuck doll that Lucy had made for him.

Jake broke in when the story moved to the Union soldier camp.

Will kicked him under the table before he could describe the hanging they'd seen. He didn't want Seth to be upset. Jake gave him the look but skipped that part anyway.

Ma got a funny look when Jake mentioned the bounty money. "You cain't spend it if you're dead."

"Still, Ma, that's a lot of money," said Jake.

Ma's face tensed. "Ain't no amount of money that'll grow back a leg or raise the dead," she said, her voice rising. "Lots of boys comin' home with arms and legs missin' an' lots more ain't never comin' home agin."

As ever, Jake was slow to pick up on Ma's growing distress. "That money would buy a whole farm, or build a nice house, or....," he said.

"Enough about the money," Ma interrupted. "I don't want to hear no more on it." She spoke slowly and quietly, a sure sign of a full-blown storm coming.

"I'm just talkin', that's all," said Jake.

Ma slapped the table and her chair scraped as she stood up and went outside without another word. Seth's eyes went wide. Nate looked up then went back to his playing.

Will leaned back from the table. "Now you did it," he said. "When are you gonna learn when to talk and when not to?"

Jake clenched his jaw, stood up and left the table. He climbed up into the loft leaving Will and his younger brothers alone. Seth looked at Will, then down at the table, clearly upset. Ike was watching Will intently.

"It's all right, Seth. It's been a rough couple of days. We're gonna be just fine."

"When will the war be over, Will?" Seth asked, his eyes tearing up. At five, Seth was at the age where a boy is embarrassed by crying, but sometimes can't help himself. He had to have been badly scared by the ordeal they'd been through.

*Hell, I was terrified myself!* Will thought. "It cain't last much longer," he said. "General Billy Sherman has a bunch of Rebels surrounded over in Georgia. And General U.S. Grant has got another passel of 'em on the run in Virginny, so it cain't last too much longer. Then things will change, and everybody can be friends again."

Seth wiped at his eyes. "Then you and Jake won't have to go off no more?"

"That's right," Will said. "We ain't goin' off no more, not if we can help it."

Now Ike had a funny look on his face. "What if those men come back, Will. What're we gonna do if they come back?"

Will thought for a minute, then he said, "They ain't likely to come back. Most of 'em are dead, their leader is dead, and the Yankees is out lookin' for the rest of 'em. Most likely they're long gone from here." Will smiled, trying to lessen the tension. "I bet they're halfway back to Arkansas by now."

"But Bloody Bill is still out there," said Ike. "An' Quantrill, too." Seth's eyes widened at the mention of Bloody Bill.

"Men like that, they're mostly cowards," said Will, "an' they only pick on folks who cain't fight back. When there's a good chance they'll be killed, they won't come around." After what he'd seen and heard, he only half believed his own words, but he wanted to ease Ike's mind. "Besides," he added, "Bloody Bill operates way out west, near Kansas, a long way from here."

Ike nodded. "Ok. But what if I wanna fight 'em? What if I wanna shoot them men that hurt Ma? I want to, Will."

For the second time that day, Will was taken aback by one of his brothers. He had no idea Ike would be this angry. Of course, Will had been angry too. But that was different, wasn't it? He decided to tell a white lie. "Seth, take Nate upstairs and play with him up there. I need to talk to Ike for a minute."

"Aw shucks," complained Seth. "Why do I have to always take Nate and go play?" He sulked, waiting for Will to change his mind, a ploy that sometimes worked.

This time Will didn't fall for it, and after a moment, Seth hung his head and grabbed Nate by the hand and pulled him up. "Come on, Nate, we gotta go upstairs.

"Don't wanna go to bed," yelled Nate, and he bit Seth on the arm.

Seth yelped with pain. "Don't bite me no more, Nate!"

"Nate! Go upstairs with Seth!" said Will sternly. Nate began crying but he climbed the ladder, Seth right behind him to keep him from falling. Will felt bad about having to be stern with the boys, but he figured they'd soon forget it and be asleep.

When Nate's wailing tapered off, Will looked at Seth and said, "You're old enough to know what I'm gonna tell you but you cain't tell Seth, ok?"

Ike sat up straight at the compliment. "Ok."

Will took a deep breath. "The Yankees killed most of those men.

An' remember I told you earlier they captured two? One of 'em was named Watt, and I got his hat right here 'cause I lost mine." He raised the hat for emphasis. "Now, the reason I got his hat is 'cause he don't need one no more."

Ike was puzzled. "Don't need his hat no more?"

"Yeah, Ike. They hung him from a tree until he was dead."

Ike's eyes widened and he leaned back in his chair.

"They do it to every bushwhacker they catch," Will continued. "Or they shoot 'em. What I'm tryin' to tell you is that we can trust the Yankees to catch all of 'em and make sure they get what they deserve, get what they got comin' to 'em. All of 'em, even Bloody Bill, even Quantrill and his gang, and even the ones that got away yesterday. The Yankees are gonna catch up to 'em. An' I believe it'll be soon, too."

Ike sat back in his chair. "So you think the Yankees will catch 'em and kill 'em so we don't need to?"

Will nodded. "Yep, that's what I'm sayin'."

Ike was silent for a while. Then he seemed to make up his mind about something. "Ok, but if they come back here, I'm gonna shoot 'em."

Will hoped it would never come to that. He looked at the old Kentucky rifle leaning in the corner. Seth had carried it everywhere, even to supper at the Carter's. "You remember how I showed you to load and shoot that rifle?"

"Yeah. I ain't no little kid."

"That's right, little brother, you ain't no little kid. An' I know I ain't never said it before, but I'm glad you're my little brother."

Ike blushed.

"You hang on to that rifle for me," Will said. "I know where to find it if I ever need it."

"Ok."

"Ok," replied Will.

Ike set his jaw firmly, grabbed the rifle and climbed the ladder to the loft, leaving Will alone with his thoughts.

Will finished his buttermilk and took a drink of water to clear the stickiness from his throat. Nature called and he headed to the outhouse to relieve himself. He expected to find Ma close-by, but she was nowhere in sight. He wondered where she'd gone.

Then, he knew. *She's been to the cemetery.* Sometimes, when she was upset, she would visit the little graveyard behind their house and sit for a while. Ma rarely let her emotions show through her tough exterior; even so, from time to time she would get into a sad spell. Will knew she still missed her second husband Frank Higgins; so much so that she'd rebuffed the many suitors who'd come calling over the months and years following his death. And she still grieved for the two little girls, just infants — Will's sisters — who'd died from the croup and the summer colic. Will sometimes saw her talking to them, over in the little graveyard, as if they could hear her. He never let on that he knew; Ma deserved to grieve in her own way. Still, it made Will sad to see her like that.

He walked back from the outhouse, stepped inside and climbed up into the loft. After sleeping on the ground, the hay-strewn floor looked like heaven to him. Will wanted nothing more than to roll up in his blanket and lay down in the soft hay and sleep for days. Seth was already asleep on his pallet in the corner, and Nate slept curled up next to him. Ike was still awake, though, and he wiggled around in the hay, trying to get comfortable.

Jake was still in a snit, lying on his blanket with his eyes wide open, staring at the ceiling. Will didn't have the energy for an argument, so he ignored him. He pulled off his shirt, wrapped himself in a blanket and leaned back into the hay.

Just when he began to nod off, Ma climbed up into the attic, carrying a lantern and the jar of salve.

"Let's get some more salve into those cuts," she said.

Will sighed. "Cain't it wait 'til mornin'?"

"No," said Ma, "It cain't."

Will sat up and threw the blanket aside. Ma sat next to him and scooted closer. He turned so she could get to the scrapes on his chest. In the dim light from her lantern, he could see her own bruises, and he felt ashamed all over again. "Ma, I'm sorry we wasn't there to protect you. Those men could've hurt you bad." He couldn't tell her what he really thought. That Jake was right, and he had failed her. They should have come down sooner.

"Now you listen Will Tanner, and you too Jake," Ma said softly, while applying the salve to Will's scrapes and his wrists where the rope had burned him. "There wasn't nothin' else you could have done. Those were hard men. Killers. If you'd a come runnin' down there shootin' your guns, you'd be dead right now. I'd druther have black eyes every day than to see you boys killed. It was bad enough when they hauled you off, trussed up like hogs that way, but you was alive. And as long as you're alive, you got a chance to stay that way."

Ma heard Ike stir, and she lowered her voice. "You know I been trying to keep you boys, both of you, out of that awful bloody mess." Her hands rubbed the salve in a little harder. "A whole lot of boys your age is comin' home shot to pieces. Or they ain't comin' home at all." She paused and said, "Turn around so I can get your back."

Will complied. The salve stung in his cuts for a few seconds and he tensed. Next to him, Jake sat up and cocked his head their way.

"You done right to hide out," Ma said, talking over her shoulder to include Jake. "It's what I wanted you to do. It's what I told you to do, an' I wish you'd stayed up there and not come down at all."

Will hung his head. "Ma," he said. "We thought for sure they was gonna kill you all. We couldn't just sit there and watch while that happened."

She sighed and paused in her dabbing. "I guess it's done now, anyhow."

*She knows I am right,* thought Will.

Ma moved over to put some salve on Jake's wrists. "That Porter boy, you sure he got away?"

Will was relieved she'd changed the subject. "He weren't among the dead, so yeah I think so."

"He's the one who set the fire," she said. "'He liked doin' it, I could tell. It seemed personal, with him, somehow. Why did he come after you two?"

Jake opened his mouth to speak, closed it again and said nothing.

"I ain't real sure," said Will. "He was at Elkhorn Tavern with us, an' he got captured by Yankees. For some reason, he blames it on me. Us."

"Why would he do that?"

Will took a deep breath. "I tried to get him to come with me an' Jake. He froze up like a rabbit and wouldn't move. When the Yankees moved up, they got him. It wasn't our fault, he just wouldn't move. We had to leave him, or we'd have got taken too, or worse."

Just as Ma was about to say something, Jake broke in. "Ma, I'm gonna join up with the Union Army."

Ma stopped applying salve, sucked in a breath, and gave Jake a long, hard stare. The silence felt like a heavy blanket over them.

Will's mouth fell open. He hadn't given Colonel Benson's words any thought since he'd left the Union camp and was caught off guard by Jake's decision. *I should've seen it comin', though. He's showed me plenty of sign.*

Ma's eyes bored into Jake's, until he looked away. The long silence was stressful; it was like waiting for the thunder after lightning had flashed.

Ma swallowed hard. "No, Jake," she said. "I aim to have my boys alive and whole when this war's done and over. All of 'em. You ain't doin' that, I forbid it." She put the lid on the salve jar and stood up. Her voice was calm but there was fire in her eyes.

Jake turned red and Will waited for him to explode; Jake was never one to take heed of a warning. Ma hardly ever raised her voice, but when she had the fire in her eyes, it was time to listen. Neither Will nor Jake had had a whipping since they were little boys, but Ma's words could skin you just as good as a willow switch.

Jake raised his head and looked Ma in the eye. "My mind's made up. I'm of age, an' I can do what I want."

Will steeled himself for one of Ma's tirades. Instead, her voice lowered and her scowl eased. "You ain't of age, Jake."

Jake's voice rose. "I was of age two years ago when them damn Rebels come and got us," said Jake. "THEY think I am of age. There's lots of boys my age an' younger already joined up. Porter ain't no older than me, I didn't hear you ask HIM if he was of age."

Ma's jaw dropped.

Will was surprised at Jake's nerve. He'd never gone against Ma like this, not out in the open. He motioned to Jake to shut up. As usual, Jake ignored him.

"Those men, Porter, and more just like him, or worse," Jake continued, "they need to be killed or at least run out of Missouri. In the Union Army, I can help 'em do it. And get paid besides. An' there's bounty money...."

Ma interrupted him. The fire had returned to her eyes. "Revenge is for the Lord to take, not you!" Ma's voice rose again, and Seth stirred. "You got to let it go for now, you hear me? When the war's done, the law will take care of them. This war WILL end, and someday soon if I ain't mistaken. Things WILL be set right again."

Her voice rose more. "An' I aim for ALL my boys to live through it. Let the Yankees handle it." She turned to go.

Ike sat up and his eyes were wide open. Seth stirred again but didn't waken.

Jake started to say something else. Ma stopped him with wave of her hand "Not one more word."

Will looked at Jake and said "Jake that's enough. Let it go for now."

Jake turned his hard glare on Will, his disgust plainly written on his features.

"Let it go. For now, Jake," Will repeated.

Jake shook his head, flopped back into the hay, and rolled his eyes to the ceiling.

*Now maybe we can all calm down,* Will thought. Hoped.

"I don't want to hear no more of this talk of joinin' up." Ma said, voice quivering. She edged toward the ladder and started to back down it. "You hear me, Jake?"

"Ok, Ma," said Will, eager to end the fight.

Jake scowled, grunted and jammed his hat over his face.

"I want to hear you say it, Jake," said Ma.

"Ok, Ma," Jake grumbled.

Will was sure of only one thing. He knew Jake, and Jake wasn't going to let this go. He may have said he wouldn't talk about it, but he didn't promise not to do something. Something stupid.

Ma clambered down the ladder and Will heard dishes and pans clattering downstairs, He figured Ma would be up a while. In a few minutes, Jake was snoring. *How can he have words with Ma and then just go to sleep like that?* Will wondered, for the hundredth time.

Exhausted himself, Will tried to sleep, but his whirling mind wouldn't allow for it. He understood Ma's desire — her need — for them to stay out of the war. Will had thought it the best course himself, for a long while. He wanted nothing more than to be left alone to run his farm and help Ma raise his brothers. Twice now, the war had come to them. Grabbed them. And they'd been sucked into it despite their own wishes. Would there be a next time? If there was, would they be as lucky again?

*Lucky? If you can call it luck, everything we owned burned up, Ma beat black and blue.* He thought about Missy the mule lying there dead and his heart fell. *How are we supposed to plant next spring with no mule? Cain't buy one, all our money's gone, too! Ain't nothin' left but ashes and a few bits of iron. Just a few hoes with no handles and a plow with no harness.* The three hundred dollars in bounty money the Yankees had offered would more than replace the mule and harness. It would buy seed, tools, and more. Maybe a few shoats and a milk cow. *But Ma ain't gonna allow it, an' I ain't sure it's worth it myself.*

The events of the last few days were still vivid in Will's mind, and they triggered memories he'd tried to forget. Memories of the fight at Elkhorn Tavern two years ago. Images of guns and cannon and thundering booms and crackling rifle fire and smoke. Men and horses screaming and dying. Blood and gore everywhere. He saw again in his mind Charley Porter's begging and pleading eyes as he and Jake made their own escape.

He wished the war would just come to an end and be done with, and he could live in peace again on his own farm. He wished things could go back to normal. After the killing, the carnage, the burning, the looting; after the revenge and all the spilled blood, could things ever be normal again?

Will didn't want to take sides in the war, didn't want to fight for either side. He wondered how many Rebels truly wanted to fight for the South? How many had been forced into it?

As Will thought about General Price's invasion, the second one, happening right now, he became angry. That a Confederate hero and former Governor of Missouri had dispatched bushwhackers to drag off anyone of age to fight, willing or not, outraged him and left him cold. *Bushwhackers! Of all people!*

Will recalled his talk with Toby and how it had all seemed so unfair, the way black folks had been treated. How slaves had suffered. He'd hardly ever looked at Ben's negroes, except in passing. He'd never paid any attention to them at all. Now that he knew how Toby felt, it bothered him that he hadn't looked at them, talked to them, thought about them.

He'd tried to talk to Old Tom in the wagon earlier. He'd thanked him for his help on the new cabin. 'I just do what Massa Ben say I do,' Tom had said. But before Tom could turn away and hide his eyes, Will had caught a flash of resentment in them. And he had begun to wonder, was Tom, too, resentful? Ben was a good master and treated his negroes well—like family, even. Still, were they not still in chains of a sort?

And all of it, the whole war, the bushwhacking, the murdering, the burning, every damn bit of it, just to keep negroes like Toby and Bo and Old Tom in bondage? It didn't sit right with him. It didn't seem right to buy and sell people. Even if, like Ben Carter's slaves, they were treated like family? *They're family all right,* he thought, *until somebody gets short of money an' then it's time to sell a slave or two. There ain't nothin' makes that right.*

Will hadn't thought about any of this before. He'd just kept his head down and plowed his land, planted and harvested his crops, layed low, stayed out of sight. Now, there was this huge nagging doubt in the back of his mind about the whole thing. Were the abolitionists right, after all? Was it time for slavery to end? It sure felt wrong, now, to keep a man or woman in bondage.

To protect their right to keep slaves, the Rebels had twice done terrible things to him and his family. They'd beat up Ma, burned their home and all their belongings, stole all their food. That couldn't be right, could it? The Yankees had never done that. Maybe it was time to choose sides.

In a way, he had enjoyed his time with Sergeant Burnes and the other Union troopers. He felt at ease around them, felt safe, felt at home, somehow. And then there was the bounty money. Three hundred dollars was more than he'd make in a year on the farm. With that money, he'd be able to buy more land, expand the farm. It might set him up for life.

Jake was right about one thing, for sure. The war was far from over. And *If we have to fight, why not fight for the right side? The good side?* Will somehow still hoped it wouldn't come to that. *If it does, what will I do?*

The more Will thought on it, the more right it felt. Maybe he could do something about all this mess, all this cruelty. Something other than hide from it out in the woods. He began to feel guilty about all the other men of his age who had already chosen sides. Who had already been fighting and dying. Could he hide anymore?

Mercifully, the whirling thoughts in his head soon slowed, and sleep relieved him of his agonizing uncertainty.

*****

# Chapter 13

A mosquito buzzed in Jake's ear and roused him from his deep slumber. He slapped it away and thought about going back to sleep, but he remembered his plan. *I need to be gone before sunup.*

The last several days had taken their toll on him, and he still felt beat up and worn-out. He had barely slept, waking up often to think about his plan. Worrying about how Ma was going to react when she found out. He felt bad about that part of it, but some things just had to be done and she would just have to accept it.

For the hundredth time, he wondered if he was doing the right thing. And for the hundredth time, he came to the same conclusion: yes, it was the right thing to do.

The birds were singing already, welcoming the first faint glow of dawn, and the morning star was shining through the hayloft door. He rubbed the grit from his eyes and eased out of his pallet of hay and blankets. He shook his head to clear the cobwebs and rose to gather his things.

The loose floorboards of the barn creaked no matter how carefully he stepped, and Will rolled over and gave him the evil eye. Jake shrugged and pointed to the chamber pot. Will huffed, pulled his quilt over his head and rolled over, face to the wall. In seconds, he was softly snoring again.

Jake threw on his new hat—the dark blue Yankee Trooper's hat taken from one of the bushwhackers. It still felt good on his head. He had slept in his pants, so he tied his shirt, socks, and brogans into his blanket, and dropped the bundle out through the hayloft door. It made a soft thud as it landed on the ground below. He winced—Ma was a light sleeper and she slept in a stall downstairs.

He waited to see if the noise woke her, but he heard nothing.

Barefooted, he climbed softly down the ladder. He made little noise as he padded from the carriage house and grabbed up his bundle. He snuck over to the barn, ducked inside and dug out his socks and brogans, and put them on. Chigger wandered over, and he gave him a good scratching. "Chigger, you take care of everybody now, you hear?"

The old dog wagged it's tail and nudged him for more. Jake scratched him one more time and finished dressing. He gathered up the little bag of food that he'd stashed there the night before, and gave the dog a bite of his leftover chicken. The dog followed him out the back door for a few feet before he stopped, rolled over and wiggled in the dust.

Jake eased down the dirt lane, keeping the barn between himself and the carriage house, out of sight of any curious eyes. The sky was glowing orange and getting brighter every second. There was no sound other than the singing birds and a rooster crowing somewhere.

Jake was so pleased with his getaway that he didn't notice the lone figure standing near the outhouse, watching him walk away.


In her borrowed nightgown, Joline watched her second oldest son disappear around the curve of the lane. She didn't have to wonder what he was up to, she knew right away. If there was any doubt, the bundle he carried made it plain. She wanted to yell for him to stop but she hesitated, not sure what to do. Her heart pounded and she felt sick.

She ran to the road, but the sharp rocks quickly reminded her she was barefoot. She padded back to the carriage house, threw on her worn brogans and raced back down the lane to retrieve her son.

Rounding the last bend she saw Jake talking to some men in a wagon. As she neared them, she saw the men were negroes. Jake threw his bundle into the back and started to climb in.

"Jake! Wait!"

Jake's head jerked up and his eyes flashed before he looked down at his feet. He mumbled something and shook his head. When he turned his face back up to her, his resolve showed in his eyes and in the set of his jaw. He crossed his arms, looked her in the eye, cleared his throat, and said, "Ma, I'm gonna do this and you cain't stop me."

Joline's eyes teared up. "Jake, please don't do this. It will break my heart if something happens to you. I don't know what I'd do if you got hurt...or...." She couldn't say it out loud, but if he got killed, she thought she might as well die too.

Jake looked at her and his eyes misted over. He shook his head. "Ma, I'm bound to do this. It's the right thing to do."

"No, no, no, Jake," she pleaded.

"Ma, listen to me. I'm a marked man," he said. "The Rebs think I deserted, no matter if they hauled us off at gunpoint. If I stay here, they'll come back lookin' for me, or others just like 'em will." He paused. "You see it, Ma? It's better this way. My chances are better ridin' with the Yankees than stayin' here waitin' on more of them bushwhackers to show up and burn us out again. You and the boys are safer if I go off. When I'm gone, they got no reason to come after us. You hear what I'm sayin'? You understand now?"

Stunned, Joline had no response to his words. She hadn't thought of the things he was saying. She also knew that in his heart, he wanted to go; this other stuff was just his excuse.

She had known in her mind — had always known — that a day like this would come. That her boys, all of them, would grow up and become men, with their own families, their own minds, their own plans. They'd leave, one by one and make their own way in the world.

But in her heart, she wasn't ready for it. Not like this. She was not ready to see them go off to war and come home mangled or not come home at all. She would never be ready for that.

"I know it's hard on you," Jake said. "But it's only right for me to do this. It feels right an my mind is made up. I am gonna help the Yankees run these god-damned bushwhacking murderers and rapers out of Missouri. I've been hidin' for way too long while other boys go off and do it. I cain't hide no more."

Joline had never seen Jake like this. Her pleadings had no effect and would not sway him. No, that wasn't true, her words did affect him. He was going to do this, despite her words, and she couldn't stop him. *This war is going take my sons away from me.* "I ain't ready for you to run off like this," she said.

Jake took her hand and looked her in the eye. "I know, Ma. I know. But I gotta do it."

"We need to be movin'," said the wagon driver. He looked at Joline with downcast eyes. "Sorry, Ma'am."

"Ma, I gotta go," said Jake. "I was willin' to walk all the way to camp, if I had to. Then these boys come along, an' I know'd em from

143

before. So it looks like I got a ride, but we got to go." He walked over and hugged her. "I'm sorry I was gonna sneak off. I didn't want to upset you no more."

Joline hugged him tight for a long time. Her tears moistened his shirt and he grew restless. She knew she had to let him go. Another feeling came to her, and she realized she was proud of him in a way, making his decision and sticking to it. *He might even be right for once,* she thought.

Still, she worried. "Jake, you be careful, I don't want to ever lose you." She turned and walked away.

"Ma, I'll be back, I promise. Soon as this is over, I'll come back."

She stopped and looked back. "You'd better, Jacob Tanner, you'd better come back home." She turned and walked on and the tears began to stream. Behind her the wagon creaked away.

Joline was not inclined to religion. She had never gone to church outside the occasional wedding or funeral. But now, as she walked, she silently prayed.

*Dear Lord, if you're hearin' me, please don't take my Jake. Please let him get through this awful war and come back home to me.*

Then the sobs came and wouldn't stop.


When Will woke, the sun was beaming through the hayloft door. He noticed right away that Jake's spot in the hayloft was empty and his blanket was gone. At first, he just thought it was an oddity. But he recalled Jake's furtive movements earlier that morning and he began to suspect something.

He heard Ma sniffling as soon as he climbed down the ladder. She was at the stove, fixing breakfast. She turned away when she saw him standing there, but not before he saw her puffy, red eyes. She'd been crying and right away he knew. *Dammit! Well, I shouldn't be surprised after the fight last night.*

"He's gone to join the Union Cavalry, ain't he?"

Ma plopped in a chair, held her head in her hands and rubbed her temples. "Yes," she sighed. "I tried to make him stay, but he was determined on it."

Will took a deep breath and blew it out in a big sigh. "Well, he's been keen on it ever since we camped with them." He picked up a tin cup. "I reckon I can catch up with him and talk some sense into him. Knock it into him if I have to."

"No, Will." She shook her head. "There ain't no talkin' him out of it this time. I tried. An' some of the things he said made some sense, though I still don't like' it. And don't you be fightin' with your brother."

"What did he say, Ma?"

"He said if he was still here, them bushwhackers might come back, and that we'd all be better off if he was off with the Army. It'd be safer for us and for him too."

Will recalled all his jumbled thoughts on the matter from last night. But Jake had figured out something Will hadn't. *Jake's right,* he thought, *an' the same goes for me. We'll all be better off with me an' Jake in the Cavalry.*

Ain't nothin' to be done now," Ma said, "'sceptin' hope and pray that he don't get killed or maimed. Jake always had that stubborn streak in 'im. It's in his blood."

Will smiled when she said that, recalling his talk with Jake on that very subject. "I'm sorry, Ma," he said. "He is a headstrong one, that's sure."

Will figured the only thing to do now was to go join up himself, and that way he could keep an eye on Jake. *If I do go, who'll look after the farm, an' Ma an' the boys?* It would have to be Ike. That was a lot to ask of him, but Will thought he'd do fine. *Wasn't I about Ike's age when I had to take over?* Still, Ma wasn't gonna like hearing it.

Ma rose and poured some coffee into his cup, breaking into his thoughts. She sighed again, but her sniffles had slowed down. "I got biscuits makin'. An' some ham, too."

"I'll eat in a little while," Will said. He'd become heart-sick over what he was about to do, and his appetite had left him. He thought about what he needed to say to Ma and how it was gonna hurt her. Hurting her was the last thing he wanted to do, but maybe it was best to get this out now so all the hurtin' could be done and over with.

Will steeled himself to take Ma's ire. "Ma," he said, "I think Jake might be right. They might come back for him. An' that goes for me, too." He paused to let that sink in.

Ma set her coffee down and stared into the cup.

"I think, Ma…." Will paused and swallowed hard. "I think the

145

only thing to do is for me to go join up too so I can keep an eye on Jake. Keep him out of trouble." *There, now it's out in the open.*

"Just like you always do?" Ma looked up and shook her head. "I know you, Will Tanner. I know you been carryin' the load your Pa run off from, watchin' out for your brothers, takin' care of the farm, bein' the man around here. An' don't think for a minute I don't appreciate it. I love you for it. I'm glad you look after your brothers, all your brothers." She shook her head again. "No, I can't let you do this. It's too much. Jake's gotta carry his own weight now and answer for his own self."

"I know you ain't askin' me to do this," Will said. "I'm thinkin' it's the best way. You know how Jake is, he'll get into trouble as soon as they start orderin' him around."

Ma's lips curled up in a tight smile. "Yes, he will do that," she said. "But you might not be able to help him."

Now it was Will's turn to smile. "He'll ask to join up with Captain Steven's company. I'll ask for that too, so I'll be right there beside him."

Ma sighed a long sigh. "I don't know, Will. I don't know what's worse, havin' Jake off by himself or having both of you off." She hung her head in her hands.

"I would be doin' it for you Ma, too, and for Ike and Seth and Nate. An' now the Carters have got involved, they might be in danger too. This whole thing just needs to be over and done with."

Ma didn't answer for a while; she seemed to be lost deep in her own thoughts. Finally, she stiffened and seemed to come to a conclusion. "I cain't talk no more about it now."

She stood up and wiped her eyes again, went to the washbasin and sloshed some water on her face and dried it with a towel. "I got to get breakfast done, an' there's all the other chores...." She held her stomach for a moment, then said, "Watch the coffee don't boil over, I'll be right back." She left the carriage house through the back door.

Will felt pretty low. Just as he feared, he had made it worse for Ma. But he was convinced that he was right—that Jake was right—that the longer he hung around here, the more danger they were in. With him and Jake both gone, there'd be no reason for Porter to come back here. Or any other rebel conscript gangs. Besides that, where would he and Jake be safer than amongst hundreds of blue-coated soldiers with all those new carbines?

146

He heard a commotion up in the loft, and Ike clambered down the ladder. He gave Will a curious look. "So, Jake's run off?" he said.

Will wondered how much Ike had heard. "He'll be back," Will lied. He didn't want Ike getting any ideas of his own.

"Uh-huh," Ike grunted. He stared at Will for another moment.

When Will remained silent, Ike shrugged. "Well, I got chores to do," he said, reaching for biscuits and ham. He poured himself a cup of coffee, and was gone.

*If I'm really gonna do this,* Will thought, *I best be getting' to it.* Then Lucy's face came into his mind and his heart fell. *What am I going to say to her?*


It was still morning, but it was already stifling in the barn. "It's gonna be another long, hot day," said Will.

"Yessir, it will," said Ben Carter. "I cain't help you with the miles or the sun but you got food an' water."

Will sighed as he put the bit into Redjack's mouth while Ben threw a saddle over his back. Ben had graciously offered him the use of one of his mules. He'd have to figure out a way to get the it back once he got to the camp.

"Cinch everything down tight," said Ben. "You don't want to slide off'n him."

Will had never put a saddle on a mule, they'd always ridden Missy bareback. He reached for a strap, and Redjack flinched when he touched him in a sensitive spot.

"Sorry 'bout that, Redjack. Steady there boy...."

Redjack turned his head and looked at Will, as if to say, 'don't ever do that again.' Will jumped back in case the mule wanted to bite.

Ben laughed. "Yeah he's a mite touchy sometimes. You watch him. He will bite."

Will nodded. Missy would bite, too, if you did something wrong. The memory of her lying dead back at the farm made him sad and angry again. The saddle secured, he put his bedroll on behind it and tied it off. The mule brayed in protest.

"He prefers the plow to the saddle," said Ben. "But he gits used to it pretty quick."

147

"You too, Redjack?" Will said to the mule. "You gonna give me a hard time too? You might as well." He sighed again when he recalled the tongue-lashing Ma had given him over his decision to join up. She had taken it pretty hard, despite what Will thought were good reasons for him to go. She had stalked off and gone somewhere. He hoped she'd get over it in time to come see him off. And then there was Lucy. He had yet to face her though he was sure she'd heard the argument. When Ma got mad, she got loud.

"If he don't, I will, William Tanner," said a voice from the back of the barn.

Will smiled though his back was still to Lucy. *Yeah, she's heard.* He finished tying the rope and turned to face her. "Well, go on then," he said.

She was dressed in an old dress she wore for working in the garden, and it did nothing to hide the swell of her breasts and the roundness of her hips. But it was her face and her eyes that drew his own to hers. Hers were a deep brown that seemed to draw him in. Her skin was tanned and smooth despite a bit of dirt on it. Her dark hair was wild and tangled — a loose strand of it was stuck on her face. She'd never looked prettier to Will.

Ben shook his hand. "Good luck to you." To Lucy, he said, "Don't tarry long," and then left the barn.

Lucy looked Will straight in the eyes. "You weren't even gonna say goodbye?"

"I was just about to come lookin' for you."

Her eyes softened. "Well, then." She looked away, her eyes misty. She took a deep breath and turned back to meet his gaze. "I don't want you to go, Will. What if somethin' happens to you?"

Will didn't know what to tell her. He knew, in his mind, that something — anything — could happen. But in his heart, he somehow knew he'd be back. He decided to tell her the truth of it.

"It's best for everybody right now, even you. With me an' Jake gone, those men, an' others just like 'em, ain't got no reason to come back here." He paused. "An' I know what could happen to me, but I somehow know that it will be ok. I just know it. I will come back home, Lucy, I promise."

"You cain't promise that, not for sure." She looked down again. "You can promise me to not do anythin' silly. You can promise to keep your head down and don't act like some hero."

"All right, I'll do my best to come back. I won't do anything...stupid, and I'll keep my head down and not be a hero." He laughed a nervous laugh. "I'm not much of a hero anyhow. That's Jake, not me."

She cocked her head at his words. "That ain't true. You're just smarter than him. You just keep on bein' smarter."

"An' when I get back," he said. "I'll have some real money and I can buy some land an'...." He stopped right there. He hadn't thought any further ahead. Could there be a future for him with Lucy? His ears burned and he knew they'd turned red.

Lucy smiled. "You just come back, safe and sound. We can talk about money and such then."

Will nodded. He turned back and checked Redjack's harness again, just for something to be doing. "I'd best be gettin' on, it's a long ride an' it's hot out there."

"Will," she said, laying a hand on his arm.

Her hand was warm and soft, and his arm tingled where she touched him. He wanted her to never take her hand away.

"I know you can't read," she said. "I'll write to you anyway. You can get somebody to read my letters, and you can have somebody write letters back to me."

He could not imagine letting anyone else hear the things he wanted to say to her — he couldn't even say them himself.

He turned to face her and took her hands in his — his calloused hands felt like cow hooves compared to hers, but he delighted in her touch. And now she was close enough to smell. She smelled sweet and flowery like honeysuckle, and there was something earthy about it, too. He liked it. He wanted to touch her hair, but that would be too much.

"Please do write to me," he stammered. "An' I will learn how to read your letters. An' I'll learn how to write back. I promise you that."

She looked surprised and she smiled. "I'll do that. And I expect you to do what you say. And keep your head down. And take care of Jake too, and both of you come back home."

Before Will could say any more, she was in his arms. She closed her eyes and kissed him, a long full kiss on his lips, her breath sweet as honey. Then she was gone, rushing out the door. Leaving an empty space. He stood there a long while, stunned to his core, savoring that kiss. His lips burned where her lips had touched his, and he wanted that feeling to last as long as it could. He stood there, thinking about Lucy and what their future might hold.

Redjack whinnied, breaking Will's reverie. The heat in the barn was becoming stifling. He put his daydreaming aside with a shake of his head and mounted the mule. When he rode out of the barn, he looked for Lucy, but she was nowhere to be seen.

Will turned the mule toward the lane and clicked his tongue. "Let's go, Redjack," he said, and the mule started off. When they reached the main road, he hesitated for a moment, then pulled the mule left toward his farm. Before it came into sight, he heard an axe thunk into a log and he stopped. If Ma was still upset, he didn't want to face her again. Best to just ride on out. He'd already said his goodbyes and didn't want to do it again. It was too hard.

But he worried he might not see the place again for a while and wanted to take a last look, so he edged closer. And there was Ma, chopping a notch into a log. Ben's negro Tom swung his own ax and wood chips flew like quail busting from the brush. Ike and Seth were working nearby, chopping away, two handed, with hand-axes. Ma wiped her brow and looked his way. If she saw him, she didn't show it, and she soon bent back to her task. Even Chigger was there, dozing in the shade of a log, completing the peaceful scene.

He watched them work for a while before he turned the mule westward and rode away.

*****

# PART 2

## North Missouri Railroad bridge
## West Fork of the Cuivre River
## September 1864

# Chapter 14

Jake was bored. It had been quiet — too quiet — along this stretch of the railroad they'd been guarding for a week. He was tired of standing guard, digging latrines, mucking horse manure and all the other odious duties the sergeants made them do. And he'd yet to shoot his carbine at anything other than a wooden post at target practice. He wanted to be out there somewhere, chasing down and shooting at Rebel guerrillas and bushwhackers. That's what he'd signed on to do, yet here he was, way out in the middle of nowhere, protecting a bridge from nobody that he could tell of.

The only excitement they had was when a train came through, its huge steam engine huffing, looking like some huge animal snorting fire and steam and smoke in all directions from its various orifices. Passengers would stare out at the soldiers and the soldiers stared back, tipping their hats to any pretty girls.

But trains were even more impressive at night with their huge yellow eyes glowing in the dark and white-hot sparks flying from the smokestacks like lightning bugs. There were few trains, though, and the days and nights seemed to drag along.

Jake was walking his beat, daydreaming about killing rebels, when something whizzed by over his head. Thinking it was a bumblebee, he swatted at it with his hat. Only then did he hear the dull boom of a rifle shot off in the distance, followed by several more. The truss next to his head splintered as something struck it, and another bumblebee zipped over his head.

"Hey!" he yelled to the corporal of the guard, "I think we're gettin' shot at!"

Corporal Smyth, Will, and their cousin, Eli Calloway were already running in his direction. The corporal raised an arm and pointed; Jake turned to look and saw Rebel horsemen about a quarter mile away now, fast approaching his post at the west end of the bridge. Dust billowed behind them and smoke puffed from their guns. A second later Jake heard more bullets thunk into the wood or buzz overhead. He could now hear, and feel in his boots, the thunder of iron-shod hooves striking the ground.

He squeezed up against a truss as tight as he could and readied his carbine. His picket mates joined him in a loose defensive position, Corporal Smyth standing behind him, with Will and Eli on the other side of the bridge.

Smyth had turned white and his voice shook. "What're you waiting for?" he yelled to Jake. "Fire on 'em!" He cupped his hands and yelled to Will and Eli, "Fire on 'em,! Fire at will!"

Jake aimed and fired his carbine to no effect on the oncoming riders. The corporal fired his own carbine, followed by Will and Eli. The horsemen rode straight on toward the bridge.

"Reload!" yelled Smyth, panic edging his voice.

Jake was already reaching for his next cartridge. His shaking hands fumbled it, and he cursed as it fell through a gap in the wooden trestle. "Shit!" he yelled with a nervous laugh. *It's gone, forget it! I got plenty more!* He shakily inserted the next one into his carbine.

More shots buzzed overhead. In full panic now, Smyth yelled, "Retreat! Back across the bridge!"

Jake pulled the trigger, and the hammer snapped down, but the carbine didn't fire. He didn't wait to figure out what went wrong; the riders were almost on them and he took off running, right behind the corporal. Will and Eli were right behind him. The Rebel fire was getting more accurate, and bullets thudded into the bridge around them, which only spurred them to run faster. They reached the east end of the trestle without a scratch, where they were met by Captain Stevens and Lieutenant Campbell. Other soldiers were crouched in a ragged line on either side of the tracks, some were still loading their carbines.

"How many?" demanded the Captain.

"Twenty or so, I think, Sir," replied Smyth.

"I think that's about right," said Sergeant Burnes, peering at the oncoming horses. He had just come up with another squad of soldiers.

"I want some men on this end of the bridge," said the Captain. "Build a barricade, get some rails and stack 'em, get some men behind it. The rest of you men spread out on both sides of the track, independent fire. Put some fire on those people over there, now!"

Jake looked at his carbine, and to his horror realized why his carbine hadn't fired. He'd forgotten to put a cap on the nipple. He quickly put one on and was ready to fire again. He hoped nobody had seen his mistake.

The Rebels had stopped about two hundred yards short of the bridge where they dismounted. A few stood with the horses, while the bulk of the force approached closer to the bridge, alternately running and crouching to fire. None were in uniform. After a hundred yards, they stopped and took what shelter was to be found, which wasn't much. Several of them lay down, and some crouched behind the shoulder of the railroad bed. One of the bushwhackers ran up from their horse picket with some torches and a strange looking bucket with a built-in funnel.

*Coal oil!* "They're gonna burn the bridge!" Jake yelled, but nobody heard him over the din. The Captain and Lieutenant were busy directing the placement of the barricade and hadn't noticed the coal oil and torches. Sergeant Burnes saw it, though, and trotted over to Lieutenant Campbell and pointed it out. Campbell promptly reported it to the Captain.

"I want ten men here behind this barrier!" shouted the Captain. "Men who can shoot! Jake fancied himself a good shot, so he hurried over and took a position beside Will. More men joined them.

"Men," said the Captain. "They're gonna' try and burn the bridge. Don't let them get to the bridge with that can!"

With a yell, the bushwhacker's firing intensified, and two of them ducked forward onto the tracks, one lugging the can, the other carrying a lit torch.

"Fire on those men!" Burnes yelled. The company fired almost as one, and dirt kicked up all around the two bushwhackers. Amazingly, the men were not hit, but they dropped the can and scurried back to their meager shelter. The can sat there upright, forty feet from the bridge.

A handful of guerillas rushed the bridge again. Those men didn't even reach the can before they were driven back by bullets. Wood splintered a few inches from Jake's head, and he ducked. When he looked up, a marauder lay sprawled on the tracks. The man's legs scratched in the dirt a moment as he tried to crawl away, then grew still.

A bullet hit the bottom of the can, and a spray of clear coal-oil gushed out onto the railroad bed. It soaked into the gravel until the flow slowed to a dribble and stopped.

The firing on both sides slowed while the Rebels regrouped. More torches appeared and another can of coal-oil was brought up. Six men took up burning torches and ran forward to throw them at the bridge.

Again, withering fire from the company drove them back, and another body lay on the ground. Two of the guerillas, braver than their fellows, managed to get close enough to throw their torches. One landed in the gravel at the foot of the bridge, and soon burned itself out. Another landed upright against a wooden truss and its flames began to lick the wood. The truss began to smolder.

Another guerilla lay on the tracks and writhed in agony. He tried to crawl away but didn't get far before he gave up and just lay there, screaming for help. None of his fellows came to his aide. Off in the distance, a little knot of guerillas gathered at the horse picket and a discussion ensued, with much pointing and gesturing at the bridge.

"Put some fire on those men!" yelled the Captain. A loose volley rang out and the smoke drifted across the bridge. The volley only served to animate the knot of men, a few flinched and ducked but seemed otherwise unaffected by the shots. A horse screamed and collapsed.

"You're shootin' too high!" yelled Burnes. "Aim Low! Remember your trainin'! Aim Low!"

By now the knot of men had broken up. A lone man picked up another can and a torch. He hobbled forward, the heavy can slapping him on his thigh. Bullets sprayed dirt near him, but he kept running and made it to the bridge. There was a lull in the firing as the company reloaded, and the man hurriedly tipped over the can and let its contents spill out onto wooden ties. Then he stood up and ran back to safety.

Another guerilla jumped up and ran forward; unencumbered by a heavy can or a rifle, he carried only a lit torch in each hand. Weaving and dodging, he managed to get within throwing range of the bridge unscathed. His first throw fell short of the bridge. He crouched and ran a few feet closer.

"Shoot that man!" screamed the Captain. Most of the men were busy reloading, so he whipped out his own revolver and fired all six shots at the man, to no effect.

Reloading himself, Jake saw what happened next from the corner of his eye. Will raised his carbine and took careful aim. He fired just as the bushwhacker drew his arm back to throw his last torch. Will's bullet struck the man square in the chest; he fell backward and his legs folded under him. The torch dropped from his hand into the gravel behind him where it sputtered and smoked.

The man's death seemed to take the wind from the bushwhacker's sails and the firing slowed. It was their last try at the bridge. They fired a few last desultory shots while running back to their horses, where they mounted up, turned and rode off, leaving their dead and wounded behind.

Jake figured they either ran out of coal oil or lost their nerve, and he didn't much care which. Sergeant Burnes was clapping Will on the back and shouting something Jake couldn't hear over the cheering of the jubilant troopers.

There was still work to be done. "Get some water on those fires!" yelled the Captain. Jake jumped up—his legs were wobbly, but they worked—and grabbed a bucket. A bucket line formed, winding down to the creek, and the troopers soon had the smoldering truss extinguished. The only damage to the bridge was some blackened, sooty wood.

Men gathered around the bodies lying on the tracks. Jake's knees shook so bad he sat down on a log instead. He looked down, surprised to see his hands shaking of their own free will. He took a deep breath and tried to calm himself. It was over, and he had survived. His racing heart began to slow down.


The smoke from the battle had barely cleared when Will walked across the bridge, kicking the dead torches over the side. More troopers joined him, putting out the small fire.

Four bodies lay on the track, all of them in civilian clothes. Only one of them was still alive. Shot through both legs, he had crawled away from the bridge. He hadn't gotten far before he gave out. A trail of blood led from where he fell to where he now lay, and more blood stained his pants legs from his thighs down. The man might survive his wounds. Till the Colonel hung him, anyway.

Two troopers stood over the prisoner, their carbines cocked and aimed at him. Sergeant Burnes squatted next to him, pulled his canteen and gave it to the man. The man took it, but his hands shook violently, and he spilled more than he got in his mouth. "Let's get him back to camp!" yelled Burnes.

The surgeon came over and started binding the man's legs with

157

white rags, and two big soldiers picked him up under his arms and dragged him off. The man yowled with pain and cursed at them the whole time.

The other bodies lay on their backs. Their open, lifeless eyes stared straight into the sun as if they sought some kind of answer there. Will stood over the man he had killed. He knew without a doubt that he had killed this man; he'd taken deliberate aim at him and had been the only one to shoot at that moment. He'd seen the man fly backward from the impact of his Minie ball.

Will made himself look at the body. His bullet had hit the man square in the chest—a heart shot. He hoped the man had died quickly. There wasn't much blood on the front of the man's shirt, but the red-rimmed hole where the bullet had entered was plainly visible. A large stain in the crushed rock between the tracks showed where the man's lifeblood had gone. Will was used to blood; he killed and butchered hogs every fall, and he knew how much a hog could bleed. But he'd never seen this much blood. It gagged him, and he had to look away to control his stomach.

When the urge to heave had passed, Will made himself look again. A few minutes ago, when the man was trying to fire the bridge, he looked fierce and violent, and he had terrified Will. Now the man just looked pitiful and Will began to feel sorry for him. "Sorry I had to shoot you," he whispered low enough for no-one else to hear.

A clap on his shoulder startled him so much he nearly jumped.

"That was some good shootin' there," said Sergeant Burnes. "You saved the bridge. The Captain was impressed." Then he frowned. "You all right there, Tanner? You look a little green…. Ah, it's your first time to shoot a man, ain't it?" He paused. "Terrible thing, killin' a man. He forced your hand, Tanner. He'd a burned the bridge sure as I'm standin' here. You did your duty, and you did not have any say in it. That's the hard hand of war."

Will nodded. "I know." Burnes' words didn't make Will feel any better.

Burnes looked at him again and frowned. "Let me show you something over here, Tanner."

Together, they walked to where the dead horse lay. A couple of troopers stood over it, cursing and shaking their heads. The Captain stood off to one side making more notes in his little book.

"Tell me what you see hangin' there on the saddle," said Burnes.

At first, Will didn't spot anything. He looked again and saw a patch of hair that didn't match the horse. Puzzled, he looked closer and thought it was a piece of animal hide. Then he realized in horror it was a dried piece of skin with the hair still attached. Human hair. His face drained and he fought back the bile trying to rise in his throat.

"You're even greener now than before," said Burnes. "You know what that is, then?"

"A scalp. A human scalp."

"A Yankee scalp," said Burnes. "Probably taken at Centralia. There's another one on the other side."

"These people take scalps from our soldiers, like some kind of damned wild Injuns?"

Burnes nodded, his eyes boring into Will's. "Yep, Tanner, that's what I'm sayin'. They did worse than that at Centralia. These people are worse than animals and they don't deserve our pity. Don't you feel bad about killin' that 'un. This might not be his horse, but it might as well be. He was ridin' with 'em. This was a good thing you done today, Tanner. A good thing. Try and remember that when you think about that man."

Will shook his head, still not wanting to believe. But what he said was, "Ok, Sergeant."

"War brings out the best in some people and the worst in some other people," said Burnes. "That man lyin' yonder was one of the worst. He'd have killed you and hung your scalp on his saddle if he could have. He prob'bly killed some of our boys over at Centralia. It's for sure he raped and stole and looted and burned all over Missouri."

Will had thought there could be no worse people on earth than the men who'd burned his farm. Now he knew he was wrong. He hardened his heart. Men who'd do this deserved no pity, no mercy, no quarter.

Burnes squatted down and searched the saddlebags. In one he found a small bag of coins. "For the company fund," he said, pocketing the money. In another he found a bag of pipe tobacco, which went into his own pocket.

He removed two revolvers from the saddle. "Look here, Will, he carried two extra Navy revolvers." Handing one to Will, he continued, "Here, you take one, you earned it."

Will didn't want the gun, he had his government-issued Starr revolver, but he took it anyway. The Sergeant stuck the other one into his own belt. The saddlebags held nothing else of value, just some old dried bread.

"Grab some shovels!" Burnes yelled out. "Let's get this scum buried afore it stinks up the place!" Burnes clapped him on the shoulder again and walked off

Will walked back to the man he'd killed, remembering smoke and flames and the terror he felt when Porter's gang burned his farm and threatened his family — and Lucy. He looked at the dead man at his feet. "You chose your path," he said, "and it led you to this. I'm not sorry no more." He turned and walked away to find a shovel.


Jake sat on a stump near the campfire, cleaning his carbine. Will, Eli and some others sat nearby, doing the same. He saw the courier gallop in, perform a running dismount of his horse, and duck into the Captain's tent. It was the third or fourth since the fight. He wondered briefly what was up. He figured he'd find out when he needed to know.

"That weren't so bad, were it?" asked Eli. "We had us a fight today boys and it weren't so bad, were it?" His knees bounced up and down with nervous energy. "We kilt three of 'em! And no more than a scratch on any one of us!"

"That, me boys, was just a skirmish," said Sergeant Burnes. "So, while ye done good today boys — and ye done good indeed — remember, that was just a skirmish. It might not go so well next time."

Captain Stevens yelled for him from the tent and Burnes strode off.

The boys were subdued somewhat by Burnes's warning, but only for a minute and they soon went back to their hubbub and noise. Someone brought out some contraband whiskey and the boys passed it around.

Jake took the jug and took a little sip. Like before, the whiskey burned his throat and nose, and he coughed and gagged. Some of the boys sniggered at his discomfort, and he felt his face go red. When the jug came around again, he croaked, "Gimme another sip." The second drink still took his breath away, but he managed not to gag.

"That's enough, Jake," said Will. He took the jug from him and passed it on to the next boy in line.

Jake bristled. Will was bein' his usual puffed-up self. "Dammit

160

Will, quit bossin' me!" He sounded like a frog when he said it, and the boys laughed again.

Eli broke into the conversation. "You sure got that danged bushwhacker, Will. You got 'im dead to rights," he said. "That was a dang good shot. Right in the heart, just like a deer."

Will frowned and his eyes moved off into the distance.

For some reason that made Jake angry. "Sometimes I don't understand you, Will. We came out here to kill bushwhackers, and now we done killed some, you seem mighty blue about it. I wish I had got me one."

"I ain't blue about it, Jake. He deserved what he got."

"Then why are you so god-awful…."

The bugler blew assembly. Will and Jake looked at each other, their argument forgotten for the moment.

"What the hell is that about?" asked Jake.

Will just shrugged and stood up.

Burnes reappeared from nowhere. "Line up! Line up!" he yelled. "Form a line, right here!" He pointed at the usual spot. "Captain's got some words for us."

Captain Stevens walked over as the men were settling into a ragged line.

"Men," he began. "Good work today. Our prisoner is squawking like a jaybird, and we know what gang these boys belonged to and where they are. I have some good news for you. We're gonna' be relieved of guard duty by some regular infantry. They are on their way here and will be here by nightfall. We're gonna' join up with the rest of the regiment and go after Bloody Bill Anderson and his scum like those that just attacked us."

The troopers erupted into cheers, and some hats flew into the air. Eli looked at Jake with a big grin on his face. Will looked like he'd eaten a sour apple.

"So, men," continued the Captain. "Prepare to break camp. You'll be issued seven days rations and plenty of ammunition. The wagons and tents will not be coming with us—we need to move fast and light. Take only what you need and be ready by nightfall. Dismissed!"

Jake was elated. *It's about time we go after them sumbitches!*

He grabbed his cartridge box and haversack and headed to the supply wagons, where he filled both and stuffed more ammunition into his pockets. Back at the campfire, he quickly fried his salt pork and corn pones and roasted his coffee beans. It might be a while before they'd have a fire again. These went into the saddlebags, along with the extra cartridges for his carbine.

Jake fed, watered, curried and saddled his horse. Bags of corn for the horse went into the saddlebags, too. He rolled his few spare clothes into his blanket, rolled that into his rubber poncho, and tied it on the back of his saddle. He was ready to go, and he sat in the shade near his horse, waiting for orders.

In the east, a cloud of dust rose high over the tree line, and soon a scout rode in with news that it was the infantry, coming to relieve them.


Will stopped packing and walked over to where Sergeant Burnes beckoned to him, waving a letter. "Yes, Sergeant?"

"Got somethin' for you," said Burnes, handing him an envelope. "Came in that last pouch."

Will looked at it. He couldn't read the words on it, but it had to be from Lucy. She'd promised to write, but the mail was slow, and this was the first letter he'd received. *Maybe it's not from Lucy. Maybe it's bad news from home.*

Will handed back the letter. "Sergeant, I cain't read. Will you read it for me? An' will you keep it between you an' me?"

Burnes chewed on his pipe-stem for a few moments. "I reckon I could do that. And yes, I'll keep it between us." He peered at the writing on the envelope. "It's from a Miss Lucy Carter, Millwood, Missouri."

Will's anxiety changed instantly into joy.

Burnes opened it. "It's dated September third. Mail is damned slow these days." He knocked the plug out of his pipe and put it away. "All right then." He began reading from the letter:

> *Dearest Will,*
>
> *I well recall my promise to you to write to you and as I have some time I will now do so. I send this letter to*

*you by post and I hope it reaches you. The little cabin is almost done. Yesterday we split shingles and Ike climbed up and nailed some on. The roof should be done in a few days and the cabin will be snug. There is some chinking left to do. Seth is doing a good job with mud and wheat straw. Your Ma is much improved now and back to her old self. I expect you will be glad to hear it. Although she misses you and Jake something awful. There was a bad storm last night wind a howlin and rain a fallin. A biblical porporshen as Papa says. I thought of my dear soldier getting all wet from this storm and I sincerely hope that you come through it ok. That is all I will can write for now I must go and tend the garden. I will write to you soon again. You must write back and do not forget the promise that you made to me.*

*Ever Your friend*

*Lucy Carter*

When Burnes finished reading, he said something, but Will wasn't listening. He was hearing Lucy recite the words he just heard. *She thought of me when the storm hit.... Ever your friend.* The words kept rolling through his mind like a song.

"Tanner!" Burnes said. "Did you hear me? I said, would you like me to teach you to read?"

*****

# Chapter 15

Jake slipped sideways, almost falling out of his saddle. He had fallen asleep atop his horse, while on the move, yet again. The company had been riding all night—after a long day filled with the normal exhausting routine of camp, fighting a battle and burying the dead. On top of that, right at dusk, when they'd normally get some supper and some rest, they broke camp, packed their saddles and mounted up. They had been in the saddle ever since. Jake rubbed his eyes again and wondered if they'd ever stop for a rest.

He looked up but couldn't see any stars for the clouds. A tiny bit of light glowed through from the waning moon, which was just enough, out in the open. Under the trees, the horse in front of him was only a darker shadow that moved in and out of the inky blackness. Only the sound of gently clopping hooves, the creak of saddle leather, or an occasional cough marked the passage of time.

Jake had dozed off again when his horse suddenly stopped. Word was passed back that they were halting for the night. He followed the column into a grove of small trees. Some of the boys were so exhausted they just dropped their reins and plopped to the ground without so much as a blanket to cover them. Other men were assigned to gather up and picket the horses so they wouldn't wander off. Jake grabbed his carbine and gum blanket before his horse was led away. He had just closed his eyes, or so it seemed, when he was shaken awake by Sergeant Burnes.

"Come on, me bucko! You've got picket duty for the first watch," Burnes sounded way too cheerful. "Wake up, Private!" he said louder when Jake didn't move.

"All right dammit, I'm comin'. What time is it anyway?"

"Don't worry about that, you just come with us now. It's only an hour's watch, then you can get back to snoozin'."

"Sergeant? Permission to go on picket with Jake," asked Will from the darkness beside him. Jake didn't even know he was there.

"Denied, Private," said Burnes.

Jake felt the anger rising in him. "Dammit Will, I don't need you out there. I can handle it on my own."

Will muttered something Jake couldn't hear and laid back down in the grass.

Still cursing, Jake rose from his blanket, grabbed his carbine and followed Burnes. Goose Zumacher and Eli Calloway filed in behind him. Burnes led them to a depression about a hundred yards from the camp and pointed to a tree line about a hundred yards further across a grassy meadow. Will could barely see it in the gloom.

"You watch this way," said Burnes. "If you see anybody out there, you fire on 'em and yell. Goose will be on your right, and Eli will be on your left. That's all you need to worry about. Stay awake. You'll get relieved in an hour. Got that?"

"Yes, Sergeant," Jake sighed.

"Good. Look sharp now." Burnes and the others disappeared into the darkness.

"Dammit," Jake whispered. *Why me?*

He fought off sleep as long as he could, then his chin fell to his chest.

A twig snapped close by.

Jake's head jerked up and his heart pounded in his chest so hard that he just knew it could be heard ten feet away. *Goddammit! I fell asleep!* He shook his head to clear it and rubbed grit from his eyes.

He peered out into the darkness looking for a deeper blackness that shouldn't be there, a shadow moving among the shadows. His ears strained so hard he swore they moved like a cat's ears fixin' on a mouse.

Sure enough, the shadows moved out there. Four — no, five men, maybe more — creeping up one step at a time through the underbrush. Shadows against the lighter open meadow. Another twig snapped behind him. His heart pounded even harder.

*They got by me! Now what am I gonna do? I cain't run, they're way too close. If I let 'em go, them bastards will massacre the whole company.*

Then he knew what he had to do. His heart clenched when he thought about it, but he resigned himself to do it. Without a sound, he raised his carbine, already loaded, primed and half-cocked. He aimed at the nearest moving shadow. He prayed that his powder hadn't gotten wet from dew. He prayed even harder that he'd survive the night. He silently prayed, *God, let me live through this and I'll take whatever punishment they decide on.*

Jake pulled the hammer to full cock, the metallic click as loud as a hammer blow in the stillness. The shadows froze in place, and before they could react, he pulled the trigger. The blast was deafening, and the flash blinded him. One of the shadows yelped and fell to the ground. Back at the camp, a sentry bellowed out an alarm. Jake had done his duty, but what price would he have to pay for it?

His muzzle flash had shown the Rebels where he crouched in his shallow hole, and Jake knew bullets would soon be aimed his way. He had to move. He rolled out of his hole and crawled toward a fallen tree that lay nearby. The sound of his movement made an awful racket, and he tensed up, expecting the Minie balls to fly any second now. He rolled behind the log just as the sharp crack and flash of rifle shots illuminated the glade. Most of the bullets went over his head. One struck the log where he lay, sending splinters flying. Jake squirmed deeper down into the soft dirt.

"Save your shots, you idjits!" yelled a voice from the darkness. "We'll have the whole damn Yankee Army on us in a minute! Reload! Now!"

Jake's lips curled into a tense grin. *He must be a dang sergeant!*

"Who got hit?" asked another voice out in the gloom.

"It were me! It's just a scratch, though!" said a third voice.

"That you Joe Simpson?" asked the second voice.

"Gol-dernit, don't be callin' out no names, you hear me!" the Rebel sergeant bellowed. "By God, there's some stupid sumbitches in this outfit...."

Someone in the darkness mumbled something in response. Jake couldn't make it out.

A carbine fired over on his left, followed by another over on his right. *That's Goose and Eli!*

"Missed that time, Yank!" yelled someone from the darkness.

Shouts and other sounds reached his ears from his camp behind him; officers shouted orders, leather rustled, brass and steel rattled as men threw on their kits. Jake could almost see the Captain buckling on his saber. Carbine breeches were being snapped shut, and hammers cocked. A horse neighed somewhere and he briefly wondered which side the horse was on.

*I need to reload! An' don't forget the damn cap this time!* He levered open the breech of his carbine and inserted a new cartridge, smashing it in hard with his thumb and closed the breech. On his first try, his shaking fingers refused to seat the new cap. He took a deep breath, tried again, and was able to get it on the nipple. He pulled the hammer back to full cock and was ready to fire. The loaded carbine re-assured him, and calming, he took a deep breath. He recalled that even though he couldn't see his comrades, he wasn't alone out here — his whole company was behind him and coming to his relief.

"Fall back to the horses and be quiet about it!" shouted the Reb sergeant. "We've lost our surprise. If they push us, though, we'll give 'em a volley."

The sounds of moving men swished around him in the undergrowth. As the Rebels backed away, Jake's courage returned and he thought he might yet live through this fight. He decided to give them a parting shot, and raised his carbine and aimed in the general direction of the retreating Rebs. He fired again. This time there was no grunt, no yell. Some of the Rebs returned fire; a few bullets thunked into the log, and Jake tucked himself in tighter against it. The smell of burnt powder wafted to him in the slight breeze.

"Cease Fire, I said! Goddammit, din't you hear me, you sumbitches. I said hold your goddam fire!" screamed the Rebel sergeant. There was more muttering in reply.

"Missed me, you Yankee sonofabitch!" another Rebel yelled. "But I won't miss you!"

"Getcha next time, Yank!" shouted a different voice.

Jake nearly jumped out of his skin when a body plopped down beside him. He breathed a sigh of relief when he realized it was Sergeant Burnes. "Damn, Sergeant! You scared the bejeezus outta me!"

Burnes calmly asked, "Whatcha shootin' at there, Tanner?" He stuck his head up and peered out at the retreating shadows.

Jake was amazed by Burne's demeanor. You'd think they were out on a turkey hunt.

"Some Rebs trying to sneak up on the camp." Jake managed to stammer. His heart was hammering, his throat was dry, and his voice crackled. "They're pullin' back now. I heard 'em say they'll make a stand if we follow 'em."

Burnes spat on the ground. "They ain't Rebels. They're bushwhackers. We'll give 'em a push anyhow and see how fast they run." To the men coming up behind, he yelled "Skirmish line!" and Jake could hear men behind him falling into a loose battle line. "You too, Jake."

Jake jumped up and moved to his place in line. His file partner, Goose, stood behind and to his left."

"Sergeant!," yelled Captain Stevens. "Give 'em a volley."

"Yes Sir!" replied Burnes. To the men in line, he said "You heard the Cap'n. One volley, then reload and hold your ground no matter what them bastards do. Aim low, boys! Fire by rank! Front rank, kneel! Ready! Aim!" Thirty-odd Sharp's carbines rattled as they were leveled at the still retreating shadows, by now almost back to the distant tree line.

"Fire!"

The front rank fired a ragged volley, except for Jake, who had forgotten to reload. The meadow lit up like there was a lightning storm, and for a split-second, Jake could see the bushwhackers across the way. Smoke belched forward, then drifted rearward with the wind, into the faces of the men. Jake held his breath until it was gone.

"Front rank, reload!" Yelled Burnes. "Rear rank! Ready! Aim! Fire!"

In the dark, Goose—who stood behind him—had moved a little too close to Jake, and his muzzle was just about in Jake's ear when it blasted. His ear rang and he couldn't hear the next order Burnes gave, but the men were reloading so Jake followed suit. He was quickly ready to fire again.

It did not matter, though, the order to fire again did not come. Out in the meadow, the bushwhackers had mounted up and were galloping away. Jake's thumping heart began to slow.

The sky was getting lighter when the order to dismiss was given. The men relaxed and some strayed from the skirmish line. Pickets were placed out in case more bushwhackers were about. Nobody slept. Some troopers made fires to cook breakfast and make coffee. Others, like Eli, paced back and forth, full of nervous energy.

Will overheard men bragging about how they'd run off the bushwhackers who had high-tailed it out of there after the first volley. After two skirmishes with no injuries on their part, the new men figured they were now veterans. They were all smiles, joshing and elbowing each other. All except for Jake. He looked upset; he just sat on a log and stared at the ground.

Will figured they'd just been lucky, and he worried how long their good fortune would last. Bushwhackers could shoot just as straight as they could. He wasn't alone in his worries. The officers and more experienced troopers wore frowns and serious, wide-eyed looks etched on their faces.

Sergeant Burnes was off a ways having a conversation with Lieutenant Campbell. Will couldn't hear what was being said, but both men looked agitated. Sergeant Burnes saluted Campbell and strode angrily to where Will stood with a little knot of troopers. "Jake Tanner, you and Eli go over and retrieve that dead bushwhacker." said Burnes. "Will, you go with 'em. Your carbine ready to fire?"

Will nodded.

"Well what the hell you waitin' for then? Git movin'. An' keep your eyes open."

The three boys swished through the dew-covered grass toward the opposite treeline. A blood trail led to a lone man, in civilian clothes, that lay face down out in the open meadow. The man was not moving.

"Looks like he made two or three steps after he caught a Minie ball," said Will.

"Look! He's shot in the back!" said Eli.

Sure enough, a small hole in his frock-coat was rimmed in blood. "Yeah, he was runnin' away," said Will.

"Let's turn him over," said Eli "Easier to drag him that way."

Will poked him with the rifle, just in case. There was no response, and they turned him over. Exiting his body, the Minie ball tore out a huge hole in his chest, and white bone gleamed amid the gore on his coat. The front of his coat was soaked with blood, and the ground underneath him was caked with it. Blow-flies were already buzzing around the dead man.

Will felt sick, and might have lost his breakfast, if he'd had any. Jake walked away and retched.

"Jesus!" said Eli. "I know the man. That's Henderson Wortman from Pike County. I know his family." Eli looked away from the body. "Neighbors of ours. They're good people. Damn."

"Well, he ain't good people," said Jake, wiping his mouth. "He's a damn bushwhacker."

Will nudged him and shook his head in warning. Eli was already upset, there was no need to make it worse. "Let's just get this done. Grab a leg and drag him back to our lines."

Eli was sick and had to walk away for a moment. When he came back, Will said, "Here, Eli, take my gun. Jake an' me'll get him." Will and Jake each grabbed a leg and dragged the man across the meadow, and Eli followed behind them.

When they told Sergeant Burnes who the man was, he nodded and dismissed the boys. "We'll let the Colonel know, and his family will get told sooner or later. We'll bury him too. Go get some coffee and a bite to eat. We'll be mountin' up soon. Be ready."

"Wonder who shot Wortman," said Eli. He looked pale, and Will saw his hands shaking.

"There ain't no way to know for sure," said Goose. "It was dark and and a with the whole company shootin' there ain't no way to know."

"Jake wounded one," said Jon, laughing. "I know that because he said so out loud. His sergeant jumped all over somebody for callin' him by name."

"I heard that, by god, I did," said Max.

Goose grinned. "Yeah, that's a damn sergeant for you."

Eli lit his pipe from a burning stick. He puffed a few times. "Well, I reckon I cain't know if it was me that shot him. Wortman, I mean. An' I reckon he'd have shot me if he had to anyhow, so I cain't feel too bad about it. Never would a thought he'd run with bushwhackers, though. His people live close by us, an' they're good people. Damn, I feel bad for 'em."

Will poured himself a cup of coffee. "Got any sugar, Goose?"

Goose pointed to a sack laying on a log nearby. "Help yourself."

Will poured a handful of sugar into the cup and swirled it before he took a sip. The coffee was strong but the sugar made it drinkable. "Good coffee, Goose."

"Odds are, it weren't you, Eli." said Max. "There's sixty-odd of us that shot at 'em."

Eli nodded and sighed. "Yeah, I reckon that's right." He straightened up. Max's words brightened his mood. "All right then. I probably wasn't the one so now I don't feel so bad."

Will walked up and stood in front of Jake. "You all right?"

Jake's cheeks flushed red. "Yeah, I'm all right. Nothin' to it."

Will studied his brother. It wasn't that his hands shook that concerned him, Will's own hands still trembled. No, it was more that Jake's eyes wouldn't meet his own. And that meant he was hiding something. "You sure, Jake? You look a little pekid."

"I'm fine," Jake hissed. "Leave me be!"

"Ok, Jake. Just askin', is all." Will now knew for sure something wasn't right. He also figured he wasn't likely to find out what it was from Jake. He decided not to push it.

Will's attention turned to the pounding hooves that announced a rider. A courier galloped in and did a running dismount. The man ran over to the Captain, saluted and handed him a dispatch. Captain Stevens read it and handed it to Lieutenant Campbell. They discussed something for a few seconds then Campbell signaled for Burnes to come over.

The Captain wrote something on a sheet of paper, folded it and handed it to the courier, who put it in the dispatch pouch. The trooper mounted up and galloped back out of camp the way he'd come.

*He's in an awful big hurry*, thought Will.

The officers and Sergeant Burnes stood in front of the Captain's tent and drank coffee while they had a short meeting. The officers talked excitedly but Will could not make out what they were saying. He felt sure something was up.

In a few minutes the meeting broke up, and Sergeant Burnes strode over. "Get ready," said Burnes. "We're mounting up in fifteen minutes."

"What's the scuttlebutt, Sergeant?" asked Goose.

"Plans have changed. We're headed to Jefferson City, to help the Union hold it against Price. The brass is expectin' a big fight there." He paused to drain his cup. "They're sayin' now that Price may have twelve thousand men with him. The generals is rounding up as many troops as they can to fight him. Infantry and artillery and all. Might get a bit hot over there. We gotta get movin'.'"

"Well, hell," said Max, pouring out his coffee. "No breakfast today, boys!"

As Jake rode, he cursed himself for sleeping on picket duty. It had worked out all right but it could have gone the other way just as easy. He had let his fellow troopers down, and he kicked himself over and over for it. He thought he'd do better when the time came, and he was ashamed that he hadn't.

Will rode up and startled him from his thoughts. "What happened out there last night? I can tell somethin's not sittin' right with you."

"Nothin, Will. Nothin' happened out there, except we fought a dang battle, if you cain't see that then you're just plain blind."

"There's that. But you look like somebody stole your last dollar."

"Maybe I'm just tired, is all," Jake hissed. He wasn't about to tell Will what he'd done. If Will knew, he'd hold it over his head and never let him forget it. *He still don't trust me. Just like last night, him askin' to stay out there on picket duty with me like I'm some child. He do that just to embarrass me? Why the hell won't he just let me take care of myself?*

"Just tryin' to help," said Will.

Infuriated now, Jake raised his voice. "I don't need your damn help, cain't you get that through your head yet? I can take care of myself an' I don't want you hoverin' over me like some damn cow mooin' over her damn calf! Just keep away from me, Will and let me be, dammit!"

Some of the men nearby raised curious eyes but soon looked away.

"All right, Jake," Will whispered. "I'll leave you be. But you need to figure out what's eatin' at you real quick, cause we got us a big fight comin' an' I'm worried about you."

Jake was now sorry that he'd raised his voice. What was between him and Will was for their ears only. He lowered his voice. "I can handle it, Will, now just go away, will you?"

Will shrugged and kicked his horse ahead to ride beside Eli. As soon as he was gone, Jake's anger abated and his shame returned.

*I will take care of it myself. I won't never let that happen again. I'll drink a whole pot of the god-awfulest coffee I can make. I'll chew raw coffee beans or stick myself with my knife if I have to. I'll do whatever it takes. I won't let the company down like that again.*

Once Jake had convinced himself, he felt better. His spirits raised, and he could look at his companions again. He hoped there was a big fight coming. So he could redeem himself.

\*\*\*\*\*

# Chapter 16

Near noon, Will saw the first refugees on the road. Some rode in wagons piled high with furniture and goods. Some were on horseback or muleback. Most walked, their backs bent from carrying their worldly possessions on their shoulders. It was a pitiful sight and Will's spirits fell.

Sergeant Burnes rode up and motioned at them with his pipe. "They're running from bushwhackers. That bastard Anderson's got 'em terrified, an' rightly so. Every Union soldier or Militiaman who can carry a gun is on his way to defend Jeff City against Price. That leaves the whole countryside undefended. Anderson's been burnin' and killin' all over. He's got a free hand out there."

They came upon an overturned wagon, its meager contents scattered about in the ditch. An old farmer looked at it helplessly, hands on his hips. Will and a few others stopped long enough to right the wagon. A feeble cheer rose from some bystanders.

"Thank ye," said the old farmer. He spat tobacco juice and some dribbled on his shirt. "They burned us out yesterday, an' that's all we got left. Much obliged."

A faint smudge of smoke appeared over the horizon to the south, and the Captain called another rest halt while scouts rode out to check it. Most of the men slipped off their horses and dropped to the ground where they were. Burnes came around and selected a few boys for picket duty.

*Thank God it's not me this time,* thought Will. He lay back against a tree, pulled his hat down, and closed his eyes. In what seemed like only seconds, someone was kicking his booted feet.

"Mount up," said Burnes. "It's not much further. You can rest when we get there."

"Don't you dang sergeants ever sleep?" mumbled Will.

"No," said Burnes. "We're like your mothers. Got eyes in the backs of our heads, too. Now get up and hop to!" He went on down the line of dozing troopers kicking them awake.

The men mounted up and the column limped on. Burnes hadn't lied; soon they topped a rise and spread out before them in a broad valley was the Missouri River. On the far side sat a large town. Above the town, sitting atop the highest hill around, a huge, square building gleamed in the mid-day sun. A bright gold-colored dome flashed from the top. A Union flag, bigger than the one in Camp Fremont flapped lazily from a tall pole set in front of the building.

The sight of the town and the prospect of a good meal and some rest invigorated the troopers and they sat a little straighter in the saddle. Their exhausted horses, though, would not be coaxed into moving any faster.

In minutes they arrived at a crowded ferry crossing and the column came to a halt. They sat there awhile, waiting for orders. They weren't the only ones waiting. Other soldiers—infantry, cavalry, militia—had also arrived and gotten caught up in a massive logjam of civilians, soldiers, horses, wagons and even two cannons. Will took it all in, but the cannon caught his eye. He'd been on the receiving end of cannon fire before, but he'd never been that close to the big guns. He recalled well the thunderous sound they made and the sight of cannonballs bouncing across the prairie.

Captain Stevens rode over and led them off the road and away from the seething morass, which had backed up a quarter-mile onto the road. He ordered the men to dismount and rest for a while. Most grabbed hardtack or salt beef from their saddlebags and had a quick lunch.

While they waited, the wagons caught up. Will was glad to see Toby and Bo, who stopped their wagon nearby. Stiff from so much riding, Will limped over to replenish his rations and ammunition. "Hello, Toby. Bo," he said, nodding.

Toby ignored him in his usual sour manner, but Bo smiled his wide grin. Will extended a hand, and Bo's smile vanished. He turned away to tighten a rope that looked plenty tight. "Some white folk won't like it if'n we act too friendly like," he mumbled under his breath. He walked to the other side of the wagon, checking more ropes, keeping his eyes on his work.

175

Bo's manner puzzled Will, and at first, it annoyed him. Then he noticed some nearby troopers watching them and whispering among themselves. Will didn't want to cause trouble for Bo, so he quickly said, "Got any ammunition in that there wagon, driver?"

Bo shook his head. "Nossir, no ammo in dis wagon." His smile returned.

Will winked before he walked away. He thought it sad that you couldn't be friendly to a man you liked just because of the color of his skin. But it was the way of the world, and he couldn't change it. He refilled his cartridge box at another wagon driven by two negroes he didn't know.

A steam whistle blew somewhere across the river, and soon, a gleaming, white steamboat appeared in the muddy current. It chugged its way across the river, sparks and thick, black smoke belching from its twin smokestacks.

Will frowned. "We gonna have to ride across on that?"

"Looks that way," said Eli.

A second boat appeared behind the first. Will's heart lurched. The steamers reminded him of his Pa who had died back in forty-nine. He was killed in a steamboat explosion in New Orleans, on his way to the goldfields. Ever since, Ma had always told anyone who'd listen to stay away from steamboats. It looked like he'd have to ride one today, and he wasn't looking forward to it. He tried not to dwell on it.

The first boat nosed into the bank and extended two thin gangplanks. Neither could handle horses or artillery, so the infantry filed across and onto the boat. Will felt relieved. Infantry soon lined the upper and lower decks, solid lines of blue that contrasted with the gleaming white of the wheelhouse. There were so many on board, with their guns and accouterments that the boat tipped heavily to one side as it backed away. Now will was doubly glad he wasn't on board, the thing looked like it might tip over any minute now.

As soon as it backed away from the bank, the other boat angled in, and it too quickly filled up with soldiers. It was a short trip across and back; the first steamer returned, and the loading was repeated. The steamboats alternated in this fashion until all the infantry was across.

It was not possible to get the heavy cannon onto the steamers, so the big guns rode across on the ferryboat. *It'll be a wonder if those big guns don't sink that tiny boat,* Will thought. But the ferry crew balanced the cannons well, and they made the trip across without a mishap.

When the ferry returned, Captain Stevens ordered the company to board, ten men at a time, with their horses. Will was in the first bunch and he led his mare carefully to the middle of the boat. He was a little queasy on the crossing; when the horses and men moved about, the boat tilted steeply to one side or another. He feared the boat would overturn and spill them into the river.

"Keep those horses steady!" yelled the ferryman.

"Quit your rubberneckin'!" yelled Sergeant Burnes. "Stand still!" The men complied, and the boat righted and steadied itself.

When they reached the far side, the unloading proved to be easier than the loading. The horses and soldiers were eager to get back on steady ground. Will more so than many. He and his horse eagerly jumped off and climbed the bank. He led his horse up the bricked landing and crossed over the railroad tracks.

Will had never seen such a bustling place as this town—he'd never been to any town larger than Mexico, Missouri. He'd never seen a three-story house before, and there were many of them here. The Capital building on the hill with its shiny dome towered over the city. Horses and wagons cluttered the streets. The sweet smell of horse manure and the stink of raw sewage assaulted his nose. A steam engine huffed smoke and steam into the air from somewhere upriver. It was hidden by the masses of people, horses and wagons, but he saw its plume of black smoke curling away into the sky and its whistle added to the cacophony.

"You seein' this?" asked Jake, who had slipped up beside him unnoticed. It was the first time he'd spoken to Will all day. Jake could hold a grudge for a long time when he wanted to.

"Yeah," replied Will. "I don't see why anybody'd want to live in a pigsty like this."

Jake coughed and covered his nose with his sleeve. "I reckon our pigsty is cleaner than this place," he said. "Dang, it stinks. I hope the rest of the company gets over here quick so we can move on."

It took eight more trips for the ferry boat to get the remaining horses and troopers over. The only mishap occurred when a panicked horse jumped off the ferry too soon, dragging his unlucky trooper into the river with him. The horse got his feet under him, and the trooper hung on to the saddle horn. Other than his ruined ammunition and provisions, no real damage was done.

Goose tapped Will on the arm. "You see them women up there?"

177

Will looked where Goose pointed and saw a row of barely clad women lined up on a third-floor balcony. He saw bare ankles, legs, knees and even thighs. Their bare skin glowed white in the shade. They whistled and cat-called down to the troopers below with vulgar suggestions. One woman flashed her oversized breasts at them. His jaw dropped.

"Oh, yeah, now you see 'em, dontcha?" said Goose. "Sporting girls. Soiled Doves."

"Whores," said Max.

"Yeah, same thing."

Will frowned. "Whores?"

"You reckon….?" asked Max.

Goose sighed. "No, we'll be movin' on, there ain't no time for sportin'."

Max looked crestfallen.

Will didn't know what to make of the conversation, but he knew one thing. The image of those huge bare breasts would stick in his mind for a while. Then he remembered Lucy and he was ashamed of himself.

He had to drag Jake away by the arm.


As the company picked their way slowly through the crowded streets, Jake gawked up at the buildings, church spires, and the capital with its gleaming golden dome and huge flag. "Where the hell did they find a tree that tall to make a pole from?"

"I don't know," said Will. "That flag'd cover our barn."

The mention of the barn brought back memories of the farmstead. Jake didn't miss the hard work. He did miss Ma's cooking. "Reckon we'll get to eat any good food? I am damn tired of rancid pork and them god-awful crackers. Chewin' coffee beans is getting' old too."

"Don't get your hopes up," said Will. "With the Rebs comin' up, we'll go right to the fight."

Will turned out to be right. The company rode right through the town without stopping. When the houses gave way to open cropland, he turned to Jake and said, "Told you!"

Will's know-it-all attitude once again annoyed Jake, and he

remembered why he was mad at him.

They crossed a newly-dug shallow ditch that curved away north and south for what looked to be miles. Men were still digging in it, many of them negroes. Other men were using mules to place abatis — trees with the sharpened outer branches facing outward — as barriers. Others placed head logs atop the outer bank of the ditch to shield soldiers from Rebel bullets. Here and there stood little knots of blue-clad soldiers manning the ditch.

"There ain't near enough soldiers here," said Will.

Sure enough, Jake saw long gaps between the soldiers. "Maybe, but we got cannon." He pointed at the cannons placed at regular intervals along the line.

"Most of them cannon ain't nothin' but logs painted black," said Will.

Jake looked again. "Shit! Reckon they'll fool anybody?"

"Fooled you, didn't they?"

Jake had had enough of Will's smugness. He gave him a quick sneer before he kicked his horse into a trot and rode up next to Eli and Jon.

Out in the middle of the grass-filled valley, a small river snaked its way through, its course marked by small willows and cottonwoods.

Sergeant Burnes rode up and nodded at it. "That's the Moreau River, boys, and that's where we'll be. We got skirmish duty."

"Shit," said Jake. "Why ain't we behind the works like the infantry?"

"Because we ain't infantry," said Burnes. "We're cavalry and we got horses."

"So we can run away faster?" asked Jon, laughing.

Jon's remark irritated Jake. "I ain't about to run!"

It was fall, the dry season, and the Moreau was low, in places only a shallow riffle They splashed across and dismounted on the far side, using the trees to hide themselves. Burnes ordered every sixth man to hold horses; the others spread out in a loose skirmish line on the far bank, each man choosing a tree or fallen log to stand or hunker down behind.

It was Will's turn to hold horses, but Burnes pulled him off that duty and assigned Jake to it. Will shrugged and handed the reins to his brother.

Jake opened his mouth to complain but Burnes cut him short. "I need Will for somethin' else," he said.

Jake clamped his jaws shut to avoid commenting. It would serve only to get him chewed out again. Burnes had been on his case the whole ride. He wondered if the sergeant knew about him falling asleep on guard two nights ago and was punishing him for it. Then again, Burnes wasn't one to let a mistake go by. He'd tell you straight away and in no uncertain manner if you'd done something wrong. So, that wasn't likely. The more Jake dwelled on it, the more convinced he was that Will was Burnes's favorite. Just like he was always Ma's favorite. These thoughts irritated Jake, but there wasn't much he could do about it. Yet.

Will was alarmed. Burnes wanted him to do what? "But Sergeant...."

Burnes cut him off. "Corporal Smyth's got the quick step. You're in charge," he repeated. "I want you and three other men out there, atop that hill. Two of ye take the left watchin' that way, and two of ye take the right."

Will opened his mouth but no words came out. *Why me?*

Burnes saw his chagrin. "I'm puttin' you in charge 'cause you keep a cool head under fire. Plus, you're used to bossin' your little brother around, ain't you?" He clapped Will on the shoulder.

"Yes, Sergeant."

"Then you won't have no trouble with these boys. You watch for any sign of Price's army. You'll see their dust a long time before you see them. When you see 'em, you send somebody back to fetch me. If they come at you in force, fire a warning shot and skedaddle back here. Got that? I need you boys back in the line so don't be stupid. You'll be relieved in two hours."

"Yes, Sergeant."

Burnes turned and walked away, leaving Will dumbfounded.

Will didn't want to be in charge of anything, but he had no say in the matter. Orders were orders. "OK, let's go," he said, and Eli and two other troopers followed him out onto the hill, where he sent flankers out to both sides. "Stay close," he warned.

"You rest," he told Eli. "I'll take the first watch," Eli sat down and took a drink from his canteen, laid back in the grass and pulled his hat over his face.

Will looked around. *What a beautiful place,* he thought. The green, thigh-high grass rippled in the wind, reminding him of the waves in the Missouri River. The sky was a brilliant blue, and fluffy white clouds edged across it in the breeze. Off to the south, a pair of red-tailed hawks circled high in the air, hunting for their dinner. Closer down to earth, a buzzard glided across in front of him, its black wings tilting in the gusts.

His weariness and the gentle rustling of the grass combined to make him sleepy. He splashed water from his canteen onto his face and turned into the breeze. The cooling effect refreshed him.

When he turned back, he saw the dust. It was a barely visible smudge over the horizon off to the southeast. He rubbed his eyes and looked again. *Yep, sure enough, somebody's coming.* His heart pumped faster, now, and his drowsiness disappeared.

"Eli," he said. "They're here. Go get Sergeant Burnes."

Eli soon returned with Captain Stevens, Lieutenant Campbell, and Sergeant Burnes in tow. They stood with Will and Eli at the top of the rise.

"Where?" asked the Captain. Then, "Never mind, I see it."

Will looked again to the southeast, where he saw the dust cloud now rising well above the far tree line.

"How many? Infantry or Cavalry?" the Captain asked. He put his binoculars to his eyes and scanned the horizon.

"I ain't seen anythin' other than dust, Sir," said Will. Even as he said it, several gray-clad cavalry emerged from the trees across the meadow and spread out sideways into a line. Will stopped counting at twenty; there were at least twice that many. Sabers flashed in the sunlight as the Rebels drew them from scabbards and raised them, but nothing else happened. They merely sat there on their horses.

The Lieutenant was skittish. "Return to the lines, Sir?"

The Captain trained his glasses on the new arrivals. "They're not gonna attack the whole regiment with fifty men. We'll hold right here for the moment."

*The whole regiment? When did they get here?* Will took a long look behind him and sure enough, the line of blue-clad soldiers on the Moreau River now stretched for a quarter-mile. The Fifteenth was now well over 900 men strong, and the line of blue was impressive. With that many men behind him, he instantly felt less exposed and alone out here.

Behind the regiment, in the freshly dug earthworks, stood thousands more blue-clad men, bayonets gleaming in the bright sunshine. Will smiled. *If the Rebels want a fight, looks like they'll get one.* He decided the Captain was right, the odds were against fifty men attacking. Will would worry when the captain worried.

The Rebels just sat there atop their horses. One man had a spyglass and was giving them a good look.

Will now saw two distinct dust clouds off in the distance. A much larger one had appeared behind the first. More riders appeared from the tree line. These men were in civilian dress and armed only with shotguns or pistols. The Captain stood unruffled. He scanned from right to left and back again with the binoculars. "The first bunch are regular Cavalry. The second bunch are guerillas." He pulled out a small notebook and wrote something in it.

More and more horsemen rode out of the trees and spread out. The Lieutenant got more nervous about their exposed position. The Captain seemed to sense it. "Steady, men," he said. "They aren't ready to charge at us yet, and they only have a few carbines. No long rifles and no cannon. We'll skedaddle at the first sign of cannon." He laughed. "Maybe they'll be stupid enough to charge. I hope so."

More gray-clad regular cavalry poured out of the trees and into the line. the Captain made no move to withdraw from the hilltop. Will glanced at Eli, who gave him a nervous look. The flankers edged back a few feet.

More sabers flashed. Not all the Rebels had them, but several hundred of them did. Some small cannon appeared, and the Rebels parted in spots to allow them through.

"Captain…." said the Lieutenant, pacing back and forth.

"Well, I think we've seen enough," interrupted Stevens "Back to the river. Slowly now, we don't want to give them the wrong impression." The Captain turned his back to the Rebels and strode off, never once looking back. The Lieutenant crabbed sideways, keeping one eye on the Rebel Line. Sergeant Burnes, Eli and Will edged backward, keeping their eyes fixed on the Rebels. Will saw another flash as the sabers were re-sheathed. The cannon never fired.

When Captain Stevens and the pickets reached the river, the order to mount was given. The whole regiment withdrew to the new earthworks just in front of the town. Will thought this was a good idea, and when he looked back over his shoulder, he saw the Rebels moving forward in a ragged line. Just as Will and his company passed into the earthworks, the Rebel cavalry reached the river and occupied the position the regiment had just left. Behind the Rebel cavalry, long rows of rag-tag men marched across the prairie. Only about half carried weapons of any kind, and most wore civilian clothes. *Conscripts,* Will thought. *Did me an' Jake look that ragged back at Elkhorn Tavern?*

Will's regiment took up their positions in the shallow earthworks. The diggers had thrown the dirt forward, and head-logs lay across the top, so there was good cover if you lay forward in the dirt. But there was no shooting. The Rebel cavalry just watched from their position on the river, and the Rebel infantry just stood there in loose formation. The Union soldiers glared at them from behind their works.

Nothing happened for a long while, then a knot of Rebel officers rode up to the tree line. Word passed down the line: It was General Price himself, on the big gray horse, come to take Jefferson City for the Confederacy.

"Where's a sharpshooter when you need one," grumbled Sergeant Burnes.

Nothing more happened, the two sides just studied each other across the prairie and Will soon became bored and sleepy. Since he was not on picket duty, he lay back against the dirt and covered his face with his hat.

Jake plopped down beside him. "Reckon we'll have a fight?"

Will kept his eyes covered. "I reckon they come a long way not to have a fight."

"Good," said Jake.

Will lifted his hat and gave Jake a stare. "Spoilin' for a fight, are you?"

"That's what we're here for," Jake said, his thumb rubbing the hammer of his carbine. "Ain't it?"

Too tired to argue, Will sighed and lowered his hat. "Yeah, they'll come at us," he said. "But we're in a good spot for a fight." He closed his eyes again.

Will slept soundly until thunder rolled somewhere off in the distance and woke him up. He realized it wasn't thunder when another boom echoed across the valley. *Cannon fire!*

"Give 'em hell!" yelled Jake. "Eat that, Johnny Reb!" Jake was standing up on the lip of the ditch, pacing back and forth, clearly enjoying the spectacle, and a clear target for any sharpshooters out there.

"Get down, Jake, you dang fool!" yelled Will.

"It's our cannon, Will, quit worryin'"

Will scooched over and grabbed Jake by a pants leg and pulled him down. He got the usual hateful glare for his trouble, but Jake stayed down.

The thundering blasts brought back the sheer terror of being the target of cannon fire at Elkhorn Tavern. Will quickly found he much preferred the shooting side, noisy as it was. The one-sidedness didn't last though; blue smoke soon puffed from the Rebel lines, followed after a second by the familiar deep booms and rolling echoes. Jake was not so happy now; he hunkered down behind the head log while cannonballs whistled overhead.

The cannon duel intensified, and cannonballs flew in both directions. The din was deafening, the ground trembled, and smoke clouded the view until a breeze came up and blew it away. Screaming horses and yelling officers added to the noise. Will chanced a peek through a crack and could see cannonballs skipping along the ground, throwing up big clods of dirt and grass where they bounced along.

Both side's gunners were terrible shots. Will didn't see much damage being done to either side. Some balls overshot the earthworks and plowed into the soft ground amongst the wagons in the rear. After what felt like an hour, but was really only a few minutes, the Rebel firing slowed, then stopped, and the Rebel gunners limbered up and withdrew back into the trees. The Union cannon threw a few more parting shots, then it, too, died away. Soldiers on both sides waved hats, jeered and yelled taunts at each other.

Will tensed now, ready for the follow-up infantry assault. It never came. The fight was over for now. After a while, Will lay back down and covered his face. Drained from lack of sleep and exhausted by the cannon fight, he was soon asleep.

He slept soundly all night, and when reveille blew at dawn, he rose to more cheering and hat throwing. When he looked out over the valley, his jaw dropped. The Rebels had gone without a fight.

*****

# PART 3

# Independence, Missouri

# October 1864

(Special Order)
Headquarters, Army of Missouri
Boonville, October 11, 1864

"Captain Anderson with his command will at once proceed to the north side of the Missouri Rover and permanently destroy the North Missouri Railroad, going as far east as practicable. He will report his operations at least every two days."

By order of Major-General Price[3]

\*\*\*\*\*

*(Price's verbal Command to Anderson)*

*"... destroy the railroad bridge. . .at the end of St. Charles County."* [4]

# Chapter 17

A week later, Will watched the long wisps of dark hair flutter in the wind from the obscenity hanging from the dead bushwhacker's saddle. He knew right off what it was—the scalp of a dead Union soldier. It wasn't the first he'd seen, and it wouldn't be the last. No matter how many he'd seen before, the sight infuriated him; his jaw clenched and unclenched, his teeth ground together, he cursed under his breath and he gripped his carbine so tight it made his hands hurt.

"You bastard!" yelled Jake, kicking the dead bushwhacker who lay nearby in the grass, blood still oozing from his body.

"Feel better, now, do you?" Will asked. He felt the same rage, but his was tinged with sadness and he knew kicking the dead man wouldn't make him feel better.

Jake turned his angry glare on Will. "Yeah. Well, no."

"Figured as much," said Will. He had mostly given up trying to lecture Jake on his fits of anger. It just made things worse.

He left Jake and walked over to where Colonel Owens and an entourage of captains and lieutenants stood over two more dead guerillas. Sergeant Burnes, who was searching one, handed Captain Stevens a blood-stained leather wallet, who passed it on to Owens. The Colonel examined a document he pulled from it, then squatted to look at the body closer. "By God! That's Todd Young!" he exclaimed.

Will's ears perked up. The Colonel wasn't prone to getting excited about dead bushwhackers. "Who's Todd Young?" he asked Sergeant Burnes.

"Young's one of Anderson's lieutenants," whispered Burnes. "Well, was, anyhow. If that's him, then we caught ourselves a big fish." He turned to the knot of men who had by now gathered around.

"Which one of you sorry troopers got lucky and killed this man?" he asked.

"We was all firin' at him." Goose shrugged. "Cain't tell who hit 'im."

Will nodded his agreement. "No way to be sure, Sergeant."

"I hope he died slow," said Max, spitting tobacco juice to the ground, hitting his boot instead. "Dang it!" he said, wiping it off on the back of his other pants leg.

"Well, whichever it was, good shootin'," said Burnes.

"Well, as we all know, it weren't me," said Jake. "I sure wish it were." He glowered at Will, who had insisted it was Jake's turn to hold the horses. "I still ain't got me one, yet, that I can tell of."

Will gave him a glare. "You think that'll make it better, do you?" Right away, he regretted his own words, now was not the time to get Jake riled up.

Jake turned red and his mouth opened, but a look from Burnes silenced any retort.

"Well, this 'un won't be doin' any more maraudin'," said Max. He spat again, missing his boot this time.

Rifle fire crackled from somewhere to the west. The officer's heads jerked up, turning about, searching for the exact direction. *They look like a herd of deer with their tails flipped up an' their heads turning this way an' that,* thought Will. He'd have laughed except he knew this was dead serious.

Soon, the officers decided what to do. "Let's move!" Came the order from the Colonel, echoed by the Captains, passed on by the Sergeants. There would be no burials for these bushwhackers.

Will mounted his horse and fell into line. "Come on, Jake, you heard the man."

Jake mounted up and glanced at the scalp dangling from the dead man's horse. "I hope you're burnin' in hell right now, you son of a bitch!" he said. "I hope the coyotes tear your insides out and scatter your bones! I hope nobody ever knows where you died, damn you!"

"Feel better now, Tanner?" asked Sergeant Burnes. "Cause if you do, would you mind fallin' in?"

Jake turned red again. "Yes, Sergeant."

Will just shook his head. *Like a dog with a bone.* That led him to think of Chigger, their old beagle, and he wondered how things were back home. They'd been riding hard and fast and the mail hadn't found them, so there'd been no letter from Lucy. He forced his mind back to the task at hand, namely, surviving the next fight.

The Colonel led them west on the dirt road and gave the order to gallop. Dust billowed into the air and Will pulled his yellow bandana up to cover his nose. They had gone only two miles before they halted, and scouts moved forward to check things out. Now that the thundering noise of eight hundred galloping horses had died away, the men could plainly hear close-by rifle fire. The familiar blue smoke from a fight billowed just over the hill in front of them. A low muttering began as the men wondered who was shooting at who over there. The scouts returned and the bugler blew "To Arms," cutting off any further conversation.

"Be ready, boys. Somethin's up!" yelled Sergeant Burnes.

Will wheeled his horse back into line and pulled out his carbine. He was checking it when the bugler called them into firing line. Though they'd drilled on fighting from horseback, this would be the first time they'd ever done it in battle, and Will tensed. Shooting at men who were shooting back at you was un-nerving enough; to do it on skittish horses was fraught with danger. He looked at Jake, sitting atop his horse right next to him, and bit his lip.

Jake leaned forward in his saddle with an angry scowl and a distant stare. He was itching for a fight. When Jake had that look, he was apt to be reckless.

Will need not have worried about a horse charge; the Colonel changed his mind and ordered the regiment to dismount. Goose had horse duty this time, and he grumbled at being left out of the coming fight.

Even Burnes appeared somewhat rattled. "You might feel

different in a little while," he told Goose. "Some good boys are gonna die here today."

Will felt a chill run up his spine and raise the little hairs on his neck.

The troopers spread out into a two-deep line of battle and walked quickly to the crest of the hill and halted. Across the valley stood a long line of motley dressed Rebels, facing them across the knee-high grass. A few bayonets glinted in the sun and two cannon pointed their gaping maws at them. On the far left of the Rebel line, smoke puffed and rifle-fire crackled as they fired at something that Will couldn't see.

Will's heart pounded and his senses sharpened. They'd finally caught up with Price's main army. A flurry of activity drew his eyes to the middle of the regiment, where the Colonel and his staff sat atop their horses. The Colonel scanned the rebel line through his field glasses—he smiled and calmly spoke to his staff like this happened every day. In stark contrast, the staff fidgeted and gestured nervously.

The regimental colors were on full display up there, a beautiful, inspiring sight, but as Will knew, also a prime target for rebel cannon. A courier left the group, in a big hurry, heading back the way they came.

"Skirmish line!" yelled the Captain, repeated by the Sergeants. Will walked forward of his file partner about ten yards and stopped, as did half of his company. "Forward, march!" The formation walked forward, keeping their intervals, till they had walked about fifty yards into the open valley, where they halted. Puffs of smoke appeared from in front of the rebel formation and a few bullets zipped overhead. The rebel skirmish line began a ragged, halting advance toward them. More puffs of smoke were followed by more buzzing bullets. Will began to get nervous.

"Steady, boys! Hold your fire!" yelled Sergeant Burnes. Will was once again amazed by Burnes' coolness under fire.

Will heard a roar as if there was a tornado coming. Something dark flashed by overhead and crashed into the ground behind him. Then came the distant boom of the cannon that had fired the ball. The Rebel line continued to advance. *They're getting too close, why ain't we shootin'?*

"Front rank, kneel!" yelled Burnes.

Will kneeled, then ducked as another cannonball burst on the ground somewhere behind him. Dirt and grass rained down. A strange trilling yell reached him over the crackle of rifle fire and the boom of cannon. The sounds all merged into one eerie crashing roar.

"Fire by rank!" yelled Burnes. "Front Rank ready, aim, fire!"

Will could barely hear the order, but he leveled his carbine, took aim and fired as one with the front rank. Their own smoke obscured his view and when it cleared, there were gaps in the Rebel line. More gunfire erupted from far off on his right. He glanced that way and was surprised to see a line of blue stretching off for a quarter-mile to his right along the crest of the hill.

Up and down the line, other companies began to fire in volleys. Smoke billowed out from the Union lines. Rebels stumbled or fell, but not enough. "Front rank reload!" Burnes yelled. "Second rank, ready, aim. Fire!"

The second volley was deafening, as it came from behind Will. His ears rang and his eyes burned from the smoke. Sergeant Burnes yelled something he couldn't hear. The rear rank moved up and men plopped down on the ground. Will followed suit. The Rebels were close now and getting closer with each breath he took.

"Fire at will!" yelled Burnes over the noise. Will was already loaded, so he aimed and shot, then took a moment to look for Jake, He found him crouched behind a nearby tree, busy reloading his carbine. Will silently implored his brother to be careful. *Keep your fool head down, Jake! I don't want to be the one to have to explain to Ma if you get killed.* Will realized he couldn't do anything else to protect Jake, and he got chill-bumps as he recalled what Ma had said: 'you might not be able to help him.' As usual, Ma was right! Will had his hands full just following orders. He turned his eyes back to the front, picked out a fat Sergeant in gray, aimed at him and fired. He saw no effect; the man kept striding forward, slightly crouched and waving his men on. He reloaded and fired again at another of the gray-clad men.

All hell broke loose as a ragged line of butternut-clad men topped a rise to their left and lowered their rifles. *They're on our flank!* Will felt his heart flop in his chest and the hair raised up on the back of his neck. He fought the urge to run and turned his carbine and fired at the new threat. He saw a man fall to the ground.

The Rebels fired, and their volley was un-nerving. Most of their shots went high, but this close they couldn't miss and a few men in blue fell. The Rebels charged, screaming that strange yell, rifles lowered and bayonets glinting in the sun. Will frantically reloaded and again resisted the urge to run. He mentally steeled himself as he realized he might die here. Today.

Someone bellowed out a cease-fire order. Will didn't know or care who or even which side the order came from. The last hour had been a whirlwind of Rebels charging, Union Troopers firing, orders and counter-orders. It was all a blur of smoke, booming cannon, crackling rifle fire, zipping Minie balls and screaming men and horses. Will had been praying for it to stop.

They had turned back the flanking attack by the butternut soldiers, but it was a close run thing. The Rebels had run short of ammunition and didn't have the heart to fight with bayonets only. They had melted away after one more volley. The wounded — those who could move — crawled or limped their way back to the Rebel lines.

The firing slowed, then stopped, and an eerie silence fell on the battlefield, broken here and there by officers shouting orders, moaning and crying men, and yells for help. Will's ringing ears added to it rather than subtracting anything from it.

A cloud of blue-white smoke drifted across the meadow until the breeze blew it away. Will wiped his powder-stained face with his neck rag and peeked out from behind his rock. He saw the rebels across the prairie melting back into the woods — leaving their dead and wounded in the tall grass.

Will crouched a little lower behind the rock. *If I can see the Rebs, they can see me.*

He spun around on his back and looked up into a clear blue sky with a few fluffy white clouds drifting by. A red-tailed hawk circled overhead, it screamed out its lonesome call and then soared away. Shadows of clouds glided across the tall grass down in the valley, and the wind scythed through the grass in great waves. He took a deep breath and let it out slowly. *I survived! Where's Jake?* He frantically looked for his brother.

He found Jake lying behind a log not twenty feet away, gazing off into the distance with a puzzled look on his face, as if asking "where'd the Rebels get off to?" Will allowed himself to breathe again and yelled his name until Jake made eye contact with him.

Jake shrugged at Will. "What do we do now?" he yelled.

"Just stay down," yelled Will. "They might have sharpshooters over there. Wait for orders."

Up near the top of the hill, some officers gathered behind a stand of trees. He made out Colonel Owens and Captain Stevens; he didn't know the others. There was some heated discussion and animated gesturing. Someone brought out a white cloth and tied it to a fallen limb. Captain Stevens held it high and waved it about, before stepping out from behind the trees and exposing himself.

Will could barely hear Stevens yell "Parley! Hey over there! Parley!" He hoped the Rebels had better hearing than he did. They did hear it, and soon, a gray-clad party emerged from the opposite woods, waving their own white flag, mounted on a cavalry saber. Their uniforms were worn but presentable, and a few even had sabers hanging from their belts. One wore a fancy hat, pinned up on one side, with a large black feather stuck in it that rippled in the breeze.

Captain Stevens and another officer stepped out to meet them halfway across, still carrying the white flag. Will could not hear any of the discussion. *Are we surrendering, or are they?* It was neither. Soon the word passed down from the officers, to the sergeants, and on down to the troopers. There would be one hour to remove the wounded and dead. Will and Jake were ordered to help recover the wounded.

Finding some of them was easy, they waved and yelled for help. Will spotted a gray-clad sergeant who had been gut shot, and briefly wondered if he might be the sergeant he shot at earlier in the battle. No, that was a much bigger man than this one.

They gingerly picked him up and laid him on the stretcher and carried him to the Union Surgeon's tent. Halfway there, the man asked for water, they stopped long enough for Jake to lend him his canteen. He took a long swig and handed it back. "Much obliged," he said, then lay back on the stretcher and covered his eyes with an arm and made no further conversation.

The surgeon shook his head after he examined him, and pointed to an area off to the side, under a tree. "I've got to spend my time on men I can save," he whispered.

The man moved his arm from his face and opened his eyes when they laid him down. Will hoped he hadn't heard the surgeon, but his eyes told him that he knew. It was likely that this man had been shooting at him just a few minutes ago, but Will found he couldn't hold a grudge. "Good luck, Johnnie," he said.

The Rebel sergeant only nodded in return and put his arm back over his eyes. Again, Will felt a pang of sorrow for the man. He shook it off and hardened his heart; the man was a Johnnie Reb, a sergeant no less, and it was his own fault he was here and got shot.

On their next trip out, two men in filthy civilian clothes waved them over to a body lying in a slight depression. "This your man, here?" one of them asked.

Will and Jake carried the stretcher over to the body. He recognized the man on the ground as one of their own, a trooper named Tilford Taylor.

Will saw right away the dirty yellow hair the other man sported, and he stopped short, stunned to his core. He felt his face flushing and his anger rising. *What the hell is Charley Porter doing here?* He pulled his hat down low on his face and looked only at the boy on the ground, hoping Porter wouldn't recognized him.

Porter did a double take and shouted, "Well, I'll be damned if it ain't Will and Jake Tanner, the Yankee-boys from Millwood!" He turned and yelled to someone behind him "Hey boys, c'mon over here and meet some old friends of mine! Got a couple of galvanized Yankees here!"

Will's hopes had been dashed to the ground and all he could do was stand there in shock.

Two more bushwhackers stomped over, muttering and cursing, anger and disgust written all over their faces. "Hangin's too good fer 'em," said one, spitting tobacco juice on Will's boots. "Bastards," said the other. They both had big knives and revolvers stuck in their belts, and they pushed back their coats and placed their hands on their pistols.

Will's heart pounded so hard in his chest he thought it was coming right out. He was shocked and confused by the sudden appearance of these bushwhackers. This was a dangerous moment, white flag or not, and he took a short step back from the men. His move caught Jake unaware and caused him to stumble backward. The bushwhackers guffawed loudly.

*Where's Sergeant Burnes?* His eyes searched for him and found him about twenty yards away. He had heard the commotion and was ambling over, his right hand on his revolver, his head cocked to listen. Will instantly felt steadier.

Trying to control his voice and ignoring the catcalls, Will cleared his throat and said, "He's one of ours. We'll take him now." Ignoring Porter for a moment, he took a closer look at Taylor, and he could see his chest heave, so the man was still alive. "Let's get him back to the Doc."

Jake didn't respond or move. He had dropped the stretcher, and his face was beet-red, his jaw clenched, and his fists balled up tight. He had recognized Porter and was about to explode.

*If I don't get Jake outta here there's gonna be blood spilt. Likely, ours,* thought Will. He yelled at Jake, "Jake! Let's get him to the Surgeon!"

Jake ignored him again.

"Jake!" Will repeated. The injured man, Taylor, moaned, and that finally broke through to his brother and he broke his stare at Porter. Together, they gently rolled Taylor over and saw a bloody gash on his forehead. It had been a glancing blow. Taylor would live. They loaded him onto the stretcher and picked it up.

Something white fluttered to the ground. Before Will realized it, Porter had scooped it up.

"Well lookee, lookee, what have we got here?" said Porter.

"That's mine," croaked Will, his throat suddenly dry as a dusty road. He coughed to clear it. "Give it back."

Porter ignored Will's protest. He opened the letter and let the envelope fall to the ground. He read out loud, stumbling on some of the words. "Well, well. From Miss Lucy Carter. I do believe I know her. Ain't she the one....? Yeah, she was at your farm the day we burned you out. Looks like you got you a sweetheart there, Will Tanner!" Porter laughed, his mouth twisted into a sneer. "Maybe we'll pay her a visit right soon. I'll be sure an' give her your regards."

By now, Sergeant Burnes had arrived; he stopped a few feet away, watching with a puzzled look on his face. "Ok, son, that's enough," he said. "That there's personal property and you can return it right now." He spoke to Porter as if he was one of their own troopers.

"What are you gonna do about it?" asked Porter. The other bushwhackers spread out a little.

"You there! That's enough!" yelled a burly Rebel Sergeant who had appeared from nowhere. "Give 'im back the damn letter. This here's a truce to remove the wounded an' we ain't gonna dishonor it like this. Git on with your work or git the hell out o' here." The men muttered and they backed away.

Except for Porter, who ignored the Rebel Sergeant and turned to stare at Will. He dropped the letter and it fluttered to the ground at his feet. "You know, Tanner, this ain't over yet. We're gonna have us another go at it here shortly. An' now that I know you're here, I'm gonna be aimin' for you."

Will stopped in his tracks, and gently laid his end of the stretcher on the ground.

"Stop right there, Private!" yelled Burnes.

Will was incensed — everything in his sight seemed to be tinged with red and his vision narrowed until it focused solely on Porter. He knew Porter was goading him, pushing him to lose control, but he couldn't stop himself. He took two steps toward him, leaned down and swished up the letter and envelope and stuffed it them into a coat pocket, his eyes never straying from Porter's hateful leer. He stood up toe to toe with him and looked him in the eyes, his fists balling up, his arms twitching with the urge to swing at his face. Jake appeared in the corner of his vision, and he too glared at Porter with a murderous look. Will was never more grateful for his brother's presence.

Charley's leer was gone and he took a step back. "Ain't this just like old times," he said. "I gotta fight the both of you again? Fine by me!"

"Anytime, Porter!" growled Jake. "You just say the word and we can have it out right here! Right now."

Will put his hand on the pistol stuck in his own belt. "Fists or pistols, Porter. Either one."

The Rebel Sergeant stepped between them and Burnes was suddenly in Will's face. "Stand down, Tanner!" he bellowed.

Burnes' yelling cut through the haze of anger but Will's eyes stayed locked on Porter's while the Rebel Sergeant pushed him away.

"Tanner!" yelled Burnes again. "Back off! Now!"

Will finally broke his stare and moved back to the stretcher. Lieutenant Campbell glanced their way but made no move to intervene.

The Rebel Sergeant walked back to face Burnes. "Apologies to ye. I don't hold with them there murderin' devils, an' I won't tolerate 'em breakin' no truce."

"Obliged, Sergeant," said Burnes, and he touched his hat in a show of respect.

The Rebel Sergeant turned to face the bushwhackers. "You thievin' devils there!" he yelled. "This here is a truce and your own Captain Anderson agreed to it. You will not break this truce, you hear me? You can git back to the lines now or ride on out, I don't give a

197

damn which it is."

"C'mon boys, git back to the line and make sure we're loaded and cocked," said one, spitting tobacco juice to the ground in disgust. The guerillas, except for Porter, backed away, cursing.

The two Sergeants eyed them as they moved off.

Porter stood in place, his eyes holding Will's for several long seconds. Finally, he glanced at Sergeant Burnes before coming back to Will with a sneer. "We'll meet again Will Tanner, maybe today, maybe here, maybe…somewhere else." A hard light came into his eyes, then, and a smirk crossed his face. "Yeah, maybe we'll see you over at old man Carter's place. That'd be somethin' now, wouldn't it? That Lucy Carter—now she's a sweet one!"

Will felt the blood drain from his face and the cold icy hand around his heart return. He tried to step forward but Burnes blocked him.

"I got your attention, now, Tanner?" asked Porter.

"You bastard!" yelled Will around Burnes.

Porter blanched, and his hand moved to his gun. "Don't you ever call me that!"

Burnes now blocked Will's view. "Enough, Tanner!" he yelled. Will took a step back, turned and walked back to the stretcher, glaring at Porter over his shoulder, who hadn't moved.

The Rebel Sergeant pushed Porter backward and away from Will and Jake.

It didn't stop Porter from yelling out, "That's right, Tanner! I'll be payin' 'em a visit 'fore too long! You hear me, Tanner?" He grinned once more, then turned, laughing, and followed his fellows back to the rebel lines.

*****

# Chapter 18

Will jumped when Jake plopped down beside him behind the rock. "When we fire, you take out Porter," he said. "You find that bastard, and you aim right at him. We need to end this right here and now. Are you hearin' me, Will?"

Will nodded. His thoughts were of the same ilk. Still, it shocked him to hear Jake say the words.

"I'll be lookin' for him too," continued Jake, "but you're the better shot. I got to get back to my position." With that, Jake turned to go.

Will grabbed his brother's arm. "Jake, listen to me for once. Keep your head down. They'll push us hard this time."

Jake must have seen the gravity in Will's eyes, because for once he didn't argue. "Ok," he said. "You too." He gathered his legs under him, getting ready to sprint. Just before he did, he said, "If you get a shot at Porter, Will, you take it." Then he was gone from Will's view.

Sergeant Burnes replaced him. Will's first thought was *now what?*

Burnes looked at him funny. "That Porter boy, he one of them who burnt you out?"

"Yeah, he was."

"Figured so," said Burnes. "You boys do somethin' to piss him off?"

"It goes way back, Sergeant," Will said. "I ain't even sure what he thinks we did to him. He blames us for gettin' captured and spending time in a prison camp. But that were'nt our fault, it was his own dang fault."

"Well, to me it looked personal," Burnes said. "That boy is dangerous, he's got cold eyes. Killer eyes."

Will sighed. "Yeah, and now he's threatened somebody who ain't even got nothin' to do with it."

"You know, Tanner." said Burnes. "Ye cain't reason with a rattlesnake, it's just plain beyond their understandin'. Sometimes, you just gotta kill it afore it bites ye."

Will's eyes widened. Was Burnes sayin' what he thought he was?

"There's gonna be another big push here," Burnes continued. "An' it's a cryin' shame, but more soldiers — honorable soldiers, good men — are gonna die here today. If one of those damned bushwhackers was to get killed, then I don't think nobody'd cry over it."

*Yes, he is sayin' just that,* thought Will. *Kill Porter.*

Burnes scanned the Rebel lines. "Well, they're getting' ready over there. It's gonna get hot. Keep your head down, Tanner," he said. Then he was gone.

Will fretted over what Burnes had said. He wasn't too surprised by Jake's feelings on Porter, he'd made that plain. But Sergeant Burnes, probably the man Will most respected in the whole regiment, had just told him the same thing.

*But Porter is a man and not a rattlesnake.* Will had killed the man at the bridge and had been morose about it for days afterward. That man was killed fairly, in battle, as much as killing someone could be called fair. The fight between Will and Jake and Porter was personal. Porter had made it personal. In some strange way, that made gunning for him feel wrong. It was one thing to shoot a man in the heat of battle, while holding your ground and protecting your fellow soldiers. This felt like planning a murder.

Will reminded himself that Porter had threatened Lucy, and he knew Porter meant it. That couldn't be allowed to stand. Will made his decision but he didn't like it. There was no reasoning with Porter, so maybe he was a rattlesnake of sorts, after all. One that was coiled up, ready to strike, and Will needed to do something about it. If it ended here, today, so much the better. He braced himself for what he needed to do.

Sporadic gunfire was already starting up from the Rebel side, and a Minie ball zipped over his head. When he peered out from around his rock, the telltale puff of smoke was directly across the meadow. Was that Porter? He scanned for yellow hair in the Rebel lines but could not find it.

Will stuck his carbine around the rock and aimed at the place where the smoke had been and waited for movement. He waited a long time and was finally rewarded when a brown hat with yellow hair underneath popped up into view. Will adjusted his aim and fired. A chunk of wood flew off the log in front of his target.

You missed me, Tanner!" Porter's voice was faint from so far away across the meadow. "Try again you son of a bitch!"

"Get 'im, Will!" yelled a grinning Jake. "Shoot that sumbitch!"

Sergeant Burnes yelled, "Not now, Tanner! Wait for 'em to come out! Hold your fire, boys! All of you, hold your fire!"

Will nodded to himself as he re-loaded. Burnes was right—he was always right—wait till they charge, then Porter'll be out in the open. He took a deep breath and let it out slowly, keeping his eyes fixed on Porter's position.

A Confederate cannon boomed, and a ball bounced over Will's head with a whirr and exploded somewhere far behind him. He ducked as dirt showered him again.

When he raised his head, what he saw made his heart flip. Hundreds of Confederates in a long, ragged line, two-deep, were stepping their way. It was the big push. He looked for Porter but had lost sight of him.

"Steady, boys, hold your fire now! Wait for the order!" yelled Burnes.

The Confederates advanced to within two hundred yards and still had not fired. "Volley fire! Fire!" came the order from Captain Carter, relayed by Sergeant Burnes.

"Pour it to 'em boys!" yelled Burnes.

Will gave up on Porter and aimed and fired as one with his regiment. A sheet of flame leapt from their carbines and smoke rolled out in front, obscuring the meadow. When the smoke cleared, the Rebels had staggered to a halt, huge gaps now in their lines where men had fallen. They began to fire back, their officers urging them forward.

"Fire at will!" came the next order. Will reloaded and scanned for Porter, holding his fire, waiting for his shot.

Then he spotted him—he was now to Will's right at an oblique angle. It should have been an easy shot, and Will took careful aim. He pulled his trigger just as Porter fell to the ground. *Did I get him?* No, Porter staggered back to his feet. Will reloaded, keeping his eyes on Porter, but he faded away into the smoke and was gone.

All Charley Porter could see of the Yankees was the dark outlines of their hats as they poked up to aim. He could not find Tanner amongst them. He knew about where he was, he'd taken one shot at him already. In the waning light and the smoke, he'd lost sight of him. He was not sure which of the smoky shadows over there was Tanner. He aimed at one of the shadows and fired, but the head had ducked just before, so he was sure he'd missed.

As he reloaded, he stumbled over something soft in his path. It was a blood-soaked body. "God-dammit!" He had dropped his cartridge, and he groped for another in his box. His right foot tangled in the man's haversack and he fell face forward in front of him. As he fell, he heard the zip of a Minie ball whizz by overhead. He lay there for a moment, stunned by his fall and the sheer noise of battle. Bullets were zipping and thumping, and more men fell.

Charley began to fear he might not survive this battle. *I ain't even supposed to be here. We should be out raidin' and burning their goddam farms. Why'd Anderson agree to us bein' in a battle line like this? I get killed so he can get hisself promoted?*

Charley's heart was racing and his hands trembled. He willed himself to stand up and reload, but all he could manage was to kneel. Another Minie ball thunked into the dead man next to him. He flung away his rifle and dived to the ground.

It was much safer down on the ground, the bullets mostly whizzed by overhead, and only a few scythed through the grass. Charley had had enough of this kind of fighting. He left his rifle where it lay and crawled around the dead man and toward the tree line they had left just minutes ago.

There was a commotion to Will's right. Sergeants were bellowing and men were screaming. Some nearby troopers were turning to shoot toward their own lines. Will was confused until Jake yelled in his ear, "They got into our lines, it's a melee! Let's go!" Jake jumped up and ran towards the fight. Men were clubbing at each other with rifles, stabbing at each other with bayonets, swinging pistol butts, even throwing rocks. After a stunned second, Will took off after Jake.

Before he got there, Will saw him swing his carbine butt-first at someone who went to his knees from the blow. Another gray-clad Rebel aimed a pistol at Jake. Sergeant Burnes appeared from nowhere and shoved the man sideways and he fell to the ground. The man rose and tried to shoot at Burnes, but his pistol misfired. Burnes went for his own pistol but it got stuck in his belt. By this time, the Rebel had cocked his gun for another shot and was aiming at Burnes. Will could see that Burnes was going to get shot. Without thinking, Will stopped in his tracks, took aim, and shot the man who fell sideways. Burnes looked at Will and gave him a little salute.

A huge volley ripped through the screams and the shouts and Will automatically ducked, though no bullets came near him. When he looked up, he'd lost sight of Jake. He didn't think about what he was doing, he just ran toward the fight. *Where's Jake?* He stopped to reload and the fight was over by the time he got there. The Sergeants were reforming the line, pulling and tugging at troopers, and Confederate prisoners were being herded by angry Union soldiers with bayonets mounted on their long rifles.

*Bayonets? When did the infantry get here? I sure am glad to see those boys!*

Will's mind was a confused jumble of thoughts. Porter was forgotten. *Where's Jake? He was in the middle of all this!*

His heart pounding like a sledgehammer, Will turned over a dead trooper that looked like Jake. It wasn't him. He scanned the walking wounded as they shambled by. Jake wasn't among them, either. Will was about to panic when Sergeant Burnes appeared in his face, yelling something. He cupped his ringing ears to hear him. "Jake's over here," Burnes yelled. "He's fine, just got a scratch."

Relief flooded into him like a drink of cold water on a hot day. He spotted Jake laying behind his log and plopped down next to him. Blood oozed from a cut on his cheek and dripped from his jaw to the ground.

Jake shook his head no when Will offered him his neck rag. "Ain't even gonna need a stitch," he said. "Prob'bly won't even leave a scar." He smiled and tugged his hat down tighter on his head. "I got me one, Will! I cold-cocked him with my gun." Jakes eyes were glazed, and he babbled on and on without pause. "Didn't kill 'im though. He was regular infantry, so that's all right. Reckon we beat 'em off, didn't we? Think they'll come at us again?" Jake babbled on and Will tuned out most of it.

Will looked around him. The hillside was strewn with wounded and dead. The dead he saw were mostly Rebels, but here and there lay a blue-coated body. There were a few wounded Union troopers being tended to or carried off. "Looks to me like we gave 'em a good beatin'," he said to Jake. "An' the Infantry's here. I think the Rebs are done. They won't come at us again, not today anyhow."

Jake looked disappointed. "I still ain't got me a bushwhacker. Kilt one, I mean. I fired at Porter, but I missed." said Jake. "I still want that sumbitch dead, Will. For what he done. Did you get him?"

Will shook his head no. "I missed him too, then I lost sight of him in the crowd."

Jake's dazed grin disappeared. "Dammit. What are we gonna do, now? We need to kill that sumbitch."

Will didn't know if he should even try to curb Jake's blood-lust. And anyway, how was it different from his own mind on the matter? He wanted Porter dead too. No, that wasn't quite right. He wanted Porter to leave them be, but that might take killing him. Will decided to forget it for now. "We done good today. You done good," he said.

Jake perked up at Will's compliment. "We did, didn't we. We beat 'em good!" He jumped up and ran over to talk with Eli and Goose.

The firing had stopped, and Will took a good long look over the log. A line of blue-clad Union infantry was advancing across the field, bayonets lowered. The Rebels had disappeared except for those who couldn't, the ones who lay writhing or crawling on the open ground between the lines. Many more lay still. Will couldn't tell from here if any of them was Porter.


Charley Porter heard the sounds of battle behind him; the yelling and screaming and grunting, the thump of rifle butts on human flesh, the ringing clash of bayonets and knives. The shooting tapered off, then there was one loud volley and bullets whizzed overhead again, and some zipped through the grass nearby. Charley crawled faster. The firing tapered off again and he heard the Yankees cheering behind him. The battle was lost.

He didn't care. "God-dammit, God-dammit," he mumbled as he crawled. "What the hell were we doin' out there anyway? Goddam useless generals."

A Rebel officer stared at him from above. "Stand up like a man, son." He looked Charley over, then said, "Oh. Apologies, soldier. Get yourself to the aid wagon. The surgeons will fix you right up."

*Am I shot?* Charley looked at his legs and saw the blood all over his pants. He frantically searched his legs, feeling them all over and found no wound. *Must be that dead man's blood all over me.* He didn't bother to correct the officer. *If he thinks I'm wounded, let him think it.* "Yes, Sir. Headed that way." The officer nodded and walked off toward the trees.

He stood, using only one leg and dragging the bloodiest one, faking an injury, and limped away. Instead of heading to the surgeon's, he angled toward the horse pickets where Darnell was holding their horses.

Darnell saw him limping then saw the blood. "You hurt?"

"Just a scratch. We got new orders. We need to mount up and head south."

Darnell gave him a puzzled look. "Ain't nobody told me."

"Well I'm tellin' you now, Darnell. Untie our mounts and let's go."

Darnell shrugged. He separated the reins and was handing one set to Charley when a Minie ball bounced off a tree and grazed the rump of his horse. The horse reared and turned, jerking the reins from his hands. The horses bolted and disappeared over the hill. Darnell just looked at Charley and shrugged again.

Charley was furious. "God-dammit, Darnell cain't you do anything right?" All his money was in his saddlebags. "I need my damn horse!" he yelled. He heard the crack of musket fire from behind and more Minie balls whizzed by, some clipping branches from a nearby bush. Charley looked over his shoulder and saw a line of blue-clad infantry advancing across the field. *We got to get the hell out of here, now!*

He saw more horses a few yards away, but the Yankees were already too close. Other men were already mounted up and fleeing from the battle. There was only one thing to do. *Run!* "Come on Darnell, we got to go now, or get captured or killed. That way!" He pointed to a gully that led down the hill. It looked like it led to the woods about fifty yards off.

Charley and Darnell ran at a crouch down the gully toward the trees. Bullets whizzed by over their heads. They continued on down the gully until they reached the trees and ducked behind them.

They each took cover behind a tree, but Charley knew they couldn't stay there long. "Keep goin'!" he yelled. They ran some more through the woods till they came out into another small clearing. Charley couldn't believe his eyes. There, on the far side of the glade, stood four saddled horses, including theirs, calmly nibbling at the tall grass. The mounts picked up their heads and perked up their ears at them, then went back to their meal.

"You're better with horses, Darnell, you go get 'em. Slowly now," said Charley.

Darnell eased his way to the horses, talking to them softly. They allowed him to grab the reins with only a gentle neigh. Charley walked quickly over and mounted up.

"They went this way, I saw 'em duck into these here woods," came a distant voice behind them.

Charley heard men crashing through the trees. *Yankees!* "Let's go, now, Darnell. We got to ride!" They spurred the horses into a gallop. Looking back, Charley caught a glimpse of blue-uniformed men entering the glade. Then the trees hid them from sight.

"Here comes the Infantry back, but they ain't in no hurry," said Jake.

"Yeah, I think the Johnnies broke off and run. I think they're all played out," said Sergeant Burnes. He gave Will a funny look. "You saved my bacon back there, Tanner. I won't forget it."

Will shrugged. "You saved Jake."

Burnes smiled. "It's what we do for each other. Thank ye, anyway."

Before Will could get too embarrassed, a commotion arose from a knot of officers up the hill. The officers broke up with salutes and handshakes, a bugler blew assembly, and the men formed up into a ragged line. They were told to get their gear together, fill up their cartridge boxes, draw rations, and be ready to mount up in fifteen minutes. Scuttlebutt was that they were riding out yet again.

As they walked off toward the wagons, Jake complained, "Now we done rode all week, day and night, fought a battle, an' now we gotta ride again?"

"I recall you bein' the first one to sign up for this," said Will.

Ain't this what you wanted?" Will was only half-joking with his brother, he was exhausted himself.

Jake looked chagrined and managed a weak smile. "Yeah I reckon you're right. Dammit."

"Well, be glad it ain't us buryin' them poor Rebs," said Eli.

"Or the other way round," said Goose.

Jake didn't reply. Instead he stuffed his uncooked rations into his saddlebags and mounted his horse with a groan.

When Will had finished his preparations and mounted up himself, he took the opportunity to ride out into the field. He scanned each body he came across, but Porter wasn't among them. He made a quick trip to the surgeon's tent. Again, he couldn't find Porter.

Porter had escaped. He remembered Porter's threat and his body gave an involuntary shudder. But he figured the bushwhackers would now head south with the Rebel Army to lick their wounds and regroup. He told himself that Porter's threats meant nothing.

Yet a small, nagging doubt remained and ate at him. What if Porter slunk off on his own and tried something? He'd deserted before, so why not. Will tried to shake that dreaded idea from his head as quickly as it came. *It's not likely he would try anything on his own. A coward like he is will need a gang around him. An' it's doubtful any of them will go along, not with thousands of Federals out lookin' for 'em.*

His worries were interrupted by the bugler blowing again. It was time to form up and move out. Will walked his horse over and took his place beside Jake and mounted up.

"Well, At least I get another chance to bag me a bushwhacker," said Jake. "We're goin' after Bloody Bill's gang. Seems that bunch is headed east, and we're going after 'em."

"East?" asked Will.

Jake nodded. "Somebody found some orders from that sumbitch General Price ordering Anderson and his gang to St. Charles to burn the railroad. An' then they found tracks where a bunch of horses crossed the river just east of here. So...."

The color drained from Will's face.

"What?" asked Jake.

"They'll go right by Millwood."

Jake's eyes widened. "Shit! That ain't good. Wait? You reckon Porter is with 'em?"

"Well he ain't amongst the dead out there in the field. An' he ain't amongst the wounded over at the surgeon's tent. So, yeah. I'd bet on it."

"Dammit!"

The order to move out came down the line. Will kicked his horse into a trot, as did Jake beside him. Sure enough, the column back tracked over the road they'd come in on.

Jake yelled over the noise, "What are we gonna do, Will, we gotta do somethin'!"

"Let me think on it, Jake. For now, we're headin' that way and it's about as fast as we can go anyhow."

Jake gave Will a hard stare. "All right, Will. But don't expect me to sit back and do nothin' this time, if it comes to it."

Will glared at his brother. This time Jake would not avert his stare. He realized that he felt the same, anyway, and he softened his gaze. Lucy was in danger too. This time, they might have to do something besides hide. He nodded to Jake which seemed to mollify him for now.

*I need to talk to Sergeant Burnes!* Will spurred his horse ahead and pulled up alongside the company guidon, where Burnes rode. He looked around, no officers were in sight.

"Sergeant Burnes?" said Will. "I need to talk to you."

Burnes took a look around himself, and satisfied, fished his pipe from a pocket. "Did you kill that rattlesnake we spoke of?"

"No, we missed him." said Will. "But that ain't what I need to ask you about."

Burnes' eyebrows shot up, "All right, what is it?"

Will took a deep breath. "I heard we're heading east—goin' after Anderson?" It was more of a statement than a question.

"Well you ain't supposed to know that just yet but I reckon you can tell which way we're goin' as good as anybody." Burnes found his tobacco pouch in another pocket. "We're trailin' him, an' right now he's goin' east. He's prob'ly tryin' to distract us from followin' Price. Price is headed west to God knows where, but Anderson is headed east, so it looks to me like it's workin'."

"I heard he's headed to St Charles," said Will. "That road will take them right through Lincoln County. Anderson and that gang...."

Sergeant Burnes interrupted, "Tanner, you ever hear of something called a telly-graph? Well they got one that runs along the railroad all the way back to St Louis. They already been warned. If Anderson gets that far, he will step right in a big ole hornet's nest. I don't think he'll go far, he ain't stupid."

Will was not convinced. "They ain't no troopers left over there to come out and meet 'im, are they? Ain't all of us over here defendin' against Price?"

"There's some infantry in St. Charles. He knows that. Trust me on that, Will. He'll go east a while, then break off and run away. He ain't one for followin' orders nohow."

Will was getting frantic. *Infantry won't get there in time, even if they get sent!*

Just then a messenger rode back to the company, stopping to talk with Captain Stevens, who rode at the front of the column. The courier saluted and then galloped away behind them.

The Captain passed the order to the Sergeants, and word filtered down the column to the troopers. What Will heard chilled him. "They cut the telegraph line....Rocheport....double quick...."

"Better get back in line," said Burnes. "You heard the man." He put his pipe and tobacco away. "If they cut the telly-graph line, there must be a ruckus goin' on."

Back in place beside Jake, he passed on his conversation with Sergeant Burnes. "Burnes thinks Anderson will break off and not go near St. Charles. We're gonna try and catch him at Rocheport. There's another regiment comin' at him from the north. If we can catch him Rocheport, there won't be any more need to worry. If we don't.... We'll worry about it then."

Jake wasn't mollified this time. "We need to get Porter and settle this thing."

Will nodded. "I agree. You an' me, we'll look for him at Rocheport." That mollified Jake for the moment. But Will still worried. *I hope Jake ain't planning to do something stupid.*

The order came to break out into a gallop and talking became impossible. But it didn't keep Will from worrying.

*If we don't catch 'em at Rocheport, then what? What if we don't get Porter? If they get to Millwood before we do, it won't matter if we catch 'em later, it'll be too late for Ma and the boys and Lucy.*

He shook off those dark thoughts. *First things first. Let's see if we can catch him.*

\*\*\*\*\*

# Chapter 19

As the fifteenth topped the rise, Will heard gunshots in the distance. The glow he'd thought to be the setting sun turned out to be from towering flames down in the town of Rocheport, now laid out below them. It looked to Will as if the whole town was afire. The flames leapt high into the air and the wind carried the sound and the sharp smell of smoke up to the troopers. He could see men milling about down there but they weren't fighting the flames; instead, they were the source of the gunfire, firing their pistols and rifles into the air.

Will's heart quickened. "That Anderson down there?" he asked.

"Well, it looks like his work," said Sergeant Burnes. "If that's him down there burnin' and lootin', then maybe we caught him this time."

The order came to dismount and form into a skirmish line. The two small mountain howitzers they'd brought were unlimbered and pointed down toward the town. Colonel Owens sent scouts forward to find where the enemy lines were. In a few minutes one rode back and conferred with the Colonel. Word passed back to the company; the men down there were the Thirty-ninth Infantry — Union Troops. The cannon limbered back up.

Colonel Owens rode forward with his staff and parleyed with some officers who rode up from the town. When he returned, the regiment mounted back up and rode down toward the town.

Scuttlebutt passed down the line; Anderson had been here and gone, they'd missed him by a few hours. Will assumed that Anderson had burned the town, but he soon saw that wasn't right. Instead of trying to douse the flames, Union soldiers were feeding the fires, throwing chairs, clothing and other items into the flames. Some hooted and danced while off to the side, sobbing women and crying children stood by, helplessly watching the flames.

"Sergeant Burnes? What's goin' on here?" asked Jake.

Burnes sighed. "Rocheport is a Secesh town." He paused. "Well, it was a Secesh town. You recall what happened over at Centralia, don't you?"

Jake nodded. "Yeah, I know."

Burnes continued anyway. "Anderson massacred our boys on that train. They were on leave and not armed. Shot 'em as they stood with their hands raised. Scalped 'em. Butchered 'em. Then they set up a trap and slaughtered a hunnert an' fifty more of the Thirty-ninth Mounted Infantry that rode to their aid. Anderson had the black flag out—gave 'em no quarter—and there weren't no survivors. They run 'em down, and shot 'em, scalped 'em, cut up the bodies, Walked on 'em. Rode on 'em." He paused. "Well, these here boys is the Thirty-ninth."

"Damn!" said Jake.

Will had heard—they had all heard—about the massacre at Centralia but he hadn't known the details. It was hard to believe. Except for the scalps. He'd seen the scalps.

Burnes continued, "So some of these boys are takin' a bit of revenge."

Jake nodded and smiled. He spat over his horse. "Serves 'em right."

"No, Jake, this ain't right, no matter if they done it, we cain't be doin' it too," said Will.

"Dammit Will, You takin their side now?"

Will gave him the evil eye before he answered. "I ain't takin their side, but we need to get the ones that done it, not these folks." He wished he'd just kept his mouth shut. He should have known better than to say anything to Jake. It was getting harder and harder just to talk to him.

"Well, maybe it ain't 'xactly right, but…." Jake shrugged. "These folks been shelterin' and supplyin' Anderson and his like. I ain't feelin' too sorry for 'em."

Burnes cut in, "Only thing I know for sure is that this is gettin' out of hand. They loot, rob and murder, then we do the same, and then they do worse."

Burnes' words silenced Jake. The only sounds now were crackling flames, sobbing women, and cursing men.

As they passed by the weeping women, most of them averted their gaze. Some were bolder and cursed at the blue-clad troopers. Will looked away, too ashamed to meet their eyes. There'd be no offers of cool spring water or a bite to eat, not from this town. He realized there was something else strange about the scene. "Where's the men?"

"If they was smart, they skedaddled," said Burnes. "These boys have got their blood up, and I reckon they'd hang 'em, if they could find 'em."

The Regiment slowly passed through the town, and the noise abated and fell behind them. Will was glad to get beyond the carnage and the hatred. Burnes was right. *This war is getting out of hand. How are we ever gonna be neighbors after all this?*

The order came to speed up and his tired horse broke into a trot. Anderson was still ahead, somewhere, and Colonel Owens wanted to catch him. The order came to gallop, and the only sound was of pounding hooves.

Charley Porter slid from his saddle and collapsed in the shade of a locust tree. The last two days had been a nightmare. They had barely stayed ahead of the Union pursuit.

Their original force of over two-hundred guerillas was now whittled down by desertion to eighty or ninety men. Exhausted men had simple peeled off into the brush and gone home. Or elsewhere. Anderson had finally called a halt at a crossroads near Florence.

"This ain't right," croaked Charley. "We shoulda had it out with them Yanks before now. They was several places we could a ambushed 'em. What's happened to Bill, he gone soft?"

Darnell just shrugged. A few seconds later, he was snoring.

Despite his exhaustion, Charley's hunger wouldn't let him sleep. His stomach grumbled and he lay there and fumed. *We coulda taken them wagons back there, with all that damn food in 'em. Yet here we are, starvin' near to death.*

He got up and searched thru his saddlebags and found a small piece of dried up ham and a few crumbs of cornbread. He bolted those down and took a big swig from his canteen. It only made him hungrier. And angrier.

He laid back and pulled his hat down over his eyes, and he'd just closed them when he woke to the sound of men and horses stirring about. The gang was mounting up to ride and the sun was considerably lower in the sky. He shook his head to clear the cobwebs and kicked Darnell awake.

He mounted up, but when the column turned west, Charley became confused. "Ain't we goin' to St. Charles?"

"Anderson changed his mind again," said Bose. "We're headed west, where Bill's got friends."

Charley felt his frustration rising. Going west would not get him closer to the Carter place. There was only one thing he could do, he decided, and his decision calmed him. *I've had enough of this. From now on, me an' Darnell, we go our own way.*

He held Darnell back until they were the last ones in the column. Then they turned off into the brush. To his surprise, there were six other riders already there. He put his hand on his pistol.

"Hold on there, fella," said one rider, holding up a hand. "We ain't got no beef with you."

"What are you doin' here? You hightailin' it?" asked Charley.

"We call it sick leave," said the man. The others laughed.

"We're starvin'," another man said. "An' Bill ain't actin' right. He got the big head from that General goddam Price makin' him a captain an' all. He's got himself some big idees now. We're out of food and low on powder. We done talked and decided we ain't goin' on just yet."

Charley smiled, relaxing his gun hand. "You boys got a plan?"

The men looked at each other sheepishly. "Naw. Just find some grub. Then some likker," one responded.

"Well I got a plan," said Charley. "If you boys want to ride with us, we could use the extra guns."

"Why should we do that?" asked the first man.

Charley grinned. "I know where there's a big bag of gold coin, and all we gotta do is take it from an old man and a girl."

"Gold? Where?"

"A bit east of here. About two day's ride."

"Cain't eat gold," said another man.

Charley leaned back in his saddle. "I know this country. I been here before. There's a farm about two miles yonder. They'll be food there. Hell, there's lots of farms hereabouts. Plenty of food."

"We'll eat first, then go get that gold?" asked the first man.

"That's my plan," said Charley.

The men looked at each other and shrugged. "Well, by God, let's go then."


Will's horse shambled along listlessly with its head down. After two days and nights in the saddle, the horses were about played out. The men, too, were bone-weary. Some were fast asleep atop their slowly walking horses. They had ridden fast and hard and light but had failed to catch up to Bill Anderson and his gang. The only bright side was that recent rain had tamped down the dust.

At a crossroads near Florence, the Colonel ordered a halt. Men slipped from their horses and collapsed into the grass while the officers conferred and the spent horses grazed. Anderson's trail had abruptly turned west, and the officers scratched their heads over it.

Sergeant Burnes assigned picket duty and Will drew the short straw. "Anderson's turned west," said Burnes, as they walked to a nearby tree. "Just like I told you he would. He ain't no fool."

The mid-morning sun had burned away the light fog from the rain and it was getting warm. Will took a swig from his canteen and wandered over to the trail of trampled earth and debris that Anderson's men had left behind. It was plain to see they had stopped here a while. When they left, they took the west road.

"Looks like maybe eighty of 'em," said Burnes. "Look over here, Will. Tell me what you see."

Will hadn't heard Burnes come up from behind. He looked at the tracks. Most of the tracks headed west, but here and there a trail cut through the brush.

"Some of 'em have peeled off," said Will.

"Good eye. I expect that's right. There's news of Price gettin' beat at Westport. I think he's played out. That may have discouraged these boys somewhat."

Will took a better look and his heart stopped when he recognized the hoofprint of Charley Porter's horse. "Dammit!"

215

"What?"

"That track there, that's Porter's horse. He cut through the brush here.

"How do you know for sure that's Porter's horse?" Burnes asked.

"It's him," replied Will. "I can tell by the shoe, see that mark there that runs crosswise? I spent a whole damn day bein' drug behind his horse, lookin' down at his tracks, and I know that's his horse." Will followed the trail into the brush a short way. "Looks like two horses."

"Tanner, get back here. It might be a trap, they might double back on you."

"Yeah, I guess that could be." He pulled his pistol from his belt and cocked it. He walked further into the brush, following the trail, checking for movement or sound.

"Well, damn," said Burnes, pulling his own pistol and following Will.

They came upon more tracks that merged together. Will made out the tracks of eight horses. The trail was now very easy to follow. The riders had turned back to the main road and headed east.

Will felt sick. He knew where Porter was going. *I know it's him. An' I know what he said he'd do!* "Sergeant," he said. "Porter split off from Anderson and headed east. I need to go after 'im."

Burnes shook his head. "No, Tanner. You got to stay with the regiment."

Will became frantic. "He's headed to the Carter place," he said. "You know what he's plannin'! You heard him say it! I gotta go after 'im!" he repeated.

Burnes stared at him for a long time. "No, what you need to do is to follow orders. Or else, they'll hang you or have you shot for desertion."

"Dammit!" said Will. "Sergeant, I gotta do somethin'. I cain't just ride on while my family gets massacred!"

"What we can do is warn 'em," said Burnes. "We can use the telly-graph to get word to them, an' they can hide out till it's over. Let's go talk to the Colonel, see what he can do."

Will sat there, thinking. The telegraph was faster than any horse. *If they can get a message to Ben Carter in time, he'll take everybody to a safe place. It just might work. What if it don't?* A plan began to form in Will's mind as he walked back to camp. Burnes's remark about being shot as a deserter sobered him, so he cast it aside for now. *Let's see what The Colonel says.*

Charley rode off from the burning farmhouse feasting on salted ham and biscuits. Behind him, smoke rose across the setting sun. The farmer had stood his ground with a shotgun, giving his wife and a small boy time to run off and hide. He had killed the man with one shot to the chest, but the woman and her brat weren't worth chasing down.

They had fed and watered the horses before firing the barn. *Too bad he didn't have no horses. I could sure use a fresh mount.*

Someone found a jug of whiskey and passed it around — before long some of the men were tipsy. When they happened on a small creek, they grumbled about making camp for the night.

"We need to put a few more miles between us and that farm," said Charley. "The smoke will bring neighbors, and there might be some Yankees around."

"So why did we burn it?" asked the man called Blake.

Porter had to think about that a second. "Hell, Blake, the dang man was a Yankee, he even talked like one."

"Dammit, Porter," said Blake. "The horses is exhausted. We been ridin' three days, and they need a rest. Hell, we need a rest."

"You can rest when you're dead, which you might soon be if they catch us here."

Blake laughed. "You skeert of 'em now, are ye? We ain't, so we're stoppin' here." He pulled up and the rest of the men stopped too. They dismounted and made camp.

This angered Charley. The men just wanted to get drunk. He considered riding on, just him and Darnell. Darnell would follow him wherever he went. These men would not. If they went their own way, he'd never see them again, and he needed these men. Charley sighed and dismounted. "All right, we'll stop for a few hours, but we're on the road again before daylight."

They made camp and built a small fire. Darnell made coffee, and Charley feasted on the ham and biscuits and molasses they'd stolen.

He looked around at the six men — they were haggard, filthy and exhausted. Their eyes were hollowed out, and in the flickering firelight, their heads looked like skulls. He figured he must look the same to them. *That's good,* he thought. *The scarier we look, the better.*

A man pulled a jug from his saddlebag and passed it around. Charley declined. Blake made introductions. "This here's Carson, and that there's Buck and that's Lonzo out there playin' sentry. These two here are the Hopkins brothers, Tim and Zell. I know you, Charley Porter, but who's your friend here?"

"This here's Darnell. We been ridin' together a good while."

Darnell didn't even look up from where he was sleeping with his head on his saddle and his hat over his face.

"So, what's the plan, Porter?" asked Buck.

Porter spun his web. "There's this farm I know of, over in Lincoln County. The owner is a fat ole rich man, he raises cotton and tobaccy, got lots of slaves, and he's got a big ole bag of gold coin squirreled away."

"An' you know where he keeps it?" asked Blake.

"Not yet, but he'll talk, soon as we put a gun to his head. Or maybe his daughter's head. She's a right fine girl, too."

The men laughed and nudged each other.

Zell perked up. "He's got a daughter?"

"Yep," Charley said. "An' a wife, but she's old."

"Well, Carson, you get the wife and I get the girl," said Zell.

Carson didn't laugh. "We'll see who gets what."

The men guffawed loud enough to get a dirty look from Lonzo. "How the hell we supposed to hide with you jackasses makin' noise like that?" he asked.

"Lonzo's right, we need to keep the noise down," said Blake. "We need one man awake at all times; this is Yankee country. What do you think, swap out every hour or so?"

Charley bristled. He didn't like Blake takin' over like that; this was his plan, and he should be in charge. He bit his lip and kept his thoughts to himself.

"Well, that's a plan," said Blake staring right at Charley. He stood and took another swig from the jug.

Charley noticed Blake's eyes wander a little. Blake was getting tight.

"Well, I reckon I'll get some shuteye," Blake said. "Buck, you spell Lonzo in about an hour."

Blake had brushed Charley aside like he was a little boy, and it rankled. It was an insult, and Charley felt it deeply. He considered his options; there was six of them against only him and Darnell, and Darnell was an unknown quantity in this situation. He needed these men, he recalled. If his plan worked, there would time enough to deal with them. For now, all Charley could do was glare at Blake as he stood there by the fire, swaying unsteadily.

Blake took another swig, set the jug down, and staggered a few feet away, unbuttoned his pants and made water.

"Hell, Blake, why don't you just piss in the dang fire?" said Buck.

Blake didn't answer. He just grunted and stumbled off to his blanket, rolled up in it and laid down.

Inside, Charley seethed with anger over Blake's gall. *I should've just shot him and been done with it.* But he hadn't, and now it was too late. The others had noticed, and Charley could see the sneers from across the fire. Especially the one called Buck; his eyes bored into Charley, a crooked smirk pasted on his face.

*We'll see who's smiling when this is done*, thought Charley, as he stood up and went to make his own pallet. He laid down and pulled his hat over his face. Underneath his blanket, he pulled out his pistol and closed his eyes with his thumb still on the hammer.


Will paced back and forth, waiting for an answer. Finally, the Captains and Lieutenants saluted the Colonel as the officer's meeting ended. The Colonel went to his tent, and the junior officers headed back to their respective companies. Two couriers jumped astride their mounts and galloped off down the southern road.

After an animated discussion with Captain Stevens, Sergeant Burnes saluted him, and strode to where Will stood, impatient to hear what had been decided. Burnes told Will that the news of Anderson's change of direction would be passed on. They'd also notify headquarters about the small group headed east and had asked for the sheriff to get a warning to Ben Carter. The Home Guard would be called up, too.

Will went white. The Sheriff leaned Southern; he had never gone out of his way to help the Yankees. The Home Guard was worthless. Burnes' words didn't reassure him. "No, Sergeant, that won't help. The Sheriff...."

Burnes cut him off. "It's all we can do, Will. We got our orders: follow Anderson. We'll be mountin' up and goin' after him in a minute. Don't fret it none, the Home Guard, they'll run 'em off." Burnes looked away as he said it, a sure tell that he didn't like what he was saying.

Will looked down at his own feet so as not to give away his own bitter disappointment. He was being torn to pieces between his duty to his regiment and duty to his family, and he agonized over what to do. When he recalled the threats Porter had made, he felt an intense dread overcome him that drained his blood and left him cold.

Will had no faith in the Home Guard—he'd seen them in action—they were just a bunch of old men and young boys carrying old shotguns and pitchforks, playing at being soldiers. He saw in his mind how this was going to play out. They would be slow to gather, if they even got the word. *Porter will get there before the Home Guard even gets out of bed. Ma and my brothers—and Lucy, they'll all be killed!*

In his mind Will replayed the scene back in August; the house and barn afire, the smoke rising high in the sky, the crackle of flames, Missy the mule screaming as she was shot, his Ma bruised and weeping. He saw again, the men with guns drawn and pointed at his family, and the crazed, gleeful look in Porter's eyes. He imagined Lucy with Porter's gun pointed at her head. At *Lucy!* And he remembered Porter's threats during the truce.

'I'll be payin' 'em a visit,' Porter had said. Will had to do something! But what?

The bugler blew assembly and Will mounted his horse without thinking. The lead horses of the regiment turned onto the road leading west. Will felt trapped like he was in a dream he couldn't awaken from. He was in a trance, lost deep in his own thoughts. Unguided, his horse moved forward with the troop.

It was then he noticed that Jake was gone.

Struggling to contain his growing panic, Will asked Eli, "Where's Jake, you seen 'im?"

"Said he had the quick step," Eli said. "He pulled off into the brush back yonder."

Will thought quick. "Tell Sergeant Burnes I got it myself an' I'm goin' back an' check on Jake."

Eli eyed him suspiciously. "All right, Will."

Will rode back to where Porter's tracks had left the road. There, just in the brush, out of sight of the road, stood Jake, holding the reins to his horse and studying the tracks on the ground. He looked up and frowned as Will approached.

"What the hell are you doin'?" asked Will. He knew it wasn't the right way to broach the subject—any subject—with Jake. It had just blurted out before he could think about it.

"What does it look like I'm doin'? I'm goin' after Porter," retorted Jake.

"No, Jake, you ain't. Ma wanted me to protect you as best I could, an' this ain't the way." Will immediately regretted saying that. *I might as well as told him to go.*

Now Jake looked puzzled. "She said what?"

Will shook his head. "I ain't got time to argue with you. Get back to the regiment."

Jake turned red. "I'll show you what I think about that!" He mounted his horse, yanked its head around and galloped east through the scrub.

"Dammit, Jake!" Will could only stare where Jake had disappeared and shake his head in disbelief. *Damn Damn Damn! It's all fallin' apart!* Jake had reacted to Porter in his usual reckless way, and now, Will would have to fix it somehow. He didn't see how it could be fixed.

Will had to make an impossible choice. If he left the regiment, he could be shot or hung as a deserter.

If he didn't go after Jake and bring him back, then Jake could be shot or hung for the same reasons.

Jake was right about one thing; if somebody didn't go and warn them, everyone he loved could die at the hands of Charley Porter. So was Jake right, after all?

Will had to make up his mind; the slanting sunlight warned of night coming. Every minute he waited was a minute wasted. He thought of Ma, Ike, Seth, Nate, and Lucy, they all could die if he didn't go help Jake. He'd rather die himself than see them hurt. The last thought was the tipping point, and he made his decision.

He took one last look westward where the dust from the regiment still hung in the air. "You're a damned fool, William Tanner," he said to nobody. "Just like Jake."

Will's mind turned to the thing he had to do. *I hope Ma will forgive me when the bill comes due.*

He turned his horse to follow Jake and kicked it into a run.

*****

# Chapter 20

Someone kicked Charley's rump and he jerked awake. His pistol was still in his hand, cocked and ready to fire, and his finger twitched on the trigger.

"Yore turn to keep watch," said Buck. The man was only a dark shadow against the faint glow of their campfire.

"All right, dammit. I'm getting' up," said Charley, as he quietly uncocked his gun. He threw off his blanket, grabbed a piece of ham from his saddlebag and a cup of coffee from the fire before walking down the trail to take his post.

He leaned against a small tree and watched and listened for any sign of pursuit. As he sipped his coffee, he refined his plan. He'd lied about the gold to get the others to go along with him. *Who knows, maybe Ole Man Davis does have some gold. Well, hell's bells, I reckon he's got to have some somewhere. An' these idiots won't know any difference. An' if they beat the old man to death to make him talk, so much the better.*

For a moment, he thought he heard muted conversation from somewhere out there in the darkness and he pulled his pistol, but it was only coyotes yipping off in the distance. He calmed his nerves and forced himself to relax. He laid the pistol in his lap and settled back for his hour of watch.

The waxing moon was nearly full, and the slanting, silvery light created deep, spooky pockets of shadow his eyes couldn't penetrate. A slight breeze rustled the drying leaves and the shadows moved like living things. Startled, he jumped up and aimed his pistol; once again, his nerves had fooled him. *Damn I'm jumpy. What the hell is wrong with me?* Something moved again, and this time his eyes picked out the tail-flick of a small doe as it grazed on the sparse grass. Relief washed over him like a cold mist, and he re-holstered his gun. The deer raised its head and looked straight at him, flipped its white tail up like a flag, crashed through the brush and was gone.

Charley sat down again and forced himself to think about other things, like how he was gonna deal with Blake when this was over. He shivered once in the cool October night, and wished he'd brought his blanket. His day-dreaming calmed him and before long, the sky brightened and the stars faded.

His long hour on watch finally over, Charley made his way back to camp and kicked Darnell awake. "Saddle our horses," he ordered.

Darnell rubbed his eyes and mumbled something, but did as he was told while Charley awakened the others.

"Time to ride," he said, ignoring the cursing, hungover men. They looked even worse today than last night, if that was possible. "I told you we were headin' out early," he said. He poured himself another cup of coffee, and watched the grumbling men throw off their blankets. Darnell returned with some jerky in his hand and poured himself the last cup of coffee.

"Damn, Porter, you coulda' made more coffee," said Zell Hopkins, as he poured out the grounds.

"Ain't my job," Charley said.

"Well I ain't movin' until I've had coffee, so, ridin' can wait," said Blake, holding his head.

*Serves you right you bastard. I hope your head splits wide open.*

Blake grabbed the pot and filled it from the creek, stoked the fire and started a new pot of coffee.

Charley mounted up. "I ain't waitin' for you," he said. "It's your own fault you got drunk and over-slept. You can catch up if you want that gold. Or not. I don't care either way. I ain't your nanny." He actually did care, he just wasn't going to let them know that.

"Well, boys, 'Captain' Porter is in a hurry," said Blake. "What do you boys think about that?" The men guffawed and made no move to saddle up. Blake glared at Charley. "I intend to have breakfast before I go anywhere today," he said. "So you two just go on ahead, we'll follow your trail. That gold will wait, and so will the women."

Charley seethed with anger. Blake had called his bluff. It was either leave them or wait for them. He walked his horse off into the woods so he could think. "Damn that sonofabitch," he said.

Darnell followed him. "We can ride," he said. "I don't like these men anyway, Charley. Why don't we just ride?"

"Cause I need 'em, for now," said Charley. "Now be quiet an' let me think."

Darnell's shoulders slumped. "Ok, Charley."

Charley shook his head. Darnell might be right, they'd be better off without this bunch of drunkards and fools. But things had already gone too far, Charley had played on their greed — counted on it — and now he knew they'd just follow him to the Carter place, and if there really was any money, they'd just take it from him. And if there wasn't, he'd be facing six angry gunmen. No, he had to play along for now and wait for a better time to deal with them, catch them off guard. Besides, eight men would spark more fear in old man Carter than two, and he might just give up without a fight.

Laughter reached him from the camp, and Charley's face turned red; he knew they were laughing at him. *Just you wait, you sumbitches! Every dog has his day an' mine's comin'.*

Charley calmed as he dreamed of his revenge and his courage returned. He put on a smile and walked back to the camp and sat down on a log. "I reckon there's no hurry," he said.

Blake smiled and raised his coffee cup. "Yessir, 'Captain' Porter." The men guffawed and snorted.

Charley hid his reaction and managed a slim smile.

The men ate and drank coffee until one pulled out a whiskey bottle. Luckily, there was only a little left in it. Cursing, he polished it off and threw the bottle into the brush.

While the men had their leisurely breakfast, Charley and Darnell sat and watched them. The sun was an hour higher in the east when the group finally broke camp and mounted up.

Blake gestured with one hand. "Well, 'Captain' Porter, lead on," he said.

Charley turned pink again but ignored the jibe. "I know a shortcut," he said. He turned his horse and led them northward on a faint trail through the brush, away from the road. More laughter followed him.


Will caught up with Jake quickly; the horses were jaded, and

Jake's horse had soon slowed to a walk. Will didn't even try to make Jake go back; he knew it would get him nowhere. Besides, they might have to fight Porter, and two guns were better than one.

As they rode silently, Will had time to think about all the ways this could go bad for them both. They might have to fight a bunch of hardened bushwhackers, and they could easily get shot. If they survived that, they could be arrested, tried and shot for desertion from the Union Army. Or, worst of all, they could fail, not get there in time, and still be shot for desertion. He had to laugh at that last one.

"What's so dang funny?" asked Jake.

"Not much, Jake," said Will. "It's just that we are now deserters from both the Yankees and the Rebs. If that ain't a recipe for gettin' shot, I don't know what is."

That brought a faint smile to Jake's stony visage. "I just hope Ma don't have to watch it."

"Or Lucy either," said Will.

Jake nodded. "Yep."

Will soon grew morose thinking of Lucy. Saving her like this — becoming a deserter — if he even could save her, was probably going to put an end to any plans they might have made. *Well, nothin' for it now. Just get there in time.* With that, he spurred his horse into a gallop. The played-out horse again slowed to a trot, and Will spurred it faster again. "Sorry 'bout that, but we got urgent business," he told the horse. It soon tired again and Will couldn't spur it beyond a fast walk.

They kept on riding, even when the sun went down. The light faded to a deep purple before the moon rose in their faces and lit the road almost as brightly as the sun would have. They'd need that moonlight — Will was determined to get there before Porter, which meant they'd have to ride all night.

*What if you don't beat them there, Will Tanner? What are you gonna do then?* He sighed. "We'll worry about that when we catch up to 'em," he muttered to himself.

As he rode, Will's thoughts returned to Lucy. He'd not gotten any more letters from her. The company had been on the move for nearly a month now, and the commissary wagons couldn't even keep up, so it was no surprise that the mail couldn't find them. He sighed with guilt when he realized he hadn't kept his own promise to write to her. Sergeant Burnes had been teaching him to read, but there'd been little time for that since the skirmish at the bridge. Will could have gotten the Sergeant to write a note for him, but his courage had failed him each time there was a chance. How could he have someone else write Lucy when he wasn't even sure he could put his feelings into words? When he wasn't even sure what those feelings were?

Will knew he was letting everyone around him down in every way. He was failing Ma's charge to keep Jake out of trouble. Going off on their own like this was proof enough of that. He was not taking care of the farm and his younger brothers, a promise he had made to Frank Higgins before he died. And he was failing Lucy. She likely worried about him; where he was and if he was safe, and he hadn't written to tell her he was ok. And there was Sergeant Burnes and the troopers in his company. What were they gonna think? He felt dismal. And he wasn't sure he could fix any of it.

Jake interrupted his worrying when he moved up beside him. "I gotta take a leak, I'm about to bust wide open," he said.

Will noticed the discomfort of his own bladder. "Ok, we can stop for a minute. Maybe grab a bite to eat, too."

They pulled up and tied the horses off. They stood side by side and urinated into the brush.

"You got a plan?" asked Will.

"We kill 'em, that's my plan."

"Well that's a start, but it ain't so simple, Jake," said Will. "There's eight of them, and if they get there before us, they'll have hostages."

"Like they did that first day? Jake's voice rose. "If we'd a shot 'em that day this wouldn't be happenin'."

Will's own anger rose in response. *Is that's what's eatin' at Jake? He still blame me for that day?* Will snapped. "You know what, Jake? You're right. This wouldn't be happenin' 'cause you an' me, we wouldn't be here, we'd be dead. An' then what would've happened to Ma and the boys, Jake? They'd be dead too. So yeah, this wouldn't be happenin'."

"No, we coulda at least got Porter!" Jake's voice grew louder.

"I know you blame me for what happened that day," Will said. "That's plain to see, and I'd bet it's been eatin' at you for a long time now. There weren't no other choice. We did what we had to do to survive, an' we did survive, and so did Ma and Ike and Seth...." His own voice had risen in response. "Everybody survived!"

Jake shouted, "And so did Porter, an' here we are!"

Will snapped. He grabbed Jake by the coat and drew him up to his face. "Don't you think I feel bad about that day? Don't you think I wonder, every damn day, if I coulda done anything different? Goddamit, Jake, when I study the facts, I cain't come to no different conclusion." He shook Jake and pushed him back. "Now either shut up about it or go back to the Regiment."

Jake opened his mouth to say something else, but his mouth closed without a word. His glare told Will how angry he still was. Suddenly, like the calm after a storm, his shoulders slumped, and he looked down at the ground. "It weren't your fault, Will," he said.

"I know. But I…"

Jake interrupted. "No, I mean it was my fault." His head dipped further, and his shoulders shook.

"What are you talking about? It weren't your fault either." Will now was ashamed that he'd lost his temper and puzzled by Jake's changing moods.

"It was my fault," said Jake. "This whole feud with Porter, it's my fault." Jake slumped even further. "There's somthin' I need to tell you about Porter, about that fight we had back at Elkhorn Tavern."

Will barely remembered the fight with Porter. He'd never known why they fought, the battle afterward had been more important, and they'd never gotten around to talking about it. Besides, Jake had lots of fights, none of them important in the long run. So why was this one so important to Jake?

A pack of coyotes yipped nearby. They sounded like children yelling and that startled Will and brought him back to the present. Talk with Jake would have to wait. "We got to ride. We can talk about it when this is over."

Jake sighed, and wiped his eyes on his sleeve.

Will was speechless; Jake was crying. Jake never cried.

"Yeah, we got to ride. And we need to kill that sumbitch Porter," Jake mumbled.

Will didn't respond. Instead, he gave his horse a drink from his canteen and a handful of corn from his saddlebag and mounted up. Jake lifted his head, set his jaw and did the same. They guided the horses out onto the road. Porter's tracks were plainly visible in the slanting moonlight.

Will was puzzled by the two Jakes he just seen. One was the old, sharp, double-edged, fight with you in a heartbeat, cut you like a knife Jake that he grew up with. He'd never seen the other Jake, the one that had secrets and carried a heavy sack of guilt on his back.

There was no time to reflect on it; they both kicked their horses into a trot and rode on down the road. The moon was higher in the sky and the road ahead was a silvery ribbon leading them eastward.

As Will rode, Jake's words and his own reaction to them weighed on him. Preoccupied trying to make sense of it, he missed Porter's tracks leading off into the brush. When he finally realized it, they were miles down the road. He pulled the reins and the horse stopped. "Dammit!"

"What?" asked Jake.

"Lost the trail," said Will. "They must have turned off."

Jake cursed and turned his horse to go back.

The sky in the east had taken on the blue glow of coming dawn. "Hang on," said Will. "Let's think about this. We know where they're headed, and we know this road will get us there."

"Maybe they know a short-cut," said Jake.

"Could be," said Will. "There ain't no roads out that way. Could be they pulled off to make camp. They don't know we're trailin' 'em, an' they ain't in a hurry like we are." Back-tracking would cost them valuable time. It would be faster, now, to keep to the road. If Jake would go along with it.

"Jake, I think they stopped, made camp maybe, and we're ahead of 'em now," said Will. "Come on, we'll stick to the road and we'll beat 'em there." To his surprise and relief, Jake turned his horse and trotted east without argument. Will followed.

*I hope I'm right! Dear Lord, let me be right!*

"Damn you, Porter! We're lost!" yelled Blake.

"You might be. I ain't," lied Charley. The riders had halted in a clearing and the trail they were following had split into three trails. "Just hold on a minute." He scanned the sky for the afternoon sun. It was low in the sky off to his left which meant they'd been trending north. They'd gone far enough in that direction—they'd crossed the Missouri Railroad line about an hour back. It was time to cut due east.

"I ain't lost," Charley repeated. "We take the rightmost trail. That should take us to the Troy road, and then we turn north on that. Take us right where we wanna go."

"Well, shit, Porter? How much further?"

"We'll be there before sundown."

"There better be enough gold there to make this worth our while."

"When we get there, you'll see. Ole man Carter, he's in the tall cotton," he lied again. Then he realized what he'd just done.

*Dammit!*

He immediately regretted letting Carter's name slip. Blake might figure out that he didn't need him anymore.

"Lead on, Porter," said Blake, smiling.

*I don't want my back to this sumbitch now.* Charley thought quickly. "I gotta check my horse's foot, he's got a rock in his shoe or something. You go on ahead, I'll catch right up."

Blake's eyes narrowed. "We'll wait for you, right here, 'Captain.' Best we all stay together."

Charley's ruse hadn't worked. He dismounted and made a show of inspecting the right rear hoof of his horse. It put him out of sight of the others, and he lay a hand on his pistol and briefly considered having it out right here. But the odds weren't good, and he still might need them.

Darnell dismounted to look at the hoof. "It looks all right to me, Charley."

"Yeah," he said loudly enough for the others to hear. "Should be fine."

Then, in a lower voice directed at Darnell only, he said, "I want you to hang back and bring up the rear. Keep an eye on them boys."

Darnell gave him a puzzled look and shrugged. "Sure, Charley."

"You understand?" he whispered. "They might make a move on me. If they do, you got to shoot em'."

He nodded to the others as he fiddled with a strap. "Almost

ready," he said to them. "Just nod if you understand," he said to Darnell.

Darnell wore a puzzled frown, but he nodded.

"Let's ride," said Charley. And with that he mounted up, clicked his tongue and nudged his horse onto the rightmost trail. The men followed single file down the narrow trail.

The trees here grew thick and tall, and the trail was like a tunnel. Clouds moved over the sun and it grew dark in there. It reminded Charley of those dark woods he been lost in, the night Darnell found him. He remembered his relief, that night, when Darnell showed up. He began to regret some of his doubts about him. Hadn't Darnell always been there when he needed him? *Maybe he just ain't no braggart like some are. He is a bit touched in the head, ain't he? I bet he's killed men, and just don't like to talk about it.* Charley knew other men that were that way. He decided that maybe he could trust him after all.

They rode on, and as the sun sank lower, the light slanted through the trees making long shadows. Red and yellow leaves rustled as the wind blew through them. Dried up leaves drifted down in spirals and crunched under the horses hooves. They were making a lot of noise, but it couldn't be helped.

After a few hours, they broke out of the woods, and a river lay before them. At first, Charley was confused — he'd expected to hit the Troy Road. Then he recognized where he was.

Blake sneered. "Where's that road?" he asked. Then he laughed. "You done got us lost, ain't ye?" The other men cursed.

"That ain't the road. It's the Cuivre River an' I know exactly where we are," Charley said. "There's a bridge about a mile north of here. An' that's where we'll find Tanner's farm."

"I thought you said his name was Carter," said Blake.

Charley smiled. "Carter lives next door to the Tanner place. We burned the Tanners out back in August."

"Whyn't you get that gold when you was here then?" Asked Buck.

Charley had to lie again. "Henry Perkins weren't interested. He was only after recruits for General goddam Price."

"He was a bit odd at times," said Blake. "Well, let's go, sunlight's fadin'."

Without another word, Charley turned his horse to follow the river.

Will snapped awake, confused for a moment, and found himself still in the saddle. His horse walked on, unguided, simply following the road.

He'd been dreaming again. In this dream, a bear had been chasing Jake and Ike. When they'd run by Will, the bear stopped, turned and faced him. It did not attack him, but when Will pulled out his pistol to protect himself, it grabbed the pistol with its teeth.

When Will fired the gun, the bear just shook his head, looked at him and said one word: "Why?"

In his dream, Will didn't know why he'd fired. It seemed the natural thing to do if faced by a snarling, growling bear. Will shot again, and again the bear just shrugged and looked at him. He fired once more, this time directly at the bear's head, and still it shook off his bullet.

"Why?" it asked again, spreading its paws. Will still didn't have an answer for the bear. Finally, with a shrug, it ambled off, apparently unhurt.

That's when he woke up, feeling sad, almost wanting to cry. In his dream, it felt like the bear had wanted to be a friend but somehow Will himself had turned it into an enemy. He could still see the bear — and it's puzzled eyes — in his mind as plain as if it were real.

He wondered what Ma would make of the dream. She had some old-fashioned ideas about dreams and omens and such. It bothered him for a while — he didn't know why, exactly — until he decided he had no time to worry about dreams. He had enough to worry about in real life.

Jake was wobbling in his saddle, head down, and snoring. His hands lay in his lap still gripping the reins. His horse's head was down too, and looked like it might plop over at any minute.

*There is a limit to what we can endure, and I think we hit it.*

Will looked around, trying to figure where they were. He relaxed when he saw a familiar treeline along a creek off to the south — he'd been hunting out here before, in his previous, more peaceful life. They were about ten miles from home — over two hours for a walking horse, less if they galloped. Their worn-out horses wouldn't run for long before they'd lay down and die. They had to stop.

"Let's stop for a while!" yelled Will. Jake didn't respond. He moved his horse to block Jakes, and Jake's horse stopped of its own accord.

He yelled at Jake, and he finally looked up, his eyes blurry and unfocused.

"Let's stop here for a while," said Will. "The horses is played out, and we are too."

Jake nodded his agreement.

Will led them off the road and into a grove of willow trees by the creek. There was shade, grass, and water there for the horses. Jake practically fell off his mount and collapsed in the grass. Will took the horses to water then hobbled them so they couldn't wander too far. He removed his carbine from its scabbard, checked its load, and sat down with his back to a tree. The wind waved the willow stems and their rustling made a lonely noise.

"I'll take first watch," said Will to nobody. Despite his intentions, his head sunk and he was soon fast asleep.

Somebody's boot kicked Will awake and when he jumped to his feet, Jake stood there in front of him. "We gotta ride, Will. We slept too damn long."

"Shit!" he said, realizing Jake was right. The sun was lowering in the west now. But first he had to relieve himself. While he did so, he yelled to Jake, "Fill our canteens here, we cain't stop again."

After filling the canteens, Jake rounded up the horses and removed the hobbles. By the time Will had buttoned back up, Jake was mounted and already yelling. "We gotta go, Will!"

"I know Jake, I know it!" he snapped.

They turned onto the road and kicked their somewhat refreshed horses into a gallop. Will knew they couldn't run all the way to the farm, but he could no longer afford to think about the horses. He was angry at himself for sleeping too long, and he kicked himself for it. He could only hope that Porter's gang had stopped too. If not, then Porter was already there, and that was too terrible to think about.

\*\*\*\*\*

# Chapter 21

The first thing Will noticed was the smell of fresh bread. Just before sundown, he and Jake exited the dark tunnel of woods over the road and there before them sat their farm. A new cabin gleamed in the slanting last light of the sun's rays. A faint wisp of smoke exited a stovepipe that exited the unfinished roof, wafting the smell of cooking to them. It made him realize how hungry he was.

"They been busy," said Jake.

Will nodded. "Yep, I'm impressed." He studied the cabin. The roof still lacked some shingles, the windows had no shutters, and there was no door mounted in the door frame. It was much smaller than their original house. But it was a house, and someone was in it.

Jake yelled "Ma! It's me, Jake!" He slid from his saddle and ran toward the door.

Will shouted, "Wait! It might be a trap." It was too late, though, Jake never even slowed down. *He ain't never gonna learn to be careful, is he?* Will pulled out his carbine and checked the load. *Be ready for anything.*

It was no trap. Ma ran out barefooted, their old shotgun heavy in her hand, and met Jake well outside the door. She hugged him, then ran toward Will who was still mounted. Chigger came out from somewhere and barked at them.

"Will! Thank goodness you two are all right," said Ma. Her smile changed to a frown when she saw the rifle in his hand. "What's wrong?"

Will jumped down and hugged her with his free hand. His brothers Ike and Seth came running out and he hugged them too. Ike still carried the old flintlock, and Will gave him an approving nod. "Where's Nate?"

"Sleepin' inside," said Ma. "Chigger, hush! It's Will and Jake!" The dog whined, waddled over and sniffed them, then wagged its entire hindquarters and yipped excitedly.

"We ain't got time for this," said Jake.

"He's right, Ma," said Will. "We got to get you over to Ben's place. Some bushwhackers are headin' this way, an' it ain't safe here."

Ma didn't argue or even ask why—she wasted no time, "Grab your shoes boys," she yelled to Ike and Seth. She ran into the house and came back out with her own shoes on, carrying Nate in her arms and the old shotgun still in her free hand. Nate wiggled and fussed in her arms.

"Let's go," said Will. "Cross the fields, straight to the Carter house."

Will was tired of riding. "C'mere, Ike," he said. "You get to ride. Put your foot in the stirrup and climb up there."

Ike smiled, his teeth gleaming in the purpling light. He handed Will the flintlock, climbed up in the saddle and held onto the pommel. Will held the reins and handed up the rifle.

Jake helped Seth climb on his horse, then took Nate from Ma and lifted him up and sat him down ahead of Seth. "Damn, you got heavy, Nate!"

"Jacob Tanner, you mind your language!" said Ma.

"Sorry Ma, been soldierin' too long."

Ma shook her head. "Never mind."

While they walked, Will told Ma about the threats that Porter had made, and that he and some other bushwhackers were headed this way. He left out the part about him and Jake leaving the regiment.

When they approached the Carter house, a negro ran into the house and let Ben know there was company outside. Ben met them on the porch, and Will explained it all over again.

Ben paled when he heard the news. "Well, you had better come on in, we need to make some plans." he said. He yelled for one of his negroes take the horses to be fed and watered, and they went inside.


Lucy jerked up from her sewing to the thumping of heavy boots on the porch, and loud voices from downstairs. Some men were talking to Papa. One of them sounded like…. *Is that Will? Can that really be him?*

She jumped up from her chair and ran down the stairs in her stocking-feet and there he was, standing just inside the door. She stopped half-way down and scanned his familiar face. His eyes found hers and a brief smile crossed his lips.

"Will!" she yelled. Embarrassed, she covered her mouth when Papa looked up at her. She couldn't help but smile behind her hand. "Sorry Papa, I'm just so…. surprised!"

Her smile soon faded. Will was haggard and worn out; the dark circles under his eyes were so black she at first wondered if he'd been fighting. His blue uniform was filthy, and he had a week's worth of stubble on his face. He had lost weight — he had tightened his belt more than once.

She ran down the rest of the stairs and hugged him, despite the looks Mama and Papa were giving her. Will smelled of horse and sweat and dust and dirt. She found that she didn't mind, at all.

"Lucy! Your manners!" cried Mama.

"Oh leave 'em be, Martha," said Papa. "You know they been sparkin' a while anyhow."

Lucy felt her cheeks redden, but she was too happy to care. "Will Tanner, I am glad to see you! Are you home on leave? How long can you stay?"

Will's jaw clenched, and his smile changed into a determined frown. The familiar twinkle in his eyes was replaced by a grim, serious look. Something about the two pistols stuck in his belt and the death-grip on his rifle frightened her. *Something's wrong! He's never looked so…worried.*

"Lucy, Miss Martha," said Will, removing his hat. "I don't mean to scare you-all, but there's some really bad men comin' this way, and they intend to hurt us. We got to get ready for 'em."

Lucy felt the blood drain from her face. Will's worried looks scared her much more than his news.

For the first time, she noticed Joline and her boys were there, too. And there was someone else — Jake — out on the porch, a rifle at the ready in his hands. Keeping watch? It could only mean they expected trouble. Soon. Bad trouble.

Papa grabbed his shotgun from over the fireplace and poured

powder and shot into it. "All right. Who's comin'?" he asked.

"Charley Porter and some of Anderson's men. We were trailin' 'em. It looks like somehow we beat 'em here, but I doubt they're very far behind us. They aim to rob you. An'...." He looked at Lucy.... "There's no tellin' what else they might do."

"How many?"

"Eight, I think."

Papa took a deep breath. Mama gasped. Papa looked out the window. "Where's the rest of your company?"

Will looked down and shook his head before he answered. "It's just me an' Jake. I'll explain later, right now there ain't time."

"Why would that man, that Porter, why would he come here again?" asked Lucy.

"It's too long a story to tell right now." Turning back to Papa, Will said, "We need to send for the Sheriff. Can you send somebody over to Troy to fetch him?"

"I'll send Old Tom," said Papa. "They know him there and they'll believe him. Maybe he can gather a few neighbors too." He glanced at Joline with her shotgun and Ike with the long rifle. "Maybe we can hold 'em off till somebody comes. Chloe, get down here!" Papa yelled. When she came down, he sent her off to find Old Tom.

The men made their plans to defend the house. Will's confidence surprised and reassured Lucy. The situation called for someone to make fast decisions, and Will was making them. He wasn't giving actual orders; he just seemed to know what needed to be done and said so without hesitation. The others followed his advice without questions, even Papa.

*The Army has changed him*, she thought. *He's not a boy anymore. He loves his family and he's doing what he can to protect them.* She paled when she realized that he must care for her too. It would have been simpler just to run away with his own family, but he had come here to protect her. That thought left her filled with awe.

The negroes, women and children would hide out in the cornfields. The slaves had special places to hide, places that no-one else knew of, and they would be safe there.

Lucy ran upstairs, donned her shoes and returned, then they headed to the back door. As she passed, she kissed Will quickly on the cheek. "I am really glad to see you, Will Tanner."

Will's ears turned red and his face took on that stunned look of his. "I hope you're still glad in a little while," he said, his frown returning.

Lucy's heart sank. Will was worried, she could see it in his eyes. And that frightened her. Still, she was glad he was here.


"Well I'll be damned," said Charley. The sun had set, and the sky was turning purple, but he could still see the nearly finished one-room log house. A quick look through the open windows confirmed it was deserted. Smoke still wisped from the chimney, so someone had been there. *That bastard Carter's been helpin' 'em. Just one more reason to kill 'im.*

"Burn it down," he said.

"What for?" asked Blake.

Charley glared at the man. "Because two boys that live here are damn Yankees. They ride with the Fifteenth Cavalry. That reason enough?"

"I reckon so." Blake smiled as he pulled a box of matches from his coat. He slid from his horse and walked inside; when he came back out, there were already orange flames licking from the open doorway. He jumped astride his horse and said, "Ok, now where is this gold you been on about?"

Smoke poured from the open windows. Charley pointed to the Carter house off in the distance, its' white paint glowing in the deepening darkness. "It's right over yonder, about a half-mile away across that cornfield there."

"Well, then let's go get it." Blake turned his horse and the others followed.

Once again, Blake's tone annoyed Charley. *Won't be much longer and I'll be shed of you.*

Charley broke into a trot to catch up with Blake. "Now, I know ole Carter, so you let me do the talkin'."

Blake eyed him suspiciously. "What's there to talk about? We make him tell us where it is, and we take it."

"He's a cagey old bastard," Charley said. "You'd best let me handle 'im."

Blake guffawed. "Jeezus, Porter! You act like you're the only one can get somethin' done! What the hell?"

Inside, Charley was furious. *Not yet.* He steeled himself to remain calm and rode on. *Not yet, you bastard, not yet. I will deal with you right soon, though. As soon as you figure out there ain't no gold, I will kill you.*

Movement in the corner of his eye caught his attention, and he stole a glance behind him. The cabin was ablaze; yellow flames licked the darkening sky, and a plume of black smoke rose high in the still air. He now realized burning the cabin might have been a mistake. Ben Carter would surely see it.

He pretended to ponder that for a moment. "I reckon you're right, Blake," he said. "Ain't no need to worry about one old man. We can just ride on in there and take anythin' we want."

Blake smiled. "Now you're talkin', Porter."

Charley dropped back and let Blake take the lead. He slowed further until he was back with Darnell at the rear of the formation. He whispered to Darnell, "You stick with me. I think there's gonna be a fight."

Darnell just shrugged.

Charley figured he was just in another of his moods. "Your pistols ready?" he asked.

Darnell looked down at his guns. "Yeah, Charley," he muttered.


From the porch, Jake saw the orange glow and the thick, black smoke rising from the new cabin. He knew that could mean only one thing.

"Will!" he yelled. "They're here! They're burning the cabin!"

Will came out and stood beside him, staring at the smoke. "Ma, Lucy, an' Miss Martha an' our brothers are gone to hide out with the slaves. You an' me an' Ben, we got to hold 'em off 'til help gets here."

"That your plan?" asked Jake. He tried and failed to keep the irritation out of his voice. He knew his brother was worried. Hell, he was worried too.

"You got a better one?" asked Will.

Jake didn't, but he didn't like this one either.

Ike stepped out on the porch, holding Pa's old Kentucky rifle.

"You're supposed to be with the women, why ain't you gone with them?" said Will. "Go, on now, before it's too late."

"I ain't no child," said Ike. "I'm fifteen now. I'm stayin' here with you."

Jake looked at his younger brother. He had grown some in the months he'd been away, and he looked older than his fifteen years. *Maybe it's time? Or is Will gonna play the boss with Ike, too, like he does me?*

Will studied Ike for a time, as if he too had just noticed that he had grown. "That's right, you ain't no child," he said. "I need you to guard the womenfolk for me, and you're the best man for the job."

"We could use the extra gun," said Jake.

Will gave him a look that could have cut leather. "Shut up, Jake, let me handle this."

Jake flushed red for just a second, then he calmed himself and stared Will right in the eye. "Maybe it's his time to be a man. Let him stay, he can shoot from upstairs."

Will shook his head. "Bad idea, Jake. If he shoots at them, they'll shoot back. He ain't ready for this."

"You cain't protect all of us all the time," said Jake. "If we lose here tonight, what they gonna do to him then?"

Jake saw the indecision in Will's eyes, saw him groping for an answer to his personal dilemma. Finally, he nodded, and turned to Ike.

"All right. I know you can shoot but shootin' at a man is different. You cain't hesitate, you cain't think of him as a man, you got to just shoot. Wait for Jake an' me to shoot first. Then, if you get a clean shot, take it and reload as fast as you can. Stay down, behind the windowsill, stay out of sight as much as you can."

Ike smiled. "I can do that. I can shoot good, Will. You taught me, 'member?" He turned to go inside.

Will grabbed his arm. "If we lose this fight," he said, "you run, you hear me? Climb out a window, sneak out any way you can, 'cause they will burn this place. Take the women and your brothers to the woods and hide out till it's over, you hear me? You protect Ma and Seth and Nate."

"We're runnin' out of time," said Jake.

Will nodded. "Your rifle loaded?"

Ike's eyes narrowed. "Yeah," he said. "'Course it's loaded. Told you I ain't no child."

"Good," said Will. "Remember, make your shots count. Go on up, find a good spot."

Ike ran inside, holding the rifle in two hands, his powder horn and bullet pouch bouncing on his hip.

"He'll be all right," said Jake.

"He better be," replied Will. "Ma won't forgive us if he gets hurt."

Jake felt his pulse throb in his temples. Will was right, there'd be hell to pay if Ike got hurt. Was letting Ike stay a mistake? Was this how Will felt? Always second guessing his decisions because he felt responsible for someone else?

There was no more time to dwell on it—he could hear shouts off in the distance, coming from the direction of their burning cabin.

Will heard them too. "Inside, now! Find a good spot."

Jake didn't hesitate. He ran inside and crouched behind the parlor windowsill. Will took a position under the dining room window. Ben Carter headed up to find his own window. "Blow out them lamps!" he yelled as he climbed the stairs.

Jake did as he was asked, then looked out the open window. He saw several dark forms riding out of the cornfield. He counted them. As he did, they turned toward the house. "They're comin'," he said. "I count eight!"

"I see 'em," said Will. "We got to make our shots count. An' Jake, if there's ever a time to get you one of them bushwhackers, I reckon it's now."

"You have to rub that in, now?"

"Yep," he said. "And remember, wait for my shot."

"I know the plan!" Jake hissed, biting back a harsher reply. He shook off his irritation, and knelt behind the window. He laid his pistol at his knees and aimed his rifle at the oncoming shadows. They made good targets against the orange glow from their burning cabin in the deep purple of dusk.

*Rattlesnakes*, Will thought, taking aim at one of the riders, a faceless shadow in the darkening sky. *They're not men, they're just rattlesnakes.* He took a deep breath and steeled himself for what he had to do.

"You ready, Jake?" he whispered.

"Yeah," said Jake.

Will centered his sights on the rider closest to him and fired without hesitation. The flash illuminated the man as he yelled out, and Will saw his pistol raise and fire at the house. The bullet thumped into the house somewhere. Will reloaded without conscious thought, his trembling hands doing it automatically while he scanned for his next target. The boom of the rifles in the small room was deafening, and his ears rang again.

Jake's rifle boomed and the flash from it made a red spot in his vision. Through the red, Will saw the man fall from his horse.

*One down!*

"Good shot!" Will yelled.

If Jake heard him, he didn't reply. The twin boom of Ben's double barrel upstairs blotted out any words. Another man cursed outside. Ike fired the old rifle, and its sharp bang echoed down the staircase and made his ears ring again. Except for more yelling and cursing, there was no effect on the riders outside.

Then it was all flash and boom as the bushwhackers opened up with their pistols, and he had to duck down behind the windowsill. Some of the shots splintered the wall behind him but none came too close.

The fire slackened off and Will yelled, "Another volley, Jake!" and they fired again almost at the same time. Another scream, and another man fell from his horse.

*Two Down!*

Will heard someone yelling. He knew instantly who it was—Charley Porter! He couldn't make out the words for the ringing in his ears.

Two of the riders ran their horses closer to the house and fired. More splinters flew, this time a lot closer to where he peered over the sill. Jake fired again, and another man pitched from his horse, and lay there on the ground moaning and writhing with pain.

*Three down!*

It went quiet as the remaining bushwhackers galloped to the carriage house and disappeared behind it.

"You all right, Jake?" asked Will.

"I got me one, Will. Did you see it?" Jake replied.

Will couldn't resist chiding him. "Two by my count! 'Bout time you figured out how to shoot."

Jake roared with nervous laughter.

\*\*\*\*\*

# Chapter 22

Charley Porter's first thought, when he heard the shots, was that those were Sharp's Carbines. He'd been shot at with them many times and knew the sound well. In front of Charley, Lonzo wobbled, then slowly slid from his horse with a thump. He lay there in the dirt without moving; his horse bolted and disappeared into the darkness.

"It's a trap!" yelled Blake, too late. A shotgun blast boomed out and someone cursed. A shot flashed from a second story window, a much sharper report, and a bullet whined by over Charley's head.

"Shoot back!" somebody yelled. "Put some fire into 'em!"

The men began popping away at the house with their revolvers. Charley held back, saving his shots for later. He wheeled his horse around and took cover behind the carriage house, yelling for Darnell to do the same.

Zell Hopkins was already there, picking lead shot from his face. Blood was running into his eyes and he wiped at it with his neck-rag. "Sumbitch near blinded me," he said.

Bullets thumped into the house and splinters flew from the wood siding as the boys shot up the place. The air filled with smoke, and flashes lit up the darkness. When the men had emptied their revolvers, there was a lull while they put them away and pulled spares. The carbines boomed again, almost as one. Somebody screamed and there was a loud thud as a man fell from his horse.

He wondered how Carter had gotten ahold of a Sharp's. *No, there's two carbines in there! Somebody else is in the house with him.* Charley felt sure there were at least four shooters in there. Two carbines, a shotgun and another gun of some kind. And they were ready. Charley cursed under his breath. Burning the cabin had been a mistake.

Whoever was in there had seen the fire and laid a trap for them.

The business end of a pistol aimed right at his face loomed large in Charley's vision, blotting out all his other concerns at the moment.

Blake cocked his gun and Charley backed up a step with his hands up. "Whoa now, easy Blake. Why you pointin' that hog-shooter at me for?"

"God-Damn you Porter!" Blake yelled. "What game are you playin' at?"

Even in the shadows, Charley could see Blake's eyeballs were bulging outward in his anger. Spittle flew from his mouth as he spit out his words.

"This was supposed to be easy money!" Blake continued. "And we get here and get suckered into a trap! What the hell's goin' on, Porter? You better get to talkin' real fast."

"How the hell would I know? They was shootin' at me too! Cool your heels, Blake."

By now, the other riders had taken shelter behind the carriage house and dismounted. "Where's Tim?" asked Zell. Nobody answered. Zell took a peek around the corner at the two bodies laying in the dirt. "Aw godammit, Tim, what'd you go an' get yourself shot fer?" He hung his head and cursed.

"There's two of my friends a layin' out there in the dirt," said Blake, still holding his gun on Charley. "I wanna know why that is, Porter!"

"One of 'em's my brother Tim," said Zell, pulling out his own gun. "Let's shoot 'im, Blake."

Charley's mind latched onto a straw. "Blake, that gold is still in there. That's what we come for. Lower that gun now, and let's talk."

"Easy, boys," said Buck, shaking his head. "He was right there with us, an' it's awful dark. He could of got shot just as easy as any of us. I don't think Porter set it up. Think about that gold, now." He removed his hat and wiped his forehead on his sleeve.

There was a long silence and Charley could see Blake's jaw working. At long last, Blake lowered the gun and un-cocked it. Charley's pounding heart eased, and he let out his breath. He hadn't even realized he wasn't breathing.

"I still ain't convinced," said Blake. "And when I find out what's really goin' on here, we will finish this here conversation. Who's in that house?"

"I don't know for sure," Charley said. "I think there's at least four of 'em."

Blake sneered. "Well, hell, you can count."

Charley figured a little humility might ease the tension. He held out his hands and said, "Lookin' back on it, burnin' the cabin might have been a mistake."

Blake glared at him. "An' that was your idea, weren't it?"

Charley spread his hands. "Yeah, it was. I ain't perfect."

"So, you tell me how we gonna get that gold now," said Blake.

Charley made a show of pondering the subject. "Well, we need ole man Carter alive, or else we'll never find it. We need to get him all by himself."

"Burn 'em out," said Zell. "A little fire will run 'em out."

Charley liked that plan. Burning would force the shooters out in the open. Before he could say so Blake spoke up.

"The gold might burn up, too, if we do that," Blake said.

Charley almost let slip that there wasn't any gold, but he caught himself. He thought for a moment. He wondered where the women and children and slaves were. A plan formed in his mind. "I might know a way," he said.

"We ain't gonna listen to him, are we?" asked Zell. "He done got my dern brother kilt." He wiped more blood from his face.

"Let's hear him out," said Buck.

"Keep talkin'," said Blake.

Charley told them the plan he wanted them to play out. It wasn't his real plan. He just had to sell it like it was.

"There's still six of us, so three of us pull off," Charley said, "An' make lots of talk about killin' the women and children and slaves. That ought to pull a couple of them out of the house, and then the other three moves on it. One in the back door an' two in the front oughta do it. Just don't kill the old man."

Blake looked at him suspiciously.

"Look," said Charley. "Me an' Darnell an' Buck here, we can storm the house. You three can go find the women."

"Oh hell no, Porter. An' then what, we come back and find you an' the gold gone? No, you'll go find the women. Buck will go with you. And that halfwit too, for all I care. Me an' Carson an' Zell, we'll take the house. You come on back when you've killed the others."

"I'm no good to ye," said Zell. I cain't see. Count me out." With that he mounted his horse and trotted off.

"What the hell?" asked Blake. He pulled his pistol halfway out as if to shoot Zell, but he was already out of pistol range. "Well, I be damned. I never reckoned Zell for a coward. An' his brother layin' out there dead an' all."

"Them two never did get along anyhow," said Buck. "Forget him."

Blake shook his head. "Well, let's get that gold. Me an' Carson can take the house. Let's move."

Charley couldn't believe his good fortune. This was just what he'd wanted Blake to do. Charley suppressed his smile and replaced it with a disgusted look. "All right, Blake, you're the captain, now."


"Y'all ok up there?" Will yelled up to Ike and Ben.

"Never better!" replied Ben.

There was no answer from Ike.

"Ike! Answer me, you all right up there?" Still no answer. Will's heart took a flip inside his chest. He jumped up and ran to the stairs. To Jake, he yelled. "Yell if they come again!" He didn't wait to hear a reply.

Ben was in the room bending with Ike. "He'll be ok. Just a scratch," he said.

In the dark, Will could just make out a cut starting near his temple and stopping above his ear. There was a lot of blood, but Ike's breath came slow and steady.

"He's all right, Will," said Ben again. I'm gonna wrap it to stop the bleedin'. He'll wake up shortly and he'll be fine. I've seen worse from a mule kick. He might have a headache for a day or two, though."

Will sighed. *This is all my fault. Ma's gonna kill me.*

"You better get back down there, no tellin' what they've cooked up," said Ben.

"I reckon," said Will. He turned to go, then added, "Thank you, Mr. Ben."

As Will ran back down the stairs, he heard Charley Porter shouting from outside, "Hallo the House! Hallo the House! Y'all need to give it up now!"

"Don't answer him." Will said.

"Wasn't plannin' on it," Jake replied.

"You there in the house!" continued Porter. "We're gonna go find your women-folk and your brats and you're gonna be sorry you didn't give up. Come on out now, an' we won't hurt 'em none!"

"They won't find 'em," said Ben from the top of the stairs. "My negroes are trustworthy, and they love Lucy like their own. They're hid where no white man can find 'em."

Will didn't have to think too long. He knew giving up would mean death for him and Jake and Ben. Maybe worse for Lucy. There was no way he would allow that. He held his silence.

"You made your choice," yelled Porter.

Will heard horses gallop away toward the slave quarters. He turned back to Ben. "You sure about that, Mr. Ben?"

Ben didn't hesitate. "I'm sure," he yelled down. "They're tryin' to split us up, then they'll be stormin' the house. Best we stick together."

*Why don't they just burn us out? That's what I'd do if I was them,* Will thought. Burning the house was a sure-fire way to get them out in the open, and the bushwhackers would know it. Something wasn't right, but Will couldn't put his finger on what it was. No matter, nobody was leaving the house.

When Will got back in place, Jake said," Three of 'em rode off looking for Ma an'...."

"I know. Ben says they're safe with the slaves."

"I heard. You believe 'im?"

"Yeah, I do. It don't matter anyhow. We cain't leave Ike. We got to trust Ben's negroes. Here's the good side. Porter's gang just split their own selves up. Ain't but two or three of 'em comin' now. You loaded?"

"Dammit Will, you think I ain't loaded? After all we been through? Jeez."

"Sorry Jake, I'm just askin'. I guess I'm just a little nervous," he said by way of apology.

Jake stiffened. "Here they come."

Will crawled to his spot and looked outside. The sky was glowing with the coming moonrise. He saw a crouched figure run up to the well, silhouetted by the soft light. *Only one? Where's the others?* He took careful aim and when the shadow moved, he fired. Jake fired as well. There was a howl of pain, and the shadow fell and writhed on the ground.

*Dammit! One of us should have held fire.* "Reload, quick!"

"Reloadin'!" yelled Jake.

The back door crashed open, heavy boots thumped on the wooden floor and a dark shadow appeared in the kitchen doorway.


The moon was now rising behind him and Charley could easily see four slave huts, laid out in a neat row behind the barn. There was no glow from cookfires or candles in any doorway or open window. The shacks looked deserted. He rode around each one looking and listening for any sign of people. *Nobody home.*

Buck sat back and spat tobacco juice to the ground. "Well, hell where'd they go? They ain't here, that's sure."

Charley wondered the same thing.

"They must be hidin' out in the fields somewhere, or maybe they run off," said Buck. "Maybe we can smoke 'em out."

Charley was wary of another ambush. But maybe he could draw them out. "Darnell, burn the huts. Burn 'em all."

"You some kind of damn firebug or somethin'?" asked Buck, shaking his head.

Charley stared at the man. *You'll pay for that, shortly.* "They already know we're here this time," he said. "Darnell, burn 'em."

Darnell looked down at his boots. "Cain't do that, Charley. Aint got no matches or nothin'."

"Well, Shit. I'll do it," said Buck.

Buck dismounted and walked inside the first hut. Soon a glow appeared from the doorway. Buck then went down the row, setting of them alight one by one. The flickering light grew, and Buck's eyes glowed like twin coals.

As Buck walked back to his horse, two closely spaced carbine shots came from behind them. There was no return fire. Charley figured Blake and Carson were now dead or wounded, and out of the fight.

*Well, It's now or never!*

In one smooth motion, Charley pulled out his pistol, cocked it, and fired point blank into Buck's chest just as he raised himself up on his stirrup.

Buck stopped halfway up, as if he'd changed his mind. In the firelight Charley could see the  look of amazement in the man's eyes as he realized he was shot. Buck's hands let go of the pommel and he fell to the ground. He pulled at his own pistol, but his strength left him, and he grew still.

"Charley! Why'd you do that, Charley? Ain't they our friends?" asked Darnell. He looked even more puzzled than Buck had been.

"No, they ain't our friends," Charley said. "They were gonna shoot us later, Darnell. You gotta trust me on that. I know these things, just like I knowd them boys back in prison was gonna steal our food. You remember that, don't you Darnell? Weren't I right about that? Well, I'm right about this too."

Darnell shook his head. "Charley, I don't feel good."

"Just trust me and do what I say, and it'll be all right."

They both heard two muffled booms from behind them.

"We need to get back to the house," Charley said. "The women ain't here. I know where they will be, though."


As Will watched the man in the doorway, he tried to reload. His fingers felt clumsy and slow, and time seemed to stand still. He saw the man shift and there was a blinding flash and a deafening boom and a cry from Jake. His ears rung so loud he couldn't hear anything else. He slammed the lever of his carbine shut on a cartridge and fumbled for a cap.

He knew it was already too late when he heard the click of the pistol being cocked for the next shot. He wondered what being shot would feel like. Then his reflexes took over and he dove down to the floor.

Another blinding flash illuminated the room and from the corner of his eye he saw the figure in the doorway topple backward with a yell and fall out of sight into the kitchen. In his ears there was nothing but ringing.

By the time he got to his knees, put the cap on and cocked his Sharp's, there was nothing to aim at. The ringing in his ears subsided and he realized someone was yelling his name. It was Ben Carter. The ringing diminished gradually until he was able to hear the words.

"Will! You Ok? I got 'im Will. I got 'em. Will! Both barrels!" Ben struck a match and cupped it in his hands. Will heard Ben suck in his breath. "I think Jake's been shot," he said.

The blood drained from Will's face and the familiar icy hand again gripped his heart. The match Ben struck blinded him; after a second his eyes adjusted, and he could see his brother slumped down against the wall. A tight grimace lined Jake's face, and his hand clutched his left shoulder. Blood seeped between his fingers despite his efforts to stem the flow.

"Dammit!" yelled Will. He glanced at the kitchen door. A pair of dirty boots stuck through the doorway. They weren't moving. Then the match went out. With a scratch, Ben lit another. This time he lit a lamp with it. He hung it up near Jake and ripped open Jake's shirt.

"Ben, we didn't get 'em all," Will said.

Ben was busy with Jake and didn't respond.

"Ben, the lamp…. There might be more of 'em," he repeated.

Ma burst through the front door and cut off any answer Ben might have made. Martha Carter and Lucy followed her and stood there staring at Jake. Ma rushed to him and helped Ben staunch the blood.

"Ma, why are you here?" he asked. "This ain't over." He had a bad feeling; Porter was still out there somewhere.

Ma looked confused. "We saw the lamp light up…."

"Ben," Martha said. "Something's afire down at the slave houses."

"I need to go see about it," said Ben. He placed Ma's hand on the rag he used to staunch Jake's bleeding. "Hold it tight, Missus Joline. I've got to go see what I can do. First, I need to tell you that Ike is upstairs.

He got grazed by a bullet but he'll be all right, I'm sure of it." Ben dragged the dead bushwhacker from the kitchen doorway and ran out into the back yard.

Ma pressed hard on the rag and Jake groaned. She looked up from him. "Jake's bad off. I'd rather not leave him just now. Martha, will you go up and see to Ike?"

Martha nodded and stepped hurriedly up the stairs.

Without taking her eyes from Jake, Ma asked, "Why is Ike here? He's too young for this. Whyn't you send him out to hide?"

Jake groaned. "My fault, Ma," he said through clenched teeth and closed eyes. His head slumped, and he passed out, as if it had taken all his energy just to say those three words.

"No, it was my choice," said Will.

Ma turned her head and her eyes bored into his. "An' it was the wrong one."

Will tried not to flinch or look away. "Yes."

Ma turned back to Jake. "We'll talk on it later," she said. "Right now, I'm just glad it's over."

Before Will could say any more, a yell reached them from the back yard, then heavy boots thumped in the kitchen. When Will looked up, there stood Charley Porter, two pistols drawn and aimed right at him.

"Lay that gun down, Tanner," Charley said.

Will had been holding his carbine in his left hand, and he knew there was no chance to get off a shot at Porter. He slowly leaned the carbine against the wall and raised his hands.


Charley couldn't believe his eyes. The Tanners were here! Right here in this room, and he had the drop on them. "Looky here, looky here, looky here!"

Charley smiled, delighted with this whole turn of events. Blake and the other fools were dead. There'd be no more problems from that quarter, and no more lyin' about that damn gold.

Jake Tanner lay in the corner being attended to by two women, blood dripping down his arm and forming a small pool on the floor. One of the women was his mother, the Higgins woman. The other was

Lucy Carter.

Charley had Will Tanner and his girl Lucy right where he wanted them. "Get in here, Darnell!" he yelled.

Behind him, old man Carter stumbled in, wobbling and bleeding from a gash on his head. His knees buckled and he fell face-forward onto the floor. Darnell stepped into the parlor, edged to his right and put his back against the wall. His eyes immediately went to Jake.

"Never you mind him," Charley said, pointing to Will and Ben. "Drag the old man in here where we can see 'im. Cover 'em both. Keep your eye on 'em." He didn't figure the old man to be a problem, but it was best to be sure.

"Okay Charley," replied Darnell. He rolled Ben over and drug him further into the parlor and dropped him. Ben's head plopped on the wooden floor with a dull thunk, and a low moan escaped his lips. Darnell inched back tighter to the wall and shifted his pistol between Will and Ben.

He saw Lucy eyeing the front door and he moved to block it. "Nobody's leavin'," he said. "This here party's just getting' started." He grinned at his own joke. "I got everythin' I want right here, in one little basket."

Tanner's eyes moved to his pistol on the floor, and he shifted his feet.

Charley stiffened. "I wouldn't try that," he said. "Don't make no sudden moves. We'll just talk a little while."

Tanner relaxed and his shoulders slumped. "I ain't got nothin' to say to you, Porter," he said, spitting his name out like it was soured milk.

"Well, I got lots to say to you," Charley replied. "I bet I can surprise you. What say we bet on that?"

"I need to see about Papa," said Lucy. "Please let me go to him,"

Charley studied her. She was just as pretty as he remembered. Still, he pointed the gun at her. "No, no. Cain't let you do that. Now don't you worry none about your Pa, he'll live." *She sure is a pretty one,* he thought, *and her voice is like pure honey.* Charley wondered what she'd be like under a blanket. It hadn't been in his plan, but plans could change, couldn't they?

Lucy stole a glance at Will, and Charley saw it. "Now, don't you be worryin' none about your beau Tanner, here," he said. "We got us some things to talk about before anythin' happens. In fact, you just step on over here, next to me."

Lucy made no move to obey; instead, she glanced at Tanner.

Tanner shifted his feet again and shook his head at Lucy. Losing patience, Charley stepped over and grabbed her by the arm, spun her around, and threw his left arm around her throat. He pulled her in close and pointed the gun at her head.

"Whoooo Wheeee," he yelled, "Ain't you a pretty one. Looky here, Will Tanner. Looky what I got!"

*****

# Chapter 23

Will's heart sank. As he had feared, Porter now had Lucy by the throat and had a pistol to her head.

"Porter!" He yelled. "Don't do this! Whatever beef you got with me, let's me and you settle it. Leave Lucy out of it!" He added, more calmly than he felt, "Just me and you, Porter. We can go outside, right now, and we can settle this."

Porter laughed. "What's the rush, Tanner? We ain't had our talk yet."

Will set his feet to charge him.

Porter noticed. He quickly moved his gun back to cover him. "No sir! You hold right there now, 'brother!'"

Ma looked at Porter funny when he spat out the word 'brother.' Will supposed he was just trying to rile him, but Ma's reaction puzzled him.

Porter grinned. "Yeap! Looks like we got us a little family reunion goin' on here, Tanner. I reckon I'm the black sheep of the family." He laughed. "But that's all right, I'm used to it."

Will shook his head. "What the hell are you talkin' about?"

Ma was now staring intensely at Porter, her eyes squinting at him in the dim light, her jaw working, her fists clenched. "Charley Porter," she said. "Who are you?"

"Well, hell, didn't Jake tell you? After all this time, he ain't said nothin'?" He shook his head. "I thought sure he'd a told you-all. Well, I'll be damned!" He kicked Jake who moaned in response.

*Porter's crazy, off his gourd,* Will thought. *Maybe if I keep him talkin' he'll get distracted and I can take him.* "Tell us what, Porter?"

"What Jake didn't tell you," Porter continued, "is that you and me, Tanner, an' Jake, we're brothers."

Will's mind reeled. *What the hell? He ain't my brother!*

Porter just stood there, grinning.

Will opened his mouth, but no sounds came out. *What kind of game is he playing at?*

"I know what you're thinkin', Tanner," Porter said. "It cain't be true, ain't that what you're thinkin'?"

Porter was right about that. Will leaned forward a bit, getting set to jump if Porter's attention wavered.

"No, no, now you stay right there, brother!" Porter moved the gun back to Lucy's head.

Will stopped short. It would be useless to charge him — Porter's gun was cocked and ready. So, he just stood there, his open mouth gaping in shock.

"Yeah, that's right, Tanner. My Pa is the same as yours and Jake's. Charley Tanner. How's them apples for you?"

Ma gasped. She turned red and her eyes went wide. "What are you talkin' about?" she asked in a whisper. "Charley Tanner's dead. He died on the way to Californy."

Porter laughed, and his gun wavered a bit. His eyes moved to Will's. "That what you been told?" He looked at Ma and grinned. "That what she told you? He run off to dig for gold and died on that steamer?" He laughed again.

Ma's face had a confused look that Will had never seen before. Ma was never unsure about anything. He knew he was pushing his luck, but he couldn't stop himself from taunting Porter, "This is crazy talk. And you're a damned liar."

Porter's grin changed into a sneer, and there was steel in his eyes. His gun centered on Will's chest. "You oughn't call a man that, not when he's got a gun on you," he said. He relaxed and his grin returned. "But I can let that one go by."

Will thought long and hard but he couldn't figure out Porter's angle. He couldn't fathom why he'd lie about such a thing, where was the gain in it for him?

Ma looked up at Will. "Will, listen to me," she said. "Charley here does resemble your Pa. He's got the same hair for one, and his face reminds me of him. I can see it in his chin and in his eyes now. I saw some of it when he was here before, but I didn't recognize it. Your Pa's been dead a long time."

Porter cackled. "Yeah well I got some more news for you," he said. "He ain't dead."

Lucy was terrified. Porter had her in a death grip, his left arm crooked around her neck so tight it was choking her; his pistol was aimed at her head one instant then at Will the next. His stink filled her nostrils—his breath smelled like rotten meat and his filthy coat reeked of old sweat and blood. She wriggled as much as she dared, trying to break free from his grasp. It was useless, he was too strong.

"You be still now, and quit that buckin'," said Porter, into Lucy's ear. She could feel his jaw muscles working as he grinned. "We'll save that buckin' for later."

Lucy turned white. She might be only seventeen, but she understood the threat in Porter's words. His grip was strong, and she gave up any hope of twisting free for now.

Porter turned back to Will. "That's right, Tanner. Your Pa, Charley Tanner is still alive. An' he's my Pa, same as yours, same as Jake's."

Lucy didn't believe for a minute that Porter was Will's brother. She did believe that he intended other things.

"You're a damned liar, Porter!" Will yelled. "Pa died down in New Orleans." He took a step forward, and Porter aimed the gun at him again.

"Will, no!" cried Lucy. She thought sure Porter would shoot this time.

Instead, Porter said, "Tanner, you need to listen to little Miss Lucy here. Next step you take I will shoot you! And then our little chat will be over. An' that's too bad, cause I got things to say."

Will stopped, his fists still clenched, his jaw working as he ground his teeth.

Lucy gave Will a slight head shake. Lucy feared for him.

"Will," said Joline, laying a hand on his arm. "There's things I ain't told you." Her eyes teared up.

Lucy felt Porter tremble as some of the tension left him, but his grip was relentless. He squeezed her neck even tighter.

"No, Pa's dead," said Will.

"You ever see his body?" asked Porter.

Joline looked down at her feet. "There weren't no body. I got a letter…."

"A man can lie in a letter easier than talkin'," Porter continued. "He was damn lively last time I saw him, about seven years ago when he run off and left me and my Ma with nothin'." He spat the last words out like they tasted bad.

Joline gasped and sagged against the wall. She hung her head and her eyes went vacant. Lucy recognized the look — the bad-news look. The look a grieving widow had for a lost husband or son. A look that spoke of memories running through your head that you couldn't stop seeing. Lucy had seen it in her own Mama when Patrick went missing down in Georgia. She couldn't imagine the hurt if you found out that your husband had run off, lied, pretended to be dead all these years. That was a betrayal well beyond anything she'd ever heard tell of.

Will just stood there, staring at Porter. Then he looked at Lucy, as if to ask her to wake him up from this nightmare.

She felt Porter tremble again, and the gun in his hand wavered and fell just a little.

"Course, he never did marry her and make her honest," Porter spat. He looked at Joline. "Ma named me after him, but Pa, he never saw fit to give me his name."

In that moment, Lucy almost felt sorry for Porter. Almost. She could feel that Porter's passions were about to burst out of him like juice from a peach. *Does he want a reunion with his family? A happy ending to this? Is that what this is all about?*

No, she decided. Porter is just bitter. He's angry at his father, angry at Will and Jake, angry about everything. His anger has eaten away any compassion that he might've ever had. The war taught him how to kill, and now he likes it. He's an animal, a foaming at the mouth coyote, and he won't stop killing. He can't stop killing. Don't forget that, she told herself. He'll kill us if it suits his purpose. He's already proved that. Whatever happened to him to make him this way, it's too late for him to go back.

Porter glared at Will. "Yeah, Pa left you his farm, and you ate well all these years. Me an' Ma, we had to eat scraps and bread crusts and live hand to mouth, dependin' on other folk's charity. An' there was damn little of that amongst the good Christian folks in Liberty, Missouri."

Porter paused and Lucy felt him tremble, then his resolve seemed to stiffen. "The only way my Ma could make a livin' was to turn to whorin'. Your Pa—our Pa—made my Ma into a whore. An' that's why I'm gonna find him and then I'm gonna kill him. Right after I kill you." He spit the words out at Will like venom.

Will didn't believe Porter. He couldn't believe him. There had to be some mistake, or some other explanation. Was he playing some cruel game?

One thing was for certain, mistake, or not, Porter was going to kill somebody before the night was over. Things had gone too far—the dead men scattered out in the yard and the kitchen proved that—and Will could see no other outcome. If they couldn't somehow shake free of him or overpower the man, there would be more death.

The gun wavered again, and Will almost made a move. At the last second, Porter's eyes met his. The gun moved back, and Porter shook his head.

And there was the other man, the silent one, the one Porter called Darnell. He was so quiet that Will had almost forgotten he was there. There was something about him that was off, not right. For one thing, he wouldn't meet anyone's eyes, like he was ashamed to be here. He didn't have the eyes of a killer. He looked more like a dog that had been whipped and made to do something he didn't' want to do.

"Find some rope, Darnell, and tie em up," said Porter.

Darnell went out the back door, his head down. Will was on the edge of panic. Tied up, there'd be no chance of taking Porter down.

He decided on another tack, after all there was nothing to lose. He took a deep breath. "Porter," he said, "If we're brothers, prove it. Put your gun away and let go of Lucy. Then we can talk about this. We don't have to be enemies."

Porter appeared to think about it a moment, then shook his head. "I cain't trust you, Tanner. You're a slippery one, you are."

Darnell came back with some leather straps and tied Ma's hands together in front. Then he bound up Ben, who was still unconscious on the floor.

He moved to tie up Will. Will resisted, but a warning head shake from Porter made him stop. He clenched his fists and held his wrists as far apart as he could, hoping Darnell didn't notice.

Incredibly, the man not only didn't notice, he didn't even tie a knot, he just looped the leather loosely over his wrists. Then he tapped Will's hands in some sort of signal. Will's eyes widened in surprise. Will's heartbeat sped up. As soon as Darnell moved away, Will got his hands free, but he kept them behind him as if they were still tied.

Will stole a sideways glance at Darnell. For the first time tonight, the man met his eyes, holding them for a moment. He looked at Porter, then back to Will, just his eyes. *Another signal?*

Darnell then tied up Lucy while Porter covered Will with the pistol.

"Afraid of a girl, Porter?" asked Lucy.

"Nope. I got plans for you later, so I don't want you to run off or anythin'," Porter shot back.

Lucy looked down at her own hands, at Darnell then her eyes moved to meet Will's. There was puzzlement written there. Her bonds were not tight either—she hadn't shown any discomfort at all when she was tied up.

For the first time, Will began to hope. It was a slim hope, but it was there. If Darnell would just stay out of it, there might be a chance. That seemed to be the signal he was giving.

*If I'm wrong, then I'm dead. I'm dead if I do nothin', too.*

Porter tilted his head. "Where's those other brats of yours?" he asked Ma.

"I told them to run away as far and as fast as they could," she replied.

Porter looked dubious. "You sent 'em to get help. Yep, that's what you did. And you been stallin' all this time." He turned to Lucy. "And the darkies too, where they at?"

"Hidin'," said Lucy.

"Right. Hidin' out." Porter sneered. "You think I'm stupid or somethin'? That's Darnell, Missy, not me."

Darnell cocked his head and glared at Porter.

Three things then happened at the same time. Ben stirred and moaned, and Porter glanced down at him. Lucy stomped on Porter's foot and when he let go of her, she spun away and ducked through the kitchen door. And a voice—Ike's voice—yelled from the top of the stairs "Drop your guns or I'm shootin'!"

Porter lunged for Lucy, but it was too late, she was gone. He ducked back against the wall where Ike had no clear shot at him.

Darnell just stood there with his pistol pointed down. He dropped it and slowly pulled his other one out handle first and dropped it as well. He slowly raised his hands.

"Darnell, what the hell you doin'?" screamed Porter.

"You been lyin'," said Darnell.

"What? What're you talkin' about?"

"You been lyin' 'bout that gold just to get them men to come here and do bad things," said Darnell. "Then you killed that man. You killed him just 'cause you're mean, Charley. You're a bad man an' I ain't your friend no more."

"Damn you Darnell, you got to choose now to do this?" Porter's gun moved back and forth between the stairway and Will and Ma who were still standing in front of the window.

Will shook free of his astonishment and dived for Darnell's pistols. He grabbed them both and rolled up behind the sofa. It was scant cover in a pistol fight, but at least he was somewhat hidden, and now he was armed. He cocked the guns and hoped Darnell had loaded them properly.

He peeked around the end of the sofa. Ma dropped and rolled into a ball, giving Will a clear shot at Porter. He fired and missed. The bullet showered Porter with plaster dust from the wall.

Porter fired back, the bullet passing through the sofa just in front of Will's face. Porter then crawled through the front door and disappeared into the darkness.

Darnell stood there with his hands up. Will ignored him, crawled over to the door and peeked out. Another shot from Porter thunked into the doorjamb just above his head. He quickly drew his head back in.

"Ma, take care of Jake and Ike," said Will. "This ends tonight."

Ma nodded. "You go do what needs to be done."

"Ike!" Will yelled. "Keep your rifle on this man down here. Shoot him if you have to."

Ike stepped into view on the stairs and aimed at Darnell. "I got 'im, Will."

"Porter!" yelled Will. "The only way you get out of here alive is to give up, right now!"

A cackle of laughter was Porter's answer.

Will dove through the door and pointed his pistols at the darkness outside.

Charley's head felt like it would explode from pure rage. *Damn you Darnell Harris! What the hell's wrong with you? I'll kill you sure, next time we meet!* "Whole damn thing's come apart," he whispered to himself as he ducked down behind the well. "Damn you Darnell!" he yelled in frustration.

*I need my horse!* They'd left their horses tied up in back of the house. Charley was just about to run around the side when he saw Tanner, framed by the dim light from inside the house, roll through the door and disappear to his right. He snapped off a shot. He heard the bullet thunk into wood. "Damn you Tanner!" he shouted, unable to contain his anger.

"Give up, Porter! Last chance!" yelled Tanner.

Charley knew what awaited him if he surrendered. The thought of the noose caused him to shiver. "No way! You know what they'll do to me, Tanner!" He fired another shot toward Tanner's voice and ducked again as Tanner fired back and missed. He jumped up and ran around to the back of the house.

The horses weren't there! Panic set in, and Charley felt the blood drain from his face. There were no other horses in sight he could steal, so he kept on running though he didn't know where he was running to. He had no horse, no plan, no friends.

*The corn! I can hide in there!* He ducked into the head-high stalks just as Tanner fired again. An ear of corn exploded above his right ear, stinging his face. He didn't shoot back, he just kept running. The dried corn leaves ripped at his shirt and tore at his skin, and made a swishing sound that he knew Tanner, behind him, could plainly hear. Tanner fired again and something slammed into his left shoulder — it was like a rock had hit him. He knew he'd been hit. Oddly, there was no pain, and he kept running. He snapped off another shot at Tanner. And another, but the pistol only clicked. *Empty!*

Then it came to him — *The river! If I can make the river, maybe I can swim downstream and hide my tracks!* He changed direction and aimed for a distant tree line atop a hill. He knew the river lay on the other side.

Charley tripped over something soft — someone grunted — and he fell forward into the crusty dirt. Something popped in his left knee, and there was pain. As if in sympathy with his knee, his shoulder now began to burn, and Porter felt something dripping from his fingers. He heard a whimpering noise and saw dim shapes in the shadows. "Who's there?" he demanded "Who are you?"

"Don't shoot Massa! We ain't done nothin'!" came the reply.

*The darkies!* Charley saw two smaller forms in the dim moonlight. *The brats!*

Charley holstered his now-empty pistol, pulled his spare from his left side and fingered the hammer. He considered killing the brats for a few precious seconds. That'd show Tanner! Without his extra pistols, mounted to his now-gone saddle, he only had six more shots. And a gunshot would give away his position. He reached for his knife, but it wasn't there. *Dammit! Ain't nothin' goin' right tonight. I ain't got no time for this.*

"If you keep your mouth shut and don't yell, I'll let you live." he whispered to the negroes and struggled painfully to his feet. He could now hear Tanner's heavy boots crashing through the corn, heading his way. He heard him call his name.

"Porter! I'm comin' after you! Give it up, you ain't getting' away!"

Charley couldn't help himself. He yelled back, "Back off Tanner, I'll kill these two brats I found out here if you don't." He reached for one of the dim shadows and grabbed an arm. It was the smaller of the two boys. He threw him over his shoulder and limped on toward the tree line. The child began to wail.

The other boy, now out of sight behind him yelled out, "Will! Will! He's got Nate! He's headed to the swimmin' hole!"

*I should have shut 'em up for good,* Charley thought. It was too late now; Tanner was crashing through the corn toward him. He sped up as fast as he could go, but there was something not right in his knee and he could only manage an off-keel lope.

He made out a moonlit break in the dark tree line and he headed for it. The corn abruptly ended and about twenty yards away, the opening that led down to the river appeared before him, clear as day in the moonlight. He headed for it, the brat on his shoulder crying even louder. He didn't see the edge of the bluff until he almost toppled over it, but he stopped just in time. A rock bounced and rattled its way down, and Charley heard it splash into the river below. He looked left, then right, desperate to find a way down. Below him he saw only darkness.

Behind him, Tanner emerged from the corn, pistol leveled. Charley turned to face him.

*****

# Chapter 24

Will came out of the cornfield to find Porter silhouetted by the moon behind him. Nate wailed, terrified, and wiggled about on Porter's left shoulder, trying to get down. Porter held on tightly. With his left arm. His right held a pistol pointed at Will.

He had no clear shot, and he knew Porter could see him plainly in the bright moonlight. Porter was having trouble aiming his gun; he wobbled like a drunk man and his gun wavered all over the place. Will saw blood pooling on the ground under Porter's left arm, just a growing dark stain in the lighter dirt. *Winged him!*

"Well, ain't this a mess, Tanner," said Porter.

"Put my brother down, and we can talk about it," answered Will.

Porter shifted Nate higher on his shoulder. "No, no. I ain't givin' up," he said. "I ain't gonna hang. I ain't dying like that." His voice quivered.

Will almost felt sorry for him. "Put him down. This is between you and me. Put him down and me and you will settle this, here and now."

Porter stumbled and Will took a step closer. Porter recovered and swung his pistol toward him. "Hold right there! You come any closer and I'll shoot you. Then I'll shoot him."

"All right, Porter." Will lowered his own gun and stepped backward. "Put him down, Porter, he's innocent in all this."

"There ain't nobody innocent, not anymore." Porter wobbled again. "You back up, Tanner. I'll put him down, but you gotta back up."

Will held his ground. "Maybe me and you ain't innocent," he

said. "Nate's only three, he's never hurt no-body."

Porter sneered. "You was three once, Tanner. Look at you now. You growed up to be a damned Yankee. This un will too."

Will shook his head. "He's just a kid, Porter."

Porter's gun wavered, but again he caught himself. "I told you to back up. Do it or else."

"Ok, Porter." Will took another step back. "Ok, see, I'm backin' up." He took another. "What happened, Porter? Why do you hate me an' Jake like you do?"

"I guess I don't rightly know no more," he said. "Maybe it's Pa — our Pa — I really hate. I thought it was because of what he did to my Ma, makin' her turn to whorin just to live. Then she got kilt by that damn two-bit john. He was the first man I kilt. But it was all Pa's fault, an' I made a promise to myself that I'd find him an' make him pay for it. I hate that sumbitch an' I will find 'im an' I will kill 'im, I swear I will do it." He shifted Nate higher up on his shoulder.

"Then you and Jake come along an' I thought maybe we could be like brothers, like a family. I ain't never had me no real family. But all Jake wanted to do was fight me, run me off, make me stop talkin' about it. Then you left me there on that battlefield to get captured. My brother! An' you just left me for them Yankees to drag off like some kind of animal!"

Porter's voice cracked before he continued, "It was an awful thing, Will, bein' in that Yankee prison camp. They did unspeakable things to us in there. So, I promised myself one more thing, that I'd make you and Jake pay and suffer just like me."

*He called me Will!* "Charley," said Will, softly, "I didn't know."

"I believe you, Will, yore eyes don't lie an' you was as surprised as can be back there. So, maybe I don't hate you for that no more. Maybe there's a way out of this yet, Will Tanner."

"Put Nate down," Will said again, "and we can talk this through."

"No, I cain't do that just yet," said Porter. On his shoulder, Nate continued to wail and cry.

"Charley," Will said, gently. "Put Nate down and I promise you I'll stand up an' speak for you, if you just put him down."

Porter hesitated. "You mean surrender? No, no, no." He shook his head, laughing. "I done too much, Will. Too much blood's been spilt. I seen what they do to men like me. They'll hang me, for sure." His pistol wavered again, and he lowered it just a little. "Ride with me, Will. Me an' you, like brothers—like we should be. Like we should of always been."

Will eyes widened and he cocked his head in surprise. "You're askin' me to ride with you?"

"Why not, Will?" asked Porter. "There ain't no future in the Yankee Army. There's lots of money out there, lots of gold and silver, just for the takin', for them that are willin' to take it. Let's get out of Missouri. Let's go out west together, me an' you. I hear Californy is bustin' at the seams with gold and silver and greenbacks. We can live like kings, out there, you an' me."

Will felt the hair stand up on his neck. He'd been here before, hadn't he? Then he remembered the dream. Was Porter the bear who wanted to be friends? *Can I be friends with a bear? Can I trust him?* No, he decided. *Porter is a snake, and if I don't end this tonight, he'll bite us again.* This was just another one of Porter's tricks.

He knew it was unwise to provoke him, but Will couldn't help himself. "You want me to rob an' steal an' burn an' loot an' murder? To burn out poor folk's homes and rape their women? That it, Porter? I think you know what I say to that."

Porter tightened his grip on Nate, who wailed again, and his pistol raised back up to point at Will. He sneered again. "Damn you. I had to try, but that's what I figured you'd say."

Nate wiggled furiously, and Porter yelped, "Ow! Little bastard bit me!" His grip loosened and Nate slid to the ground, but Porter kept him pinned against his legs. Nate wailed ever more loudly.

The corn rustled to Will's left, and from the corner of his eye, he saw someone step from the cornfield. He recognized him instantly. *Ike!*

Porter turned to face the new threat and he took his eyes off Will. Just for a split-second, his gun moved away from Will, giving him the best shot he'd had all night.

Will almost took the shot. His heart jumped and he felt the blood pulse all the way down into his gun hand and his finger twitched on the trigger. But he didn't follow through, and he wasn't sure why. *Am I feelin' a little sorry for him?* He shook his head to clear it. *He's a damn rattlesnake. You cain't feel sorry for him!*

"Well, looky here," Porter said. "You aim to shoot me too, boy?"

"You hurt my Ma," said Ike. "You burned our house, killed our mule. You hurt Jake. An' you been mean to my little brother, so yeah, I aim to shoot you."

Even in the dim moonlight, Will saw Porter's nervous grin. The old, bad Porter was back. Will chanced a glance to his left and saw Ike with the rifle pointed in Porter's direction. A bloody bandage circled his head, but he was steady on his feet and his aim was true.

Still, Will worried he might hit Nate. "Hold off, Ike."

Nate bit Porter again.

"Ow! Dammit!" yelled Porter. He loosened his grip just enough for Nate to wriggle out of his grasp. His hostage was gone but now his left arm was free, and he pulled another pistol and turned toward Ike.

*No!* Will took the shot. The gun in his hand seemed to jerk backward of its own accord, and the ball struck Porter in his left shoulder and spun him around.

Porter's left hand dropped the gun he held there. The gun in his right hand began to arc up and point at Ike.

"Now, Ike!" yelled Will, cocking the pistol again. There was a flash and a sharp crack and Porter jerked, but he didn't fall. Instead, he turned back to Will and snapped off a shot.

Will felt the wind from the bullet as it passed by his ear, but he stood steady. He pulled the trigger and his pistol bucked again.

Will's shot spun Porter even further to the left, and his right hand dropped the gun into the dirt. He continued spinning until he fell over the edge of the slope and disappeared into the darkness.

Will heard him tumble and slide down the loose rocks and then there was a splash. He ran over and picked up Nate, who hugged Will tight and wailed. Will looked him over, there was not a scratch on him. "You did good, Nate. Good boy," he said, crooning to him and rubbing his hair. Nate's wailing subsided to sniffles.

Ike, however, was stunned, and just stood there, the long rifle pointed at the ground.

Still hugging Nate, Will said, "Reload, Ike, always reload." Ike reached for the powder horn attached to his waist and began to fumble with it, his eyes as wide as saucers.

Will edged closer to the bluff. Nate stiffened in his arms and gripped him tight. Will searched for Porter, but he couldn't see anything in the darkness down there. He listened for any sound, turning his head this way and that; there was only the peaceful murmur of rippling water to be heard. Satisfied, he backed away from the edge, and Nate relaxed.

Someone else crashed out of the cornfield, and a shotgun glinted in the moonlight. He instantly recognized the burly frame of Ben Davis. Then two of his negroes, Seth with them, glided silently from the cornrows. One held an ax handle in his hand, the other had a shovel slung over one shoulder.

Near his feet, Will saw a gleam in the moonlight, and he reached down to retrieve one of Porter's pistols. He soon found the other and stuck them both in his belt.

"It's over. Porter's dead," Will said. He took another long look for Porter's body and still saw nothing. There was no moaning, no cursing, no rustling of movement coming from down there. No sound of splashing. After a few seconds, the crickets started chirping, and Will's racing heart began to slow. He felt tired, suddenly, and he turned away once more.

"Let's go home," he said. He shifted Nate to a higher, spot on his shoulder, put one arm around Ike, and with Seth following, they entered the corn-field, leaving Ben and his negroes standing, stunned, atop the bluff. The only sound was the swishing of clothes against dried corn stalks.

*****

# Chapter 25

"You did good tonight, Ike. I am proud of you," said Will.

Ike's teeth glowed in the moonlight when he smiled. "You're the one taught me how to shoot," he said, as they walked back through the corn.

"Well, you took to it real natural like," Will said. "How's the head?"

Ike shrugged. "Hurts some."

Will turned to Seth. "I'm proud of you too," Will told him. "If you hadn't yelled out when you did, I wouldn't a found them in time."

Nate, still in Will's arms, sniffled from time to time. Will hoped he'd soon forget his ordeal. "An' I'm proud of you too, little brother. You're a brave boy," Will said.

"Nate bite!" said Nate.

"Yes, you did," said Will, with a grin. Nate laid his head on Will's shoulder and closed his eyes. Before they got back to the house, he was sleeping.

The first thing Will noticed when they emerged from the corn was the bodies laid out in a neat row by the carriage house. He counted; there were five of them. Someone had covered their faces with gunny sacks. Old Tom leaned nearby on a shovel, watching the bodies as though he expected them to rise up and attack again. The moonlit scene raised the hair on Will's neck, and he was glad Nate was asleep.

Ma ran out and hugged them each. Tears came to her eyes when she saw they were not hurt. "We heard the shots. Is it over? Are you all ok?"

"It's over, an' we're all right." Will said. "Nobody's hurt."

She sniffed and wiped her eyes. "Is the Porter boy dead?" she asked.

Will thought about his answer. *Is Porter really dead? I cain't prove it. With four bullet wounds, he had to be dead, didn't he?* "Yeah, I think he's dead," he finally answered. "He fell down into the river. If the bullets didn't kill him, then he drowned."

"You don't sound so sure about it," said Ma, frowning.

Ben appeared beside them "We'll go back with some torches, try an' find him," he said. "It don't feel finished, somehow, without no body." As he turned to go, he yelled, "Come along Tom. Fetch some torches."

"What happened out there?" asked Ma.

"I'll tell you all about it later, Will said. "What about Jake, is he....?"

"He'll live," Ma said. "It's gonna take a while for him to heal, though. He's shot clean through his shoulder. No bones are broke that I can tell. Doc Calhoun is on his way."

Will took a deep breath and let it out with a sigh and some of the stress he felt left him. He felt a great weight lift from his shoulders; he'd been more worried about Jake than he realized. He nodded, not trusting his voice, and fought back tears.

"We need to talk," Ma said. "But you need coffee first. Let's go inside."

"Ok," he said. Still carrying Nate, he followed her into the house.


In the Carter's kitchen, Joline poured her eldest son a steaming cup of coffee from the stove and found him a biscuit and some molasses. When he had wolfed down the biscuit and gulped some coffee, some of his color returned.

"I never knew molasses could taste so good," he mumbled around a mouthful. "I don't know how long it's been since we last ate." He licked his fingers and wiped them on his pants.

Joline studied him in the dim lamplight of the kitchen. His dark stubble had turned into an almost full beard, and his unkempt hair had grown long and shaggy. He was thin and had deep hollows and dark circles under his eyes. He needed good food and rest.

Joline sighed. His rest would have to wait. It was time to have the talk she'd been dreading; if she didn't tell him now, she might never have the nerve again. She looked at Chloe, who knelt on the floor, scrubbing on a large bloodstain. She looked at Will and said, "Let's go outside."

Will said nothing; just rose from his chair and headed to the door. Joline followed him out to the back porch and they sat on the steps. She looked up at the stars and sighed. The night was not cold, but she could still see her own breath, like fog in the air.

"Ok Ma, let's talk," said Will.

"First, tell me what happened tonight," she said. "The whole story."

Will explained how Porter had found them on the battlefield and threatened them. He described how he and Jake had rode day and night to get here to warn everyone and he took the blame again for Ike's involvement in the shooting.

He told her about the stand-off at the riverbank. She blanched when he told her that Porter had used Nate as a shield. He described the final moments and Ike's role in it. He smiled. "Nate bit him," he said. "An' Porter dropped him. That gave me a shot. Then Ike shot him, then I shot him again." He shook his head. "It was a family affair."

"Is he dead?"

"I think so," Will said. "I must have winged him out in the cornfield—he was already bleedin' pretty good, and me an' Ike put three more bullets in him. He fell down the slope into the river—I heard the splash—an' I never heard another sound—no splashin', no yellin' or nothin'. I listened a good while. If he survived the shootin', he surely drowned."

It was a strange feeling Joline had. She was relieved that the danger was over, but she was also sorry that the Porter boy was dead. If the boy hadn't been so twisted by his own hate, he'd still be alive. Maybe they could have talked more and reconciled with him somehow. Now, any chance of that was gone forever.

Joline sighed. "I need to tell you about your Pa now, your real Pa, Charley Tanner." she said, pausing to look up at the stars again. She didn't want to do this. She had hoped she'd never have to do this. But now was the time. Will needed to know.

"I didn't want to ever say anythin' bad about him," she began. "I reckon now you need to know. Charley Tanner was a good man—for the most part—that's why I fell in love with him. He could be sweet and kind and gentle. I want you to always remember that, Will."

"All right," said Will.

Joline sighed again and continued, "He had flaws, too. Some people would call it 'em bad habits, I suppose. One was his drinkin'. The man had a taste for whiskey, like many a man does. No big matter, that, if that was all there was to it."

Will nodded. "The drinkin' led to other bad things, didn't it?" he asked. "I seen it in the army."

She took a deep breath. "He was a mean drunk. We had many a fight over the drinkin' an' sometimes Charley would get a little rough with me. It weren't nothin' too bad, but I worried it would get worse."

Will looked down at the ground and nodded.

"He took up with other women," said Joline. "I got tired of it all, Will," she said, looking straight at him. "I just plain got tired tired of him drinkin' all our money away, and him gamblin' an' fightin' and cheatin' an' lyin'. So, I made him go away." Her voice grew hoarse and her eyes stung with tears. "He didn't want to go. I made him." She wiped a tear from her cheek with one hand.

Will leaned back in his chair and sighed. "Sounds like you didn't have much choice, Ma."

"I don't know, maybe. I know I was scared, and there was you two boys to worry about. Still, there was many a day, afterward, when I thought maybe I was wrong to do it. I still do sometimes. Maybe I should've just tried to live with it, just let it go."

Will looked at her straight in the eye. "No, I believe you were right. I seen what too much whiskey can do to a man, it makes people mean."

"Still," she said, "I cain't help but wonder sometimes, if I could've helped him. How do you know when to give up on somebody?"

A puzzled look came across Will's face, and he leaned back against a post. He shook his head. "I think that when a man turns mean, that somethin' inside of him changes, and then there ain't no goin' back. I think that's what happened to Porter, and maybe that's where Pa was headed." Will took a deep breath. "Maybe it was just in his blood."

Joline stiffened. She'd said that about Jake, often, as a kind of joke, and maybe as an excuse for some of his milder misdeeds. Jake had his faults, but they were minor compared to Charley Tanner's. Jake wasn't like his father, he was just a rowdy, rambunctious boy. She vowed never to say that to Jake again, ever, if she could help it.

Will interrupted her musings. "You think he's still alive out there somewhere, Ma? Charley Tanner, Pa, I mean, What about that letter? The one you got that said he was dead?"

She pondered that for a moment before answering. She recalled the day Ben Carter came to her door, sadness written all over his kind face, his hat in his hands, and read the letter to her. Even now, she recalled the hurt the words brought. Even though she'd sent Charley Tanner away, she still had deep feelings for him, and it hurt her to think he was dead. It took her a long time to get over it. But there also had been a sense of relief, and she was ashamed of herself still, for that. It was such a confusing jumble of feelings.

Will deserved an answer, so she said, "It was some newspaper man down in New Orleans that wrote it. I cain't recall the name, and now the letter is burned up. Blowed to pieces or drowned in the river is what it said, an' there weren't no body. I had no reason not to believe the letter, and I thought he really was dead after that, I truly did." *Charley Tanner let me think he was dead all these years! I ought to be angry, but somehow I ain't.*

"I reckon he wanted it that way," said Will, shaking his head.

"Joline nodded. "Lookin' back on it now, maybe I should have known he'd do somethin' like that. It was always his way to run away from a problem."

Will sighed. "This is a lot to take in, Ma. It just don't make sense." After a minute, he asked, "Do you think Pa really was Charley Porter's father?"

"Maybe," Joline said. "Prob'bly. He has the looks — I didn't see it right off but if you look close, he does — did — look like your Pa. It might explain the hate he carried for you an' Jake. So maybe he was tellin' the truth, or some of it, anyhow." She paused for breath.

"It's still hard to believe, Ma." said Will. "It's a lot to think on."

She laid a hand on Will's arm. "It is, an' I am sorry for it. Sometimes life just reaches up and slaps us in the face, whether or not we deserve it." She looked away again and thought for a while. There wasn't much else to say. She noticed the darkness of the night had turned a lighter shade of purple. *Another day is coming; what will this one bring?*

"Ma," said Will. "When the fightin's done and I come home, I promise you I will go look for Pa and if I find him...."

Joline frowned "An' do what?" she asked. "What if you do find him? What will you do then? No, Will, let that sleepin' dog be an' don't stir up no more trouble about it. I got over him a long time ago. I had another husband that I loved. an' three more boys. I made another family. I don't begrudge him the same thing. Let it be, Will."

She searched Will's face for an answer, and finally he nodded.

"Ok, Ma," he said. He rose and put a hand on her shoulder.

She held it for a minute.

"You know," Will said. "I never really thought much on it, but Frank Higgins was my real Pa. I don't even remember Charley Tanner."

She kissed his hand. "Yes, he was. He never showed a lick of difference between you boys. He was a good man, and he raised you up to be a good man, too. You're just like him. You always treated your brothers all just the same. You're a good man, William Tanner." She rose from the step herself, hugged him, and gave him a peck on the cheek.

He hugged her back for a long minute, and whispered in her ear, "Thank you, Ma." He released her and stepped back.

"I suppose you're still starvin'," she said, wiping more tears from her eyes. "An' I got to check on Jake. Let's get some more food in you. Thank God for the Carters, where'd we be without 'em?"

A strained smile crossed Will's face. "Yeah," he said. "Something to eat would be good."


Lucy couldn't take her eyes off of Will. He wolfed down biscuits and ham and drank coffee until she thought he'd burst. She believed him when he said he hadn't eaten in three days. When he finished the last crumb and washed it down with the last of his coffee, he sat back and told her his story.

Lucy was astonished by all that led to the strange events of last night.

When he finished, he asked a favor of her. "Please don't tell Ma that Porter wanted me to ride with him," he said. "Or Jake, either. It might upset 'em both. And I don't even know myself if he was just stringin' me along or not. I don't see no reason for him to think I'd do it. He either was a fool, or he took me for one. Or he was just stallin' for time."

"I promise, Will," she said. "Don't you worry about that."

"There's something else, too," he said. "You have to promise me you won't think bad of me no matter what happens after today."

Lucy was puzzled. "How could I think less of you after what you did for us?" she asked.

Will's mouth turned down and his head fell.

That worried Lucy. "What is it, Will?"

He raised his head and looked her in the eye. "Jake an' me, we might be in for some trouble," he said, clenching his jaw and rubbing his temples.

Will was plainly still worried about something. What kind of trouble could he possibly be in? He wasn't one to get into trouble. Jake, maybe, not Will. Then it occurred to her. "You aren't supposed to be here, are you?" she asked. "You an' Jake, you left your post to come here."

Will's eyes turned misty. "I had to," he said. "I couldn't let Porter do what he planned to do to here. To my family. To you and your family. I tried to get Jake to stay out of it, but you know Jake—he won't take no advice from me."

"How much trouble are you in?" she asked.

Will shook his head. "I don't know. They might charge us with desertion. We might get the stockade. We might go to prison, or worse. It might get real bad."

Lucy felt light-headed all of a sudden. "But you're heroes for comin' here and fighting off those killers, surely they'll see that, won't they?"

"Maybe," Will said, shaking his head. "Whatever they decide, I ain't runnin' from it. I'll take whatever punishment they decide on. It was the right thing to do, an' I'm glad I done it. I just hope I'm still glad when the time comes to pay up." He ran his fingers though his hair. "There wasn't no other choice. I had to come here and try to warn you-all." He paused and looked up at her again. "It was that or lose everybody I care about."

Lucy's sat there with her mouth half-open. Will was a hero, surely anyone with half an eye could see that. He and Jake had saved them all, and yet they might be punished for it? It made no sense.

Will sat up straight and leaned back in the chair. "Lucy," he said. That was all he said before a commotion on the front porch distracted him.

"There's riders comin' up the road!" Ike shouted.

Will jumped up and ran into the parlor, pulled back the curtain and peeked out through the open window

Miss Joline ran down the stairs

"It's ok, Ma." said Will. "It's Union Troopers—Sergeant Burnes an' some of the boys. I'll go out and talk to 'em. They're here for me and Jake."

"What do you mean?" asked Miss Joline.

Will didn't answer her. Instead, he straightened up his uniform as best he could and squared himself to the door.

Just before he strode out, Lucy hugged him and gave him a peck on the cheek too. "Don't you worry none, Will. It's gonna be all right. I just know it is."

Will hugged her back. "Remember what I said." He squared his shoulders and walked out into the rising sun.

Lucy ran to find her Papa.

*****

# Chapter 26

Will strode out onto the sunlit porch to meet his fate. His heart was pounding but he was determined not to let his fear show. He and Jake had known the possible outcome of what they were doing, and they'd done it anyway. *We've danced,* he thought, *and now we got to pay the fiddler.*

He heard stumbling steps behind him, and Ma and Martha Carter emerged, holding Jake between them. His color was off—a pale gray—he'd lost a lot of blood, and his knees wobbled. His lips were compressed with pain. He stood as straight as he could with the two women supporting him on either side.

Will looked at Ma and cocked his head. "What's he doin' down here?"

"He wouldn't take no for an answer," Ma replied. "Said he had to be down here and stand with you."

Will stared at him, then smiled. "I guess you're gonna be all right then."

"Yeah, I reckon I will," said Jake, his voice weak and raspy.

Seven Union troopers halted in a line in front of the porch and spread out sideways. Will knew them all.

Sergeant Burnes, a serious frown etched on his face, glared at him from his horse. His eyes took in the bodies laying off by the carriage house, the bullet holes in the walls and window sills, the bloodstains still evident on the hard-packed ground. "Well, I'd say there's been a little shootin' here," he said.

"More like a full-blown battle, if you ask me," said Eli Calloway.

"Umf," grunted Burnes. "Well now, nobody asked you, Calloway."

Burnes was angry. No surprise there. Will expected it.

Goose, Jon, Max, and two others that he knew only by name — George Brown and Sanford Hunter — sat astride their horses and looked on. They were his brothers in arms, his tent-mates, his friends, his comrades. Now, they wouldn't even meet his eyes. Will knew he'd let them down and he was ashamed of it. He looked Sergeant Burnes in the eyes, stood up straight and snapped to attention.

"At ease!" said Burnes, dismounting. "Ma'am," he said to Ma, "you can let Jake sit down in that chair."

Burnes climbed the steps onto the porch, stood in front of Will and looked him in the eyes. "Well, I'm waiting for an explanation," he said. "It better be good."

"Yes, Sergeant," said Will. He stared straight ahead, and explained what had happened, starting with finding Porter's tracks and ending with him tumbling off the bluff, presumed dead. He left nothing out and embellished nothing. He stated just the facts and did not justify any of his actions. *I'll take what's coming,* he thought, *like a soldier.*

After Will finished speaking, Burnes inspected the bullet holes in the house. He looked at smoldering remains of the slave quarters. At the smoke still curling from their new cabin that lay in ashes across the cornfield. He walked over to the bodies lined up near the Carriage House, pulled back the sacks and inspected each body, mumbling something Will couldn't hear.

"You say you have a prisoner too?" Burnes asked, when he came back.

"Yes, Sergeant," said Will. "This prisoner helped us escape and he gave up when he could've helped Porter. But he didn't...."

"That's enough, Private. Save it for later. Let's see this prisoner."

"Here he is, Sergeant!" yelled Ben. He limped around the corner from behind the house, pushing Darnell Harris ahead of him. Harris was bound with his hands behind his back and his eyes locked onto the ground in front of him. Lucy followed close behind them both.

"You Mister Carter? You own this place?" asked Burnes.

Ben spat blood from his mouth. "Ow, that still hurts," he said. Turning back to Burnes, he said, "Yessir, that's me." His hat was askew because of the blood-stained rag tied around his head. Both of his eyes were swollen and purple, and he was missing a front tooth. He extended a hand to Sergeant Burnes.

"You look a mite rough yourself," said Burnes, shaking the hand.

"I'll heal, thanks to your two soldiers," said Ben.

Burnes looked puzzled by the remark. He turned to the prisoner. "Whats' your name?"

"Darnell. Darnell Harris."

"You got anything to say 'bout all this?" Burnes asked.

Darnell shook his head no but spoke anyway. "Those were bad men." He nodded to the bodies. "They done some bad things. They was gonna do some more bad things."

Burnes stared at him for a minute, then called Eli over. "Tie this prisoner up under yonder shade tree and stand guard over 'im. There will be hell to pay if he gets away." Looking sternly at Harris, he added, "Shoot him if you have to."

Darnell looked at the ground. "Ain't runnin' no more," he said.

"Come on, git over here, you sumbitch," said Eli, leading him away.

"Sergeant," Ben said, removing his hat. "I cain't tell you how glad I am you sent these two boys here to warn me. Why if it hadn't been for them, I'd be dead, and my wife an' daughter, they'd be...." Ben choked up. "Well, I don't know what might have happened. Will and Jake here, they saved our lives. "

Burnes opened his mouth but no words came out.

Lucy spoke up, "That's the truth of it, Sergeant. We'd be dead by now.... or worse...." Her eyes teared up and she sniffed... "If not for these two brave boys. And likely his own mother'd be dead and his brothers too." Her hand covered her mouth and she began to cry. Then she wailed.

Burnes stared at her, blushing. "It's all right now, Missy. It's all over now."

Will was amazed. He'd never seen Lucy cry before, not like this. And he'd never seen Burnes blush.

"These men were here back in August, an' burned out the Tanner place," Ben continued, patting Lucy on the shoulder. "They threatened

280

to shoot me an' mine way back then. They are bad men, terrible men." He looked over at the blankets. "Well, they were. The Tanner boys accounted for all of 'em."

Will knew that wasn't true, but he was grateful. He now understood what Ben and Lucy were trying to do.

"Carter," Burnes said. "Let's have us a chat over here." He grabbed Carter's elbow and led him off to one side.

Will watched them from the corner of his eye and listened hard. He could only hear snatches of their conversation.

Ben's hands moved rapidly as he talked. "Good soldiers...." said Ben. "....tell the Colonel...."

"....those boys...." said Burnes, shaking his head. "...deserters..." Will's heart thumped hard at that word.

Ben shook his head and said something Will couldn't hear. Then he heard, "Ain't there been enough sufferin'?"

Will braced himself to be taken prisoner by his fellow soldiers.

After an eternity, Sergeant Burnes and Ben finished their talk and they strode back to the porch. Burnes looked grim. He stared a hole right through Will, then Jake.

Will stood still and kept his eyes forward. He steeled himself to accept whatever came.

Burnes stepped back onto the porch and removed his hat. "Gather 'round me everybody!" He looked at Martha Carter, at Lucy, at Ma, at Jake, and took a long look at Will. He nodded again to Ben and put his hat back on. He laid his stern gaze on Jake and Will and said, "This is the way I see it, and I'm only gonna say this once, so you two better get this right." He yelled, "Attention! Except you, Jake. You stay sittin' down."

Will stood ramrod straight and looked forward.

Burnes took a long breath and said, "Of all the cockamamie stories I ever heard tell of, this one beats all. I don't know why you think you can lie to me, Private, and get away with it. An' I never want to hear that lie you told me again, ever. Is that clear, Private?"

"Will felt all the color drain from his face. He was puzzled. What lie? He'd told him the truth. He squeaked out a "Yes, Sergeant."

"'Cause if you two actually were a couple of no-good deserters,"

Burnes continued, "I'd have to take you back in irons and you'd likely be shot. Ain't that right, Privates?"

In unison, Will and Jake answered, "Yes, Sergeant!"

Ma gasped and her hand moved to cover her mouth.

Burnes smiled. "But the truth of it is that you two are genuine heroes, ain't that right, Private?"

Will could only cock his head in confusion.

"That's a yes or no, Tanner," said Burnes.

"Yes, Sergeant," said Will, almost whispering. He cleared his throat. "Yes, Sergeant," he said, more firmly.

Burnes nodded and went on. "So, listen up, here's the true story." He poked at Will's chest. "Your horse went lame and you had to drop out of the column. Your brother Jake was assigned to stay with you till the farrier's wagon came up. But then you got captured by these here bushwhackers. You with me so far, Tanner?" His eyes bored straight into Will's.

Will didn't dare even blink. "Yes, Sergeant!"

Burnes continued, "You were brought here by force of arms, and with the help of that man Harris over there you two escaped your bonds and while defending this here family, you two killed these five men here, and that Porter fellow over by the river. You men are bona fide heroes." He paused again and shook his head. "I still cain't believe it yet, myself. But that is the truth as I see it, and that's the report I will make to Captain Stevens and Colonel Benson."

As he spoke, his voice raised in volume and his face reddened. "Now, here is the important part, Private. As 'heroes', you two are keen to return to your duty and continue killin' bushwhackers and rebels and followin' my orders faithfully until I, your First Sergeant, say otherwise. Or, until this god-damned war is over!" He paused again. "You two 'heroes' understand that?"

By this time Burnes was yelling and had pushed up so close that Will smelled the pipe smoke in his beard and saw the purple scar underneath it. He wanted to smile but didn't dare. "Yes, First Sergeant!"

Burnes moved his eyes to Jake. "And you, Private Jake Tanner?"

"Yes, Sergeant!" croaked Jake.

"At ease!"

Will sagged. He felt like he'd been resurrected from the dead, which in a real sense, he had been. He could hardly believe what had just happened. He'd expected punishment of the most severe kind, yet Burnes had called him a hero?

Ma, who by this time was in tears, ran over and hugged Sergeant Burnes, who turned even redder than he'd been just a moment before. He nervously searched through his pockets for his pipe and tobacco, then when he had them, changed his mind and put them away.

Lucy jumped into Will's arms, hugged him, then stood back and blushed. Ma hugged Jake, then Will.

Burnes surprised Will yet again when he turned to Martha Carter and said, "Ma'am, would it be possible for some poor soldiers to get a bite of breakfast and some coffee?"

"Chloe!" Martha Carter yelled, smiling. "Put on some more coffee!"

Will was amazed. It looked like he and Jake had gotten off easy. He was amazed even more when a smiling Ma took Sergeant Burnes by the arm and walked him into the house.


Jake passed out again, still sitting in the rocker, on the Carter front porch.

When next he awoke, he was stretched out on the front porch in the sunshine, a blanket under him and a pillow under his head. A dog was licking his face. *Chigger!* He scratched the old dog between the ears and his tail thumped on the wooden planks.

The mid-morning sun was getting high and its warmth was all the blanket Jake needed. He delighted in it. Chigger laid down beside him and rolled over so Jake could rub his belly. "Where were you when the shootin' was goin' on?" he asked the dog, in a dry, raspy voice. His shoulder throbbed when he so much as talked.

Will sat next to him, cross-legged on the porch. He handed him a cup of broth. It smelled wonderful and his stomach rumbled. His hands shook when he tried to lift it. His brother steadied the cup and helped him drink.

He gulped some down and nodded his thanks.

"Finally got me a bushwhacker, din't I?" he managed to croak.

"You got two, I think," said Will. "It's about time you learned how to shoot straight." He grinned. "I'm just joshin' with you. You did good, Jake."

For once, Jake didn't mind Will's teasing. He looked at his brother with more than a little new-found respect. Will started out slow sometimes, but he always finished up all right.

"You're some lucky sumbitches, 'ats all I got to say," said Jon. Jake hadn't even noticed him standing there by the porch. Max stood nearby, watching the road. Both sipped coffee from tin cups.

"Coffee's good," Jon continued. "Been a long time since I had good coffee."

"That's cause you're the one what makes it," said Max.

Jon snorted coffee out of his nose laughing.

"Yeah, you're right, Jon, we were lucky," said Will.

"Yeap, beats all I ever did see," said Jon. He smiled and held out a hand. "I wanna shake your hands. I never knowed no genuine heroes before. They's five god-be-damned bushwhackers a-layin over yonder that won't never raid no more."

Will shook his head. "Ain't shakin' with you Jon, we ain't no heroes, just lucky is all."

They all had a laugh at that. Except Jake. His shoulder was too painful. *My brother is a hero. He killed most of them men lyin' over there.* Will had saved them all and solved the Charley Porter problem, too. Jake just couldn't find the energy to say it out loud.

*I finally got me one! No, two!* He had thought that would make him happy, but it didn't. It only made him sad.

"The regiment," Will asked. "Where are they?"

"Well we never did catch up with Anderson," said Jon. "We chased him like a jackrabbit—right into another outfit. He ran right dab-smack into the Thirty-Third Mounted Infantry, and word is, they killed 'im. Ole Bloody Bill is dead, an' that's for sure. His men scattered. An' that Rebel bastard General Price is skedaddlin' back to Arkansas. He got beat up bad, and he's all used up. Missouri is safe for the Union. For now, anyhow."

"He asked where the regiment was, Jon, not for a general history of the damn war," said Max.

Jon turned red. "Oh, yeah. Well, we're headin' back to Camp

Fremont so I reckon that's where they are."

"Not you" said Will, turning back to Jake. "You get to stay here till you heal up."

"Lucky dog, you," said Max.

Jake tried to grin. "I suppose you could call it that. How 'bout we trade places?"

Max grinned. "Nah, I reckon not."

*Yeah*, thought Jake. *I'm a lucky dog all right.* He drank some more broth and marveled at how lucky he'd been. How lucky they'd both been. Will wandered off to take care of something. Ma came out and fed him a spoonful of laudanum, and the pain began to ease. It made him sleepy and he closed his eyes, Chigger still lying next to him.

When he opened his eyes, it was night and he was in a warm bed. In his drug induced haze, he saw an angel sitting next to him. At first, he thought the angel was Lucy. Then his eyes focused in the dim lamp-light, and it wasn't Lucy. He didn't know who she was, but she was the prettiest girl he'd ever seen.

*****

# Chapter 27

## One month later

"Corporal Tanner get those men into line!" yelled Sergeant Burnes.

"Yes, Sergeant!" answered Will, smiling, as he ordered his troopers into a precise line. It was a chilly November day and a thin dusting of new snow lay on the ground. A slight breeze rattled the few remaining leaves in the trees behind their camp on Bean Branch. The duty was boring; Company G of the Fifteenth Missouri Cavalry was back on railroad picket duty. Will welcomed the boredom. It gave him plenty of time to think.

As they rode out to relieve the current guard, Will looked up and down the line of troopers and smiled again. He was proud of his regiment, his company and his squad. Hard fighting and hard riding had molded the fifteenth into professional soldiers, and it showed. Their uniforms were clean, if somewhat worn, their horses well groomed, and their equipment in top shape. Most of all, they displayed it in their attitude. They had beaten the enemy on the field of battle, and the enemy knew they had been beaten. The Union troopers now had pride in themselves and trust in each other.

Union soldiers had run General Price's ragtag Confederates out of Missouri. Bushwhackers like Bloody Bill Anderson and William Quantrill were dead, their gangs scattered and broken. Bushwhacking and marauding had become a rare occurrence in this part of the state. Northern Missouri was peaceful once again. The troopers were still on guard; there was still the occasional attempt to burn a bridge or derail a train. Until the war was over, there would be no loss of vigilance.

There was now some free time. Time to relax, time to think, time to learn new things. Will spent most of his free time learning to read the occasional newspaper that got passed around. He could now read the letters that Lucy sent to him, without help from Sergeant Burnes. His writing still needed work—he could only print his words, and he had to ask how to spell sometimes—but Burnes had taught him how to sign his own name. He had written to Lucy just this morning, and he pulled the letter from his pocket to read it again.

> *Dearist Lucy, I hope this leter finds you well and in good spirits. In your last letter you ask me if I longed to be at home and on the farm again. Lucy I must tell you now I hope to not find myself behind a mule never agin, now that I been out here and find I like this life of a solder. I know that might not be what you wish to hear. But I say to you now it dont get in the way of my feelin for you for I feel just as strong abut you today as I did when I saw you last. Do not despair at my words for I know that my heart is true to you and my hope for the futur will make you happy and proud of me. forever and truly your frend and lover,*

> *Wm Tanner*

Will knew that he had changed. The war and the killing had changed him. He could not imagine going back to the farm now. His mind was made up, the farm would now go to Jake—if he wanted it—or to his younger brothers. Will wasn't sure what he would do after the war, but he knew it wasn't going to be farming. He hoped Lucy could live with that.

He missed Jake. He even missed the arguments they always had. Jake had been home on convalescent leave since the shootout at the Carter place. His shoulder was slow to heal, and he couldn't ride or even hold a gun. Will suspected that Lucy's cousin Annie had something to do with it as well. Jake and Annie had hit it off pretty well, and she had taken over his care. Will laughed. He had heard that Annie treated him like a baby and Jake allowed it! Maybe the war had changed him too.

He wasn't sure how Lucy would react to his new plans. *I might not send this letter. It might be better to tell her face to face, when I get back home, and this is all over.*

He stuffed the letter back in his pocket. He'd have to write another one now.

The Lieutenant shouted, "Column Halt!" and the column came to a quick stop. The guard was relieved — replace by fresh guards, and the column started onward again. At the Littleby Creek Bridge, it was Will's turn to relieve the six men on guard there. The old guard had no news to report, all had been quiet. The relieved men mounted up and took their place at the end of the column, "About Face" was ordered, and the column moved off. Will made his assignments. As the sixth man, he would take his own two-hour watch with one of the other men.

Two hours later, the sun had gone down, and the temperature dropped. Will pulled his overcoat tighter around him. In the east, an early rising full moon gave a glow to the sky even before the orange in the west had died away. Will watched the moonrise. A gust blew and leaves rustled as they fell to earth. A blue jay scolded him from a tree-top and a chickadee warned him not to come any closer. He welcomed the birds and their noise, it meant no-one else was around.

As he walked his beat across the bridge, his mind went back to the night he'd shot Charley Porter. Many secrets were revealed that night, and his newfound knowledge haunted him. His real Pa, Charley Tanner, was still alive out there somewhere. *Maybe I'll go lookin' for him, someday.* Then he remembered Ma's advice on the matter, so maybe he wouldn't, after all. *Do I even care enough?* He didn't know the answer to that. It seemed that secrets, once revealed, just led to more questions that didn't have answers.

He didn't have an answer, either, for what Porter had asked of him. Was Porter serious about them riding together, or was he just stalling for time? He must have known it would never happen. Why would he stall? There was no advantage for Porter in hanging around, nobody was coming to his rescue. Will was just as confused as ever about it. Finally, he shrugged. Porter was dead. There was no use in trying to figure him out now.

Lucy's last letter told him that Porter's body still had not been found. Seth had told her he was probably eaten by turtles. He'd gotten a cuff on the head for that from Ma. Will could just see that in his mind, and he smiled. Lucy swore she'd never eat turtle again.

Turtles or no, Will figured that someday some poor farmer would discover Porter's bones half-buried somewhere along the riverbank. Will was sure he'd hit him square, despite the darkness.

Still, it was possible that Porter had survived. Will almost hoped he had. *He was my brother, after all. But he was a killer! A bushwhacker! A thief and a scoundrel, a merciless, cruel man! Can I ever call a man like that a brother?*

*Was there ever any good in him?*

Will concluded, that yes, there once had to have been something good in Porter, as there was in everybody. The war had changed Porter, too. It had made him evil. *Funny, how war turns some people into better men and turns others into animals. There just ain't no answer for it. I just need to be the best man I can be, no matter what.*

Will's mind turned back to his duty. He hefted his carbine to a more comfortable position, turned and walked his beat back the other way.

*****

# THE END

# An excerpt from book II in the Tanner Series

# Coming soon

## Chapter 1

## Jefferson Barracks, St Louis, Missouri

## January 1865

"I tell you one thing, I ain't a-goin'!" yelled an angry, familiar voice.

His mind numbed by exhaustion and dulled by sleep, Will Tanner couldn't match the voice to a name. He groaned, rolled over, covered his head and tried to get back to his dream of their snug and warm cabin. The dream was gone, though, replaced by this drafty, cold and smelly log hut.

Somebody shook him by the shoulder. "Will! Will! Wake up!"

Will burrowed deeper into the covers. "Arrrrgggghhhh! What the hell is it this time!" His first thought was that Jake was fighting with somebody again. Jake was always fighting with somebody. *But Jake ain't here,* he recalled. *He's still home nursin' that shoulder wound.* He flung back the covers, sat up and raised his hands. "Hold on, dammit! Gimme a minute," he said, shaking his head and rubbing grit from his eyes. Sentry duty in January was long and cold. He'd only been asleep for minutes.

He opened one eyelid and recognized his cousin Eli Calloway.

"Will! Will!" Eli said, shaking his shoulder again. "Dammit, Will. Have you heard? They're sendin' us down river to New Orleans!"

Will rubbed his eyes. Surely he had not heard that right. Why would they be going to New Orleans? "It's just more rumors. Go away and let me sleep." He fell back into the bed and covered his eyes with an arm.

"No, Will!" said Eli again. "Wake up! It's true. They're sendin' us down south." Other voices chimed in with their assent.

Will groaned again. An army of angry privates surrounded him. Privates who couldn't tie their own shoes or wipe their own noses without his help. Sometimes he wondered if a corporal's extra pay was worth the trouble. He shook his head and pushed back his hair. "Eli, you know they cain't do that. We're Missouri State Militia, they cain't send us anywhere 'cept Missouri!"

"Well, that's what we're hearin.' An' they sound serious...."

Will sighed. "All right, all right, let me go see what's goin' on." There'd be no more sleep this morning. He'd go talk to Sergeant Burnes. Sergeants always knew what was really going on. But first, he needed to clear the cobwebs. "We got any coffee?"

Eli wiped out a tin cup with his coattail and poured a cup from the pot sitting on the wood stove that sat in the middle of the barracks.

Will took a sip and spat it right back out. "Dang Eli, you tryin' to poison me?

"Sorry. It's army issue coffee. We ran plumb out of the good stuff. Shoulda' warned you, I reckon."

Will took another sip. It was bitter and foul, but the taste cleared the fog in his brain. He suppressed his gag reflex and swallowed it, but he couldn't hold back his grimace. "Jeezus that's bad."

The men surrounded his bed, all talking at the same time.

Will waved them back. "Ok! Shut up and let me go find out! Gimme some room!"

The men nearest him backed up a foot and Will grabbed his boots from under the bed and shook them out. More than one trooper learned that the hard way that spiders liked to hide in their boots. Will tried hard not to learn things the hard way. He shook out his coat for the same reason, threw it on, then his great coat went over that.

Outside, the weather had not changed from last night, but at least he could see in the dreary light. A brisk northwest wind blew from a gray sky and sleet struck his face with tiny little needles of ice. The cold wind sliced into him as if he wasn't even wearing a coat. He slipped and slid across the frozen ground to the hut where the sergeants slept. He could hear angry voices from inside despite the howling wind, and he opened the door. Stepping inside backward, he pulled the door closed, tiny crystals of ice flying in with him.

Before he could turn around, he bumped into someone who cursed. When he turned, he found the one-room hut was filled by irate soldiers, all talking at once.

The din echoed off the walls and roof and drowned out any conversation until a bellow silenced the hubbub. "Quiet Now! All privates GET OUT NOW! We'll let you men know something as soon as we know ourselves."

Will recognized Sergeant Burnes' powerful voice with its faint Irish brogue. The privates filed out and cold air filled the hut.

"Not you, Tanner. You stay," said Burnes.

Will's eyes adjusted to the dim, smoke-filled interior. Several corporals stood around the stove, warming their hands. Burnes refilled his pipe and lit it with a match. Playing cards, scattered bills and coins littered a small table, and an opened bottle of whiskey sat on the mantle.

There was another man there, a gaunt and haggard looking sergeant, holding an opened bottle of whiskey. His blue frock coat was faded and patched, his infantry brogans worn and muddy, and two Colt revolvers stuck out from his belt. His long scraggly beard, streaked with gray, lay on his chest and his matted dark hair fell to his shoulders. In the flickering lamplight, the dark hollows under his eyes gave him a haunted look.

The man gave Will a puzzled look. "Has it been that long, Will Tanner? Have I changed so much you don't recognize a kinsman when you see him?"

Will instantly recognized the voice, firm and deep, though it didn't match the skeletal figure standing before him. "Uncle Lige! What the hell...." Will extended a hand to him, and they shook. Lige then pulled him into an embrace. He was as thin under his clothes as he looked, but his muscles were hard and his back ramrod straight. Will could feel the strength in him.

Will broke off and backed away, embarrassed but smiling. "It's been a long time. It's good to see you." Ma's oldest brother, Elijah Miller, had joined the Union Army soon after the war broke out. He'd marched off to fight and no-one had heard from him since.

"I see you know each other," said Sergeant Burnes. "Good. Saves me the introduction." Burnes gestured with his pipe. "Sergeant Miller here has volunteered to serve with us. He's been assigned to G Company to replace Sergeant Jackson."

"Replace Jackson?" Puzzled, Will recalled that Jackson was in the hospital with measles, as were many of G company's men.

Burnes took a puff from his pipe and sighed. "Jackson died," he said, eyes shining with moisture.

Will was taken aback. He recalled Jackson, a decent man and a good sergeant. He and Burnes had served in the east together and knew each other well. Will often found them playing euchre and sharing a bottle together. "Well, damn," said Will, for lack of anything else to come to mind.

Uncle Lige's eyes found his. "So how is everybody, Will. How's your Ma? An' Jake and Ike, an'...." He paused and pulled his beard. "Well, I know you had another brother, but I'm damned if I can recall his name."

"Seth," said Will. "An' then little Nate was born about two years ago. Maybe longer. You ain't met him yet. He come a little while after Pa — Frank — died."

"You two can swap stories later," said Burnes. "Right now, I got news. Grab a seat, all of ye."

"Yes, Sergeant," said Will, dragging over a chair. He recalled why he was here. "I heard from some of the boys somethin' about going south?" Chairs scraped on the wood floor as the corporals and Uncle Lige pulled up chairs of their own.

"First thing you need to know," said Burnes, "is that it's strictly voluntary. They cain't make anybody go. This is a Missouri Militia outfit, and they just cain't do that. So put a stopper in that rumor as fast as ye can."

Will and the other corporals nodded. Will felt vindicated, he'd said the same thing just a few minutes ago.

"Second thing is, they'll sweeten the pot with a three hunnert dollar bounty if ye sign up." Burnes paused. "That's in addition to any bounty you was promised for signin' up with the Fifteenth Cavalry."

Will's ears perked up at the mention of the money. Another three hundred, with the three hundred already coming to him, plus what he saved from his monthly pay, would build up a pretty good pile of greenbacks. He did some quick math in his head. If his luck held, he might come away from this with seven or eight hundred dollars in his pocket, more money than he could make in years of farming.

"Here's the catch," said Burnes. "You got to resign from the fifteenth and sign up with a regular Federal outfit."

"That don't sound so bad," said Will.

"Well, not if you don't mind walkin'," said Burnes. "You'll be infantry."

\*\*\*\*\*

About the author:

Robert Daniel Mumford is a retired IT worker bee, former Civil War re-enactor, History buff and genealogist. He had ancestors on both side of the war, two Rebels and two Yankees. He has written family history books about both sides of his family. (Soon to be released on Amazon.) He was born and raised in West Tennessee, lived almost thirty years in the Mountains of East Tennessee, and now lives in Marietta Georgia with his wife and two rescue dogs.

Thank you for reading!

# Endnotes

---

[1] Source: Original Records: War of the Rebellion, Series II, Vol. 1, Chapter 2, p, 270.

URL: http://www.simmonsgames.com/research/authors/USWarDept/ORA/OR-S2-V1-C2.html#e6

[2] Source: Original Records: War of the Rebellion: Serial 084 Page 1040 LOUISIANA AND THE TRANS- MISSISSIPPI. Chapter LIII.

URL: https://ehistory.osu.edu/books/official-records/084/1040

[3] Albert Castel and Thomas Goodrich, *Bloody Bill Anderson, The Short, Savage Life of a Civil War Guerrilla, StackPole Books, Mechanicsburg, PA: 1998. pp: 114, 115.*

[4] Ibid, p. 115

65825041R00163

Made in the USA
Columbia, SC
14 July 2019